D1265483

# THE
# OUTCAST

Also by Michael Walters

FICTION

*The Shadow Walker*
*The Adversary*

# THE
# OUTCAST

MICHAEL WALTERS

Quercus

First published in Great Britain in 2008 by

Quercus
21 Bloomsbury Square
London
WC1A 2NS

Copyright © 2008 by Michael Walters

A CIP catalogue record for this book is available
from the British Library

ISBN 978 1 84724 419 2 (HB)
ISBN 978 1 84724 420 8 (TPB)

10 9 8 7 6 5 4 3 2 1

Typeset in Plantin by Ellipsis Books Limited, Glasgow
Printed and bound in Great Britain by Clays Ltd, St Ives plc

To Hazel and Murray –
for making it possible in the first place
And, as always, to Christine
for making it possible now

## Medley for Morin Khur

The sound box is made of a horse's head.
The resonator is horse skin.
The strings and bow are of horsehair.

The morin khur is a thoroughbred
of Mongolian violins.
Its call is the call of the stallion to the mare.

A call which may no more be gainsaid
than that of jinn to jinn
through jasmine-weighted air.

A call that may no more be gainsaid
than that of blood kin to kin
through a body-strewn central square.

A square in which they'll heap the horses' heads
by the heaps of horse skin
and the heaps of horsehair.

Paul Muldoon

# SUMMER

There was nothing. Nothing for miles. Nothing for days.

After all these years, it had overwhelmed Sam – the rolling steppe, the distant mountains and, far to the south, the vast terrain of the desert. He was dizzied by it, unable to comprehend the distance, the sense of space. So different from the confined clutter of what was now his home.

If anything, it was better than he remembered, better than his imagination.

He had forgotten the deep intensity of the colours, the expanse of the liquid blue skies, the lush richness of the northern landscapes. And the sheer vastness of the space that lay around them on all sides.

And now, at last, he was free. His hosts had understood what he was looking for, and identified Sunduin, an unemployed graduate, to act as his guide. They would travel east, out into the empty grasslands – the supposed birthplace of Genghis Khan himself.

Sunduin spoke excellent English, but it was easy to see why he had failed to secure more permanent employment. He was a slovenly creature, dressed always in a faded tee-shirt and battered jeans, his lank, too-long hair overhanging his pallid forehead. He was surly and taciturn, clearly unenthused by the prospect of acting as a guide and interpreter to an over-indulged Western visitor. Sam kept a watchful eye on his bags and money, certain that Sunduin would not miss an opportunity for an easy profit.

As they flew out on the bumpy MIAT flight, watching the grasslands open up before them, Sam felt both excitement and trepidation. Sunduin was slumped next to him, apparently asleep.

He had barely spoken since they had met at the airport, doing just enough to get them through the check-in processes. He woke only as the aircraft touched down at Ondorkhaan, and was equally taciturn in leading them through the primitive airport and out into the sunlight.

As they emerged from the airport, Sunduin gestured across the road and moments later, a truck pulled up. The driver had clearly been waiting for them.

Sam pulled out his wallet to pay the sum that had, according to Sunduin, been agreed. The owner had insisted on US dollars, and to Sam the amount was pitifully small. He half expected a demand for some additional payment, but the man simply counted the notes carefully, stuffed them into the breast pocket of his shirt and nodded. He spoke a few words to Sunduin, and climbed out of the truck. Sunduin threw his own bag into the back seat and took the man's place behind the wheel, gesturing that Sam should follow.

Sam looked at the driver, who had lit a cigarette and was watching them expressionlessly. 'Is he staying here?'

Sunduin shrugged. 'He has other business.'

It was a mile or so into town. Sunduin, for the first time showing some enthusiasm, slammed his foot down hard on the accelerator, and they sped along the narrow dirt road. It was not yet nine a.m., but the sun was already growing hot. The landscape was bare but beautiful, mile upon mile of open rolling grassland.

Sam stared around as they approached the outskirts of Ondorkhaan. It was the regional capital, but there was little to the town – a few wooden houses, with an occasional larger, more official-looking edifice along the main street. Sunduin made no effort to reduce the vehicle's speed as they entered the town.

'Are we stopping?' Sam asked. He had left Sunduin to deal with the detail of their accommodation.

Sunduin shook his head. 'I thought we should head straight across there. I've booked us a hotel in Dadal.'

Sam nodded. Genghis Khan's supposed birthplace was close to the small township. 'That sounds good. How far is it?'

Sunduin shrugged. 'A little way. Eighty, ninety kilometres. Maybe a couple of hours. It's not a good road. Sleep if you want to.'

Against his expectations, Sam did sleep, lulled by the bouncing rhythm of the truck and when he opened his eyes, the sun was higher in the sky, the temperature still rising. Sunduin glanced over and said: 'Not far now: ten, fifteen minutes.'

'Do you know this area?' Sam asked.

'It's my country. I know it well enough.'

'It's a beautiful country.' Sam was conscious that his words were a tourist's platitude. There was no way he could convey how much this country meant to him, even after all these years.

They were still on the grassland, but the altitude was increasing. There were sparse clusters of trees, tall conifers that threw dark shadows across the intense green of the steppe. Ondorkhaan was far behind, and there was no sign of human habitation.

'That's it,' Sunduin said. He took a hand off the wheel and gestured ahead of them. 'That hill, there. The birthplace of our great leader. So they say.' It was impossible to interpret his tone.

'I look forward to seeing it.'

They drove another half mile, and then Sunduin hit the brakes and pulled them off the road on to the grassy plain. 'We stop here.'

Sam looked around, startled by the suddenness of Sunduin's action. 'Is this it?'

'You want to see the birthplace?' Sunduin looked bored suddenly, as though this whole expedition was a waste of his precious time.

'Yes, but I thought we'd go to the town first.'

Sunduin glanced wearily at his watch. 'It's only eleven,' he said. 'There's no point in going to the hotel. I thought you wanted to see the birthplace.'

'I do.' Sam realised that, for all his plans, he wasn't sure what he had been expecting.

Sunduin opened his door, and climbed slowly out into the warm air. 'Are you coming?' he said.

Sam watched him for a moment. 'Yes,' he said, finally. 'Of course.'

3

He opened his door, and climbed down. The high sun was hot on his back.

And then, as he straightened, the sky went dark, and a chill ran through his body. It was as if all the light and heat had been drained from the world.

He looked up, startled, half-expecting some unpredicted solar eclipse. In the otherwise empty sky, a single small dark cloud had momentarily drifted across the sun. In a minute, the light would return.

Sam stared across at Sunduin, striding away across the grassland. The sun was already brightening again, but the chill stayed with him. The truth was clear: two of them were setting out on this journey. Two of them would see Genghis Khan's birthplace.

But only one would return.

PART 1

## WINTER 1988

He had found a public phone, just off Sukh Bataar Square, but there was no way he could use that. He cursed himself, and he cursed this whole bloody country. The state that it was in. At least at home he understood things. Here, he was operating on instinct, guesswork.

And there were no fucking phones.

He hadn't planned for this, which was a mistake. But what did he expect? This was his first time on mission. He couldn't be expected to think of everything.

Public call boxes were out; they were bound to be monitored. The same went for his office phone; the line would be bugged. They kept an eye on everyone, just as they did back home. Especially if you were foreign; especially if you were Chinese.

In the end, he broke into one of the offices at the university. It wasn't difficult, and if the phone was monitored, it couldn't be traced back to him.

Even so, his hands trembled as he dialled. The phone rang for endless minutes until he became sure it would never be picked up. Then there was a click and a voice. 'Yes?' In just that one word, Sam recognized authority.

'I'm sorry,' he said. 'I'm trying to call the museum. I thought I'd dialled 237 1505.' The agreed format. The venue, and, in the last four digits, the time they should meet, the following day. All planned.

'I'm afraid you've got the wrong number.'

'Oh. I'm sorry.' He pressed his finger down and cut the connection. That was all they needed. Tomorrow they would meet. Face to face. For the first time.

# CHAPTER ONE

## SUMMER

It was instinct. Instinct and pure dumb luck.

Tunjin wasn't even aware of thinking, let alone taking aim. He dragged out the pistol and fired, his mind lagging a lifetime behind what his eyes were seeing, what his body was reacting to.

Afterwards, all that remained were sensations: the jarring kickback from the gunshot; the memory of the impact through wrist and arm; the noise, sharp, explosive, but somehow muffled, as though coming from somewhere far away; the figure crumpling to the ground, a startled expression on his face; the bleaching hot sunlight across the square. Everything fragmented and distant, like someone else's photographs. The blood. The crowd. The sirens and the endless screaming.

And finally it was as if the sky had darkened and closed in on him. There was a sudden sharp pain across his chest, and he stumbled, his legs unable to support his hefty body. The pistol dropped clatteringly from his hand, and his last image was the startled face of the young uniformed officer beside him.

It was several hours later when he woke. In the square, the sun had been high in the empty sky, relentless in its midsummer glare. Now, its low reddening rays were angled across his bed, glittering on the trolleys and medical equipment. His waking mind was a matching blaze of half-impressions, a brilliantly illuminated swirl that told him nothing.

From his supine position, Tunjin could just glimpse through the windows the startling black and pink monolith of the Hotel Chinnghis Kahn. Beyond that, there was only the sky, a translucent mauve in the dying sunlight. Even now, it looked warm out there.

He tried to move his head, but found the effort too great. He stared up at the blank white ceiling, suddenly conscious that there really was something wrong with him. Not just tiredness, or shock, or the after-effects of unconsciousness. Something more serious.

He couldn't move. He could – just about – twist his head from side to side. But when he tried to turn his head fully or move his limbs, there was nothing. Just deadness, numbness. No sensation at all.

He stared up, trying not to panic. There had to be some explanation. After all, he didn't feel ill, did he? No. He didn't feel anything. His mind felt as numb as his body.

He became aware that he was not alone. There was a chatter of voices, a buzz of white noise that had scarcely impinged on his senses before now. And somewhere a voice he knew.

'How is he?' Doripalam asked. They were standing just inside the door, whispering, as if trying not to disturb the vast figure on the bed.

The doctor shrugged. His demeanour and his expensive-looking Western-style suit suggested that his presence here was interrupting some more attractive engagement elsewhere. 'It's too early to say,' he said. 'He's been unconscious for a long time.' He glanced at his watch as if calculating precisely how long.

'A coma?'

'No.' The doctor smiled, adopting the patronising manner unique to his profession across the world. 'Not what we would call a coma.'

'So what precisely would you call it?' Any member of Doripalam's team would have warned the doctor to avoid superciliousness when dealing with their boss.

'He's been unconscious, that's all. It's part of the recovery process.

He's been through a lot. But we don't know quite how much. We don't know how bad it is.'

'You don't know how bad what is? What is it exactly?'

The doctor stared at Doripalam for a moment, as if wondering whether to challenge his right to enquire into this matter. 'There are no relatives?' he said at last. 'No next of kin?'

Doripalam shook his head slowly. 'No,' he said. 'Not as far as we know.' He paused. 'Look, he works for me. But that's not why I'm here. Not the only reason, anyway.' He hesitated again, unsure how to phrase his next words. 'Let's just say I owe him one. He once saved my life.'

'It may be a stroke,' the doctor said, finally. 'We're doing tests. But it wouldn't be surprising.' He was looking almost embarrassed now. 'I mean, he's massively overweight. He drinks—'

'Like a fish,' Doripalam said. 'Though rarely water, I understand.'

'His blood pressure was through the roof. He's really been very lucky. It could have been much worse.'

'So how serious is it?'

'We don't really know,' the doctor said. 'He's still alive. That's a good sign.' He caught Doripalam's expression. 'No, I mean it. This could easily have killed him.'

'That might have been preferable,' Doripalam pointed out. 'Depending on what else is wrong with him.'

The doctor nodded. 'We have to see. He might be paralysed, or partly paralysed. It might be minimal. Or it might not.'

There was a sound behind them. Both men turned and looked along the length of the quiet private room. Beyond Tunjin's bed, the city skyline was dark against the reddening glare of the setting sun. A nervous-looking nurse was staring at the monitors. She looked up at the two men, her eyes wide. 'He's awake,' she said. 'He's looking at me.'

The minister barely raised his head as Nergui entered. 'Okay,' he said, 'so what's this all about? What's going on?'

Nergui had grown accustomed to this absence of preliminaries, the lack even of common courtesy. There had been a time, not so long ago, when it had irritated him, but now he knew that it was all just part of the show. Occasionally, he could even feel a degree of sympathy for the old man.

Nergui lowered himself into the seat opposite the minister's desk without waiting to be invited. 'We're trying to find out,' he said.

The minister looked up, with an expression that suggested that Nergui had just admitted to an act of criminal negligence. 'You don't know yet, then?'

'No,' Nergui said. 'Except that it's not what it looks like.'

'And what does it look like?'

'An attempted suicide bombing. Maybe something like Madrid or London but on a smaller scale.'

'Everyday life in Basra or Baghdad,' the minister said. 'Well, that's what it looked like to me. But you know better.' The last words had an undertone of scepticism in them, but it was half-hearted. The minister knew better than to underestimate Nergui's judgement.

'I think so,' Nergui said. He stretched out his legs, looking untroubled. His socks, the minister registered, were a pale green. Inevitably, they matched the tie he was wearing beneath his usual dark grey suit. 'There are factors that need to be explained.'

The minister stared at him for a moment, as though contemplating whether to enquire further. Finally he said, 'We're keeping a lid on it, though.'

'As best we can. We've put an embargo on the media.'

'Can we make that hold?'

'For a while. They like to keep us sweet. But we can't push our luck.'

'What about witnesses?'

'Lots of them. But they don't know quite what they witnessed. We just have to accept that the rumour mill will be churning.'

'But they'll know we're concealing something.'

'That's hardly new territory. They'll make up some story about government iniquity that'll be even worse than the truth.'

'You always know how to reassure, Nergui,' the minister said. 'But you're on top of things?'

'As far as it's possible to be.'

'Why do I have the feeling that you're keeping something from me?'

Nergui shrugged. 'Because that's my job, I imagine. It's what you pay me for.' He paused, weighing up his next words. 'I'm saying what I know. It's not my job to engage in idle speculation, Bakei.' Not many people called the minister by name, when Nergui did so, it was always with an undertone of warning, an invocation of their shared history.

The minister shook his head. 'You never engage in idle anything, Nergui. What about the shooting?'

'That's in hand.'

'You knew the officer involved, I understand? One of your people?'

Nergui gazed back at the minister, his face blank. It never paid to underestimate the minister, either. 'He was, yes. Before.'

'A good one?' In the circumstances, the question was far from casual.

'As good as they come.'

'And it's under control?'

'Trust me,' Nergui said. 'It's in hand. All of it.' He paused. 'All we need to do is find out quite what it is we're holding.'

'Tunjin. Can you hear me? Can you hear what I'm saying?'

It didn't seem appropriate to shout in a hospital, not in circumstances like these. But he wasn't sure what Tunjin could hear, what was getting through to him. His eyes were open, but there was no expression, no indication that he was awake. Without the remorseless pulsing of the monitor behind the bed, Doripalam could have imagined that he was looking at a corpse. He glanced back up at the doctor, who was watching the scene, his face barely more revealing than Tunjin's. 'What do you think?' Doripalam asked. 'Can he hear?'

The doctor shrugged. 'Who knows?' he said. 'Keep trying.'

Doripalam looked back down at Tunjin. 'Tunjin, it's me. Doripalam. Can you hear me?'

There was something there, he thought. Definitely something. He tried again, louder this time, trying to ignore the doctor's presence. 'It's Doripalam, Tunjin. Can you hear me?'

Tunjin's pale fleshy head was slumped back on the bed, but something in his eyes indicated recognition, acknowledgement, awareness of who he was or what he was saying. It was, Doripalam thought, like reaching into a cave or into deep water, sensing there was something to be grasped if you could only reach it.

Tunjin blinked unexpectedly. 'Tunjin,' Doripalam said again, 'can you hear me? Can you understand what I'm saying?'

Tunjin was blinking repeatedly now, as if trying to clear his vision. Swimming up from the depths, awareness filling his eyes. The set of his face changed, concentration welling up from within, and his mouth began to move.

'Ungh . . .' It was little more than a plosive exhalation of breath, but it was the first sound that Tunjin had uttered since they had brought him in here.

'Tunjin. Can you hear me?' Doripalam looked back at the doctor, wondered whether he could somehow use his authority to make the laid-back bastard *do* something. Though he had no idea what it was that needed doing.

'Umph . . .' Tunjin's mouth and jaw were working, wrestling with the air. His eyes were bright, now full of expression, staring upwards at Doripalam.

'Gun,' Tunjin said. It was the first distinct word he had spoken.

Doripalam looked at the doctor, who gave another of his characteristic shrugs. The familiar intelligence was returning to Tunjin's eyes, but his body looked like a beached whale on the hospital bed, his immense chest rising and falling as he struggled to speak.

'Can you hear me, Tunjin? It's me, Doripalam. Are you all right?'

'Gun,' Tunjin said again, his intonation growing more urgent. 'I shot—' His eyes were darting backwards and forwards, as though trying to work out who was present, who was listening. It was still not clear he recognised Doripalam.

'It's all right,' Doripalam tried to sound calm. 'You don't need to worry. You did the right thing.'

'But—' Tunjin stopped, as though trying painfully to work his way through a complex argument. 'But . . .' He stuttered to a halt once more.

Doripalam turned to the doctor. 'Is he all right, do you think?'

The doctor was watching Tunjin's movements with apparently casual interest. He nodded towards the monitor behind the bed. 'Better than I would have believed possible,' he said at last. 'I don't know what was wrong with him, but it certainly wasn't a stroke. Or if it was we've just witnessed a miracle. Perhaps I should get one of the priests in here. Those Western born-again ones who hang around the square. They're very keen on the hand of God stuff, I understand.'

Doripalam gazed at him for a second, then redirected his attention back to Tunjin. Tunjin's mouth was opening and closing. Finally, he spoke again: 'Gun – I shot—' He paused again, holding his breath as though making a final effort to articulate whatever idea he was wrestling with. 'It was the gun,' he said at last, quite distinct this time. 'Whose gun? Whose gun was it?'

It suddenly struck Doripalam that this was more than a succession of random stuttered words. He had assumed that Tunjin was simply trying to come to grips with the whirl of ideas and images filling his brain. But he was trying to say something quite specific.

'Tunjin,' he said, 'what is it? What do you mean?'

'I think,' a quiet voice said from behind them, 'that he's enquiring about the ownership of the weapon.'

Doripalam looked round, startled despite the gentleness of the voice. Startled, above all, because he recognised the speaker. 'Nergui,' he said, turning to face the tall figure standing in the now open doorway.

Nergui said nothing, his impassive gaze fixed on the figure on the bed.

'I left you a message,' Doripalam was aware that his voice sounded almost accusatory. For the first time, he realised that Nergui was not alone. Two men in plain dark suits were standing behind him, only half visible in the shadows of the corridor.

Nergui nodded. 'I know. Thank you. That was good of you.' He paused, his blue eyes still fixed on Tunjin. 'But I'd already been contacted.'

Doripalam finally grasped the significance of the words that Nergui had spoken seconds before. 'What did you mean, "ownership of the weapon"?'

'The ministry is investigating what happened in the square.'

'I know,' Doripalam said, bluntly. 'They made that very clear when they arrived on the scene.'

'I am very sorry. The ministry is not known for its courtesy, I'm afraid.'

'Look . . .'

Nergui nodded. 'This does not fall into your remit. We are dealing with it. But they – we – should have kept you informed. Especially in the circumstances.'

'Circumstances?' Doripalam could see that Nergui was gazing straight past him, his blue eyes fixed on the prone figure on the bed.

'I am here formally to detain Tunjin in custody,' Nergui said, his voice toneless.

'Custody? The man's ill. After all he's been through.'

Nergui nodded. 'I understand that. But he is a witness to what may have been a terrorist act. And there are aspects of the situation that we need to investigate.' He paused. 'I am sure you understand.'

'I don't understand anything, Nergui,' Doripalam said, his temper rising. 'You come muscling in here, throwing your weight around, just like your people did in the square. This man isn't just a colleague, he should be a friend of yours. He saved your life. What's all this stuff about custody?'

Nergui nodded again, his face grave, his expression suggesting that Doripalam's words had simply confirmed his own thoughts. 'I know. I have no wish to be difficult. But I'm afraid we're taking over now.'

'Look, Nergui, you can't just—'

'You know that I can, Doripalam,' Nergui said, gently. 'And you know I wouldn't do it lightly.' He paused. 'I've no problem with you staying around for a little while to keep an eye on Tunjin, if you wish. But he's our business now.'

# CHAPTER TWO

'So how many am I making?'

Odbayar was sitting cross-legged on the floor, a tattered paperback book splayed on the carpet in front of him. 'As many as you can. There won't be a shortage of support.'

He sounded confident enough, Gundalai thought, but then he always did. Regardless of the circumstances or the facts. It was a talent, there was no question about that. Quite an impressive talent, and so far Odbayar had come a long way on the back of it.

'You could help,' Gundalai pointed out, gesturing with his paintbrush. 'We'd get twice as many done. If you think the numbers will justify it.'

Odbayar pushed the book aside. His expression suggested that Gundalai had made a proposal which was novel, perhaps intriguing, but fundamentally absurd. He nodded. 'Oh, the numbers will justify it,' he said. 'That's why your contribution is so critical. That's why everything needs to be done properly. That's why it needs our full commitment. Every one of us.' He nodded again, more slowly this time, as though reflecting on the profundity of these statements. Then he picked up the book and continued reading.

Another talent, Gundalai supposed. The ability to respond, at length and with impressive fluency, without actually answering the question. And implying that, even by asking it, you were somehow failing to live up to Odbayar's own irreproachably high standards. He was not a politician yet – not a conventional politician at any rate – but it was clear that Odbayar was already perfectly fitted to the role.

'These all right, then?' Gundalai held up a sample of his crafts-manship.

Odbayar put his book down again, looking only momentarily irritated by the further interruption. He tipped his head on one side and squinted at the banner that Gundalai was holding. It was a primitive affair – stiff cardboard tacked to a piece of old wood – but Gundalai's draughtsman's skills were undeniable. Odbayar nodded thoughtfully. 'Yes, looks okay,' he said, as close to enthusiasm as he was ever likely to get. 'Good slogans, too.' The wording of the slogans had, needless to say, been Odbayar's own.

In truth, Odbayar's slogans had a tendency to be wordy. It was a pity, he thought, but there was no point in underselling the sophistication of their core messages. Odbayar saw himself as representing the popular will, but he was no populist. There were too many people peddling false hope, easy solutions. It was time to tell the truth, Odbayar declared, even if the truth might take a little longer to explain.

The slogans were all variations on a common theme: selling out the people's birthright, betraying their heritage, giving away their inheritance. Theft. But not just the theft of money or possessions – though there was certainly that as well – but something more profound. The theft of their history. Everything that made this country what it was. Everything they were supposedly celebrating this year.

And it was worse even than that. It was also the theft of their future. Everything that this land might one day become.

Odbayar wasn't the only one to see it. He could feel that things were moving in his direction. It was evident in the opinion columns, the editorials, in the privately owned newspapers. He could hear it in the grumblings of the old men gathered in the square, smoking their cigarettes, playing their endless games of chess. People were finally beginning to realise how serious this was.

'You think people will still come?' Gundalai said, with his uncanny knack for timely intrusions into Odbayar's train of thought. He had his head down, painstakingly working on the lettering of the next placard.

'Why wouldn't they?' Odbayar said. 'We've got all the student bodies behind us. And some of the opposition parties are beginning to come on board, unofficially at least.'

'But after yesterday people are jittery.'

'That was nothing to do with this. No one knows what that was about.'

'So how do you know it was nothing to do with this?' Gundalai said, with unarguable logic.

'Why would it be? This is just a peaceful protest. We've informed the authorities.'

Gundalai shrugged. 'Maybe that was a peaceful protest as well. Maybe he'd informed the authorities.'

'That was—' Odbayar stopped, realising just too late that Gundalai was winding him up again. 'Yes, all right. Very funny.

Gundalai looked up, his face as deadpan as ever. 'But there was a man shot,' he said. 'Killed. Whatever the story, it's bound to have an effect. Things like that don't happen here. And they're hushing it up. There was nothing on the TV news.'

'If anything, I think it's going to increase the turnout,' Odbayar said, with his familiar self-confidence. 'It's just another example of how we can't trust this government. And of how they won't trust us with the truth.'

Gundalai had moved on to his next placard, and was carefully drawing a pencil mark to align the lettering. 'Me,' he said, 'I'm just worried about who they might want to shoot next.'

'This is ridiculous.'

Nergui's expression, as always, revealed nothing. He glanced across the room at the huge bulk of Tunjin on the bed. 'I have a job to do.'

'What is your job these days, Nergui? Do you even know?'

It was a reasonable enough question, given everything that had happened in recent months, but Doripalam could feel that he was stepping onto dangerous ground. He had no idea what Nergui was thinking or feeling these days.

Nergui looked back at him with the faintest of smiles on his lips. 'My job's the same as it ever was,' he said. 'I just have to keep on finding new ways to carry it out.'

'And that's what you're doing, is it?'

'That's exactly what I'm doing.' He shrugged, the smile growing more definite now, with, at least for a moment, the first signs of some warmth. 'I don't expect you to like it. But it's what I do. Nothing's changed.'

'And what you do is take into custody someone who saved your life? Who probably saved dozens of lives yesterday? I don't begin to understand this, Nergui.'

Nergui shrugged. 'It's not your job to understand it. Not this time.'

Doripalam opened his mouth to respond, then bit back his words. 'It's my job to protect Tunjin's interests,' he said. 'No one else is going to do it. And he's part of my team now.'

'And we will keep you fully informed.' It was the tone, Doripalam thought, that Nergui might use with a particularly inquisitive member of the press or some junior representative of one of the opposition parties. It felt like a calculated taunt, the dismissal most likely to sting Doripalam.

'So what are you planning to do, then?' he said. 'He's in no state to be moved.'

'So I understand,' Nergui said. 'Though perhaps his illness is not quite so severe as you first feared?' He looked over at the doctor, who had been following their exchange with his usual mild curiosity. 'Would you say so, Doctor?'

The doctor shrugged, clearly no more intimidated by Nergui than he had been by Doripalam. 'He's certainly made what appears to be a remarkable recovery. But we'll need to do tests. We won't be able to release him for some time.'

'How long?' Nergui said. 'Twenty-four hours?'

'That should be enough. Depending on what the tests tell us.'

'Of course,' Nergui said, smiling now. He looked back at Doripalam. 'Everything must be done properly. That is why I brought my two colleagues. To ensure that Tunjin is looked after while he's in here.' He gestured to the two figures in suits, who had moved silently into the room.

Doripalam did not recognise them, though he knew most police officers and ministry agents, at least by sight. Both men were heavily built, self-consciously muscular, their close-cropped hair and rigid stance more indicative of the military than any of the civilian services. What, Doripalam wondered, was actually going on here?

'If you're planning to detain Tunjin formally,' Doripalam said, 'you'll have gone through the proper procedures. Nothing's changed since you moved on.'

'Do you think so?' Nergui asked, as if sincerely seeking a response. 'I hope you're right. But my fear is that everything has changed.'

Doripalam walked back across the square from the hospital to police headquarters, still seething, his repressed anger only just competing with his profound bafflement. What the hell was Nergui up to?

He was accustomed to this: the game-playing, the inscrutability. And he knew Nergui well enough to recognise that it would not be arbitrary, that there would be some underlying plan. But that didn't excuse it. Not this time. Not in these circumstances. And certainly not involving Tunjin.

In the past, he had at least known where he stood with Nergui. Nergui balanced his loyalties with a politician's skill, but in the end he and Doripalam were on the same side. But, for all the time he had known Nergui – and what was it? five, six years? – everything had been much more straightforward than it was now. For much of that time, Nergui had held the role that Doripalam now occupied, head of the Serious Crimes Team. The political world had rarely intruded into their lives, and Nergui had always been skilful at protecting his underlings from its noxious effects. Doripalam knew now how challenging that could be.

But Nergui had been promoted to bigger, and supposedly better, things. Much of his life these days seemed to be glorified pen-pushing, preparing endless reports to the ministry or to the committees of the Great Hural on organised crime, drug trafficking, international terrorism. All interesting and important stuff, but not activity likely to keep him engaged for very long.

The two men had met occasionally over the past year, as Doripalam struggled with the corruption uncovered by the Muunokhoi case. His investigations had identified an increasing number of officers, in the Serious Crimes Team and other parts of the service, who had been tainted by Muunokhoi's operations. In a few cases, there was definitive proof of corruption, but more commonly, there was only uncertainty. With Muunokhoi dead, his entourage had largely melted back into the underworld from which it had briefly emerged.

In the end, only five officers were prosecuted, and one prosecution was subsequently dropped due to insufficient evidence. Doripalam believed that at least another ten officers had been on Muunokhoi's payroll. But there was no way of proving it, even to his own satisfaction. The best that Doripalam had been able to do was arrange for them to be transferred back into operational roles where the impact of any future corruption would be limited. In his darker moments, he wondered whether he had unjustly ruined some poor innocent's career, but he could see little alternative.

It had been an unpleasant period, and Nergui's support had been invaluable in accessing the required resources and political clout. Doripalam had restructured the Serious Crimes Team, working with the small number of senior officers that he could still trust. They had brought in a raft of new recruits – most from outside the service, with thorough vetting of their background and circumstances – and ensured that they were properly trained and resourced. The basic stuff that should have been done years ago.

In the meantime, Nergui had forged a wary, but mutually

respectful, relationship with Bakei, the security minister. Bakei had been a senior officer in the security services under the old regime – a born survivor who had moved into political office, and progressed, often against the odds, through a succession of political and operational crises. Over the past six months, as the prime minister had struggled to hold the ruling coalition together, Bakei had played a key role in negotiating between the competing factions, keeping the show on the road. And much of that, Doripalam guessed, would have been down to Nergui's astuteness. The minister's stock was on the rise, and Nergui's influence was rising with it. But what he was planning to do with that influence was anyone's guess.

By the time he reached the Khanbrau Bar, Doripalam's anger was mellowing, replaced by a growing curiosity about Nergui's actions. There would be no personal animosity behind any of this, that wasn't the way Nergui worked. If he thought he was doing the right thing, nothing else would matter.

The tables outside the Khanbrau were crowded on yet another warm evening. Doripalam preferred to sit inside, in the shadows, enjoying the cold dark beer while the world went on with its business outside.

This place had become something of a habit with him. He had started coming here months before, initially as a useful place to meet with Nergui, conveniently located near the central square. The bar was attractive, too, because few of their ministry or police colleagues drank here, most preferring the German beer in the Chinggis Club. The Khanbrau attracted more of a tourist crowd, particularly as the summer approached.

Doripalam's visits to the Khanbrau with Nergui were his first experience of drinking regularly in the same venue, and he found that he rather liked it. It was a place of respite – a brief buffer zones between the challenges of work and the demands of domesticity. He could feel the temptation to stay in here, have just one more drink, to stave off the real world just that bit longer.

He had taken to coming here more often, sometimes with one

of the team, but often, as tonight, by himself. He enjoyed sitting with a newspaper or book, sipping one of the dark beers, watching the couples and the groups and the other lone drinkers. It was peaceful, quiet, and no one made any demands on him.

Solongo didn't approve. It was another part of his life that lay outside her control, that didn't fit in with the neat plans she had mapped out for them both. In any case, her attitude to alcohol had always verged on the puritanical. Although he'd seen no evidence himself, he'd heard rumours that her father, Battulga, a senior Party official, had had a drink problem towards the end. She talked a lot about her father – usually with the unspoken implication that, in most respects, he had been everything that Doripalam wasn't – but she never discussed this.

But she had other things on her mind right now. She was doing what she enjoyed, battling against the odds. She looked tired but also as if she was enjoying life again – as if she was finally engaging with something real, rather than living vicariously through her father's past or Doripalam's present. And, he thought with mild satisfaction as he ordered a beer at the bar, the fact that she had taken up smoking again at least meant she couldn't occupy quite her usual altitude of moral high ground.

He took the beer carefully across to a table in one of the darker corners and sipped the drink slowly, enjoying the first cold bitter taste after the dry heat of the afternoon. It was turning into an unusually hot summer – days of baking heat, clear blue empty skies. It would be good, he thought, to be somewhere other than here. Somewhere outside the city. Somewhere among the trees, where there was shelter, cooler air. He wanted more than anything simply to get away.

He was beginning to reflect on the possibility of taking a few days' leave – unlikely, with the deadlines that Solongo was facing – when he felt his mobile phone vibrate in his pocket. He pulled it out and glanced idly at the number. Batzorig, who was rapidly taking on the mantle of his unofficial deputy. He sighed and thumbed the call button, wondering why he was needed now. 'Hello?'

'Doripalam? Wanted to check where you were. I tried the hospital first, but they said you'd left. I just tried your home number.'

Doripalam paused, wondering what to say about his visit to Tunjin. 'I was just on my way back,' he said. 'Called in for a beer.'

'It's just – well, we've got an incident.'

'What sort of incident?' Batzorig was, like most of the team, young and inexperienced, promoted too quickly and struggling with the challenges that were thrown at him. But he was bright and honest and enthusiastic – none of which were particularly common characteristics in the service.

'We have a body,' he said. There was a moment's pause before he added: 'It looks like murder.'

'Where is it?' Doripalam swilled the beer in his glass, watching the pale foam against the dark liquid. He could see his evening disappearing.

'It's at the city museum.' Doripalam could hear his breathing down the line. His own mind was already making the obvious connection.

'There's one other thing.' Batzorig went on.

'What?' Doripalam could see the evening sky through the large windows at the far end of the bar.

'The person who reported it,' Batzorig continued hurriedly. 'It was your wife. It was Solongo.'

## WINTER 1988

The museum was as good a first rendezvous as any. He could spend hours wandering through its largely deserted halls, staring at the exhibits, a notebook in his hand. From the walls, the images of Genghis Khan stared down, grimacing as though to express disapproval.

He was slightly surprised that the museum had survived through the more stringent days of this regime. But the Party had always had ambiguous views about places like this, just as in his own country and in the USSR. They talked about erasing history, but they were keen to foster national pride and identity, and they recognised where that identity had its roots.

So the museum had survived, even though its exhibits had seen better days. Labels had become detached, items were missing, the glass itself was stained to the point where it was almost opaque. He suspected that the more valuable items had been looted or misappropriated years before.

Nevertheless, people were beginning to visit the museum again, a sign of how things were changing. Even now, on this freezing winter's afternoon, light already draining from the streets outside, there were some visitors wandering purposefully about the dim corridors.

The contact was standing in one of the galleries on the ground floor, staring fixedly into a glass case filled with what looked like random trinkets from the later empire. He glanced up, his face betraying no emotion or sign of recognition.

This was it. The moment that had been planned for. The point from which they could start to build their future.

# CHAPTER THREE

## SUMMER

Nergui was at the window, gazing down at the street below. It was nearly six, and Peace Avenue was still busy with traffic, the usual mix of clapped-out Russian vehicles and newer Korean models, moving slowly and decorously out of the city. The western sky was deep red, a few thin clouds straggled against the setting sun.

'How is he?' he asked, not looking back.

The doctor looked up from his examination of Tunjin. 'Who exactly *are* you, anyway?' he said. He looked untroubled either by Nergui or by the presence of the two suited men who were sitting, impressively upright on hard-backed chairs at the far end of the room.

Nergui turned back towards the doctor, smiling broadly. 'I showed you my ID,' he said. 'I trust you found it satisfactory?'

The doctor shrugged. 'I've honestly no idea,' he said. 'You're from the ministry of security, that's all I know. I haven't a clue whether you have the authority to be here.'

Nergui's smile widened even further. 'I have the authority. Don't worry about that.'

'I'll try not to,' the doctor said. 'So I presume you outrank the one who was here before?'

Nergui looked puzzled for a moment, until the doctor prompted: 'The policeman. The one who left. I had the impression he was something senior.'

Nergui nodded. 'Very senior,' he said. 'But, yes, I suppose I outrank him, if you want to put in that way.'

'I don't want to put it any way. Not really any of my business.' The doctor watched Nergui closely. 'But, then, I'm not sure that the condition of my patient is any of *your* business.'

'He's a friend,' Nergui said.

'Do you often put your friends under arrest?' the doctor said.

'Not exactly arrest. And only when I need to.' Nergui stepped away from the window towards the bed. Tunjin was breathing steadily, apparently asleep, and the monitors were sounding with comforting regularity. 'How is he?'

'Remarkably well. We're doing more tests. But at the moment he seems to be as fit as you'd expect someone in his physical condition to be. Nothing abnormal. He's just sleeping now.'

'So what was wrong with him?'

'I don't know. That's the main reason I'm doing the tests. If you'd asked me a few hours ago, I'd have guessed that he'd had a stroke. But that wasn't much more than a guess, largely based on the fact that he looks like a stroke waiting to happen. He was unconscious, appeared partly paralysed. From what his colleagues said, it happened very suddenly, with no obvious prior symptoms, so it was a logical starting point. But then he woke up, and seemed pretty much to have recovered.'

'Doesn't that usually happen with strokes?'

'Well, a stroke can be many things, sometimes the patient barely notices. But, no, it wasn't a stroke.'

'So what was it?'

'That's what we're trying to find out. But my guess is that he was drugged.'

Nergui nodded, as if the doctor was only confirming what he had assumed. 'What sort of drug?'

'Could be various things. Could be something like Rohypnol or Ketamine. What they call the "date rape" drugs.' He glanced across at Tunjin's massive prone body. 'Perhaps not the most appropriate description in this case.'

Nergui stared at him for a moment. The doctor held his gaze momentarily, then was forced to look away. 'We'll find out what it was,' he said.

'And how long before it's safe to wake him?'

'You could wake him now, but I'd rather let him sleep on for a while. This must have been traumatic for him. It would be traumatic for someone in a much better physical condition than his. If you're planning to question him, I think you should wait a couple of hours.'

'No sooner?'

'I can't stop you waking him. But he's my patient and you claim he's your friend. Leave it for a couple more hours.'

Nergui nodded. 'You're the doctor,' he said. 'I just hope you appreciate the implications.'

'Only the medical ones,' the doctor said. 'But that's my job. I can't speak for any other implications. Maybe you can. Maybe that's your job.'

'This way, sir. You can come round the back. It's quicker.'

Doripalam blinked up into the shadow. Batzorig was at the top of the stone steps above him. He had been there for some time, awaiting Doripalam's arrival.

'Where is it?'

'It's at the back. It's a kind of delivery area. A loading bay. I'll show you.' Batzorig bounded down the steps with his usual slightly uncontrolled enthusiasm, and jumped past Doripalam into the street. Doripalam hesitated for a moment, wondering whether Batzorig was going to tumble backwards into the passing traffic.

'This way.' Batzorig turned and disappeared round the corner, down the side of the museum's imposing entrance. Doripalam stepped after him, finding himself in a narrow passageway. Batzorig was a few steps ahead, looking back. 'Down here.'

'Where's Solongo?' Doripalam asked, walking with some nervousness into the shadowy alley.

'She's upstairs with a museum director,' Batzorig said. 'I think she's okay. It was a bit of a shock for her. But she seemed to be coping all right when I saw her.'

In any other officer, Doripalam might have suspected an undertone of irony, but the concept was alien to Batzorig. 'She's not easily fazed. But it might have been more of a shock than she's realised. I'll go up and see how she is once you've filled me in.' It suddenly occurred to him that he hadn't stopped to think about what the impact might have been on Solongo. He was accustomed to assuming that she could handle anything, but perhaps some things were beyond even her capabilities.

'I think anyone would have been disturbed,' Batzorig said. 'It isn't a pretty sight.'

They were too much alike, Doripalam thought, he and Batzorig. It probably wasn't a good idea to have as your putative deputy someone who thought and acted pretty much as you would have done. He could recognise in Batzorig the same combination of naïve enthusiasm and considered thinking that had characterised his own early days in the service. It was a potentially powerful combination, he thought, but then he would, wouldn't he? Perhaps he needed something different, a different set of traits, to challenge his own preconceptions. Doripalam thought back to his previous deputy, Luvsan – a different kind of enthusiasm there, certainly. A loose cannon. Far looser than they could have imagined. Pointing in entirely the wrong direction, in fact.

'In here, sir.' Batzorig was standing in a doorway. He ducked back, and Doripalam followed him into a courtyard surrounded on three sides by the internal walls of the museum, with rows of blank windows. The fourth wall opened on to one of the main streets leading to the central square. In the wall opposite the street, there was a loading bay, designed to accept large-scale deliveries.

'This is the place.'

Doripalam stopped and looked around. There was sufficient space for large delivery trucks to back into here to offload exhibits or other materials.

Batzorig had jumped up on to the loading bay. 'The body's still here. The scene of crime people haven't got here yet. They said about forty minutes.'

Always keep them waiting, Doripalam thought. He was never entirely clear what the scene of crime team treated as a priority but he knew it was never his own assignments. He followed Batzorig up on to the loading bay, choosing the more dignified option of the steps.

It took a moment for his eyes to grow accustomed to the shade. The delivery area was typical of the kind of facility found in any large-scale commercial or public operation. It was a broad space, with a concrete floor and bare walls – a contrast to the marble-faced splendour of the public areas of the museum. There was little clutter, just a few crates and boxes stacked at the far end of the room, a large roll of heavy-duty wrapping paper, a workbench neatly arrayed with packaging materials. In one corner, there was a cubicle, presumably used as an office, with a shabby desk topped by the ancient-looking computer. The room was lit, not particularly effectively, by strips of bare fluorescent bulbs. Two uniformed officers stood by the door at the rear of the bay, positioned to prevent anyone from entering.

Apart from the packaging materials, the only item visible was the large dark bulk of a clumsily rolled carpet, set a few yards back from the edge of the bay.

Batzorig gestured to it. 'That's it.'

'It's not been touched since the body was found?' Doripalam hoped it was an unnecessary question, but it never paid to take anything for granted.

Batzorig shook his head. 'No, one of the assistants here found the body first. Then they went to fetch Solongo.'

Doripalam nodded. Of course, they had. If it had been anyone else in charge here, the first action would have been to call the police. But nobody would have been willing to take that step without consulting with Solongo first. He couldn't say that he blamed them.

He took a step forward and caught sight of the body, half-hidden in the folds of the carpet. 'So what's the story?'

'The carpet arrived earlier today, part of a consignment of support materials for the exhibition. You know . . . ?'

'I know about the exhibition,' Doripalam said. Everything there is to know about it and possibly more, he added silently to himself. 'We can presumably track down the firm who delivered it?'

'We're on to that,' Batzorig said. 'It wasn't specialist stuff, I mean, not part of the exhibits. Just things like lights and stands and background materials. So it would have been just a standard courier company, not one of the specialist firms.'

'And the carpet was part of the background material?'

Batzorig shrugged. 'Presumably. They assumed that one of the specialist curators had ordered it. Anyway, all the stuff was unloaded. They'd moved most of the items up into the museum, but left the carpet – I think partly because they weren't sure where it was supposed to go, and partly just because it looked awkward to move.'

Doripalam leaned over and peered down at the body. Most of it was still hidden by the carpet, but the eyes were staring blankly upwards, the face a ghostly white. 'When did they find the body?'

'About an hour ago. Someone started messing about with the carpet, wondering why it was so badly rolled. It had been tied up with string, which was really all that was holding the body in there. They cut the string, the end fell back and – well, you can see.'

Doripalam nodded. 'It presumably wasn't intended to be hidden for very long?'

'It wasn't even rolled into the centre of the carpet. The intention was clearly that it would fall out as soon as the ties were cut.'

'Nice. Any clues about the victim?'

Batzorig shook his head. 'I haven't wanted to disturb anything, so haven't got too close. But he's not a local.'

Doripalam looked up at him. 'Not a Mongolian?'

'No. You can see if you look closer. Not sure what he is. Turkish, maybe. Or Middle Eastern.'

'And definitely a "he"?'

Batzorig smiled. 'Well, again, I've not looked too closely. But there's a moustache.'

Doripalam bit back an inappropriately facetious comment. 'You've put out an enquiry for any missing persons?'

'Of course. The fact that he's not a local may make it easier.' Or, as they both knew, might make it considerably harder. There were fewer illegal immigrants here than in many countries – not least because there was relatively little to come here for – but there were enough. And if this was one of those transients without documentation, without a history, without any official identify, they might never discover his name.

'Any ideas on the cause of death?'

Batzorig shook his head. 'Not for sure. There's some significant bruising on the face, but I don't know what else there might be on the body.'

Doripalam nodded slowly. 'And we're still waiting for the pathologist as well, of course?'

Batzorig nodded apologetically. 'I'm assured he's on his way.'

'Or will be eventually. What about witnesses?'

'Well, apart from Solongo—'

'You'll need to do the formal interview. We need to do all this by the book.' Which was true, but it didn't entirely account for Doripalam's reluctance to deal with his wife on what was now very much her home territory. 'Who else?'

'Well, there are four or five assistants who were down here. It was one of them who actually found the body.'

'Museum employees?'

'One of them is, I think. The rest are volunteers – mostly students getting some experience by helping out with the exhibition.'

Doripalam knew all about these. He had heard plenty from Solongo about their inexperience, their incompetence, their general ability to disrupt the smooth implementation of her plans. 'Are we likely to get anything useful from them?'

'I doubt it. They might be able to tell us something about the delivery. But even the one who first found the body – well, he's not seen much more than we have.'

'Where are they?'

'I've put them in one of the meeting rooms upstairs. Made sure nobody left before you got here.'

That was Batzorig's strength: simple reliability. You knew that everything that should have been done would have been. He was unlikely to have done anything very innovative or unexpected – though he had surprised Doripalam once or twice. But, for all his experience of working alongside Nergui, Doripalam still held the view that inspiration was over-rated. At least this way nothing would be missed.

'Okay,' he said, wearily, tasting in his mind the clean cold edge of the beer he had left behind in the Khanbrau. 'Let's get on with it.'

It was a smaller gathering even than Gundalai had expected – scarcely a dozen in total. Predictably enough, most of them were students, eager-looking young people with the light of idealism bright in their eyes. One of them, a young man in a fake Nike tee-shirt, had brought a bottle of vodka, and two or three of them were taking covert sips and becoming increasingly rowdy. An old man, dressed in a thick grey *del* that looked far too hot for the summer weather, sat behind them, exuding disapproval. All of them were looking expectantly towards Odbayar.

Odbayar himself was sitting behind the desk at the front of the hall, an overhead projector beaming the familiar image of Genghis Khan on to a screen behind him. He seemed entirely unfazed by the low turnout. With this size of audience, the platform and microphone seemed absurdly superfluous, but Odbayar was impervious to potential ridicule. He tapped on the microphone and leaned forward slowly.

'Ladies and gentlemen,' he began, not entirely accurately since there was only one woman in the room, 'comrades. Thank you for taking the time and trouble to attend our meeting this evening.'

He paused, as though expecting a smattering of applause. 'We are a small gathering, but we are the start of a great movement. It may be that, in the years to come, this meeting will be seen as a turning point in the history of our great nation. You will be proud to tell your children, and your children's children, that you were here tonight.'

In his way, Odbayar was an impressive orator. His style was unvarying – a string of platitudes and clichés designed to flatter whatever audience was in front of him – but the effect was genuinely impressive. Even the vodka drinkers had momentarily put aside the bottle and were listening intently.

'All of you know,' Odbayar went on, 'that we are living in the midst of scandal. Our government has betrayed us. No, it is worse than that. Our government continues to betray us, hour by hour, day by day, week by week. Each sunrise brings a new scandal, a further betrayal. Each day another piece of our wealth, our history, our heritage is given away for little more than a handful of coins. Each day we hand over another part of our nation to those who lie beyond our borders; to those who wish only to exploit our wealth and resources, to diminish our power and, yes, perhaps to rule over us as we once ruled over half the world.' His voice had risen to something of a climax, although Gundalai knew from painful experience that there was plenty more to come. He had heard this speech twenty or more times over the preceding days as Odbayar had rehearsed his delivery. Odbayar would be delivering the same speech again and again in coming weeks, in student halls and public meetings, trying to drum up the level of popular activism that would match his own heart-felt indignation.

There was no question, at least in Gundalai's mind, that Odbayar was sincere. Some would see him as an opportunist, an aspiring politician on the make. But Gundalai had known Odbayar for years – they had been schoolchildren and then students together – and, whatever faults he might have, hypocrisy was not among them. With Odbayar, what you saw was exactly what you got, often painfully so. He simply assumed that he was right and that his view should take precedence over everyone else's. It was the kind of personality that might just be capable of changing the world.

Odbayar's oration had increased in both volume and intensity, and he was leaning forward over the desk, jabbing his index finger towards the scattered figures in the audience. 'This is the truth,' he said, in a tone which implied that he was providing them with access to verities previously undisclosed to mankind. 'Over the past decade, the government – *your* government – has consistently failed to protect your interests. They have made deal after deal. They have talked about inward investment. They have talked about the vast wealth supposedly flowing into our country. They have talked about improving our standard of living. They have talked about creating a future that is the equal to our glorious past. But what have they really done? What have they really achieved? All they have done is sell our precious assets – our minerals, our mining rights, our copper and our gold – and gained nothing, or next to nothing, in return. All we have done is make the rich Western world still richer, and mortgaged our own future to those who wish us only harm.'

Gundalai couldn't quite buy into all this rhetoric, though he agreed with the broad thrust of Odbayar's words. Like many of his countrymen, his attitude towards the government – any govern-ment – was one of deep cynicism. He was just old enough to recall the dying days of the self-serving communist era, and he had seen little evidence that things had changed much since then. It was essentially the same party in charge now, and even when the parties and the individuals were shuffled, the personalities remained much the same. They were all in it for what they could get out of it. Sometimes the self-interest was naked – there had been a growing number of corruption cases in recent years, and probably count-less more that went unreported or even undetected. But often it was more subtle, and perhaps more insidious. The old regime had created its own elite, its over-class, and the new order had quickly done the same, often with the same individuals benefiting.

He envied Odbayar's clarity of focus, his unswerving belief that he could be the one who would finally change all this. But he didn't believe that change was really possible. And even if it was, it was unlikely to be for the better.

Gundalai realised with a start that he had ceased to listen to Odbayar's speech, lulled by the all-too-familiar cadences. Odbayar already reaching the climax of his speech, the rapt audience hanging on each word, eager to see how he would conclude.

As Odbayar raised his voice to embark on the final, climactic passage of his speech, there was a deafening explosion from the rear of the hall. Gundalai heard the sound of something shattering, and then screams, and suddenly he was pushed violently backwards and he heard nothing more.

# CHAPTER FOUR

The interviews had seemed interminable, but had told them almost nothing. Between them, Doripalam and Batzorig had interviewed all the museum staff on duty that afternoon, including the volunteers working with Solongo. Most had been in other parts of the building and could tell them nothing of value. The small group who had been present in the loading bay when the body was discovered added their individual perspectives and colour but little of substance.

It wasn't even clear who had actually discovered the body. At least two of the young men claimed this dubious honour, each reporting confidently that he had been the one to notice the odd bulging of the carpet and cut the restraining strings.

In the end, Doripalam had interviewed Solongo after all, deciding that it was cowardice rather than protocol that had prompted him to suggest Batzorig should take on the task. Even so, the interview had proved largely unilluminating. She seemed amused to find herself facing her earnest-looking husband in the untidy office they had commandeered as an interview room. 'I'm obviously privileged if I'm being dealt with by the man in charge,' she said, her face betraying no expression. 'Are you sure that's quite in order?'

Doripalam shrugged. 'Probably quite out of order. I just wanted to find out how you were.' He glanced across at the uniformed officer who was sitting at the side of the room, taking notes, but the other man studiously avoided his gaze.

Solongo said nothing for a moment, as though weighing up the significance of what he had just said, and then suddenly smiled with what seemed genuine warmth. 'I'm fine,' she said. 'Really. It takes more than a dead body to put my off my stride. And, to be honest, it's the least of the problems we've got round here.'

'How's it going? The exhibition, I mean.' It was a question he hardly dared raise at home these days. He wondered whether she might be more forthcoming in this formal environment.

She smiled. 'Oh, you know. Could be worse. I'm not sure how, though. But that's not really what this interview's about, is it?'

Doripalam nodded, understanding the unspoken message. Not in front of the junior officers. Well, fair enough. He did have a job to do. 'Let's get down to business, then. You were called when they found the body?'

She nodded. 'Just because I'm the person in charge, I think. They didn't know what else to do.'

'Who fetched you?'

'Batdorj. He's one of the volunteers. A bit more experienced than some of them.'

'Did he actually find the body?' Batdorj was being interviewed by Batzorig, and was not one of the two young men who had so far laid claim to this distinction.

'He didn't say so. There was a group of them down there. Once one of them opened the carpet, they'd have all seen it pretty much simultaneously, I imagine.' She paused. 'I can't say I reacted very calmly myself, even though I'd already been told that something was wrong.'

Doripalam glanced up at her. That was part of it, he thought, part of the reason she was reacting like this. She was disappointed with – ashamed of – her own reaction to finding the body, as if she had exposed some unacceptable weakness.

'Anyone would have been shocked,' he said. 'Even in this job, it never gets any easier.' He hesitated. 'Can you tell me what you saw? I mean, we can wait till later—'

'It's not difficult now,' she said briskly, 'but I can't imagine I can add anything to what others have told you.'

He shrugged. 'You never know. You might have seen something that the others didn't.'

'I know. You've told me often enough: the need to be rigorous. Attention to detail.'

He smiled. 'I'm glad you were paying attention.'

She glanced across at the uniformed officer, her smile unwavering. 'I hang on your every word, darling. So let me think it through. Batdorj came to find me.'

'You were upstairs?'

She nodded, and he thought he detected an unfamiliar flush of embarrassment. 'I was outside. Having a cigarette, actually.' For a second, she had the air of a schoolgirl caught out by a stern teacher. Then she laughed and the image was instantly dispelled. 'Bloody typical, really. First time in the day I grab five minutes off, and they find a dead body.'

'Did he tell you what they'd found?'

'No. I think they were all a bit shocked. Didn't quite believe it. Batdorj just told me I needed to come. I assumed it was another breakage.'

Doripalam had heard plenty about breakages over the past few weeks, along with Solongo's broader litany of complaints about the incompetence of those charged with transporting, delivering and displaying the exhibits. He still couldn't quite understand why she had allowed herself to get caught up in all this: the anniversary exhibition – the centrepiece of the summer's celebrations of the founding of the Mongol empire. A pretty big deal, and somehow Solongo, with undeniable ability but limited experience, had found herself in charge of it after the museum director, a world-renowned expert in Mongolian history, had suffered some kind of minor nervous breakdown and had departed on indefinite sick leave, only weeks before the exhibition was due to open. 'And, knowing what I know now,' she had added, 'I can't say I'm surprised he did.'

There had been no time to spare so they couldn't re-advertise the job or take any formal steps to find a replacement so they'd turned to Solongo. Or, more accurately, Doripalam thought, she had realised how desperate they were and had offered her services. She was a trustee of the museum, and had been involved in various exhibitions. She had some experience in organising public events after leaving university. But she had never been involved in anything remotely like this.

As soon as she'd taken over, she realised that her predecessor had had no capacity for organising or managing an event of this magnitude. Solongo's challenge, in the absence of any other willing volunteers, was simply to ensure that the exhibition actually happened. Which, when she'd taken over, had been far from a foregone conclusion.

Doripalam knew that it was the challenge that had attracted her. She was an extremely capable woman, who had felt wasted hobnobbing with the great and the good, and she had desperately wanted to prove that she could do something more than that.

'There are exhibits coming in from all over the world?' Doripalam said, mainly for the benefit of the note-taker. He had heard all about this too many times already. 'How are the materials delivered?'

'There are specialist transport companies – people who are supposedly expert in dealing with this kind of material, though you wouldn't always believe it when you see what they do. Most of the specialist stuff is transported like that – a complete nightmare in terms of insurance and so on.'

'And this carpet – that would just have been a standard delivery?'

'I presume so. A whole stack of background stuff turned up this morning: two or three deliveries. As always, it wasn't clear who'd actually ordered what. I have an overview, but there are specialist curators who are looking after specific aspects of the exhibition. They have their own budgets to hire any background materials they need – stands, specific lighting—'

'So you wouldn't be involved in those kinds of ordering?'

'Not usually. So long as they were in budget and weren't ordering anything out of the ordinary.'

'And that might include carpets?'

She frowned. 'I wouldn't see a carpet as part of the standard requirements. I suppose I can envisage how it might be used but I'd expect it to be cleared with me first. I'm not even sure where it would come from – most of our stuff is organised through a small number of specialist suppliers.'

'Have you found out who ordered it?'

'I've not really had an opportunity to check properly. But there are records of all the orders placed – I can get the details for you. And there are itemised records of all deliveries down in the loading area.'

'I'll be surprised if we find anything. What about the group downstairs? Did any of them see how the carpet was delivered?'

'Well, you're no doubt interviewing them all yourselves,' she said, pointedly, 'but nobody seemed very clear. There'd been several deliveries and everyone assumed it had arrived with one of them, but nobody knew which. I don't think anyone noticed it for a while. It's even possible it came the day before.'

'I think if the body had been there for more than a few hours, it would have been hard not to notice it,' Doripalam said. 'Especially in this heat.'

'I bow to your expertise,' she said. 'As always.'

Doripalam smiled faintly, but ignored the bait. 'Anyway, we'll check the records properly, and we'll contact the transport companies who've delivered in the last couple of days. I take it there's no CCTV in the loading area?'

'No. There probably ought to be. We've done some improvements to the security – the insurance companies insisted for some of the pieces in the exhibition – but it's not exactly state of the art.'

'What about the body itself? Did anything strike you about that?'

'Other than it being dead, you mean? That was quite enough for me.' She paused, as though wrestling with some idea. 'No, not really. I mean, it was wrapped in the carpet – though "wrapped" is probably an exaggeration. It was positioned just inside the carpet, barely covered over.'

'So somebody wanted it to be found?'

'Rather than waiting for the summer heat to do its work? Yes, I assume so. It was bound to be discovered as soon as anyone touched the carpet.'

'And what about the body itself?' He knew Solongo well enough to recognise that there was something on her mind.

'I don't know. Nothing really. I didn't really look that closely. I – well, I guess I panicked a little bit.' She closed her eyes, as if conjuring the scene up in her mind. 'Anything else? Well, I don't think he was Mongolian, but you probably know that.'

Doripalam shrugged, reluctant to give out any more information than he had to, even to Solongo. 'We're still waiting for the pathologist for a definitive view,' he said. 'But he doesn't look Mongolian.'

'And there was bruising on the face,' she said. 'A lot of bruising. As though he'd been beaten or kicked.' She paused. 'That's what—' she stopped again, as if unsure how to continue.

'What?' Doripalam could hear the scratch of the uniformed officer's pen across his pad.

'It's probably nothing,' she said. 'It's what comes of being overwhelmed by the Mongol empire twenty-four hours a day.'

'What is?'

'Well,' she paused again, and then plunged on, 'It's just that the carpet, the bruising, it reminded me of a story about Hulagu.'

'Hulagu?' Doripalam struggled to recall his schoolboy history. 'Genghis Khan's grandson?'

She smiled. 'Well done. Yes, Genghis's grandson. He led the siege of Baghdad in 1258. They eventually captured and killed the caliph of the city.'

The story had begun to come back to Doripalam – one of those memorable historical tales that, in his school days, he had never quite managed to position in its authentic context. He knew it had supposedly happened but he had never been quite clear when or why. 'But they knew that it was against Mongolian ethics to spill a king's blood on the ground,' he interrupted.

She nodded, smiling, as if her husand were a slow student who had managed, against the odds, to come up with the correct answer. 'Exactly,' she said. 'So they wrapped him in a carpet and trampled him to death.'

Doripalam stared at her. 'You're not suggesting that—'

She shrugged. 'I'm not suggesting anything. It's probably just the first symptom of my own impending nervous breakdown. I'm living with this stuff day and night at the moment, so these stories just pop into my head. But even so.'

'Go on,' Doripalam said. It sounded pretty bizarre to him, but the positioning of the body in the carpet was strange enough. And he knew that it never paid to underestimate Solongo's judgement.

She shook her head. 'I don't know. It's just that the capture of Baghdad was one of the final stages in our war against the Muslims. Our genocide of the Muslims, some have called it. Ethnic cleansing. A clash of civilisations. Anyway, it just seemed to me that – well, it all has a certain contemporary resonance, don't you think?'

An hour later, Doripalam met with Batzorig to compare notes. He had arranged for one of the uniformed team to drive Solongo home, saying that he would follow her as soon as he could. She had given him a look that suggested that the promise sounded as hollow to her as it did to him.

The two men worked painstakingly through the interview transcripts, but the information remained unhelpfully thin. Most of the volunteers had visited the loading area during the earlier part of the day, but no one could remember who had delivered the carpet. One of the young women interviewed by Batzorig had been sure that she had seen the carpet being off-loaded from a delivery truck during the early part of the morning.

'Which truck?' he had asked. 'Do you remember which company?'

She had shrugged. No, she hadn't registered the name of the company. Was it one of the usual companies, or an unfamiliar name? She didn't know. So perhaps that meant it was an unfamiliar name. Or perhaps it had just been too familiar.

'Could you describe the men who unloaded it?' Batzorig's hopes were fading now.

Not really. They had been Mongolian, she thought. Or Asian. At least, one of them had been. Probably average height. Normal build. Dark hair. Dressed in overalls. Or, at any rate, she was sure they were wearing the kind of clothes that the delivery drivers usually wore.

'But it was definitely early this morning that you saw them?'

Definitely. Unless it had been yesterday afternoon. But then they'd have noticed the carpet earlier, wouldn't they? So it must have been this morning. Assuming, that is, that it really was the carpet that she'd seen being off-loaded. Now she thought about it, she couldn't be absolutely sure.

It was always like this. It was one of the standard grumbles within the team – just how hopeless most witnesses turned out to be. Even when an incident had occurred right in front of their noses, they generally managed to misremember or misinterpret it. In circumstances like this, with witnesses struggling to remember apparently mundane events, the chances of extracting any reliable data were minimal.

Resorting to more definitive sources of information, Batzorig had checked the formal documents relating to the ordering and delivery of the museum's goods. There was no record of the carpet being ordered, and none of the specialist curators had any knowledge of how or why it might have been requested. There had been five recorded deliveries that day, but none of the delivery notes mentioned the carpet. They were in the process of checking with the relevant delivery companies, but Doripalam held out few hopes of any success. It was quite possible that there had been a further unrecorded delivery.

All in all, they were little further forward. They sat in the relatively luxurious office belonging to the absent director, and leafed morosely through the pages of notes. Artefacts of the Mongolian empire surrounded them on all sides, and an enormous print of the familiar face of Genghis stared down from behind Doripalam's head.

'An awful lot of nothing,' Doripalam said, tossing the wedge of papers on to the desk. 'So do you have any theories?'

'Nothing,' Batozrig said. 'We don't know who the victim is, and I can't begin to imagine why the body would have been dumped here of all places. It's not likely to be internecine warfare between archaeologists, I imagine.'

Doripalam smiled indulgently at the half-hearted attempt at a joke. 'Maybe it's just random; the body had to be dumped somewhere, so why not here?'

'Because it would have been risky,' Batzorig pointed out. 'I mean, much more risky than just dumping it in some waste ground, or outside the city somewhere.'

Doripalam nodded. 'So why here? What significance could this place have?'

Batzorig looked up. 'What do you think about your wife's idea? About Hulagu, I mean.' He had noted the comment in the transcript of the interview, though Doripalam had not drawn attention to it.

Doripalam shrugged. 'I don't know. It sounds pretty far-fetched to me. But I suppose that it would explain the carpet. And it would begin to explain why the body was brought here. If you're going to re-stage an episode from the glory days of the Mongol empire, you'd want to do it where someone will pick up on the reference.'

'And where it would have most resonance.'

'Exactly.' Doripalam shook his head. 'But it's all speculation. We don't know who the victim is. We don't know where he was killed. We don't even know for certain how he died, until the pathologist's finished.' He paused. 'Even so . . .'

'Sir?'

Doripalam looked up at the young man. 'If Solongo's right – I mean, if there's anything at all in what she's suggesting.' He stopped again, as if unsure how to articulate the ideas running through his mind. 'If she *is* right,' he said, finally, 'it suggests that we might be facing something very nasty indeed.'

## WINTER 1988

At first, he was sure he was being followed.

He shivered, pulling his padded coat more thickly around him, making a point of not looking back. Bloody cold. It was sometimes cold at home, but nothing like this bone-freezing chill. This close to the central square, the streetlights cast an eerie glow across the ice-lined road. Just a few blocks back, the lights ended, throwing the far end of the road into blackness.

He set off walking again. There were few people about, even though it was not late. Most people, he assumed, had more sense than to expose themselves to these cold temperatures for longer than necessary.

He felt more comfortable once he emerged from the narrow street that led from the apartment block into the main thoroughfare. Here the lights were brighter and more frequent, a pale pink chain stretching down towards the central square. There were more passers-by now, mainly young people, huddled in their thickly quilted clothing, rushing past in their eagerness to find warmth. Occasionally a vehicle passed, its driver cautiously navigating the potentially lethal road surface.

In some respects, the fierce cold was a blessing. Although he felt isolated and exposed, there were few around to observe his passing. Even if he was being watched, the brutality of these midwinter temperatures might dissuade any observer from pursuing the task too assiduously.

Had he been right to come here, right to pursue this? It was a major risk, even though it had been officially sanctioned. The authorities would always grant approval if they thought there was anything to be gained. But he had no illusions about how much that would be worth if anything went wrong. Then he would be on his own.

Finally, he steeled himself to look back. The street was empty. The only footsteps he could hear were his own. It was all under control. He was ready for his next meeting with the contact. Soon they would be able to talk properly.

It was all under control.

# CHAPTER FIVE

## SUMMER

'So you *are* here,' Tunjin said. 'I thought I was still dreaming.'

'You must have very disturbed dreams.' Nergui was sitting with his legs stretched out, looking as relaxed as the straight-backed hospital chair would allow.

'You couldn't begin to imagine,' Tunjin agreed. He tried to raise his hefty body, but the effort was too much. He was beginning to hope for some change of view, something other than the cracked whitewash of the ceiling, the partial glimpse of Nergui's face if he craned his head sufficiently. 'How long am I supposed to stay here?' he asked.

'They said twenty-four hours. I asked for less.'

'You wouldn't have had any complaints from me.' Tunjin paused. 'I'm under arrest, then?'

Nergui expression revealed nothing. 'I wasn't sure if you'd understood. I was waiting till you woke properly. But, no, not arrest.'

'I'm helping you with your enquiries?'

Nergui nodded. 'Something like that.'

'In my experience, that's usually just a euphemism.' Tunjin's eyes moved towards the door. 'You're not alone, I notice.'

Nergui smiled. 'Observant as ever. I'm just taking precautions, that's all.'

Tunjin dropped his head back on the pillow, letting out his breath suddenly. 'Should I ask against what?' He twisted his head and stared at Nergui. 'What's this all about? Not just you turning up here and throwing Doripalam out, I assume you've got your reasons for that, though forgive me if I don't quite follow them at the moment. But all of it. What happened yesterday?' He frowned, as if the question had only just occurred to him. 'What did happen yesterday, anyway?'

'Several questions,' Nergui said. 'All of them good ones.'

'Thank you. Not much chance of a satisfactory answer, then, I take it.' Tunjin stared up at the ceiling. The place looked less pristine up there. A spider had taken up residence in one corner, ignored by the assiduous cleaners who took care of the lower parts of the room. 'About as much chance as there is of me getting a drink in this place.'

'Abstinence will do you good,' Nergui pointed out. 'You've been ill, after all.'

Tunjin twisted his head again. 'That's another thing,' he said. 'I thought I was dying. At one point, I thought I was probably dead already. Now I feel, well, not healthy exactly, but a long way from dead. I'm sure this place is good, but I didn't know they were miracle workers.'

'You'd be surprised what they can do,' Nergui said.

Tunjin opened his mouth to speak, then decided there was little point in asking more. He stared up at the dense tapestry of the web in the high corner of the room, trying to make out the spider presumably lurking somewhere in the middle of it. 'I've known you for too long,' he said finally. 'You'll tell me when you're ready.'

'I'll tell you when I'm ready,' Nergui agreed. 'Some of it I can tell you now. So long as you tell me some things in return.'

'Fair enough. I'll tell you everything I know. That shouldn't detain you long.'

Nergui nodded, as if taking the proposition seriously. 'Okay, so tell me what you remember about yesterday.'

Tunjin frowned. 'Yesterday? Easy. I remember it as if it was—' He stopped. It was, after all, a good question. What did he remember about yesterday?

Nergui leaned back, rocking on the two rear legs of his chair like a restless child at school. 'Start at the beginning,' he said. 'If you can. First thing in the morning.'

Tunjin thought hard. Had yesterday been any different from most of the days that preceded it? There was no reason to think so – except that somehow he had ended up here. But all he had were images, pale half-memories that had flooded his head on waking but were now dissolving like last night's dream. Those drifting memories of gunshots and crowds and screams.

He closed his eyes and saw again, as though imprinted on his retina, the searing brilliance of the muzzle flash. Somewhere behind that, crowding in, a string of other thoughts, ideas, memories. Yesterday.

'I remember waking up,' he said at last. 'It was just another day. I was on the afternoon shift. So I woke up late. A bit hungover, but better than a lot of days. Just a few vodkas. I'd been on lates the previous day, too, so didn't go mad.' He looked at Nergui. 'Is this what you want? Is this any good?'

'Keep going,' Nergui said.

'I got up, got dressed. The apartment was a mess, so I thought I'd grab a coffee on the way in.' He paused, trying to concentrate. 'It was another hot day. I had plenty of time. I decided to walk into work.'

'You hadn't any other plans?'

'No, just walk in, grab a coffee, maybe a shot of vodka. Just one. Set me up for the day.'

'Hair of the dog,' Nergui agreed.

'I left the flat – I'm still in the same place, you know. Thought I might want to move after all that happened. But I feel at home there, despite everything. Anyway, I left there, walked up the street towards the centre.'

'What time would this have been?' Nergui asked.

'Not sure. Twelve? Twelve thirty, maybe? I had to be at HQ for two, so something like that. Wanted time for the coffee.'

'Go on.'

'I got near the square, and I heard a lot of noise. Shouting. Crowds of people, it sounded like. I didn't know what was happening.'

'What did you see?'

'I was still a few blocks away. I could just hear the noise. Not the kind of noise you expect to hear at twelve thirty on a . . .' He stopped. 'What day was it?'

'Wednesday,' Nergui said. 'Today's Thursday.'

'That's right,' Tunjin said, as though confirming Nergui's lucky guess. 'Not the kind of noise you expect to hear at that time on a Wednesday.'

'But then you saw the crowd?'

'Eventually, yes. It was a smaller crowd than it sounded, actually, the shouting was echoing round the buildings so it sounded as if there were more of them. But still a lot for that time on a Wednesday.'

'What happened then?'

Tunjin paused. The memories had been coming back clearly, but suddenly they were fading again, like a film unexpectedly going out of focus. 'I'm not sure,' he said. 'Let me think. I had to go through the square to get to work, so I carried on walking forward.'

'Is this what you're remembering, or what you think should have happened?'

'I don't know.' Tunjin closed his eyes again, willing the images to return, seeking confidence that he was recalling reality rather than assumptions. 'Yes, I can remember. I walked forward down there. I remember stepping into the sunlight as I made my way down the street. The crowd was clustered at this end of the square, near to the government buildings.' He stopped once more, now visualising the white faces of their banners and placards. 'It was a protest,' he said. 'Against the government. About corruption. Selling off our heritage. The usual stuff.' He was trying to retrace the pattern of his thoughts during those moments. 'It wasn't something we'd been warned about. The protest, I mean. No one had told the police. Or, if they had, no one had bothered to tell me.

Or I hadn't bothered to listen.' He shrugged, 'That happens sometimes.'

'So I recall,' Nergui said. 'What happened next?'

'I was standing at the edge of the square, wondering how many
people there were. How long they were going to be there. Whether
there was any chance of me being able to squeeze my way through
to the bar.' He was staring up at the blank white of the ceiling,
trying to envisage the scene. There was still no sign of the spider.
'I stood there for a while. Then I saw someone I recognised.'

'One of the crowd?'

'No. One of the police officers patrolling the edge of the square.
There were a few uniforms – not many. I don't think the police
knew quite how to handle it.'

'We're not used to this freedom of expression,' Nergui said.

'That's the trouble,' Tunjin went on, 'nobody knows quite how
to behave at these things. Nobody. The protesters. The police. We're
making it up as we go along. Anyway, yes, it was one of the uniforms.
We'd worked together a couple of times. So I went up to him and
we chatted. I was just asking him what it was all about.'

'Who was he? The uniform?'

Tunjin frowned, momentarily halted by an unexpectedly difficult question. He concentrated hard, wondering why his memory
had stuttered at what should have been the easiest question. 'There
were two of them,' he said, suddenly. 'Two uniforms. I knew one
of them. I don't know his name, but you can track him down easily
enough. He works out of the city-central station.'

'And the other one?'

Tunjin tried to shake his head, moving it as far he could on the
hard pillow. 'No, I didn't know him.' He paused, a thought suddenly
striking him. 'He didn't either.'

'Who didn't what?'

'The uniform. The one I knew. He didn't know the other guy
either. They'd never met before.'

Nergui looked up, with the air of someone who had finally heard
something of interest. 'Why do you say that?'

'You always know what to ask, don't you?' Tunjin said. 'I don't know. It was obvious, somehow. They were both being professional, both doing their job. But the first guy – the one I knew – he didn't know who the other uniform was, what he was doing there. He was treading warily round it, but you could tell he was curious.'

'So there was more than one team operating?'

'Well, that's it,' Tunjin said. 'Now you mention it. I don't think this was any kind of official operation. It wasn't a big deal. It was just being handled by whoever was on duty from the city-centre crew.'

'So who was this other uniform?'

'That's the question. If he'd been from the city-centre team, my guy would have known him. If he wasn't—'

'Then why was he there?' Nergui nodded. There were times when he resembled a patient teacher calmly waiting for his students to catch up with his thought processes. 'So what happened then?'

'I'm not sure,' Tunjin said. 'The protesters were shouting, chanting something. There was a bunch of tourists at the far side of the square. It looked pretty calm, no sense that it would get out of control. We were just chatting, watching it all. It was baking hot, and I was feeling a bit dehydrated. The uniform – the one I didn't know – offered me a bottle of water –' Tunjin paused, considering the implications of what he had just said.

'And then you saw something?'

Tunjin blinked. 'You can be scary, you know that? But, no, I'm not sure that I saw something.' He paused. 'I think my attention was drawn to something. Subtly.'

'The uniform? The other one, I mean.'

'The other one. Yes. I didn't register it at the time. But, thinking back, yes, I think he somehow made me aware of it.'

'It.'

'It. Him. The man. At the far end of the square.' He stopped, reconstructing the scene in his mind. 'The man in the overcoat. Too heavy for the weather. The man opening his coat.'

'How did you recognise it?' Nergui said. 'What was happening, I mean.'

'Doripalam,' Tunjin said. 'One of those briefings. The US stuff on the war on terror.'

'I'd never seen you as the seminar type.'

Tunjin shrugged. 'Easier than working. No, I thought it was quite interesting. Probably not very useful, but interesting. I take these things in, you know.'

'I'm sure. But you recognised it from that?'

'I suppose so. The stuff on suicide bombers. The film that Doripalam had. How to handle it. I thought it was nonsense here.'

'But you knew what to do when you saw it?'

'Yes. It was strange. I knew exactly what I was seeing. I knew how I ought to handle it. I knew there was only one way.'

'Immediate termination.'

'That's what they say. No time to give warnings, no time to disable the bomber. If you get it wrong, they've triggered the bomb anyway. All you can try to do is halt them before they can do it. Immediate termination.'

'And that's what you did.' It wasn't a question.

'That must be what I did.'

'And you had a firearm?'

Nergui had asked the question quietly, but the words again derailed Tunjin's train of thought. 'No. Of course not. I don't carry a gun. Not off duty. Not on duty, if I can help it, these days.' Tunjin had trained as a firearms officer years before. He'd been a decent shot, once upon a time. Now, he wasn't sure he could keep his hand still long enough to pull the trigger.

'So where did the gun come from?'

It was growing dark outside, Tunjin realised. The sun had set, and the shadows were creeping into the pale room. The lights were on in the ward, but now he could barely make out the spider's web. 'That's it,' he said. 'That's what I've been asking. I don't know. It was there, suddenly. I didn't hesitate. I didn't think. I just used it.' He stopped. 'I shot him.'

There was a long silence. 'You did the right thing,' Nergui said at last. 'You did the only thing you could have done. If you hadn't done it – well, you didn't know what the consequences might have been.'

There was something in Nergui's tone. There was, Tunjin reflected, very often something in Nergui's tone. 'But you do,' Tunjin said. 'You do know what the consequences would have been.'

Nergui was staring past Tunjin, his eyes fixed on the blank glass of the window. 'I do,' he said. 'I do now. I have a luxury you didn't have.'

'Which is?'

Nergui shrugged. 'Information.' He hesitated, as if suddenly aware of Tunjin's emotional state. 'He wasn't a suicide bomber,' he said. 'We know that now. He wasn't real. The bombs were fakes.'

The call came just as the pathologist arrived. It was typical, Doripalam thought. They'd spent all afternoon here, achieving very little, waiting for something that might shed some light. The scene of crime people had arrived with their usual lack of urgency, strolling in just as he'd begun to assume they'd deferred their contribution to the next day. They were painstaking enough, there was no question of that, but Doripalam wanted to urge them to move faster, cut a few corners, just to start getting some results. At that point, after an afternoon of fruitless interviews, he'd have settled for anything.

But there was nothing. He hadn't seriously expected that there would be. After all, this wasn't, actually the crime scene; it was just a place to which the body had been delivered. And, except for the blood of the victim, even the carpet seemed empty of any potential evidence. It had been removed for more detailed exam-ination but he had little confidence that anything would be found.

Which left the body itself. The corpse had been removed earlier that afternoon, and the pathologist had been working on it since then, with all his usual mutterings about needing more time. Doripalam had insisted on an update that evening. There was little point in all of them dragging back across to headquarters, so he had asked the pathologist to come back to the museum.

And then, literally as the pathologist walked through the door, Doripalam's mobile rang.

He gestured for the pathologist to sit down next to Batzorig, and impatiently answered the call. His mind was already distracted, focused on the thickness of the files under the pathologist's arm, wondering whether the size of the material would correlate to its value, but knowing from experience that the opposite was usually the case.

'I'm sorry,' he said at last. 'Can you repeat that?' He had misheard or misunderstood what the caller was saying.

The caller, one of the control room team at headquarters, patiently repeated what he had said, 'We think it may well be a bomb.'

Doripalam looked up at the two men sitting opposite. Batzorig looked as eager as ever, his enthusiasm undiminished by the hours of fruitless interrogation. The pathologist, a short mousey man with a constant air of grievance, wore an expression that suggested he had been unreasonably interrupted in some duty of far greater significance.

'A bomb?' Doripalam repeated.

'Well, we don't know for sure, but all the signs—'

'Where? I know you told me before, but tell me again. I'm not sure I'm taking this in.'

'A hotel, sir. On the south side of the city. Not one of the big tourist places.'

'Well, that's something,' Doripalam said and immediately regretted the words. That was the way things were going, he thought. His first instinct, faced with something like this, was to worry how it would play in the media, how it would affect his own position. 'Are there any casualties?' he asked, conscious now that the question sounded like an after-thought.

'We're still trying to get in there.' The officer stopped, as if he had run out of breath. 'The army team have just arrived. We're trying to find out if it's safe to go in.'

Doripalam nodded. He was listening to someone in mild shock, he thought. There were no precedents for this, no guidelines about how it should be handled. 'Okay,' he said. 'I'm on my way.'

He ended the call and looked back up at Batzorig and the pathologist, who were staring at him quizzically. The pathologist was thrusting forward the pile of bulky files, with the air of a child trying impatiently to conclude the formalities of delivering a birthday present so he could get on with enjoying the party.

Doripalam stared down at the files. 'Is there anything useful in there?'

The pathologist looked startled, as though he had been asked some unexpected and wholly unfair question. 'Well, you know we can never be definitive, and there's even less to go on here than—'

'Nothing, then?'

The pathologist glared at him. 'There's a lot of detail—'

'I'm sure there is.' For a moment, Doripalam gazed back at the hunched figure, wondering whether there was anything to be gained from this conversation. 'We're very grateful for your hard work. And thank you for taking the trouble to bring it over.'

'Yes, but—'

'You'll appreciate,' Doripalam said, waving his mobile phone gently in the other man's face, 'that it's not really the priority just at the moment.'

# CHAPTER SIX

There was smoke and dust everywhere. It was difficult to distinguish between the two, but the smoke caught suddenly in the back of the lungs, acrid and choking. It hit Gundalai unexpectedly, as he stumbled blindly down the corridor, his eyes still unaccustomed to the dull glimmer of the emergency lighting.

This was how people died, he thought. Not from the blast or the flames, but quietly, when they thought the worst was past. Their brains ceased to function, and they succumbed to a threat they hadn't even known was there.

He thrust out his hand against a doorway, trying to work out where he was. He didn't think he'd come far. Although it was difficult to be sure. He recalled the blast, the sudden glare, the extraordinary noise, as if the whole place was collapsing in upon them. The screaming . . .

And then what?

There was a period of time he couldn't grasp, that had somehow slipped beyond his memory. He had no idea how he came to be in this gloomy smoke-filled corridor. And he had no idea how long it had taken.

He took another step forward, his head still bowed, unseeing, uncaring about his direction but just trying to keep moving. To keep breathing. To keep alive.

And then his hand touched something cold and smooth, but noticeably a different texture to the plaster wall he had stumbled against before. Wood, he thought. A wooden door.

He pushed it hard with both hands, and then nearly fell back in despair as it failed to move. His fingers slid across the smooth surface of the door, searching for a handle, some form of purchase. There was a raised rectangle at head height – a window. His hands moved down, fumbling to the left and right until he found the cold stainless-steel doorknob.

Grasping it in both hands he turned it frantically. For a moment there was no movement and panic threatened to overwhelm him. Then he twisted it round once more and felt the door open in front of him.

Cool, clean air struck him in the face, and the dense grey fog was replaced by a battery of dazzling lights. He staggered out, retching, his throat and eyes raw from the rasp of the smoke. Almost immediately, overwhelmed by the glare and his own confusion, he lost his footing, slipping on the smooth tiled floor. He rolled, striking his shoulder painfully on the hard ground, and lay for a moment, trying to regain his breath and his bearings.

As his coughing subsided, he opened his eyes and stared up at the high ceiling above him. He was back in the hotel lobby, only metres from the room where the meeting had taken place. Apart from his own coughing and the internally exaggerated sound of his own breathing and heartbeat, there was an odd, unexpected silence. He had envisaged a mêlée of screaming and shouting and police sirens. Instead, it was as if there was a breathless audience out there waiting patiently for the next development.

He twisted his head, trying to work out what was happening. The frontage of the lobby was a series of large plate-glass windows, stretching across the façade of the hotel, facing out on to the street. The glass had been shattered by the blast, and innumerable glittering shards lay scattered across the polished tiles. Outside, there was darkness and the temperate air of the summer's evening.

And then, from his low vantage point on the floor of the lobby, he saw them.

Ranged across the deserted street, a line of blank-faced, uniformed officers and an array of unwavering rifle barrels.

Beyond the window, the pale glow of the streetlights was faintly echoed by the scattering of stars in the clear summer sky. Nergui glanced at his watch. Ten thirty. There were still a few people wandering through Sukh Bataar Square, mostly students and tourists enjoying the end of the warm evening.

From this high vantage point, Nergui could see most of the square. At the far end, flood-lit, was the newly constructed memorial to Genghis Khan. Another symbol of the 800-year anniversary. Another symbol of the state of this country.

The project had been vastly behind schedule. There had been serious doubt about whether it would be completed in time for the country's national day, the date of the memorial's official launch. Another embarrassment for the government, although only of the kind that most people expected these days. Nergui had observed the minor scandal with equanimity, his own minister was not involved. The security minister was, indeed, likely to benefit from any political fall-out, as he witnessed yet another of his rivals over-whelmed by the irresistible force of events. The minister had, to date, been a lucky politician. As Nergui was only too aware, this was a kind of skill in itself, but one that tended not to last for ever. And now Nergui wondered whether the minister's luck was finally running out.

In another mood, Nergui might have enjoyed the irony. Bakei had never been one to let the facts stand in the way of a career opportunity. He took every chance to talk up the terrorist threat, astutely applying phrases such as 'homeland security' to ensure that any proposed response sat squarely within his remit.

It was a smart enough tactic. You create a perceived threat, and then make sure that you're the only one with the capability to deal with it. Your colleagues defer to you because they don't want to risk being proved wrong. And they're quite happy for you to face the consequences if you are proved right. But that means, for the present, they have to let you take the credit for being courageous enough to face up to that possibility.

Nergui had never had any doubt about the minister's courage, at least not in political matters. He struck while others were still wondering whether to risk picking up the knife. That was why everyone – especially Bakei himself – saw him as a future prime minister or even president.

In any case, Nergui had no doubt that if anything did go wrong, it would not be Bakei who took responsibility. It was no accident that over the last year or so the minister had assiduously built up Nergui's public profile alongside his own. By raising Nergui's profile, the minister gained a ready made scapegoat. If things went wrong, it would be Nergui's neck on the block.

The thought didn't particularly trouble Nergui; there were more important things to worry about than political machinations. And clever as Bakei was, Nergui thought he was probably smart enough to keep at least half a step ahead.

But suddenly it was beginning to look as if these questions were no longer merely academic. Something was happening out there. Nergui didn't yet understand quite what it was, but a suspicion was stirring in his mind. And if he was right, then it really did look as if the minister's luck might finally be running out.

He pulled his thick coat tighter around his shoulders, and strode slowly across the square, worried about losing his footing on the icy ground. To his right, there was the equestrian statue of the revolutionary hero, stark against the gloomy bulk of the government buildings. He could see the squat tower of the Hotel Bayangol rising up ahead on his right, the monastery-museum of Choijin Lama on his left. Beyond that, there was the park itself.

He had visited here by day and found it pleasant enough – grassland, a murky-looking lake, a run-down amusement park. He could imagine it thronged with children at the height of Mongolia's brief summer. In the depths of winter, it retained a welcoming, if slightly desolate, air.

In the frozen night, however, its atmosphere felt entirely different. The lines of conifers were blank shapes, empty spaces cut into the star-speckled sky. Although the moon had not yet risen, the stars ensured that the night was not quite pitch-black. Even so, the park was nothing more than an expanse of dark, its silence potentially concealing all manner of threats.

The path stretched off from the gate into the dark interior, a pale luminous ribbon. He glanced back again. The hotel was behind him, a squat array of dimly lit windows, a slightly run-down frontage. From here it looked enormously welcoming, a warm and inviting contrast to the darkness in front of him.

He walked forward a few more metres into the park. This was the spot they had arranged. The next meeting.

# CHAPTER SEVEN

## SUMMER

At first, Doripalam could make out almost nothing. There was a glare of lights, harsh and unremitting after the darkness of the back streets. He could hear shouting, and his throat caught the acrid smell of burnt chemicals, the aftertaste of smoke.

He stood for a second by the rear door of the car, trying to get his bearings. This wasn't a part of the city he knew well, and the police driver had confused him by taking a twisting route to avoid the clusters of vehicles gridlocked around the site of the explosion.

'Where is it?' he called to Batzorig across the roof of the car.

Batzorig squinted into the gloom and then gestured off to their left. 'There, I think. That's the hotel.'

Doripalam walked forward a few paces, wanting to get a sense of what was happening. It seemed to be largely chaos. There was a growing crowd of passers-by – a mingling of local residents drawn out of their own apartments and those who had been out on the town – standing watching, as if waiting for some event that had not yet taken place. Which might conceivably be the case, Doripalam thought. It surely wasn't wise for all these people to be milling around, unprotected, in the proximity of an explosion. If this had been a bomb, there was no reason to assume that it was the only one.

But no one seemed to be making any serious effort at crowd

control. People were chatting and laughing, treating the event more as a social occasion than anything else. Doripalam pushed his way through, Batzorig close behind.

The crowd thinned, and there, facing Doripalam, was a line of police officers surrounding the entrance of the hotel. At both ends of the line, there were armed officers, firearms trained on the hotel doorway.

Doripalam blinked, his mind still not quite comprehending what he was seeing. He peered over the shoulders of the police cordon into the dazzling glare, trying to see the justification for the array of firearms. All he could make out was the shattered frontage of the hotel, the gaping doorway.

He gently tapped the shoulder of the officer nearest to him, who turned, glaring into the darkness.

'What's going on?' Doripalam asked.

The officer stared at him as though he were insane. 'Just get back,' he said. 'It's not safe here.'

'You can say that again,' Doripalam said. He reached into the pocket of his jacket and pulled out his ID, thrusting it, perhaps slightly too vehemently, into the man's face. 'Where's your commanding officer?'

The officer stared at the ID card, obviously trying to work out its significance. Finally, he looked up. It wasn't clear whether he'd succeeded in reading the card, or had simply decided not to bother. He gestured vaguely towards the end of the line. 'Over there,' he said.

Doripalam nodded and pushed his way to where an older officer was standing, a portable megaphone in his hand. The local area chief, Doripalam thought, a couple of ranks below his own.

'Excuse me,' Doripalam said. The chief was a short, stout man, with a familiar air of self-importance. He turned blankly towards Doripalam, his attention clearly elsewhere. 'I'm sorry, sir,' he said, 'if I could just ask you—'

'"Sir" is right,' Doripalam said, uncomfortably aware that his own self-importance seemed to be growing by the day. He already had the ID card in his hands. 'Serious crimes,' he said. 'What's happening here?'

The chief stared at him. 'Sir,' he repeated, as though now uttering some kind of incantation. 'I don't think this need concern you,' he said, after a pause. 'With respect—'

'With respect, I'd like to know what's happening.'

The chief nodded, with the air of one dealing politely with a particularly troublesome member of the public. 'We're not entirely sure,' he said at last. 'It was reported as a bombing, but we're not clear whether that's really the case.'

'But it was an explosion?'

'Yes. It was an explosion. But it could have been a gas leak, anything—'

'If it's a gas leak, do you think firearms are entirely wise?'

'I've had to make some very quick decisions.'

Doripalam nodded, deciding on the emollient approach. 'Of course,' he said. 'I'm just trying to understand what's going on.'

The chief gestured towards the hotel entrance. 'We understand most of the guests were evacuated immediately. There was some kind of political rally here tonight. We don't know who else might be in there. We can't be too careful.'

Doripalam sensed a man out of his depth, struggling to retain control of the situation in the only way he knew how. 'If there are people still in there,' he pointed out, 'they're more likely to be casualties than potential terrorists.'

'We can't be too careful,' the chief repeated. 'Sir.'

It was the dismissive tone of the last word that galvanised Doripalam into action. 'Tell your men to stand down,' he said. 'I'll take control of the situation now. It falls under our jurisdiction.'

The chief stared at him. 'Look—'

'Tell your men to stand down,' Doripalam said. 'That's an order.'

The chief had turned and was squaring up to him. 'It's not really your position to give me orders,' he said. 'I don't accept that this sits within your jurisdiction. This is my patch; I'm in charge here.'

It was clear that some of the officers around them had been listening in to the discussion. Doripalam cursed inwardly, berating himself for his handling of the situation. No senior officer with any self-respect would allow himself to be publicly brow-beaten. It was time to offer an escape route.

'I'm not challenging your authority,' Doripalam said. 'But I have a responsibility as head of the Serious Crimes Team.'

The chief allowed a faint smile to play across his face, clearly sensing a weakness in Doripalam's position. 'Of course, sir,' he said. 'I fully understand that. But, again, with respect, this really doesn't fall within your jurisdiction. If it's some kind of accident – a gas leak or whatever – then it's at most a matter of public safety. If it's a bombing, well . . .'

Doripalam glared back at him. 'Well, what?'

'Well, our orders are to report all potential terrorist activities to the ministry of security. And to retain command until their representatives arrive.' His smile was serene now. It would probably not remain so, Doripalam thought, if Nergui really had been summoned from the ministry to deal with this.

'So you've called the ministry?'

The chief blinked. 'Well, not yet, we've only just arrived ourselves—'

'So don't you think you should?'

'As I say, sir,' the chief resumed, 'I think it's my call as to whether—'

Doripalam had pulled his mobile phone from his pocket. He shrugged. 'I'll give them a call,' he said. 'I know people there. I'm sure they'll be interested, even if it turns out to be a false alarm.'

'Yes, but—'

Doripalam's thumb was already on the speed-dial code to Nergui's office, wondering if his bluff might be called. But before he could dial a shrill voice cut through the darkness beside them.

'Sir! Sir!'

Both Doripalam and the chief turned. It was a young uniformed officer, breathlessly approaching from the rear of the hotel. 'Sir, I think you ought to see this.'

The chief glared at him. 'What is it?'

'I was checking the hotel's function rooms at the back, sir.' The young man tried to catch his breath. 'We've found a body, sir. A dead body,' he added, as if to remove any ambiguity.

'Killed by the blast?' the chief queried.

The young officer stopped, noticing Doripalam for the first time. 'Well, no, sir, that's just it.'

'What is?' Doripalam said, stepping forward.

The young man's mouth opened and closed again, as he tried to work out whether he should respond to Doripalam's question. Eventually, he compromised, answering but staring fixedly at the chief.

'The body, sir, he wasn't killed by the fire. It looks as if he was stabbed.'

The chief glanced across at Doripalam. 'Stabbed?' he said. 'But that means—'

Doripalam leaned smoothly forward. 'With respect,' he said, 'what that means is that this is now in my jurisdiction. Tell your men to stand down.'

The full dimming of the lights was unexpected. Nergui blinked, aware that his mind had been drifting in the silence. He had been staring blankly at his own reflection in the window. With the sudden gloom, his image vanished, replaced by the black rectangles of the buildings across the square, the pale glimmer of the streetlights.

He glanced towards the doors of the hospital room, and then down at his watch, wondering whether the lights were on some kind of timer, or whether some member of the nursing staff had made the decision. There was no sign of movement in the corridor.

Tunjin slept on under the effects of a sedative. He was lying on his back, snoring heavily, but looking calm. It might all be coincidence, Nergui thought. It might all still be coincidence. Tunjin's involvement.

But it was strange that this had so suddenly come so close to home. Nergui was never inclined to dismiss the power of coincidence – more prevalent than most people recognised, particularly in a population as small as this. And the coincidence was remarkable, which was why he found himself sitting here, watching over Tunjin's corpulent sleeping figure.

The first connection was the supposed bomber, the young man who had died under Tunjin's gunfire. Tunjin had done the right thing but it had been unnecessary. Not only because the bomb itself had turned out to be a fake, but because Nergui's team already had the young man under close surveillance. They had been watching him for a couple of weeks, along with a number of other visiting students. There was growing unrest among the student population, which over the last year or so had seemed to take on a more sinister form than the usual youthful rebellion and student politicking. There was an increasing involvement of overseas students in anti-government activism. Those involved were a mixed bunch – some Chinese or Russian, some from the West and some from the less stable former Soviet republics and other satellites. And while much of it was straightforwardly political – including those who still hankered for a return to the old regime – there was an undertow of religious fundamentalism.

After much deliberation, they had focused on a small number of students whose activism seemed the most serious and threatening. These included three students – intriguingly, all from the West rather than from any of the territories closer to hand – who had been actively preaching potentially threatening Islamist messages.

There was little real enthusiasm for the exercise on Nergui's part. He thought they were unlikely to uncover anything more than another peculiar manifestation of post-adolescent behaviour. The young men might well be juvenile fanatics, but it didn't necessarily mean that they had any criminal intent. If their objectives were malign, why would they draw attention to themselves? More likely, that was their sole intention – to attract attention. Nergui understood that it was one of the things that young people were prone to do.

Nevertheless, he allocated an experienced agent to the task, reckoning that one capable officer should be able to keep tabs on all three students. Nergui didn't want them watched twenty-four hours a day – he just wanted to ensure he knew what they were up to.

And three days ago the agent conducting the surveillance, a middle-aged, nondescript officer called Lambaa, had appeared in Nergui's office doorway holding up a cassette tape. 'You need to hear this.'

Nergui recalled the meeting in detail now as he gazed sightlessly at his reflection in the hospital window. He had worked with Lambaa only peripherally since his arrival at the ministry. But he knew he was well regarded by his colleagues as thorough and meticulous: a safe pair of hands. The undramatic qualities that distinguished the most effective intelligence officers.

'What is it?' Nergui was already beginning to feel the stirrings of unease. 'The students?'

'The students,' Lambaa confirmed. 'Recordings of some of their mobile calls, plus some stuff we bugged in their rooms.'

Nergui nodded, feeling his usual mild discomfort with this intrusion into others' privacy. 'Suspicious?'

Lambaa shrugged. 'Well, odd, anyway.' He lowered himself gently into the chair opposite Nergui, and began to tap the corner of the cassette gently on the desk, looking as if he had just wandered in for a casual chat.

'In what way odd?' Nergui asked. 'Death to the infidel, that kind of thing?'

Lambaa looked back at him, his eyes almost as expressionless as Nergui's own. 'Some of that, but there's more.'

'Go on.' Nergui leaned back in his chair.

'The conversation is more business-like than I'd assumed. I was expecting either nothing much or the usual kind of youthful posturing. But it's not like that. It's as if they're planning something.'

Nergui frowned. 'Planning what?'

'That's more difficult to say.' Lambaa flipped the cassette into the air, then deftly caught it. 'Look, I've been keeping a close watch on these guys. It's an easy enough job, since they've spent most of their time in one another's rooms in the university. They seem to have become acquainted very quickly since their arrival.'

'But then they have a common cause,' Nergui said. 'You think they knew each other before?'

'Who knows? But I don't think it's an accident that they've come together here. I think it's been co-ordinated.'

'Co-ordinated? By someone here?'

'I don't know. But what's interesting is that they've already tapped into some kind of local network.'

'Within the university?'

'No. If they had connections in the university, that wouldn't be so surprising. It's wider than that. They've had continuous phone calls since they arrived – mostly from mobiles or numbers within the city. They've had two or three meetings. Again, locals from outside the university.'

'It's intriguing,' Nergui said. 'But I don't think we frown on people fraternising with the locals in quite the way we used to.'

Lambaa's expression suggested that this change in official attitudes was perhaps regrettable. 'The question is what they're fraternising about.'

'Quite,' Nergui said. 'And who they're fraternising with. You've checked that, I assume?'

'Naturally. It's an odd mix. Some students, as you'd expect. But, more interestingly, some numbers we haven't been able to trace, which suggests people who know what they're doing.' He paused. 'Professionals, I mean.'

'People who are one step ahead of us, in other words.'

'At least one step. But that's worrying. It suggests something more organised. But we've managed to identify some of the numbers they've called. And there does seem to be a link with some radical political types,' he stopped, allowing the words to hang in the air.

Nergui was interested now despite his previous scepticism. 'Fundamentalists?'

Lambaa smiled faintly, as though he had been leading up to this. He was good, Nergui thought. Definitely one to bear in mind for the future.

'Some of that,' Lambaa said. 'But some of the links go further. Not really what you'd expect at all.'

Nergui stretched himself back in his chair, lifting his feet to rest them on the corner of his desk. 'Go on.' He decided to allow Lambaa his moment of drama.

'We've tracked some of the numbers back to other groups. Nationalists. Not the major nationalist parties, but fringe groups.'

'Racists?'

Lambaa shrugged, looking is if he didn't quite understand the term. 'Patriots, I suppose, sir. People who think the government doesn't represent the glorious heritage of our nation.' He paused. 'You know the type.'

Nergui nodded. He knew the type very well. There were plenty of them around – groups who hid behind the name and image of Genghis Khan, the father of this nation. Those who had never quite come to terms with the loss of the Mongol empire. Those who saw the decades of Chinese and then Russian subjugation, not just as a political burden, but as an unbearable suppression of the national spirit. It was perhaps not an entirely unreasonable point of view.

'So who are we talking about?'

'Fringe groups. The kinds of people who've been organising the protests.' He spoke with a contempt for extra-parliamentary action that could only be mustered by a former secret policeman. 'They're hardly an organised force – a cluster of idealists, I guess you'd say, sir.' He paused, allowing the ambiguity of the second-person pronoun to hang in the air. 'But potentially a threat to public order.' He succeeded in implying that this was the very worst kind of threat.

'So why would our young men be in touch with this group?'

'Well, that's the question, sir. It's not clear who initiated the contact, or whether the students were in contact with this group before their arrival here. Or even whether the students even knew quite who they were talking to. We've listened repeatedly to the recordings we have of their conversations and calls, but they didn't give much away. Obviously we missed their initial discussions.' There was the faintest implication, perhaps, that this had been the fault of Nergui's tardiness in authorising the operation. Nergui had already detected in Lambaa an instinct for political survival that easily matched his own.

'So what were they talking about?'

'Some kind of operation. The nature of it wasn't clear, but there were refererences to something being planned.'

'Doesn't sound like much, given we've had them under full surveillance for a week. Maybe they were just planning another tribute to the birth of the Mongol empire. Students are generally looking for an excuse for a party, I'm told.'

Lambaa looked pained, though it was unclear whether he was more affronted by the implied criticism of his own performance or by the flippant reference to their national heritage. 'Something more than that, sir, I think. Some kind of covert operation.'

'But what kind of covert operation?' Nergui said. 'Assuming they're not just ordering the vodka and beer.'

Lambaa sat back in his chair, as if the whole conversation had been leading up to this moment. 'Terrorism, sir,' he said.

Nergui blinked at the quietly spoken, anonymous-looking man sitting opposite him. 'Terrorism,' he repeated, trying to keep any note of cynicism out of his voice. 'And you're sure about that?'

'Pretty sure, sir.'

'But you don't know what the nature of this covert operation actually is?'

'Not in detail, no.'

Nergui shook his head slowly. 'Forgive me if I'm being a little slow on this one, Lambaa. But do you actually have any evidence to support any of these assertions?'

Lambaa looked up, smiling broadly now. 'Yes, sir, as it happens, I do.'

It seemed to Nergui now that this meeting had occurred a lot longer ago than just three days. It was like looking back into another life, a world where all this discussion had been hypothetical. In Nergui's mind they had been two professionals speculating on possibilities, his own scepticism buoyed up by decades of experience of over-stated threats, imagined enemies.

But now suddenly it was real. It was here, on his doorstep, impossible to ignore or rationalise away. It was baffling, incomprehensible, illogical. But it was here, and it was as real as Tunjin's sleeping body.

# CHAPTER EIGHT

Doripalam had borrowed a flashlight from one of the uniformed officers, but the thin beam made little impression on the hazy dark. The smoke and dust hung motionless in the warm summer night, the fumes harsh at the back of his throat. Ahead, he could make out the occasional flicker of another flashlight, but he had lost sight of the officer who was leading them to where the body had been found.

'I suppose it would be possible for them to be less helpful,' he called back to Batzorig. 'Though I'm not quite sure how.'

'Never high on the local agenda,' Batzorig said, inches behind him. 'Helping out the visiting team from HQ. Especially when we've just snaffled a juicy case from under their noses.'

'We're here to lighten their load.'

'But always unappreciated. I don't know why we bother.'

Doripalam was placing his feet warily. The narrow alleyway was cluttered with several years' worth of accumulated rubbish. At this time of the year, it might be a favoured sleeping area for some of the city's homeless. Directing the flashlight warily around him, he spotted, behind a row of overflowing refuse bins, a bundle of blankets that might well be someone's stowed bedding.

The end of the alleyway came suddenly, and Doripalam stumbled out into a small open area, his flashlight beam lost in the smoky space. To his left, along the rear of the hotel, he saw a rectangle of deeper darkness – a double doorway, gaping open. He flicked the light across the wall and found the local officer, leaning against the doorway, a lit cigarette in his mouth.

'Maybe not the smartest move,' Doripalam said, 'if there really is a gas leak.'

The man shrugged. 'I don't smell it,' he said. 'Do you?' Nevertheless, he tossed the cigarette to the floor and ground it out under his boot.

Doripalam stared at him for a moment, trying to make out the officer's expression in the dim torch light. 'This the place?' he said, finally.

The officer gestured towards the open doorway. 'In there,' he said. 'I'll wait out here, if that's all right with you.'

Doripalam stepped forward, playing his flashlight across the gaping doorway. 'Not really,' he said. 'We're all in this together, you're supposed to be guiding us.'

The officer stared at him for a second, as if wondering just how much Doripalam's authority was actually worth down here. Then he nodded. 'If you insist,' he said. 'I don't think any of us will want to stay in there any longer than we can help.' He switched on his own flashlight and shuffled slowly through the doorway, Doripalam following close behind.

The smell struck him at once. Not strong – the body had clearly not been here for long, given the heat of the day – but unmistakeable even through the acrid burn of the smoke.

'Where is it?' Doripalam said, trying not to breathe too deeply.

'There,' the officer said, lifting his torch. The pale light ran across a row of wooden crates, piles of some kind of fabric, a clutter of old machine parts.

The body was lying behind all of this debris, face up on the filthy concrete floor. Doripalam had to concede that the local officers had carried out their jobs with some rigour – it was surprising that the body had been spotted at all.

He moved forward and shone the flashlight into the narrow space. The body was wedged between the cold stone of the wall – dripping with damp even in the height of summer – and the jumble of discarded rubbish that dominated most of the room. The limbs were twisted awkwardly, the head at a disturbing angle, as if the neck had been broken. On the face of it, though, that did not appear to have been the cause of death. The cause of death was, most likely, the ornate-handled knife protruding from the victim's tee-shirted chest.

'Probably not an accident, anyway,' Batzorig said, inches behind Doripalam.

'Not overcome by the fumes, either,' Doripalam replied, moving slowly forward. He looked up at the local officer. 'Nobody's touched the body since it was found?'

'What do you think? Don't imagine anyone's been down here to do an impromptu post mortem.'

Doripalam glanced up at the young man but said nothing. Instead, he leaned over the body, getting as close as he could without touching or disturbing it. He had already put in a call to the scene of crime team and the pathologist, but he recognised that neither would be in a hurry to arrive, given the demands they had already faced that day.

The body was male, its hair trimmed very short, balding slightly at the crown. The head was thrown back and angled towards the wall, but the cast of the face did not look Mongolian. It was difficult to make out much more. The body was clothed in the now blood-stained tee-shirt, a leather jacket – apparently fairly new, good quality – and a pair of denim jeans. Probably a relatively young man – no more than thirty or so at the most. Thin, but quite muscular.

Doripalam played the flashlight beam gently around the supine body. There was no sign of any other possessions, nothing that the victim might have dropped. To the left of the body there was a rapidly coagulating pool of blood, evidence that the murder had indeed been committed here.

He flashed the torch beam back towards the door, where the young local officer was leaning. 'Was it you who found him?'

The young officer nodded, less cocky now, more sombre. Perhaps, Doripalam thought, he had been more shaken by his first sight of a dead body than he had wanted to admit. 'There were two of us,' he said, after a pause. 'We'd been asked to check out the back of the hotel – make sure the fire was properly out, check if there was any other damage. You know.'

Doripalam nodded. 'Where's your colleague?'

'Out front somewhere. I think the chief asked him to look after things out there. I'll find him for you if you need to speak to him.'

'Later we will,' Doripalam said. 'You didn't spot anything else?' His voice was less dismissive now of the young man. He wondered whether he had volunteered to act as their guide back here, or whether the local chief had given him no choice.

The young man frowned, clearly taking the question seriously. 'I don't think so,' he said. 'I mean, it was too dark to see much at all. We were just looking around, looking for anything obvious. We didn't want to get too close to the building.'

'In case there was another explosion?'

'Yes. Or some damage done to it. You know, falling masonry, things like that.'

'So what made you look in here?' Doripalam said, shining his torch around the narrow storeroom. The walls were badly plastered, cracked and stained with damp. The dark corners were thick with dust and cobwebs. 'It might have been risky.'

The young man nodded, his eyes wide as if the reality of this had only just occurred to him. 'I – We just thought we ought to look in here. At least to check. I mean, after the guy out front—'

Doripalam looked up sharply, glancing across at Batzorig, who had been systematically shining his own flashlight around the floor of the room, peering for anything the young man might have missed. 'What do you mean?' Doripalam said. 'What guy out front?'

The young man blinked, his eyes bewildered. 'Well.' He stopped, as if searching for the right words. 'The man with the gun. The man they picked up.' He halted again, obviously now reading the expression on Doripalam's face. 'Didn't the chief tell you?'

For a long moment, Gundalai had been dazzled by the spotlights. Then, as his vision cleared, he remained crouched, transfixed by the row of rifle barrels. He could make out no faces, just blank silhouettes, helmets glinting in the brilliant light, and behind them the endless clouds of dark billowing smoke.

It took him several seconds to realise that, though the rifles were pointed in his direction, they were not specifically aimed at him. He was still crouched in the shadows at the rear of the hotel lobby, outside the unrelenting glare of the spotlights. The rifles were aimed at the main doors, which, like the glass frontage of the hotel, had been shattered by the force of the blast.

Gundalai shifted forward tentatively, trying to work out what was happening.

He didn't know who was out there. The police? The army? Or someone else? He didn't know who or what they were looking for, or why their weapons were trained so fixedly on the hotel entrance.

He didn't know what might make them shoot.

Gundalai looked behind him. He had no desire to make his way back into the smoke-filled corridors. On the other hand, it was a preferable option to being gunned down.

He moved back slowly, inch by inch, trying to ensure that his movements would not be detected by the gunmen outside. Already, he could feel a catch in his throat as the smoke caught him. He closed his eyes, imagining the stinging fumes, the slowly thickening air.

He had almost reached the doorway to the corridor before he felt the cold, clean air. Not the breeze that had stirred from the hotel entrance. He was too far back for that. Something different.

He looked to his left. Beyond the hotel reception desk, almost hidden in the dark corner of the lobby, there was another doorway. It was open, blackness beyond it. The scent of fresh air.

Gundalai climbed slowly to his feet, edging backwards, his eyes fixed on the gaping frontage of the hotel. In a moment he was at the doorway, and he stepped out into the cool dark.

His eyes grew accustomed to the gloom, and he realised he was in a short passage. The walls were bare plaster, the floor nothing more than stone slabs. A route for the hotel's staff rather than its guests.

The passage opened into an unlit alleyway, its gloom intensified by the shade of an adjoining building. He hesitated for only a moment; behind him, the options were either gunfire or asphyxiation. To his left, the alley ended in the blank glare of the spotlights at the front of the hotel. To his right, there was only darkness.

His instinct told him to head towards the light. He would have more options in that brightly illuminated space than in some unlit uncertainty. He began to make his way down the alley, keeping his back to the wall of the hotel. He could hear voices, the sound of movement. Somewhere, there was the distant hum of traffic and, beyond even that, the far-off sound of a siren. He couldn't be sure whether it was moving closer or drawing further away.

Scarcely breathing, he reached the end of the alley, and peered cautiously round the corner of the building. There was a crowd of people there, still clustered close to the hotel, though uniformed officers were present, easing them back; other men in overalls were anxiously struggling to erect metal barriers.

Gundalai moved to his right, away from the building, back into the darkness, and slipped unobtrusively around the outsides of the barriers. He shuffled along behind the crowd, attracting an occasional curious glance. He must look a mess, he thought. His clothes and face were grimy from the dust and debris in the hotel corridors and he reeked of smoke.

He didn't know what he was doing or why, and it occurred to him, as if observing someone else, that he was probably in a state of shock. He stopped, trying to clear his head, apologising automatically as someone in the jostling crowd bumped into him.

There was no reason to be running away. He had nothing to hide. He was a victim here. The police would want to speak to him, would be trying to tally the numbers of those who had been in the hotel. He should make himself known, tell them he was safe.

And that thought brought another. He needed to find Odbayar.

He needed to check that he had emerged from the explosion unscathed. Gundalai had given no thought to the wider effects of the explosion. He had no idea how close they had been to the blast, or how much damage it might have done.

He twisted round, struggling against the crowd surging against him. He began to push his way back towards the police cordon, intent now on making himself known.

Then he stopped, his eyes caught by something to one side of the barriers. To the left of the hotel, past the alley from which he had emerged, was a patch of waste ground. Some building had been demolished, perhaps with the intention of developing the land, but to date nothing had been done and the space appeared to have been abandoned.

It lay unlit in the shadow of the hotel, but was given some illumination by the battery of spotlights erected on two police vans facing the hotel. In the corner of the waste ground, there was an unmarked white van. Next to the van there were three figures engaged in some kind of altercation. Two of them – apparently uniformed police officers – were holding the third. And it was the third figure who caught Gundalai's attention.

It was Odbayar, his arms pinioned by the police officers. For a moment, Gundalai thought his eyes were deceiving him – that he was seeing his friend, perhaps injured, being supported by the officers clustered around him. But he peered into the darkness, and knew that he had been right. Odbayar was struggling, pulling against the men's grip.

As Gundalai watched, Odbayar ceased struggling and fell forward, limply, as if he had been struck hard on the back of his head. At the same moment, the battery of spotlights shifted momentarily – Gundalai glanced around and saw that one of the police vans had moved to allow another metal barrier to be erected. By the time he looked back, the three figures had gone and the van was pulling away, disappearing into one of the streets to the rear of the hotel.

For a moment Gundalai wondered whether he should try to

prevent whatever might be happening to Odbayar. Perhaps he should try to attract the attention of one of the officers behind the barrier, explain who he was, explain – since they had clearly made some dreadful mistake – who Odbayar was.

But his better judgement held him back. If they were behaving like that towards Odbayar, why should they treat him differently? He moved slowly back into the crowd, trying to think what he should do next. There was, he thought, one obvious place he could go. One place that, perhaps, he should go. But he wasn't ready for that yet – he didn't know what the implications might be. He had to think it through. He needed someone he could talk to, someone with the right connections, the right knowledge. But someone he could trust.

He could think of only one person.

## WINTER 1988

He held his breath for a moment, then walked forward into the icy darkness. Before there had been the occasional distant hum of traffic, a car or truck passing on the main road. As he stepped into the park, the sound fell away with an unexpected suddenness, lost behind the shelter of the trees.

He was taking a risk, he knew that. But he'd been taking a risk throughout. This was what his life had been leading to. The contact was his now. He had built the relationship from a distance, unwilling to trust any of the local agents on the ground. He knew this was his one chance.

He stopped, deep in the darkness of the park. There was some illumination from the richly starred sky, but he could see only a few yards around him.

And it was freezing now, far below zero. How long should he wait? How long *could* he wait in this temperature? The chill was already eating through his clothes, entering his limbs.

He turned again, wrapping his arms tightly around himself, trying to keep the cold from his body. Straining his eyes against the dark, his ears against the silence, searching for some indication that he was not alone.

And then, even though he had spotted no sign of any approach, a voice said quietly in his ear: 'Good evening. I'm glad you could make it.'

# CHAPTER NINE

## SUMMER

Nergui had allowed himself to doze for a while, his feet propped on another chair next to Tunjin's sleeping form. In some ways, he envied Tunjin's slumber. Nergui had never needed much sleep, and over the years had acquired a habit of staying awake till the small hours, whiling away the time reading or listening to music, occasionally watching what passed for overnight television in this country. But sometimes he missed the repose, the opportunity to escape from the pressures of the day.

He had been thinking, over and over, about that last discussion with Lambaa, trying to make sense of what he had heard, of what he now knew.

'You think they're terrorists,' he had said. 'These students. You think they're terrorists?'

Lambaa had shrugged. 'I can only give you the evidence. I think it suggests terrorism. Or at least subversion. Disruption.' Nergui suspected that, in Lambaa's conservative mind, these terms were all essentially synonymous.

'Take me through it properly. You followed two of our subjects to a location in the south of the city – an abandoned storage unit.'

'In the industrial sector, yes. I was just keeping tabs on them, as you ordered.'

'And do you know why they went there? Were they responding to a message, some kind of signal?'

'Probably. We don't know for sure yet. There were calls, some again from numbers we haven't been able to trace.'

'But you had them tapped?'

'Of course. There was nothing suspicious. Not in what was said. But that doesn't mean that there wasn't a code of some kind.'

'And they seemed to know the way to this place, did they?'

'More or less. Not like natives of the city – they were using a streetmap – but they seemed to have a reasonable idea of where they were going. It wasn't the easiest place to find, or somewhere that tourists would frequent. The whole place is a dump – abandoned factories, burned-out shops. Needs razing to the ground and re-building.'

'It will happen,' Nergui said. 'It's happening everywhere else. The whole city is one big building site.'

'When they got there, they didn't hesitate, seemed to know it was the right place.'

Nergui glanced up at the doughy, misleadingly complacent face of the man sitting opposite. 'You think they'd been there already?'

Lambaa shrugged, almost imperceptibly. 'Maybe. They've not been here long, but they were here for a few days before we starting keeping tabs on them. Perhaps someone took them there before, which is why they needed the streetmap. But once they were in the area, they seemed pretty confident.'

'And they had keys?'

'I think so. They both clustered round the door. It was one of those big industrial doors with a bolt and a padlock. I presume they had to unfasten the lock, but it might have been undone already. I couldn't get too close. There was no one else around, so I'd have been too conspicuous.'

Nergui didn't doubt it. He knew, from his own painful experiences, just how deserted the old industrial parts of the city could be, particularly once the working day was over. And, in many of those former factories, the working day had been over years before.

'But, yes,' Lambaa went on, with the air of one accustomed to precision, 'I imagine they had keys and that they unfastened the padlock. They closed it up again afterwards, but they wouldn't have needed the key to do that.' He said all this slowly, as if re-checking the facts in his mind. Years of training, Nergui thought. Committing everything to memory, noting all the facts with as much detail and accuracy as possible, resisting any speculation beyond what had actually been seen. And nothing on paper. Deniability, the mantra of the police state. Corrosive, he thought, in the new democracy.

'But that didn't stop you getting in there after them?' Nergui asked, superfluously.

'It was hardly a challenge,' Lambaa said, with apparent regret. 'Whole place was falling apart. I didn't even try to get past the padlock – it was new, though it wouldn't have stopped me for long. I went round to the rear – always worth looking there first,' he spoke as if instructing a junior officer in the finer arts of trade-craft. 'There were a couple of windows at the back. Boarded up, but it only took me a few seconds to pull away the wood. Wasn't even any glass in them. Climbed straight in. Made a bit of a mess of the suit, though.'

Nergui knew the ways of the agency well enough to recognise that a disguised expense claim would be forthcoming in due course. 'How long had they been in there?' he asked.

'Not long. Fifteen, twenty minutes. I waited outside, keeping back in the shadows, till I saw them come out. I thought they might be carrying something, but I couldn't see anything.'

'We can check their apartments later,' Nergui said.

Lambaa looked back at him, a glint of amusement in his eye. 'I already have,' he said. 'I was in there this morning, as soon as they'd gone off to the university. Did each in turn – they're just student flats. Nothing.'

'Okay,' Nergui went on, 'tell me what you found. Not just the headlines, but all the details. Let's go through it.'

Lambaa nodded, and then closed his eyes momentarily, mentally reconstructing his experiences. 'The window led into a storeroom. A warehouse. That's what the building had been. There was nothing there, as far as I could see. I shone the flashlight around it – it was getting dark outside, and the windows were mostly boarded up, except for a few of the high ones, so I couldn't see much.' He paused. 'I had to be careful with the flashlight – I didn't want to risk alerting anyone outside.'

Nergui nodded. 'But there was nothing there.'

'Not in that part of the building, no. There were old metal shelves, all of them empty. A few crates, but nothing much in them – bits of packaging, old newspapers, some pieces of rusty machinery. But nothing significant. I almost gave up because I thought that, if there was anything, it would be in there. There were two other rooms. Just wooden constructions, really, each side of the front entrance.'

'Where the students came in?'

'Yes. There was a heavy wooden double door there, with these two rooms either side. The rest of the building was just the warehouse space, with a loading bay at one end, near to the window where I got in. Anyway, I thought I should look in the two smaller rooms – they looked as if they had been designed as offices in the original layout.'

'And that's where you found them?'

'That's where I found them,' Lambaa agreed. 'There was a wooden crate, in the room on the right as you came in through the front entrance. It had a lid but it wasn't nailed down. It was new – not more than a few weeks old. You could see the track-marks in the dust. It had been dragged in there quite recently.'

'And what was in it?' Nergui said, determined now to be methodical, to draw on the precision of Lambaa's delivery.

'I've told you,' Lambaa said. 'It was a crateful of arms. All kinds of stuff. Semi-automatic rifles. Handguns. And explosives. Detonators, fuses, timing devices. You name it. A pretty motley selection, but some of it lethal enough. Potentially, anyway. And there were some replicas, too.'

'Replicas?'

'Fakes. Quite decent ones. The sort of thing you might use in a movie, I suppose. They were mixed in with the real ones.'

'What about the explosives?'

Lambaa shook his head. 'Even for the real guns, there wasn't much in the way of ammunition. And there weren't any explosives. Just all the paraphernalia. The stuff to cause an explosion – even down to a suicide bomber's belt. But nothing that would actually explode.'

Nergui tried to make some sense of this. 'Maybe that's being stored elsewhere.'

Lambaa shrugged. 'Maybe. Or maybe they haven't got the ammo yet. I just report what I saw.'

Now, three days later, sitting in this silent hospital, watching Tunjin's steady breathing, Nergui was even less sure what to make of Lambaa's report.

He leaned back against the uncomfortable hospital chair and closed his eyes, willing sleep to come. Moments later, he jerked fully awake, disturbed by the sudden buzz of his mobile phone in his jacket pocket. He had the vague idea that mobile phones were not allowed in the hospital.

He pulled the phone from his pocket and stared at the caller's number displayed on the screen. It was a number he recognised, but not someone already in the phone's limited address book. He kept no personal names stored, always conscious that the phone could be lost or stolen.

He thumbed the connect button. Before he could speak, a voice said, 'Nergui? Is that you?'

He paused, recognising the voice but unable, for a brief moment, to identify it. 'Sarangarel?' he said at last.

She laughed. 'You don't have my number in your phone. And you still pause a second too long before you say my name.'

He smiled to himself, holding the phone balanced in his hand. Nothing much had changed here. 'No one's in my address book,' he said. 'You're not under-privileged.'

There was an unexpected pause at the other end of the line. It occurred to him, finally, how odd it was that she was calling him after all this time. And even odder that she should do so in the small hours of the morning. 'Sarangarel?' he said. 'Is something wrong?'

'I'm not sure. Can you come to my flat? As soon as possible.'

'What's going on?' Nergui said. 'Are you in some kind of trouble?'

'Not me,' she said. 'But someone is, and I don't know how much. It's the minister. Your minister. He's the one in trouble.' She hesitated again. 'Or, rather, his son is – he's been arrested.'

'Dragged out of some protest?' Nergui said. 'It wouldn't be the first time.'

Another silence, and he could hear the echo of static down the line. 'I don't think so,' she said. 'I think it may be a lot more serious.'

Doripalam coughed abruptly as he and Batzorig left the dank storeroom, his throat catching on the cool fresh air. A welcome change from the damp and the smoke. The scent of decay.

They had left the young officer in there, with instructions to keep watch over the body until the scene of crime people arrived. He looked much less self-assured now, and Doripalam felt almost guilty. It wasn't this young man's fault that Doripalam was angry. On the other hand, the young man hadn't gone out of his way to find Doripalam's better side. It wouldn't do him any harm to cool his heels in this bleak spot for a short while.

Doripalam edged his way back down the passageway, shining his flashlight around to avoid the heaps of rubbish. 'Bastard,' he muttered, just loud enough for Batzorig to hear.

'Who would that be, sir?' Batzorig said. He was, as Doripalam had frequently noted, skilled at defusing his boss's temper while not challenging the generally legitimate targets of Doripalam's anger.

'Don't be smart. The local guy. The chief. The bastard who didn't tell us he'd picked up some character with a gun.'

'Oh, yes. Him.'

'So why didn't he tell us?' Doripalam went on, rhetorically. 'All that stuff about how it might have been a gas explosion.'

'Probably wanted to keep it a surprise.'

'It's that all right,' Doripalam said, grimly. 'Especially as we also have at least one victim.'

'He wasn't shot,' Batzorig pointed out.

'Are you looking for a transfer to pathology? I saw he wasn't shot. But he didn't die of old age, either.' They were approaching the end of the passage, and Doripalam could see the glare of orange spotlights across the front of the hotel. 'You won't believe how heavy the book is that I'm going to throw at that bastard.'

'Literally, quite possibly,' Batzorig murmured, in a voice just too low for Doripalam to hear.

The line of armed officers had dispersed, and instead a small cluster of uniforms was easing the assembled crowd back behind freshly erected barriers. There were fire engines drawn up in front of the hotel, and several tired-looking fire officers were stowing away equipment.

Doripalam walked forward and flashed his ID at the most senior-looking of the fire officers. 'All under control?'

The man nodded. 'More or less. There wasn't much of a fire. We delayed before we went inside in case there were more explosions. But it was a pretty small blast in that room,' he gestured to one of the street-facing windows. 'More noise than anything else. Window had blown out and we were able to dowse the flames from out here. We've been in to check the rest; the building looks safe enough but they'll need to get it assessed before we allow the public back in.'

Doripalam nodded. 'What's the room?'

'Just an office. Doesn't seem to be in use at the moment. Lots of junk stored in there – old files, paperwork. Perfect if you wanted to start a fire.'

'You think that's what it was?' Doripalam said. 'Arson?'

The fire officer shrugged. 'That's for your lot to say. But I'd check the insurance policies on this place if I were you.'

'You think it was deliberate?'

'It's not my job to speculate. But there was definitely an explosion.

Might have been gas, but there were no obvious appliances in there. Didn't spot anything else that might have caused it.'

'We'll find out soon enough,' Doripalam said. He turned and watched the gradual extension of the police cordon. 'Main priority now is to get this place sealed off.'

He made his way slowly forward, looking for the local police chief; there was no sign of him. Finally, Doripalam spotted one of the officers he had seen near to the chief earlier. He was a middle-aged man, overweight, standing back from the rest, hands in his pockets, watching the receding crowd with an air of profound boredom.

'Not too busy?' Doripalam asked.

The officer started slightly and turned to face Doripalam, his expression betraying that he had recognised the senior officer only just in time. 'Sir?' he said, finally.

'You're coping okay?' Doripalam said, gesturing towards the crowd. 'With the pressures?'

'Yes, sir. More or less.' The man frowned, impervious to Doripalam's irony.

'Where's your boss?' Doripalam said. 'The chief.' He looked around. 'Is he helping with crowd control as well?'

'Sir?'

'Is he around? I don't see him.'

'I think he went, sir.' The officer blinked, clearly trying to work out the most appropriate response.

'Went?' Doripalam said. 'You mean left the site? In the middle of a live operation?'

The officer nodded. 'He told us you were in charge now, sir. That it was your operation.'

'So you're reporting to me?'

There was a long pause. Behind, Doripalam heard the burble of the crowd, the angry shouts of the officers trying to gain control. 'Well, yes, I suppose so, sir. For the moment.'

'For the moment,' Doripalam agreed. 'Okay, then, just for the moment, tell me about this man you picked up.'

'Man, sir?'

'Man, sir. You probably remember him. He was carrying a gun. Those things usually stick in the mind.'

'Sir.' The officer looked around, as if searching for someone who might help him out.

'Not too difficult a question, is it? You picked up a man. With a gun. Tell me about him.' Doripalam's voice was icy calm. Just behind him, Batzorig involuntarily took a step back.

For a second, it looked as if the officer might try to brazen the matter out. Then, finally, he said, 'He came out of the hotel. Just after we arrived. He was staggering, shouting something. He had a gun in his hand – some sort of handgun. I didn't see what, but he was waving it around and shouting.' He paused. 'I think we were all a bit on edge. Not knowing what was happening. What had caused the explosion.'

'So what happened?' Doripalam asked, suddenly fearing the worst.

'We had a bunch of armed officers here,' the man said. 'We didn't know what we might be facing so we thought we'd better be cautious. One of them fired.'

Doripalam was staring at him, his face aghast. 'You shot him?'

The officer shook his head. 'No, no. I mean – well, I suppose one of us tried to. But we missed. At first we thought we'd hit him. He staggered suddenly, just as the shot was fired and fell forward, dropping the gun.'

'But you hadn't shot him?' Doripalam said, trying to follow this narrative.

The officer shook his head. 'No. I mean, there was someone behind me cheering because we'd got him—' He stopped, seeing the expression on Doripalam's face. 'It was nerves,' he said. 'We were all scared. But, no, we didn't shoot him. We hesitated for a moment, then someone went forward and touched him.'

'Go on.'

The officer breathed out suddenly, as if he had been holding his breath for a long time. 'It was a real shock. We assumed he was dead or badly injured. Then, just as the guy got near him, he rolled over. We thought at first that it had been a trick. Then we realised he was choking and coughing. He'd been caught by the smoke. Couldn't breathe. That was why he'd collapsed.'

'So what happened?'

'Not much. We turned him over. Someone gave him artificial respiration. We'd placed him under arrest, but I don't think he was conscious enough to know that.'

'You got him medical treatment?' Doripalam prompted, hoping that the answer was going to be in the affirmative.

To his relief, the officer nodded. 'We'd called for some ambulances, along with the fire support. One of them turned up in the middle of all this. So he must have been put on to it, I suppose.'

'You saw him put into the ambulance?'

The officer blinked. 'Yes, I think so.' He stopped. 'There were a couple of uniformed officers with him. I'm not sure, exactly. It was all a bit chaotic.'

'It sounds it,' Doripalam said. 'So where do you think he was taken?'

'To the city hospital, presumably,' the policeman said. 'I mean, where else?'

'Where else,' Doripalam repeated, tonelessly. 'And some of your people – these officers – they went with him?'

There was a longer pause this time. 'I think so.'

'You think so?'

'Two officers went with him. Two uniforms. I suppose the chief must have told them to . . . yes, the chief must have told them to.'

'The chief was overseeing all this?'

The officer clearly suspected he was being led into some sort of trap to incriminate his boss. 'No, not exactly. He was behind us. I think he got there a few minutes later.'

'While this man was still there?'

A pause. 'No. He'd gone. I didn't see him after the chief arrived. Didn't really think about him, to be honest. Assumed he was being dealt with, I suppose.'

'Lucky for your chief that you didn't manage to shoot this guy,' Doripalam pointed out. 'Given that he wasn't even there to take command. So who were these officers who went off in the ambulance.'

'I'm not sure. I didn't recognise them.'

'But they were from your division?'

'I don't—' He frowned, as if suddenly making a mental connection. 'There was no one else here. Not till you arrived. So no they weren't. Part of our division, I mean. I hadn't seen them before. I thought—'

'You thought what?' Doripalam glanced behind him, trying to read Batzorig's expression.

'Well, I don't know. It was dark, there was a lot of smoke. I wasn't sure what I was seeing. Maybe some back-up had arrived from another division.'

'Had you called for back-up?'

'Not as far as I knew. But the chief might have, without telling us.'

'But there isn't any back-up here? No one else you don't know.'

The officer shook his head. 'No, there's nobody else. Just us.'

'So who took this man?'

'I don't know.'

Doripalam looked past the officer towards Batzorig, who was staring back at him, his expression neutral. 'I'll get a call back to HQ,' Batzorig said. 'Get them to check the hospitals. See who's been brought in.'

Doripalam nodded. 'And tell them to get hold of this guy's bloody chief. Tell him to get his backside into our offices. Immediately, if he doesn't want to be disciplined.' He turned back to the officer, who was listening to all this with evident interest. 'What about the gun?'

'Gun?'

'The gun. You said he dropped it. Where is it?'

'It – I think someone took it. Bagged it up as evidence. It was all done by the book.' There was a note of pleading in his voice now, as he recognised that there was something serious behind all of this. 'But, well, I'm not sure.'

Doripalam turned to look at him. 'You're not sure what?' Batzorig had already moved away and Doripalam could hear him talking on his mobile phone, liaising with his counterparts back at HQ.

'Well, I'm not sure how much it really matters, sir. The gun, I mean.' He hesitated, clearly unsure now about the significance of anything he might say. 'It's just that – well, we had a look at it before it was bagged up. And – well, it wasn't real.'

Doripalam stared at him. 'What do you mean it wasn't real?'

'Just that, sir. It looked pretty convincing, but it wasn't.' He looked back at Doripalam, as if trying to find the means to convey a complicated idea, then he went on, 'It was just a replica.'

# CHAPTER TEN

It was nearly dawn by the time Nergui left the hospital. To the east, the clear sky was lightening, shading to a deep rose pink in the minutes before the sun appeared. It was set to be another hot day. The unchanging weather was beginning to wear Nergui down – day after day of unfamiliar heat. Hotter than the average summer this far north, and without the familiar relief of the breezes from the mountains.

He wasn't built for this. He felt much more comfortable in the winter, even in this country's frozen depths. That was his natural habitat, wrapped up, sheltered, watchful. The world slowed down to its essence.

He scraped together the necessary handful of *tugruks* and grabbed a coffee from a machine in the hospital lobby. As he sipped the scalding drink, he stared down the empty street towards the central square. The skyline was altering. You hardly noticed as each day passed, but the centre was unrecognisable from even a few years before. There had been a time when the angular monolith of the Chinnghis Khan Hotel had stood out, a unique edifice in a low-rise city. But now it was surrounded by a growing number of equally striking tower blocks, dotted with the neon of Western brand names. The horizon was littered with tall cranes, a visible manifestation of the investment pouring into the country.

He had no great problem with that. Things were lost, things were gained. Some of the losses he mourned, some he celebrated.

Some of the gains he regretted, some he welcomed. It was how things were.

He made his way slowly down the steps, wondering whether he was wise to leave Tunjin in the hospital ward. He had left the sleeping figure in the charge of two trusted agents, with Lambaa and another agent on their way to relieve them for the morning shift. Even as things stood, all this resource was being deployed to no clear purpose, and many in the ministry team no doubt already thought Nergui eccentric. But he knew his track record spoke for itself.

There was little he could do now at the hospital, and he couldn't ignore Sarangarel's summons. He had to take seriously anything that might affect the minister. And even if the matter had not involved the minister – well, he told himself that he would have responded in the same way to any call from Sarangarel. He did not want to think too deeply about whether or not that was really true.

He was almost back at Sukh Bataar Square, and the first red rays of the sun were appearing between the clusters of surrounding buildings. His car was still in the car park behind the ministry where he had left it the previous evening. He stopped for a moment in the centre of the deserted square, gazing at the imposing blocks of the new memorial, the government buildings, the towering statue of the great leader. Not for the first time, he wondered quite what Genghis would have made of this modern nation.

He bounded up the steps of the government building, heading towards the ministry block. And that brought him suddenly back to the object of his journey. Bakei's son. Who had supposedly been arrested in mysterious circumstances. Sarangarel had told him little more on the phone, except that she was with someone who had witnessed the arrest. It was a complicated story, she said, and it would be better if Nergui heard it for himself.

As he climbed into the car, Nergui heard the first sounds of the birds in the trees surrounding the ministry. There was no other traffic and he cruised uninterrupted up University Street, out to the orbital road designated the Big Ring. Sarangarel's apartment was relatively close, up in the north of the city in the area near to the US embassy.

He was unsure how to approach this meeting with Sarangarel. He was even a little nervous about the encounter – and less about the potential subject of their discussion than simply about the prospect of seeing her again. How long was it since he had last seen her? Six, seven months? Probably longer.

At one stage, Nergui had thought that their relationship might develop into something more serious. But that had come to an abrupt end after what had happened with Muunokhoi. It had been a combination of factors, Nergui supposed. His own confidence had been shaken, even though it was hardly his first experience of that kind. Sarangarel had been shattered by the events, and had felt that her own conduct had been far from impeccable. Even if that were true, Nergui – ever the pragmatist – felt she applied standards to herself that could not reasonably be expected of any human being.

Whatever the reasons, she had resigned her judicial role and returned to private practice as a lawyer. She had initially rejoined her old firm, but had subsequently moved on to one of the US-owned practices that were increasingly opening branches in the city. She was clearly doing well enough. Nergui had not visited her new apartment, but the address was in one of the more upmarket areas of the city, in a block largely occupied by foreign diplomatic staff and other visitors with access to Western currencies.

The apartment block was a striking, newly constructed building, with rows of shaded glass windows giving on to views of parkland and the mountains in the far distance. It was a long way from the squalid state apartment where he had first encountered Sarangarel many years before.

He pulled his car into the curb and parked outside the main entrance. He realised that, consciously or not, his thoughts about Sarangarel had been a distraction from the real focus of his visit here. The minister's son.

Nergui had met Bakei's son only once, as far as he could remember, and his superficial impressions had not been positive. The encounter had been at some ministerial reception, two or three years before. The son – Nergui was struggling to recall his name – had been in his early twenties, not too long out of university, but confident of his own impending worldly success.

The confidence was probably not misplaced. The young man had all the qualities that he would expect of the minister's offspring: a ferocious, if ill-focused, intelligence; boundless self-assurance; and a general disregard for others' feelings or sensitivities. It was no surprise to discover that the young man had, like his father, ambitions to follow a political career.

However, it had been more of a surprise to discover that the son's political aspirations were rather different from his father's. The minister had been a communist, and was now a reformer, one of those who felt that the only feasible way forward for the country was through the gradual introduction of Western capitalist ways, ideally supported by matching Western capitalist investment.

But that wasn't how the son saw things. Nergui remembered the young man holding court at the reception, surrounded by listeners who, individually and collectively, had a breadth and depth of political experience far beyond that possessed by the callow graduate. Somehow the young man had held their attention and his words had been greeted with evident respect.

There was nothing new about the words themselves. Nergui had heard the same sentiments from drunken bar-room philosophers and street-corner demagogues, as well as from the far-right politicians who appeared, garnering some public support, at every election. In Nergui's view, it was all based on the most irresponsible kind of political delusion, the belief that it was possible to recreate a unique grandeur and glory from eight centuries before. Of course, this prospect was attractive to those struggling to eke out an existence in the face of economic privation and the unrelenting demands of a pitiless climate. It was attractive to those who had seen their homes and livelihoods destroyed, or who had found that the challenges of freedom were even greater than the penalties of oppression.

It was just a dream. And Nergui believed that any serious attempt to pursue that dream would lead the country back into the dark ages – back into subordination to one of its larger neighbours or into the economic and political chaos that now seemed endemic in many of the former Soviet satellites.

Young men were prone to dreaming, and the legacy of the Mongol empire – the power that conquered and ruled much of the known world – was a suitably romantic one. Above all, Nergui could easily understand how the young man would have rejected his father's utterly unromantic cautious pragmatism.

It was clear that the son was no less ambitious than the father. The difference was that – as he had declared to the admiring crowd – he did not expect to further these ambitions through the tedious conventional routes that his father had followed. He didn't see himself scrambling up the greasy pole of party politics, or serving his political apprenticeship by paying sycophantic homage to those of less ability or talent. He didn't see himself paying his dues listening to endless tiresome speeches in the Great Hural.

He would by-pass all that. He would communicate directly with the people. That was the future of politics. Not today's endless bureaucracy, the pointless time-serving, the futile passing of worthless laws that made no difference to anyone. That wasn't how the empire had been built.

No, Nergui had thought at the time, the empire had been built through murder and pillage and genocide and oppression. And, at the other end of the political spectrum, that was also how the Soviet empire had been built and sustained. Nergui knew more than enough about how that had worked. That was the problem with populism – perhaps it really was how change was achieved, but it transmuted all too quickly into tyranny and totalitarianism. The last two decades had confirmed to Nergui that, for all its faults, there was a lot to be said for the tedium of democracy.

He had said none of that at the time, of course. He had simply watched with reluctant admiration as the boy had dominated a prestigious gathering with a string of platitudes and his own natural charisma. The young man will go far, Nergui had thought, though he was unsure about the likely direction of travel.

The minister spoke of him from time to time, largely in tones of condescending amusement. Though their respective politics, and indeed their personalities, differed markedly, Nergui had the impression that the father and son remained fond of each other, if only from a cautious distance.

Since then the son had followed a more activist political route, and had been involved in a number of protest movements – against government policy, against foreign investment, against the Russians or the Chinese or the Americans. Some of these protests had made an impact – in at least one case helping opposition parties to block legislation aimed at loosening restrictions on the movement of foreign capital into the country. But most were little more than short-lived publicity stunts, at best gaining a mid-page headline in some of the private newspapers.

Nergui had half-expected that at some point he would have to intervene to protect the minister's reputation in the face of some half-baked antic of his son's. There was, after all, some potential embarrassment in the minister's offspring adopting such a defiantly anti-government stance. But nothing ever really arose. The son's profile had not yet risen sufficiently to appear on the radar of the authorities – or even of the opposition parties.

At least until now. Perhaps that moment had finally arrived. If so, it might prove to be the worst possible time.

He climbed out of the car and walked across to the apartment-block entrance. The sun was over the horizon by now, throwing Nergui's shadow the length of the deserted street. The distant mountains were glowing with the dawn, the summits sharp against the pearl of the northern sky.

Odbayar, it suddenly came to him as he approached the entrance. That was the son's name. Odbayar.

\*

'What the hell's going on here?' Doripalam demanded. 'I mean, will somebody tell me?'

Batzorig was sitting next to him in the back seat of the police car heading back towards HQ. 'I couldn't even offer a wild guess, sir.'

Doripalam gazed at him for a moment, as if suspecting some irony. 'We've got an apparent bombing, we've got a dead body—'

'Two dead bodies, sir. Don't forget the museum.'

'Oh, yes, thanks for reminding me, Batzorig. It had entirely slipped my mind.' His own irony was, as always, inescapable. 'Two dead bodies. One of them beaten to death inside a carpet. Let's not forget that.'

'No, sir,' Batzorig murmured.

'And we've got some bloody local police chief waving weaponry around as if he was in the wild west.'

'Rather than the wild east.'

'Quite. And then they manage to nearly shoot somebody who is half-dead from asphyxiation anyway—'

'He was waving a gun around,' Batzorig prompted.

'A replica gun,' Doripalam said. 'And on top of all that, they manage to lose the man in question.'

'We don't know that for sure, sir.'

'You called the hospital,' Doripalam pointed out. 'What did they say?'

'They said they had no record of anyone being brought in who met that description. But you know how reliable they are, sir.'

It was true enough. The hospital was never a good source of information on anything that had happened recently – usually meaning within the last two or three days. Doripalam had never worked out the reasons. Perhaps the medics didn't communicate with the administrators, or vice versa. Or perhaps they were slow in getting their records up to date. Or more likely they just didn't like releasing information, even to the police, until they were compelled to. Doripalam had lost count of the times that the hospital had denied all knowledge of some patient who subsequently turned out to be sitting up cheerfully on one of the wards. It had even happened, briefly, with Tunjin, the previous afternoon. Which, Doripalam thought, took them back to where they'd started. 'And then there's the question of what happened with Tunjin.'

Batzorig nodded. 'If this was a bombing, then that means that the incident in the square—'

'Might have been exactly what we feared it was. The start of something bigger.'

'But I thought—'

'You thought right,' Doripalam said. 'For once the grapevine's telling the truth. It wasn't a real bomb yesterday. It was just—'

'A replica,' Batzorig said, echoing both their thoughts. 'So where does that leave Tunjin?'

Doripalam hesitated, realising that he had told Batzorig nothing of what had happened at the hospital. 'In the same place, legally and ethically,' he said. 'As far as I can see.' He paused again, recalling that all of this had been taken out of his hands. 'As far as I can see, Tunjin did exactly what he was supposed to. He couldn't have known. But I imagine there'll have to be some kind of inquiry.'

'That seems to be Tunjin's fate,' Batzorig said, with what sounded like an uncharacteristic note of bitterness. 'To generate inquiries.'

Doripalam nodded. 'Probably because he takes his job seriously.'

'A lesson for us all, sir,' Batzorig said, ambiguously. 'But you still think there might be a connection? To all this, I mean.'

'Well, maybe. It would be easier to judge if we knew what all this actually is. It just seems like a hell of a mess to me.'

They were pulling out into Sukh Bataar Square, turning right towards the offices of the Serious Crimes Team. Doripalam glanced at his watch. It was much later than he had though – well into the small hours. He wasn't sure where the time had gone. The endless arguments with the local chief, the time spent reviewing the body, waiting for the crime-scene team to arrive, negotiating with the fire service to get the police experts into the building. Hours spent not getting very far.

At close to midnight, it had occurred to him that he had not spoken to Solongo since she had been taken home, hours before, and he was anxious to make contact, to see how she was coping. She had looked drawn when he'd interviewed her, lacking her familiar self-confidence and assurance. He knew she was a strong woman who could cope with most of what the world might throw at her. But she had her limits, and more often than not, what appeared to be complete self-control often concealed near-panic. Doripalam was worried about her. She had always seen herself as an under-achiever, someone who had failed to live up to the intimidating standards set by her father, and that led her always to be talking on new tasks, new demands, pushing herself to the limit. Just as she had done with this museum exhibition.

And that had been before she'd seen a dead man rolled up in a carpet. Doripalam recalled the shock of seeing his first dead body. He could imagine that this shock, combined with the other pressures she had been facing, might have been too much even for Solongo.

He had tried to call home during the endless period they had spent outside the hotel. But the phone had simply rung through to the answering machine, and he heard his own voice apologising for not being at home. Hopefully she had already gone to bed, but Doripalam feared that it was more likely that she was listening to the phone ring, knowing it would be him and choosing to ignore it.

He wondered whether he should try her again. But it was too late. There was no chance of her answering the phone at this time, and he would get no thanks for disturbing her sleep.

The driver pulled into the HQ car park, and Doripalam and Batzorig climbed out. It was still very mild, Doripalam thought, almost as if night hadn't fallen. In this country of bone-chilling cold, warmth was unexpected, something to be cherished for the brief period it lasted. It would be dawn soon, in any case. Another day.

'You okay, sir?'

He looked round at Batzorig, who was standing by the entrance to the HQ, holding the door open for him.

'Yes, fine. Just tired, I guess. It's been a long night.'

'After a long day,' Batzorig agreed.

'Too right.' How many hours had it been since he had been sitting in the Khanbrau, knocking back that cold beer? And just how much did he want another one of those right now? 'And not over yet.'

He entered the building, breathing the familiar scent of stale air, the metallic office smell. His own office – formerly Nergui's – was on the first floor, an unprepossessing room with an outlook on to a bleak courtyard at the rear. He climbed wearily up the stairs and pushed open the door.

The short, stout local police chief from outside the bombed hotel was sitting in Doripalam's chair, angrily tapping an empty mug against the surface of the desk. He looked up as Doripalam and Batzorig entered. 'This better be good,' he said. 'This better be bloody good.'

Doripalam stared at him blankly, his brain fogged by lack of sleep. How long had this guy been here? More to the point, who had let him up here in the first place? Involuntarily, he glanced around, checking that the cupboards and filing cabinets were locked as they should have been.

'Make yourself at home,' Doripalam said. 'We're all friends here.'

'Look, you've dragged me out of bed at—'

'It goes with the territory,' Doripalam interjected before he could go on. 'You're a policeman. Does it look like I'm preparing to go home?' He slumped pointedly into one of the visitors' chairs facing the desk, gesturing for Batzorig to sit in the other. 'And since you ask, it is. It is bloody good. Or bloody bad. I don't know yet.'

The chief glared at him. 'You might enjoy staying up all night playing games but I don't have to join you.'

'Who was this man?' Doripalam said. 'The one who came out of the hotel with a gun. And why didn't you think to mention him?'

The chief opened his mouth and then closed it, as if about to deny any knowledge. 'It was nothing,' he said. 'Just a fuss about nothing.'

'You weren't there,' Doripalam said. 'So you can't really know, can you?'

'I had good people there. People I trust.' He looked from Doripalam to Batzorig, managing to imply that the same might well not be true of their relationship.

'But that's not enough, is it?' Doripalam said. 'You had an armed team there. There was a man brandishing a gun. Your team came within a whisker of gunning him down. And the gun was only a replica.'

'They couldn't know that.'

Doripalam shrugged. 'True enough. These things happen. But usually the commanding officer is there to take charge. So I can understand why you didn't want to mention it.'

'That wasn't—'

'Well, I can't see any other reasons,' Doripalam said. 'I could have you disciplined.' The chief opened his mouth, but Doripalam ploughed on. 'I *will* have you disciplined if you don't show a little co-operation.'

The chief stared back resentfully. 'Make it quick.'

'What do you know about this man? Who was he?'

The chief shook his head. 'Like you said, I wasn't there. Didn't even see him.'

'So what did your trusted team tell you?'

'Not much. Youngish guy. Dark hair? Don't know – nothing else distinguishing. Scared the hell out of them, though. They didn't mean to fire at him – just got the jitters.'

'I can see why you trust them,' Doripalam said. 'So what happened to him?'

'What do you mean?'

'Afterwards. What did they do with him?'

'He was taken to hospital. That's what they told me.'

'Under arrrest?'

The chief paused, clearly reaching the limits of his ability to bluff. 'I don't know,' he said, finally.

'You don't *know*?'

'It wasn't a priority. I mean, it was a fuss about nothing. The gun wasn't real – we don't know what the guy was up to—' The chief stopped, realising he was floundering. 'Okay, I screwed up. I should have been there. I wasn't. But there was no harm done.'

Doripalam nodded slowly, as if giving serious consideration to this interpretation of events. He leaned forward slowly, holding his thumb and forefinger a few millimetres apart. 'I'm this close to invoking formal disciplinary procedures,' he said. 'You allow an armed team to arrive at an incident without your being present. Your people nearly shoot a man who can barely breathe and who turns out to be unarmed just because they – what was your phrase? – they got the jitters. And now you tell me that, not only do you not know where this man is, you don't even know if he's under arrest. How is it possible not to know? Did your people arrest him? Was he in custody? Who went with him to the hospital?'

The chief slumped back in his chair, shaking his head angrily at Doripalam. 'I don't know,' he said. 'It's as simple as that. When I got there, it was all over. They told me he'd been taken to hospital. They said someone – some officers – had gone with him. But I don't know who – and, no, I didn't bother to think about it again after that. I was more concerned with making sure that we cleared the area, and that we were prepared if any more lunatics with guns, replica or otherwise, should appear.'

'And then you left the scene?'

'After you arrived, yes. You made it very clear that you were in charge, so I left you to it.'

'I wasn't in charge of your men.'

'I thought you'd made it very clear that you were.'

The two men glared at each other. Batzorig leaned back in his chair, balancing momentarily on the two rear legs. 'I checked the city hospital,' he said. 'They've no record of this man being admitted.'

'So what?' the chief said. 'That bunch haven't a clue who's in there half the time. Probably somebody didn't bother to register it when they brought him in.'

'Maybe they didn't think it was important,' Doripalam said. 'Sounds familiar.'

'And why is it important? Who is this guy, anyway? Why've you dragged me out of bed in the middle of the night because of some lunatic with a fake gun?'

Doripalam shrugged. 'I don't know if he is important. I don't know who he is or where he is. But I do want to know what's going on. We've got a bombing. We've got a dead body. We've got a man brandishing a fake gun. We've got a man who was supposedly taken to hospital with your officers, who's now mysteriously gone missing. And we've got another incident yesterday which might or might not be connected to all this. And, to cap it all, I've got a local police chief who can't be bothered to do his job properly.'

'Look—'

'Did your officers take this man to hospital or not?'

The chief shook his head. 'No. None of my men went with him. I checked before I left – the whole team was still there at the hotel.'

'So who went? Were there officers from another division there?'

'No, not as far as I'm aware. There's no reason why there should have been. At least not until your people turned up.'

'So who went with him?' Doripalam repeated.

The chief shrugged. 'Maybe nobody. Maybe he never went. Maybe he just recovered and went off on his own. Who cares?'

Doripalam shook his head. 'You really are a piece of work. Has it slipped your mind that this is a murder enquiry? That we're also investigating a suspected bombing? I don't know who this man is, but at the very least he's potentially a key witness.' He sighed deeply. 'Forget it. Just get out of my sight.'

The chief glared at him for a further long moment, before slowly rising to his feet, clearly determined to retain some dignity. 'This is how you get your kicks? Pushing the local guys around. It's the same old story. You get crapped on from above, so you come along crapping on us.'

'No doubt you'd know,' Doripalam said.

The chief opened his mouth as if to say something more, then shook his head and strode out of the office, slamming the door heavily behind him.

Batzorig stretched out in his seat, yawning faintly. 'Looks like the Serious Crimes Team just won itself another friend and advocate,' he said.

He turned round, startled by the unexpected voice.

The figure was just a few metres from him, little more than a silhouette, a deeper darkness against the background glow of the city.

'I'm sorry. I startled you.' The speaker didn't sound particularly regretful.

'No. I was just—'

'It's all right,' the voice said. 'No one can observe us here. You can say what you like. I understand you have a proposition.'

'Well, yes . . .' He really had no idea what he should say next. Suddenly, everything he could think of sounded gauche. He pulled his coat more tightly around his shoulders, aware how cold it had grown.

'My only question,' the contact said, finally, 'is whether you can deliver.'

'Yes, I can understand.' He stopped, barely able to think clearly. How could he persuade this man that he really spoke with authority? 'I've been told to tell you—'

'I know what you've been told,' the contact said, with a faint emphasis on the last word. 'The question is whether you've been told the truth. Whether they trust you enough. Whether you're good enough to have earned their trust.' The contact paused, as though considering the matter. 'What sort of person you are.'

'I—' He stopped, because the contact had taken two steps forward. He could think of nothing further to say as the contact slowly reached out and touched his arm, the pressure firm through the layers of glove and sleeves.

'I think,' the contact said, 'we need to find out.'

# CHAPTER ELEVEN

## SUMMER

At first, Nergui hardly noticed the young man. He looked scarcely more than a boy, curled up on the sofa, his arms wrapped round his knees, watching warily.

Nergui followed Sarangarel into the main living room. It was impressive – larger and more opulent than Nergui's own. It seemed that Sarangarel was benefiting from her return to private practice.

She had greeted him warmly enough at the door of the apartment. The block offered the security typical of apartments occupied primarily by Westerners, with CCTV cameras and electronic security locks prominent in the entrance lobby. He had no doubt that she had observed him on the internal screen before unlocking the external doors. The elevator had been open waiting for him, presumably again activated from within the apartment. He had wondered, as the elevator rose soundlessly, whether the security had been her primary motive in selecting this particular apartment. After everything she had experienced, it would have been understandable.

But the apartment had other attractions, not least the vast panoramic windows that, raised above the surrounding buildings, opened on to a vista of open grassland, the distant curves of the mountains. This early in the morning, the low sun cast elongated shadows across the steppe, a tapestry of deep emerald and jade greens.

'That's why I moved here,' she said. 'You can forget you're in the city. You can see the seasons change, watch the weather come in across the plains.'

'It's extraordinary.'

'Especially at this time of the day,' she said. 'I'm sorry to have dragged you out so early.'

He shook his head. 'I was working.'

'You don't change, then?' she said, half-smiling.

'Apparently not,' he agreed. 'Does anyone?'

She shrugged. 'I seem to have changed more times and in more ways than I can make sense of,' she gestured vaguely round the flat. 'I even seem to be becoming wealthy – relatively so, anyway. That takes some getting used to.'

'It's not a challenge I've ever had to face,' he said, 'as a humble public servant.' It sounded like a rebuke, though he had not intended it that way.

It was only then that he registered that they were not alone. The young man had been sitting motionless at the end of the sofa, in a darker corner of the room.

Sarangarel following Nergui's gaze. 'This is Gundalai,' she said. 'He's the reason you're here.' As she spoke, the young man slowly raised his head and stared at Nergui, as if he too had only now realised that there were others in the room. Nergui nodded in acknowledgement, and turned back to Sarangarel with a quizzical expression.

'My nephew,' she explained. 'My elder sister's son.' She lowered her voice slightly. 'I think he's in shock,' she said. 'He's normally a lively boy – amusing. But he's hardly said a word since he arrived.'

'When was that?'

'Just before I called you. A couple of hours ago. He called me first, to check I was here. Just as well – I wouldn't have heard the entry-phone if I'd been asleep. But he called from down the street on his mobile. He got here five minutes later.'

'But why's he here?' Nergui said. 'What's all this about? You said something about the Minister's son?'

She nodded. 'He's here because I'm the only lawyer he knows, I suppose. He thought I might be able to help him, though I don't know how I can. Except by calling you, that is.' She ran her fingers slowly through her thick black hair. 'Look, I'm not sure I'm making any sense. Let me get us some coffee, and I'll try to be more coherent.'

Nergui followed her through into the kitchen. It was well-appointed and modern, demonstrating a minimalist good taste equal to that of the living room. Sarangarel busied herself making coffee with an expensive-looking espresso machine, pouring cups of the dark liquid for the two of them.

She was looking well, Nergui thought. Prosperity suited her. And, after all she'd been through, she deserved it as much as anyone. Even now, in the first light of morning, hurriedly dressed in jeans and a sweatshirt, she still possessed the elegance he remembered. For a moment, Nergui caught himself wondering if there was anyone else in her life.

'Let's stay in here,' she said. 'I can talk a bit more freely. Not that there's anything to keep from Gundalai, but I want to get things straight in my own mind first.'

They sat at the polished wooden table that dominated the large kitchen. She added a spoonful of sugar to her coffee, and then sipped it slowly for a moment, gathering her thoughts. 'You know the minister's son?' she said, finally.

'Not really. I've met him,' Nergui said. 'I didn't take to him. Some kind of political activist.'

'That's right,' she said. 'He was running some sort of political campaign, Gundalai tells me. Anti-government, ironically enough.'

Nergui shrugged. 'You've seen what his father's like. You couldn't expect any self-respecting son to follow in his footsteps. Not straight away, anyway. Give it a year or two.'

She smiled. 'Still as cynical as ever?'

'Realistic. But I can't say I warmed to Odbayar. I think he'll turn out to be another politician on the make. Just a different variety.' He paused, as though considering the matter. 'Not that there's necessarily much wrong with that. Probably preferable to a starry-eyed idealist, anyway.'

She smiled, with what appeared to be genuine affection. 'I never know how to take you, Nergui. I never know how serious you are. I never know how much is just an act.'

'I'm always serious,' he said. 'Especially when I'm acting.'

'If you say so.'

'So what's the story? What's happened to Odbayar?'

'I'm not sure,' she said. She briefly repeated the account that Gundalai had given her of the previous evening – the gathering in the hotel, Odbayar's speech, and then the explosion.

Nergui looked up at her. 'An explosion? Last night?'

'Don't tell me I have some news that hasn't reached the all-knowing Nergui?'

'No one tells me anything these days. It's just that there was another incident yesterday.'

'Another bombing?'

'A long story. Tunjin was involved, so you can imagine it wasn't straightforward.'

'Tunjin saved my life,' she said. 'And yours.'

'I haven't forgotten. Where does Odbayar fit into this? You said Gundalai was caught in the explosion?'

'That's right. I don't know what happened to Odbayar. Neither does Gundalai. He's still got no memory between hearing the explosion and regaining consciousness in the hotel corridor.'

'You said Odbayar had been arrested?'

She paused. 'Well, that's what Gundalai thought. It seemed strange to me.' She recounted the events that Gundalai had witnessed outside the hotel – the pair of officers striking Odbayar and apparently dragging him into the van. 'Does that sound like an arrest to you?'

Nergui shrugged. 'It could be, though I wouldn't expect an unmarked van. But some of the local forces aren't as well-trained as they might be. If Odbayar had annoyed them – and from my limited experience of him, that's not unlikely – they might not have treated him too gently.' He smiled. 'Mind you, they'll probably regret it when they discover who he is.'

'I'm not sure it's particularly funny,' she said. 'He might be injured.'

'Probably not,' Nergui said. 'They might be incompetent, the locals, but they're not completely stupid. They'd have recognised that Odbayar wasn't your typical off the street activist, so they wouldn't have treated him too badly. They'd have just done enough to stop him sounding off.'

'And what if he had been some "typical off the street activist"? Would it have been okay for them to beat him up?'

Nergui was unsure whether she really was as angry as she sounded. 'You know what I think about that. But you asked me whether Odbayar might have been hurt. I think the answer's no.'

'But you don't know for sure.'

'No. You can't legislate for incompetence.' He pulled out his mobile phone. 'Okay. We need to track down Odbayar, find out where he's been held. I can try the city-centre police.' He stopped, his finger poised above the phone. 'But I'll just get the runaround. Let me start at the top and see where that gets me.' He looked up, and she was looking back at him quizzically. 'I'll start with Doripalam,' he explained. 'Let's see what he knows. About the arrest. And about the explosion.'

'So what do we have?' Doripalam said.

'With what?' Batzorig said. 'I mean, which case?'

'Is there more than one?' Doripalam was doodling on his notepad, an endless network of tiny squares spreading from the corner of the page.

'What do you mean?'

'I don't know. I mean, I don't know where things begin or end here. I don't know what's cause and what's effect. So just talk me through it, item by item. Forget what fits where. Forget what makes sense. Just tell me what we've got.'

Batzorig sucked gently on his pen. 'Okay,' he said. 'So where do I start? With the incident in the square?'

Doripalam nodded. 'That's the first thing we have.'

'Some kind of terrorist—'

'Some kind of suspected terrorist,' Doripalam corrected. 'We don't know who he was or what he was. The intelligence people took it out of our hands before we could find out.' There was no rancour in his voice. He had spent his life accustomed to this suppression of news, the blanketing of information. Even now, as a senior policeman, it didn't surprise him.

At the time, Doripalam had shrugged and moved on. It was the way things were. He thought back to the local chief's words: you get crapped on from above, so you come along crapping on us. Perhaps that was right. After all, his own behaviour at the hotel had not been very different from that of the intelligence officers who had taken over in Sukh Bataar Square. And not very different from Nergui's behaviour in the hospital.

'Okay,' Batzorig said, interrupting Doripalam's thoughts, 'a suspected terrorist. Shot dead by our colleague, Tunjin. Who collapsed and was taken into hospital. That's all I know about that,' he said, expectantly.

Doripalam realised he was expected to contribute something. 'There's not much more,' he said, finally. 'But Tunjin's okay,' he added. 'He was awake when I left.'

Batzorig nodded. 'So that's all we have on that. Some sort of terrorist. Some sort of attempted bombing.'

'Perhaps,' Doripalam said.

'Perhaps,' Batzorig agreed. 'Gunned down by Tunjin. And then immediately covered up by the intelligence services.' He hesitated, clearly thinking about something. 'Do we know why Tunjin shot him?'

Doripalam looked up at the young man, wondering if there was some significance to the question. 'Training, I suppose. He did the right thing. Handled it like we're supposed to.'

'Assuming it was a terrorist,' Batzorig said.

'Assuming Tunjin had reasonable grounds to suspect he might be.'

'I didn't know Tunjin was that good a shot.'

'He was in the firearms team. One of the best we had. It's only in the last few years . . .'

Batzorig nodded. 'Yes, of course. But that's all we have on the incident in the square? So I suppose the next thing is the museum. A young man – not Mongolian – beaten to death and delivered in a carpet as if he might be an additional exhibit in the tribute to the Mongol empire.'

'Anything in the pathologist's report?'

'I've only skimmed it. But not much we didn't know. He confirms that the cause of death was the beating. In fact, it looks as if the victim was kicked to death. Pretty ruthlessly.'

'Nice,' Doripalam said.

'And then we've got the hotel. Some sort of political rally going on in there.'

'Do we know anything more about that? About the rally, I mean? Who it was, what it was all about.'

'I've got someone on to it. It wasn't big time. Just activists sounding off about government policy.'

'What government policy?'

'Usual stuff. Selling off our assets. Betraying our heritage. Corruption.'

'Was there anything else going on in the hotel?'

'Not that I've been able to find so far. It was pretty full. Mainly tourists here for Naadam and the anniversary celebrations. But there weren't any other events going on.'

'So what else do we know?'

'Not much. There was an explosion. We still haven't got any information on the cause – whether it was a bomb or something accidental. They're still investigating the site. It wasn't a large blast. Broke a few windows. There was a fire, but it was extinguished pretty quickly. Doesn't seem to be any structural damage.'

'And then there's the man with the gun.'

Batzorig nodded. 'The replica gun. Not clear if he was really intending to be threatening, or whether he was just confused. We know he was nearly overcome by smoke fumes.'

'And we know he was nearly shot down.'

'And then he vanishes. I've got a couple of men trekking round the hospitals, seeing if there's any sign of him. But that's taking time.'

'And then finally we have our dead body in the storeroom. Any more information on him?'

Batzorig glanced down at his notes. 'We haven't got the pathologist's report yet.'

'He doesn't feel like doing something immediately, just for a change?'

Batzorig smiled. 'We'll get it soon enough. What we know for the moment is that the victim was stabbed, and we're assuming that was the cause of death. He was male, pretty young – probably early twenties. Not Mongolian.'

'Like the victim in the museum?'

'Very similar. In fact, it looks as if both of them were probably Asian but not from here. Probably Indian sub-continent – in terms of ethnicity, anyway. We've no information on where they actually came from.'

Doripalam rose from behind his desk and walked wearily across to the window. The view was as depressing as ever – a bleak empty courtyard, hemmed in on all sides by tall grey buildings. It was barely possible to be sure that it was even daylight out there, though the sun must be up by now. 'And we think he was killed where we found him?'

'Well, we don't have—'

'The pathologist's report. But I imagine we'll cope. What do you think?'

'Well, that would be consistent with the bloodstains.'

'So that's what we have?' Doripalam said, slumping back into his seat. 'Not much.'

'With respect, sir, it sounds a lot to me.'

Doripalam nodded. 'A hell of a lot. On its way to being chaos on wheels. But not much that makes any sense.'

'What about the two murders? That suggests some sort of pattern.'

'One kicked to death in a carpet, the other stabbed in a store-room? Doesn't suggest a very clear pattern to me. Except that both were Asian, but not local. I presume we're checking on where they might have come from?'

'I've got someone on to it. Checking all arrivals – over the past year to start with. We've checked fingerprints but there's nothing matching. Of course, they might be illegals.'

Doripalam nodded. It was possible. The number of illegal arrivals was, so far as they could judge, still pretty low – though there was some influx from the former Soviet Union and even some from China. But someone would have to be fairly desperate to come here rather than staying put. On the other hand, there were count-less reasons, illegal and otherwise, why someone might want to travel anonymously.

'Okay,' he said. 'A fragmented set of events. Which might suggest the end of the civilised world as we know it, but might just be a set of coincidences. And no sense to any of it. I think it's time for me to go and get some sleep.' Doripalam was getting to his feet, when his mobile phone rang from somewhere deep in his jacket pocket.

He fumbled for the phone and thumbed the call button. 'Doripalam.'

There was a long pause while he listened to whatever was being said by the caller. 'No,' Doripalam said, at last. 'No, we've heard nothing. But it's funny you should ask.'

There was an edge to his voice, and Batzorig watched with mild curiosity.

After another pause, Doripalam said, 'No. Nothing. It's a long story. We've not been able to identify anyone who's been arrested. But we do have an account that sounds as if it corroborates yours. So who was it? Who do you think has been arrested?'

There was a long silence. Batzorig, watching, was unsure whether the caller was still speaking or whether – as appeared to be the case – Doripalam was simply staring blankly into the air.

Finally, Doripalam spoke: 'Oh, sweet heaven,' he said. 'Now that does make it interesting.'

# CHAPTER TWELVE

At first Tunjin couldn't be sure he was even awake. He lay with his eyes wide open, uncertain whether this was darkness or light, sleeping or waking. Perhaps this was what death was like. If so, it was a disappointment.

He moved slightly, and felt the weight of the bedclothes, the discomfort of the hard bed, the drip still clinging to his arm. The hospital.

He twisted in bed and tried to make out his surroundings, realising that now, finally, he was able to move. The room was apparently deserted. Beyond his bed, there was a jumble of unidentifiable medical equipment, but no sign of life. The lights were out, though light was creeping through the uncurtained window. He shifted awkwardly and looked at his watch. Five fifteen. It was summer, he remembered. Grey light at five fifteen must mean morning, rather than afternoon. Not long after dawn.

Nergui had been sitting here, he thought. Nergui had been watching him. So where was he now?

He grabbed hold of the bed sheet and tried to manoeuvre his body upright. It wasn't easy. But, given Tunjin's bulk, it was never easy. He jerked his torso up, and then, in a painful movement, swung his legs on to the floor. Gasping, he sat up.

He felt okay. Probably much better than he had any right to. A slight headache. His heart beating unnaturally fast. Short of breath. Nothing unusual.

The room was definitely empty. He dragged himself to his feet and stumbled over to the window. The room looked out on to a main street, adjacent to the central square. The sun was up, but hadn't been for long, and the street was drenched in rich sunlight and long dark shadows.

He walked slowly across to where a door opened on to the corridor beyond, and peered through the small window. A man in a dark grey suit sat in a hard-backed chair immediately opposite. As far as Tunjin could judge, he was fast asleep.

I should stay here, Tunjin thought. I should wait for Nergui to return.

He paused, his hand on the door handle. But I don't know why I'm being detained, he thought. I don't even know – his addled mind went back to the confusing conversation he had had with Nergui – if Nergui has the authority to hold me here anyway.

Those unfamiliar with Tunjin's capabilities were often surprised that someone of his bulk could move with such grace and dexterity. He pulled back the door and peered out soundlessly. For a moment, he hesitated, looking down at himself. He would not get far dressed in a hospital gown.

He moved back into the room. There was a free-standing cupboard to the left of his bed. He pulled it open and identified his clothes. Trousers, an old tee-shirt, shoes. That would do.

He dressed quickly, leaving the shoes off for the moment. Then he moved back to the door and glanced through the small window.

The man was still in the chair, his head slumped forward. Maybe it was a trick, but Tunjin could always claim that he was looking for a lavatory. He slowly pulled open the door and stepped out into the corridor. The man moved slightly, and for a moment Tunjin expected him to raise his head. But he remained motionless. Tunjin moved silently past him. Moments later, he had turned the corner and was hurrying down an adjoining corridor, less concerned now about making a noise. He turned another corner, then stopped briefly to put on the shoes.

He passed innumerable closed doors, and finally found himself facing the hospital's main bank of lifts. He was about to press the call button when he realised that one of the lifts had just arrived at his floor. He moved quickly back into the stairway beside the lifts, as the lift door opened and a man emerged.

Tunjin watched as the man disappeared towards the room that Tunjin himself had recently vacated. He moved quickly back towards the lifts and pressed the call button. The lift was still waiting and opened immediately.

It took him seconds to reach the ground floor and the deserted entrance lobby. He looked around, half expecting to see some security guard or receptionist, but there was no sign of anyone. He looked back over his shoulder, conscious that, if the man from the lift had been one of Nergui's people, it would not be long before his own departure was discovered.

He reached the main door and pulled on the handles, but at this time of day the entrance was securely locked. For a second, he stood wondering what to do, considering the likelihood of finding another, unlocked exit.

Then it occurred to him that the door was locked electronically. On the outside there was a security keypad, requiring a code number. But the door could be opened from inside simply by pressing a control behind the reception desk. Finding the switch easily, Tunjin was soon pushing open the double glass doors and stepping out into the summer morning.

'You can close your mouth now,' Doripalam said. 'And put your eyeballs back in their sockets.'

'It's some place, though,' Batzorig said. He was still staring up at the apartment block, trying to take in its sleek contours, the lines of dark metal and glass.

'It won't weather well,' Doripalam commented. 'Give it a few of our winters.'

'It'll still look a lot better than my place.' Batzorig said. 'I knew I chose the wrong career.' He was joking, but the undertone of regret was real enough.

'We all chose the wrong career,' Doripalam said. It was true, he thought. There would have been a time, not so long ago, when people like Batzorig and he would have been part of the elite – the trusted servants of the state. Now the elite were the businessmen, the lawyers, the property dealers, the traders in everything from gold to energy. It was strange that Sarangarel was now part of that world.

The sun was well up, but it was still early and there was no sign of life along the street. The apartment block looked equally unin-habited, its blank windows giving no clue as to what or who lay within. Doripalam found Sarangarel's name among the array of buzzers, and pressed. After a moment, the door clicked open and they entered into the cool marble lobby.

Air-conditioning, Doripalam thought. Still rare enough here, except in some of the large hotels and office blocks. To the right of the elevator, there was a closed door with a mirrored window which might perhaps lead to a concierge's room. The elevator doors were open, waiting. He hesitated for a moment, as if expecting some further signal. Then he led Batzorig into the lift, pressed the button for the third floor as Nergui had directed, and waited while the almost imperceptible ascent began.

When the doors reopened, Nergui was standing in the corridor waiting for them. Doripalam had half-wondered whether Nergui might make some apology for his behaviour in the hospital. But Nergui would already have moved on, disregarding any impact his actions might have had on Doripalam's sensibilities. Doripalam recalled how Nergui had behaved when Sarangarel herself had been kidnapped: an icy detachment, an absolute focus on the practicalities, his personal feelings buried beneath a shell of prag-matism, as solid as the winter earth.

The thought led him, as so often before, to curiosity about Nergui's relationship with Sarangarel. As far as he knew it had never blossomed into anything more than a cordial acquaintance, though there had been a time when Doripalam had expected some-thing more substantial to emerge. Now, Sarangarel had called Nergui first, and, presumably, had chosen to call him in the small hours of the morning. Doripalam wondered what the significance of that might be.

'How's Tunjin?' Doripalam said, determined that, if nothing else, Nergui would have to acknowledge their previous encounter.

'Improving, I think,' Nergui said. 'I left him sleeping.'

'With your people?' Doripalam had no real expectation that Nergui would shed any further light on his dealings with Tunjin.

Nergui nodded. 'Keeping an eye on him.' He gestured towards an open door, halfway down the corridor. 'Sarangarel's apartment,' he said.

Doripalam noted with some amusement Batzorig's silent but expressive reaction to the dimensions and furnishings of the room that they entered. It was difficult not to be impressed – everything was striking, from the careful understatedness of the décor to the enormous windows framing the pure blue of the morning sky.

Sarangarel was sitting on an expensive leather sofa, cradling a cup of coffee. To her left was a young man – skinny, anxious-looking, his long hair swept back from his stubbled face. There was something mournful about him. He had the air of someone accustomed to treating life lightly who had unexpectedly stumbled upon a hidden darkness. He looked up as the three men entered as though hoping they might bear some positive news.

Sarangarel rose to greet them. She looked even more remarkable than Doripalam remembered. A year ago, she had been a striking woman, her elegant beauty matched by a self-possession that had been strengthened rather than undermined by the challenges she had faced. But it was clear now that at the time some spark had been dimmed by those pressures. There was a new energy in her movements, a brightness in her eyes. Even at this time in the morning she had an extraordinary presence, looking ready to take on the world and anything it might throw at her. Doripalam glanced at Nergui and wondered what he might be thinking. But, as always, his dark face gave away nothing.

'Have you found out anything?' she said. 'About Odbayar, I mean.'

Doripalam shook his head. 'Not really. Not so far. We've got corroboration of what . . .' he gestured towards the young man.

'Gundalai,' she said, and the young man nodded as though being reminded of his own name.

'We've got some corroboration of what you saw,' Doripalam said, addressing himself to the young man. 'We were there ourselves, outside the hotel—'

'You saw it?' Gundalai said, suddenly scrambling to his feet. There was an unexpected flash of anger in his eyes. 'You let it happen?'

Doripalam held up his hands. 'No. We didn't let anything happen. We arrived afterwards. It was the local police handling it.' He briefly recounted what the local officer had told them about the young man with the gun.

'They shot at him?' Gundalai said. He was still on his feet, swaying slightly. Doripalam suddenly realised how exhausted the young man looked, his face grey, his eyes red with strain.

'They missed, fortunately.'

'And they arrested him?'

'That's what we don't know,' Doripalam said. 'Two officers helped him away – presumably the two you saw. And at some point an ambulance arrived. They assumed he'd been taken away in it.'

'Under arrest?' Nergui said.

'It's not clear. What is clear is that we haven't tracked him down yet.'

Gundalai was in front of him again, inches from his face. 'What do you mean you haven't tracked him down yet? How difficult can it be?'

'Gundalai,' Sarangarel said. 'They're here to help.'

'It's okay,' Doripalam said. 'I know how he's feeling.' He looked back at Gundalai. 'No, it shouldn't be difficult. But we've checked the main city hospital and we're going through all the other surgeries and medical units. So far, there's no record of his arrival.' He shook his head. 'Not that that necessarily means much. I've got officers going round all the wards to check.'

'They've got a description?' He looked at Doripalam, then back at Nergui. 'Oh, yes. I suppose they would have.'

'And plenty of photographs,' Nergui said. 'We've kept tabs on Odbayar from time to time. But mostly in the way of what you might call parental concern.' He made the concept sound vaguely frightening.

Gundalai shook his head again, as though trying to shake the dust from his mind. 'But what about the police?' he said. 'I mean, the local police. They must know where he is.'

Doripalam was silent for a moment. 'That's where the story gets strange. The police don't know where he is; they don't know who arrested him.'

Gundalai started to say something, his eyes wide. But Nergui stepped forward and placed a hand on the young man's shoulder and he fell quiet. Nergui was looking at Doripalam. 'They don't know who arrested him,' he repeated. 'So who were the two officers?'

'They weren't from the local team. At first they thought they might be from another unit, but there was no one else there till our people arrived.'

Nergui was watching him closely. 'You think they were fakes?'

Doripalam took a step back and glanced over at Batzorig, as if looking for some support. 'I don't know. It sounds ridiculous. Maybe it's some sort of joke or stunt.'

Gundalai looked ready for another outburst, but Nergui's hand tightened on his arm and he remained silent.

'I don't think it's a stunt,' he said. 'Or if it is, it's a spectacular one. I don't know what's going on, but there are things we need to talk about.'

Doripalam nodded. 'There's too much going on, and I don't understand any of it.' He paused, as a thought struck him. He assumed that Nergui always knew everything, that he was at least one step ahead of all those around him, but Nergui had been in the hospital with Tunjin all night – it was possible that, for once, Nergui's famous grapevine had not yet been in contact. 'Nergui,' he said, finally, 'there may be even more happening than you realise.'

'Go on.' Nergui's eyes held a look that Doripalam couldn't fathom.

'I'm talking about the killings,' Doripalam said, abruptly. He caught the expression on Gundalai's face and wished he'd chosen a different word.

'There were two bodies found yesterday. It looks as if they were both murdered.'

'Where?'

Doripalam paused, looking at Gundalai. 'The second was at the hotel. In a storeroom at the back.' Before Gundalai could interrupt, he went on, 'We know it's not Odbayar. The victim wasn't Mongolian. And he wasn't a victim of the smoke or the flames. He was stabbed.'

There was a long silence. Finally, Nergui said, 'And the first?'

'He was found in the museum. Downstairs in the loading bay.'

'Another stabbing?'

For a brief moment, Doripalam felt an incongruous sense of triumph at finally being one step ahead of Nergui. But the feeling vanished immediately, leaving no pleasure. 'No,' he said. 'Not a stabbing. This one was wrapped in a carpet and kicked to death.'

Nergui was staring at him. 'Hulagu,' he said unexpectedly, his tone suggesting that his mind was elsewhere, his brain rummaging through the dense databanks of his memory. 'The siege of Baghdad. The killing of the caliph.'

Doripalam glanced across at Batzorig, somehow gratified that Nergui had lost none of his capacity to surprise. 'That was what Solongo said. You've an impressive knowledge of ancient history.'

Nergui shook his head. 'No,' he said. 'Not ancient history. Old. But not ancient.' He paused, and smiled faintly, though there was no obvious humour in his expression. 'No more ancient than me, anyway. I think we're talking twenty years.'

The glare of the flashlight was unexpected. Dazzled, he twisted his head away, his vision dancing with after-images.

'Not bad,' the contact said. 'You look okay. Better than your photographs.'

The light had gone now, switched off as quickly as it had been turned on.

It took him a moment to register what the contact had said. 'You've seen photographs of me?'

'You don't think I'd go into this without some checking up.'

'No, I suppose not.' The truth was that he had no idea. But the contact was no fool. He would not have stepped into something like this blindly.

'Just as you've no doubt checked up on me. That's why we're here.'

He had, of course. There were endless files on the contact. He was someone that they had been running for years. Though, looking back, it was not always clear who had been running whom. The contact had provided them with some useful information. In return, they had fed him various morsels – the information that kept him one step ahead of his political competitors. Information that had made him the public figure he was today.

'I think we can do business.' His voice sounded more tremulous than he would have liked.

The contact laughed. 'You think we can do business? We'll have to see about that.' He took another step forward, so that he was standing very close. 'Once we get to know one another.'

'We can't—' He stopped, the words dying in his throat, as the contact's gloved hand reached out and touched the skin of his cheek. The touch was as unexpected as the previous glare of the flashlight, soft through the rough surface of the leather.

'They would have warned you about me, in any case,' the contact said. 'That's why you're here.'

'I don't know.' The leather-clad fingers were stroking his cheek now, moving gently up and down. 'They didn't—'

The contact laughed again, more harshly. 'Are you saying they didn't warn you? Nobody told you?'

Of course, nobody had told him. Nobody really knew what he was up to, out here. He had been surprised when they had agreed so readily to the trip. He had told them he wanted experience in the field, that he was ready for something more demanding. This would just be a routine liaison with an established contact. A good entry point for an inexperienced officer. That was the line he had fed them. While he had been building up this relationship, picking up on the hints scattered throughout the contact's case history.

And they had gone along with it. They had given him the authorisation he needed. Allowed him to come, while making it clear that, if anything went wrong, he was on his own.

But no one had warned him about anything.

# CHAPTER THIRTEEN

## SUMMER

Tunjin moved as quickly as he could away from the hospital, almost achieving a slow jog as he crossed the grass verge to the narrow street beyond. He looked for his watch, then realised with a mild curse that he had left it behind in the hospital room. Along with any cash that was still left in his wallet and his mobile phone. Not to mention all his other possessions.

As so often before, Tunjin wondered why he had acted so precipitately. His departure from the hospital had seemed like a good idea at the moment he embarked upon it. Now he wasn't so sure. He had no money. He had nowhere to go. And, in all honesty, he had no idea of what he might reasonably do next.

For a moment, he was tempted to go back, claim that he had just popped out for a stroll. But, whatever the motives, that wasn't really Tunjin's way. He couldn't imagine himself lying on that bed, unclear what he was supposed to have done, waiting for Nergui to come back to make everything clear. That wasn't his style.

No, his style was to throw himself out of the frying pan and into the fiercest fire he could find. His style was to to stir up as much trouble as possible in the hope that somehow, in all the confusion, he would save his own sorry neck. And, in fairness, so far in his life this approach had tended to work. The only question was how much damage was done in the meantime.

He turned the corner of the narrow street and found himself

back on one of the main routes leading to the city centre. For all his familiarity with the city, it took him a moment to regain his bearings. The hospital wasn't a regular haunt of his, and he had no real desire that it should become one, despite his doctor's frequent warnings about his lifestyle.

How long did he have? Once the guy from the lift got back to his colleague, they'd soon discover he was missing so he probably only had a few minutes. If he'd been smarter, he'd have rolled some blankets under the bedsheets, make them think he was still there. But he wasn't smarter, and anyway that kind of thing only worked in films.

And then what? They could run out after him or put out a call to the city police to have him picked up. But would they do that? He had barely been conscious during Nergui's conversation with Doripalam, but even in that semi-sentient state he had been struck by the peremptory way that Nergui had dismissed his former protégé.

It didn't make sense. Or it made sense only if Nergui was trying to get Doripalam out of there as soon as possible, to terminate any debate, to prevent any possibility that he might take things further. If Nergui wanted to be fully in control of the situation. If he wanted to keep something under wraps.

This was a ministry matter, then. Nergui had actively excluded even Doripalam's elite team. He wasn't going to involve the local force.

So that might buy Tunjin another few minutes. But he had to make good use of them. He was heading out across the main street, away from the centre of town but with no clear idea of where he was going. He passed bars, shops, offices, an apparently endless row of tenement blocks, taking left turns, then right turns, trying to put as much distance as possible between himself and the hospital.

He was not built for speed. His jog had long ago slowed to a walk – relatively brisk by Tunjin's standards, but hardly the basis of a rapid getaway. And he was already breathless, acutely aware of the weight he was carrying, wondering how soon he might need to take a rest.

The streets were still deserted, though he could hear the occasional car or lorry on the main roads behind him. Then, turning a corner, he saw someone moving unsteadily towards him. Instinctively, he ducked back into the doorway of one of the tenements. There was a smell of garbage, and somewhere in the corner the scratching of rats.

The footsteps came closer, a steady scraping and stumbling. Behind it was a rasped mumbling, almost melodic, reminiscent of the chanting of the monks up in the temple. Tunjin was tempted to look out, but held back, realising that whoever had been walking down the street must be almost upon him.

Just as he was expecting the figure to pass the doorway, the footsteps and muttering stopped. Tunjin held his breath, trying to work out if he had missed a trick.

And then suddenly somebody reeled round into the doorway, one hand clutching at the wall. Two glaring eyes stared blankly at Tunjin.

Just in time, Tunjin understood and reacted. Grabbing the man's hand, he thrust him into the corner of the entrance and stepped back with his customary lightness of foot, watching as the drunk vomited copiously in the corner.

An occupational hazard, these days. On another night, that might have been him. Not that he usually found himself out on the street. Tunjin knew how to take himself well into the depths of drunkenness while still knowing more or less when to stop, how to get himself home, how to make sure he was in a fit state to work the next morning. He could carry on like that for as long as it took. Until it killed him.

The question was whether something else would kill him first. He took a last look at the drunk lying comatose in the corner of the tenement doorway. It was time to come up with an idea.

He crossed the street, still heading away from the centre, keeping his ears alert for any sound of pursuit. He was moving into a more upmarket area. In Ulaan Baatar, even more than in most cities, real poverty existed virtually adjacent to substantial wealth – or, as in this area, the rising affluence of the emerging middle classes. And the classification was often fluid – the semi-nomads in the *ger* camps scattered around the city often had as many, or as few, assets as those in the state-owned apartment blocks.

It took him a moment to realise that he recognised his new surroundings. He had been here before, and not too long ago. Doripalam had moved into a new apartment a few months back and Tunjin had given him a lift one evening, because he'd had some problem with his car. Doripalam had a reputation for keeping his private and work lives very separate, so Tunjin had been mildly curious.

It had been a decent enough place, a step up from his previous flat and a good few steps up from the run-down block in which Tunjin lived. He had had a suspicion, though, that the neighbourhood would still be insufficiently upmarket for Doripalam's wife, Solongo. Her background was high status and her aspirations even more so. It was difficult to see how those aspirations would ever be realised while Doripalam remained a public servant. Or, at least, while he remained an honest public servant.

The memory gave Tunjin half an idea. He had nowhere else to go, and if he stayed on the streets much longer Nergui's people were bound to track him down. Although he was still inclined to trust Nergui, he was reluctant to be drawn into the labyrinths of the security services without some notion of what was going on. That had been his unease in the hospital. Whatever his motives, Nergui had chosen not to play by the book. Tunjin was an expert at not playing by the book, and he knew that its major advantage – or disadvantage, if you were on the receiving end – was that your actions were unaccountable. He trusted Nergui – just – but he didn't know who or what else might be behind this.

So the answer was to throw himself on Doripalam's mercy. Of course, Doripalam, being Doripalam, would feel duty bound to turn him in, whatever he might privately think about Nergui's behaviour. But equally Doripalam would play everything strictly by the book. That would afford Tunjin some protection – he was confident that his actions in the square could be defended. And it might also buy him time to work out what was going on.

The first step, though, was to track down Doripalam's apartment. He stopped on the street corner and looked at the endless faceless blocks. This is the street, he thought, though there was little to distinguish it from those immediately adjacent. But the road opened on to a small area of parkland that he recalled, a small oasis of green in the urban anonymity.

He identified the block easily enough, halfway down the street. He had no idea of the number of the apartment but there was an array of named buzzers beside the intercom. He found Doripalam's name and pressed.

There was a lengthy pause before a voice answered, unrecognisable through the speaker. 'Yes?' Female. Presumably Solongo, and sounding as irritable as he might have expected, so early in the morning.

'It's Tunjin,' he said. 'I need to see Doripalam. It's something of an emergency.'

There was a protracted silence which somehow managed eloquently to express Solongo's likely response. Tunjin glanced over his shoulder, but the street was still deserted. At last, the speaker crackled back into life. 'He's not here,' Solongo said, bluntly. 'I don't know where he is.' Stripped of its intonation, her voice gave no clue as to her feelings.

Tunjin cursed silently. Not only was Doripalam not here, it looked as if Tunjin had wandered into a domestic dispute. 'I'm sorry,' he said into the microphone. 'Look, I'd better . . .' He had no way of completing the sentence. He had better what exactly?

Unexpectedly, the main doors suddenly buzzed open. 'You'd better come up,' Solongo's voice said. 'Maybe you can give me some idea where he is.'

Tunjin stared at the speaker for a moment, and then grabbed frantically at the handle of the door, thinking that he should get in there before she changed her mind. At least it would buy some time.

He crossed the polished marble of the lobby to the waiting elevator. Like everything else here, it was impressive but not quite impressive *enough*. He imagined that Solongo saw this as a stepping stone to something better. He wondered whether she would ever achieve it.

When the elevator doors opened, she was standing in the corridor waiting for him, an unlit cigarette in her hand. Not for the first time, looking at Solongo, Tunjin thought that Doripalam was both a lucky man and also possibly playing dangerously outside his league. She was a remarkable woman. Not just beautiful, though she was certainly that. It was something about her air of unquestioned superiority. She was better than you, and it had never occurred to her to doubt it.

'This way,' she said. She turned on her heel and strode down the corridor, not looking back to check whether Tunjin was following.

It was a decent flat, no question. And it looked even more impressive now than when Tunijn had first seen it. Then, the couple had only recently moved in and the apartment had seemed tasteful but anonymous, its walls largely blank, its furniture betraying nothing of its new owners.

It was still tasteful but now someone's tastes – Tunjin assumed Solongo's – were much more visible. Much of the content reflected her role at the museum – replica artefacts from the founding of the Mongol empire, statuettes, the familiar ubiquitous image of Genghis Khan, rendered distinctive by some contemporary artist whose name Tunjin should probably have known.

'Nice place,' Tunjin said, nodding appreciatively.

'You've been here before,' she said, with a touch of accusation. There was little she missed. 'Doripalam mentioned it.'

He nodded, as though acknowledging the truth of an unlikely proposition. 'It looked different then,' he said. 'You'd not been here long.'

'I'm glad you like it.' The note of irony was barely discernible.

'I need to get in touch with Doripalam,' he said. There was only so much small talk he could take. Especially when he was the one left feeling small.

'That makes two of us,' she said. 'I thought you might know where he was.'

'I assumed he'd be here.'

'He's at work,' she said. 'At least, as far as I know. But then I thought you'd be aware of that.' She raised her eyebrows.

Tunjin gazed back at her, wondering how to take this. Did she really think Doripalam was lying to her, that he was – what? Having an affair, claiming in the most clichéd manner to be working late? Tunjin's relationship with Doripalam had never been the easiest, but he thought he knew his boss well enough to discount that possibility. More likely, it had just not occurred to Doripalam to phone home.

'I saw him yesterday afternoon,' he said. 'Not since then. I don't know where he is.'

'I've seen him since then,' she said. 'Late afternoon. At the museum.' For the first time, as he listened to Solongo's precise intonation, it occurred to Tunjin that she might have been drinking. It wasn't that she sounded drunk. It was more that she sounded excessively sober, a condition that Tunjin knew only too well.

'But he didn't come back with you?'

She shook her head. 'He had to go off somewhere else, with . . . ?' She stopped, frowning. 'The young one.'

'Batzorig.'

'That's the one. Chip off the old block.'

'Something like that,' he agreed. 'Are you all right?'

She appeared to consider the question, then said, 'I'm fine.' She paused. 'I found a dead body yesterday, you know.'

He looked up at her, startled. 'A dead body?' Perhaps she hadn't been drinking, perhaps she was going quietly mad.

'I know,' she said. 'Amazing, isn't it? Not what you expect in a job like mine. Would you like a coffee?'

He was struggling to keep pace with this. 'Coffee? Yes. That would be good.'

She turned and walked through to the kitchen, Tunjin following close behind. There was a half-empty bottle of vodka sitting on the kitchen table, he noticed. She hadn't drunk all that this morning. But maybe she had drunk it last night.

He watched as she made coffee. She had a cast-iron percolator, and she seemed to be concentrating painstakingly as she unscrewed it, filled the base with ground coffee, filled the top with water and placed it carefully on the cooker.

'Do you know where Doripalam went?' he said. 'After he left you at the museum?' He decided not to pursue the matter of the dead body for the moment.

She nodded. 'There was a bomb.'

'A bomb?' She really has lost it, he thought. 'At the museum?'

She peered at him as though suspecting some kind of irony. 'No, of course not at the museum. Somewhere else. Some hotel, I think. He was with . . .'

'Batzorig,' he said again. 'You mean there was some kind of bombing in the city last night.'

'Apparently.' She sat herself slowly down at the kitchen table, tapping the coffee spoon against the polished surface. 'But you must know about this,' she said. 'You're one of his team.' The accusatory note was back, as if she thought he had been lying to her.

He shook his head. 'We weren't in touch yesterday. Not later. It's a long story.' At that moment, something in his mind snapped, sick of being silently patronised. 'I'm on the run, actually,' he added. 'Or something like that. Possibly suspected of murder.'

To his slight disappointment, she seemed unperturbed by this information. 'That thing in the square? That seems a little harsh. From what Doripalam said, I thought you were a hero.'

Maybe she had been drinking, he thought. But she was still several steps ahead of him. 'So did I,' he agreed. 'But maybe not. Anyway, Nergui didn't think so.'

'Nergui?' She sat up, looking interested for the first time. 'Where does he come into this?'

'Who knows? Where does Nergui ever come in?'

She appeared to consider the question seriously. 'When it matters, in my experience.' She smiled. 'Though I'm not Nergui's biggest fan.'

'I don't imagine Nergui's too troubled by that.'

She laughed, apparently relaxing slightly for the first time. 'I don't imagine he is. But it was Nergui who arrested you?'

'Well, not arrested exactly,' he said. 'But, yes, it was Nergui.' He was suddenly very weary, as much by this tense bantering as by his experiences over the last twenty-four hours. He pulled out one of the kitchen chairs and sat down, feeling the wood creaking under his weight.

She frowned. 'I'm probably being a little slow,' she said. 'But if you're on the run, what are you doing here?'

'I didn't know where else to go.'

'Right. I see. So I'm an accessory after the fact?'

'I suppose so. I'm sorry. It's nothing personal. I was hoping for Doripalam.'

'Fair enough,' she said. 'We were all hoping for Doripalam.'

'Have you tried the office?'

She nodded. 'Funnily enough, it was the first thing that occurred to me. They said he'd come back there – sometime in the small hours. But he'd been called out again, with . . .'

'Batzorig. A busy night for him.' But busy with what? The news of an apparent bombing, combined with the previous day's incident in the square, made Tunjin feel uneasy. If Doripalam had been out all night, that suggested something serious.

'What was all this about a dead body?' he asked, casually. He glanced across at the vodka bottle. No, she hadn't drunk all that this morning.

'I found one. Yesterday,' she said, simply. 'At the museum.'

'Had it been dead long?' It was an inane question, but thoughts of mummies were running through his mind.

'I've no idea,' she said. 'Not really my field. But not more than, well, a day, I'd assume.'

He nodded. Not a mummy, then. 'I'm sorry,' he said, 'I think I'm the one being slow now. Where exactly did you find this body?'

'In the loading bay,' she said. 'I mean, strictly speaking, it wasn't me that found it.'

'No?'

'No. It was one of the students. But they all panicked. So one of them came to fetch me because I'm the person in charge.'

'Of course.' He had little doubt that Solongo was always the one in charge. 'So one of them found a body and came to tell you?'

She nodded, impatiently. 'That's what I said.'

'So whose was this body?' He was uncomfortably aware that he sounded as if he was humouring her. He didn't imagine that Solongo appreciated being humoured.

'How would I know?' She frowned, as if seriously considering the question. 'Not Mongolian, apparently. That's all they told me.'

'And how did this person die?'

She was staring at him, as if finally beginning to suspect that he might not be taking this entirely seriously. 'Well, he was murdered, of course. At least, I assume so.'

'Why do you assume so?' Tunjin's tone was as light as ever, but his mind had reverted to his police training, gathering evidence, questioning, challenging assumptions.

'Well, you don't get kicked to death by accident, do you? Or kick yourself to death?'

It was Tunjin's turn to stare. His face was pale, his eyes now lacking any trace of humour. 'He was kicked to death?' he repeated.

'Exactly. And wrapped in a carpet.'

Tunjin half rose from the table, then sank back down again.

'Not very well wrapped, actually. Just covered up, really, so there was no chance that we wouldn't spot it as soon as the carpet was moved.'

'But you're sure? I mean, wrapped in a carpet?'

'Of course I'm sure. It's not the kind of thing you could easily mistake.'

'But – wrapped in a carpet? And kicked to death? You mean like the Hulagu story? In Baghdad?'

She laughed, and rose to get the coffee pot from the cooker. 'I'm impressed,' she said. 'You're obviously more educated than you look.'

He shook his head, ignoring the implied insult. 'Not educated,' he said, 'just experienced. Painfully experienced.' He pulled himself slowly to his feet and stepped across to the kitchen window. The vodka bottle was in front of him, and he thought how attractive it looked. He could drink all that in maybe four or five large mouthfuls. It wouldn't be enough, but it would be a start.

He pushed the bottle determinedly away from him and gazed out of the window. It opened on to the broad street below, golden in the risen sun, the dense green of the parkland visible beyond the line of apartments. A figure in a dark suit stood at the far end of the street, apparently talking on a mobile phone. Perhaps one of the Nergui's people. But it hardly mattered now.

He looked back at Solongo, who was carefully pouring the coffee. 'Painfully experienced,' he repeated. 'A painful experience.' He paused. 'And I think it might be coming back to haunt me.'

# CHAPTER FOURTEEN

'It's a long story,' Nergui said. They were in Sarangarel's kitchen, bunched around the marble-topped table. He looked around. Doripalam was watching him, serious as ever, his pen poised over the virgin page of a notebook, ready to follow in detail wherever this might lead. Sarangarel had been pouring coffee, playing the attentive hostess, but no doubt taking in every word. Batzorig was leaning back on his chair, his head tipped back, his eyes fixed blankly on the ceiling. But, from everything he had seen of the young officer, Nergui had no doubt that he was also registering everything being said. And would be able to repeat it back, more or less verbatim, if required.

Only Gundalai seemed distracted, his body hunched into the chair, away from the rest of them, rocking gently backwards and forwards, his hands clutched around his stomach as though he was feeling nauseous. Nergui half-expected that at any moment he might explode in anger and demand an end to all this talking.

'This was nearly twenty years years ago,' Nergui said. 'I was new to the police service, just out of my intelligence role. Tunjin was working with me. It was a difficult time. The late 1980s. Russia struggling with reform, not far from collapsing into chaos. We'd lost our Soviet banker, but we didn't know what that might mean.' He looked across at Doripalam, catching his eye for the first time that morning. 'It wasn't like it is now,' he said. 'I didn't really even know what my job was.'

Doripalam returned his gaze, unblinking. 'You've always known what your job is, Nergui.' It was hard to tell if there was any undertone of bitterness.

Nergui smiled. 'Okay,' he said. 'But at that point we were just trying to hold things together.' He stopped. 'If it doesn't sound too pompous, we were trying to hold the nation together.'

'Trust me,' Sarangarel said. 'It sounds too pompous.'

'Russia was in turmoil, and we knew how dependent we were on her. We were moving towards democracy but too slowly. And there were plenty out there who didn't wish us so well.'

'China,' Gundalai said, unexpectedly.

Nergui glanced at the young man. 'Among others,' he said. 'But, yes, China has rarely wished us well. China still thinks that, rightly, we should be her colony.' He smiled. 'Whereas, of course, for most of the last century, Russia has known that was her prerogative.' Gundalai was still gazing fixedly at the floor, showing no sign of taking in what Nergui was saying.

'But Gundalai is right,' Nergui went on. 'It was China we were most concerned about. The country was full of observers. From everywhere. Plenty from the USSR. But they had other things on their minds. And a presence from the West. Mostly interested in our mineral reserves. They didn't much care what happened to us, so long as they were in pole position to stake their claims to whatever assets we might have.'

'Observers?' Batzorig said, suddenly, as if he had just woken up to the conversation. 'You mean spies?'

'Spies,' Nergui agreed. 'Or close enough. Most were here legitimately. Or semi-legitimately: government representatives; diplomats; attachés; the odd academic, conducting some sanctioned research.' He took a sip of the coffee that had grown cold in front of him. 'The one we're talking about was one of those. A very odd academic. Chinese. Wu Sam.'

'You allowed academics in?' Doripalam said.

'If they had legitimate reasons to visit. This one was an expert on Mongol history. An enthusiast for the great Mongol empire. A bit of an eccentric. Buried in his books, supposedly. He wanted to conduct some original research, to delve among whatever artefacts he could find.'

'And you trusted him to do that?' Sarangarel said.

'Up to a point. We consulted with our own experts and they confirmed that his track record was legitimate.'

'But you said he was a spy?'

'We expected it. It went with the territory. The Chinese wouldn't have wanted him to come here if they didn't think that he might be able to feed something back. But it wasn't likely to be anything of great significance.'

'It sounds like a perfect arrangement,' Doripalam said. 'So what was the problem?'

'The problem,' Nergui said, 'was that Wu Sam was a genuinely odd academic. We thought he was a homosexual.'

'Which is still a problem for most of our countrymen,' Batzorig said.

'As you say,' Nergui was unperturbed. 'And which was even more of a problem in those days. There were, as I'm sure you're aware, no homosexuals in the former Soviet Union.' He smiled. 'So I am assured, anyway.'

Batzorig looked as if he was about to speak, but then closed his mouth.

'We're not really sure what happened in this case,' Nergui went on. 'We later received some information that our academic had propositioned a number of young male students—'

'But you had him under surveillance?' Batzorig said.

'To a degree. But we weren't really interested in his private life.' Nergui gazed impassively at the young man, as if daring him to respond. 'That wasn't the issue. The issue was that there was some apparent falling out between him and one of the young men in question. We don't know why.'

'A lover's tiff?' Batzorig said, sardonically.

'We don't know why,' Nergui repeated. 'But whatever the cause, the student was killed.'

There was silence in the room. It was as if a light-hearted anecdote had suddenly been transformed into tragedy.

'Killed?' Doripalam echoed. 'By this . . . ?'

Nergui nodded. 'Wu Sam. Well, apparently. The circumstances weren't clear. It may have been manslaughter. I suppose it may even have been an accident. The student's head was crushed, as if struck with some heavy object.' He paused. 'I am not telling this story very well. It was only later that we linked the death to Wu Sam. And by then there were other considerations.'

'I'm not sure I follow.'

'The student's body was found up in the north-east; in the area reputed to be the birthplace of Genghis Khan. The local militia received an anonymous tip-off. They sent out a couple of officers and their dogs discovered the body. At first, they assumed he was the victim of an accident – that he had somehow fallen from the path and struck his head. But the head was too badly damaged. It was difficult to see how a blow of sufficient force could have been administered by accident, unless the body had fallen from a greater height than was suggested by the surrounding terrain.' Nergui sounded as if he were quoting from some long-remembered forensic report.

'So the tip-off came from the killer?' Doripalam said.

'Maybe. But perhaps just some herdsman who didn't want to get involved. People usually tried to steer clear of the police in those days.'

'So what made you connect this death with Wu Sam?' Doripalam asked.

'Nothing, at first. It took a while even to identify the victim. He had papers with him, an identity card that confirmed he was from the city, but communications were not so good in those days. It was a few days before the locals contacted the city police, and some days after that before he was identified. A university student, son of two low-ranking Party members. No one knew that he had been out of the city. No one had any idea why he was visiting that area, or who might have been with him.'

'I thought you kept close tabs on everyone in those days,' Doripalam said.

Nergui shrugged. 'Everyone was paranoid, everyone thought they were under surveillance. But the truth was—'

'That someone could get murdered without you having a clue who'd done it.'

'Quite so. Whatever the nature of the crime, we assumed that the motive would be trivial. Petty robbery or a brawl. Tunjin was the investigating officer.' Nergui allowed the silence in the kitchen to build. 'One of his first cases as a detective. He'd recently joined us from the uniformed team. Very capable, of course. And he made the breakthrough, eventually. He went through the usual routine. Tracking down anyone who knew the victim, anyone who might have known the victim. It took us a long while to reach Wu Sam. Their subject areas were different – the victim was a scientist. Wu Sam had never taught or worked with him. But we received some information that the two men had been seen talking. There was a suggestion that the relationship might have been more than simply an acquaintance.'

'It hardly sounds like the basis of a robust prosecution,' Doripalam pointed out.

'It wasn't,' Nergui agreed. 'It was just a lead, the first indication we'd had of anything out of the ordinary.' His eyes flickered momentarily across to Batzorig. 'But it was little more than gossip.'

'But surely you'd have been keeping some sort of track of Wu Sam's movements?' Doripalam said.

'Up to a point. But we weren't that bothered in constraining his travel out of the city, particularly as he'd shown no interest in visiting the areas that might have given us cause for concern, such as the mineral-bearing regions. He'd made a couple of trips, both sponsored by the university and both to areas appropriate to his work – to Karakhorum, for example. As far as we knew, he'd not left the city during the period when the student had been killed.' He smiled. 'Which just shows how pitiful our surveillance was. It's fortunate that our great populace never realised this, or the democratic revolution might have arrived much earlier.'

'So he did leave the city?' Doripalam asked.

'So it appeared, yes. Tunjin eventually uncovered a witness –
one of the university's records clerks, someone with an eye for
detail – who remembered seeing Wu Sam driving out of the
university in the passenger seat of a truck. A truck driven by the
student who subsequently became the victim. We identified
another student – a family friend of the victim – who had lent
him his parents' truck, supposedly for a weekend trip to the
mountains. We found another witness who talked about a friendship between the two men – with some innuendo about how
close the friendship might have been. And then we found two
more students who claimed to have been propositioned by Wu
Sam.'

'An unreciprocated proposition, presumably?' Batzroig said.

Nergui shook his head. 'I've no idea. We were only interested
in Wu Sam. We had taken our eye off the ball. We had not taken
him seriously as a spy. We had not taken him seriously at all.' He
stopped, his eyes staring into the far distance, as though his mind
was replaying the events of twenty years before. 'Which was a
mistake. A serious mistake.'

'He was the killer?' Doripalam said. 'He'd killed the student?'

'We never knew for sure. The evidence was there, but it was
purely circumstantial. He'd been seen leaving the city with the
student. It was presumed they'd been together when the student
was killed. But it was little more than anecdote. Even the one who'd
seen them couldn't be sure if they were really travelling together,
or if they'd just encountered each other leaving the campus. There
was no forensic evidence to link them. We didn't have access to
DNA analysis in those days.' He spoke with evident regret. 'So we
never knew for sure. We interviewed him, but he claimed to have
no idea what we were talking about. We couldn't prove otherwise.'

'But you were sure?' Doripalam said. It was the curse of the
policeman's life. The instances when you knew – you knew with
absolute certainty – who the perpetrator was, but lacked the evidence
to substantiate it.

Nergui shook his head. 'I can't even say that. But all of that was superseded in any case.'

'Superseded?' Doripalam repeated. It was a perfect piece of Nergui terminology – formal, precise, euphemistic, undeniably ironic.

Nergui's eyes were sharp, though Doripalam still felt that they were focused on something he would never see. 'You remember the murders that winter? Two years ago?'

It was an entirely rhetorical question. Neither of them would forget that tortuous sequence of events.

'At the time,' Nergui said, 'I said that that was the first real serial killer I had encountered in this country. But I still don't know if that was true.'

'And it wasn't quite a serial killer,' Doripalam pointed out. 'Not in the sense that people would normally understand.'

'Not a straightforward psychopath,' Nergui agreed. 'Whereas Wu Sam—'

'Was a straightforward psychopath?'

'I don't know what he was. All I know is that, too soon, we had another corpse on our hands.'

Doripalam was staring at Nergui, his brain belatedly making the connections that had been implicit in the narrative from the start. 'Another corpse?' he prompted, already knowing and dreading what Nergui was going to say.

'Another student, barely out of his teens. An exchange student. He'd come here from one of those eastern republics – Turkmenistan, I think. Had hardly been here long enough to make any friends.' His voice faltered, as though even he was struggling to make sense of his own memories. 'But you know how he died. Twenty years ago. He was wrapped in a carpet and kicked to death.'

There was a protracted silence. And then Gunlundai dropped his head into his hands and began to weep.

## WINTER 1988

No one had warned him.

But it was worse; more than just a sin of omission. Out here in the frozen night, the truth was suddenly clear to him, and it chilled him more than the biting wind.

He had been set up.

He had thought that he was so clever, that he had spotted an opportunity others had missed. He would forge new alliances, build a new world. A new empire. But they were laughing at him all along. They had spotted his pretensions and taken the steps needed to steer him here.

This man was behind it all. A man with certain predilections. And, to keep him sweet, from time to time they would feed him a young titbit. A young man who would do what he was told, go along with it for the sake of his career.

He could see exactly how it worked. It kept the contact happy, made him feel valued. But it kept him vulnerable, too – engaged in acts that were illegal here. Exposure would be devastating for one of his seniority. It was like feeding heroin to a user. It kept him dependent, kept him wanting more. It meant they had the contact exactly where they wanted him.

The contact was smiling. 'They really should have warned you,' he said, again. 'Although perhaps then you wouldn't have come. And that would have been a pity.'

He had no words to respond. Repulsion was rising in him, like bile in his throat. He was repelled by the prospect of acts that he had been taught were abhorrent, that were illegal in his own country as here. And he was angry and resentful at being used in this way.

But it wasn't only that. There was something else. A creeping contempt for his own stupidity, his naivety, for allowing himself to walk into this. For wanting to walk into this.

He had no idea where the unexpected thought came from. And at that moment the contact reached out and began gently to stroke his face again, his gloved fingers harsh against the cold skin.

'There is a place we can go,' the contact said. 'It is warm and discreet. No one will know we are there.'

It was all suddenly too much. He thrust the contact's hand away from him, and turned on his heels, walking with increasing speed back down the path to the road.

He half expected that the contact would follow, try to change his mind. But when he reached the park gates and glanced back, the contact was still there, a motionless silhouette against the paler dark of the sky.

He hesitated a moment, almost considering going back. His role was to obey, to be one of the pawns in this unfathomable game. But he knew that he could not.

There was no way out of this now. He would not be allowed to remain here, a walking threat to the contact's reputation. And he would have no career to return to. Failure might be tolerated but disobedience – and he had disobeyed, even though no orders had ever been articulated – was beyond the pale.

He looked back again, but the contact had gone, melted back into the icy darkness. He stayed for a moment, peering into the blackness, but he could feel the cold cutting through his clothes, eating into his skin and bone.

He pulled his coat around him, and began the lonely walk through the empty streets towards the central square.

PART 2

He had been expecting it. The only question was how soon.

A week went by. He spent it crouched in his tiny apartment, trying to work but unable to make sense of the words in front of him. He had been passionate about this history, about Genghis Khan, the legacy of the empire, the potential for the future. The vision that would unite their two nations. But now none of this meant anything to him any more.

He sat at the rickety desk, waiting for the knock that would announce the end of his trip here, the beginning of his expulsion back to – what? He had no idea, except that his career would be finished.

But the week went by and nothing happened. Finally, he regained the confidence to leave his apartment. He had barely eaten for days, surviving on the remnants of a stale loaf of bread and some old biscuits. Now, he felt able to visit the university refectory, eagerly wolfing down a plateful of their bland, fatty mutton stew. And later he took a walk into the city. The sky was a clear empty blue, the air fresh and sharp, and he felt alive again. He had spent the week tense with anxiety, convinced that he would be picked up at any moment. Now he decided that he had been deluding himself, more idiotic self-aggrandisement.

As he returned from his walk, he saw two men in heavy coats and trilby hats, emerging from the apartment block. One of them – a heavily built man, already lighting up a cigarette, his hands cupped against the chilling wind – gazed at him, as though with mild curiosity. 'Your name Wu Sam?' he said, his voice gentle around the bobbing cigarette.

Wu Sam nodded. 'I've been expecting you,' he said.

The man raised his eyebrows slightly and glanced across at his colleague. 'Have you?'

Wu Sam felt it was necessary at least to state his position clearly. 'You can see my papers,' he said. 'Everything is in order. I have permission to stay for three months. My visa—'

The man held up his hand, with the air of one accustomed to directing traffic. 'That's not why we're here.'

'Then what?'

'We're here to ask you some questions.' The man shook his head, an expression of vague regret crossing his face. He took another drag on the cigarette, and then tossed it, barely smoked, into a lingering pile of grimy snow. 'About a dead body.'

# CHAPTER FIFTEEN

## SUMMER

Out here there was nothing. Just endless undulating grassland, miles of dusty dirt road, and occasionally a copse of fir trees providing the only shade. Earlier in the morning, with the first sunlight appearing above the low-lying eastern hills, they had passed a nomadic camp. There was no sign of human life but a scattering of tethered goats and horses had simultaneously raised their heads as the truck sped past. Since then, more than an hour later, they had seen no further evidence of habitation.

'How long do we give them?' Odbayar said. He flicked his cigarette butt out of the truck window.

The Chinese man, Sam, glanced at him irritatedly. 'If you have to smoke, at least use the ashtray. The grass out there is dry enough to ignite.'

'There's hardly any grass to ignite,' Odbayar said. 'I've never known it so dry this far north.'

'We are ruining the planet,' Sam said, piously. 'We will pay the price.'

'That'll be your country ruining the planet. And the rest of us who pay the price.'

'And which country would that be?' Sam said. His knuckles were white around the steering wheel as he held the truck straight on the uneven road.

'Either. Both.' Odbayar shrugged. 'You tell me. They're both the same in that respect. Each as bad as the other.'

Sam nodded solemnly, considering the merits of this judgement. 'No doubt,' he said. 'And not just in that respect.'

Odbayar pulled another cigarette from the packet in the breast pocket of his shirt and lit it carefully, blowing the first stream of smoke expertly out of the window. 'So,' he said again, 'how long do we give them?'

Sam's eyes were fixed on the long straight road. It stretched out apparently as far as the mountains, though in the far distance it was lost in the deep green shade of the forests. The shadow of the truck extended lengthily behind them, an endless black companion to their journey. 'Not too long,' Sam said finally. 'We need to get far enough away. And give them time to become uneasy.'

'That could take a while,' Odbayar said. 'They probably don't even realise I'm missing.'

'That's true,' Sam agreed. 'It was all too chaotic last night. Maybe we overplayed that a little.'

'It would have been too risky otherwise. If things had been calmer – well, either we wouldn't have been able to stage it at all, or it would have been spotted too quickly. I think it was just right, with the gun and everything. Dozens of people must have seen us, even if they didn't understand what they were supposed to be seeing.'

Sam laughed. 'No doubt they will realise quickly enough when the police come to collect their witness statements. Which the police will do as soon as they register what has happened. What has apparently happened,' he corrected himself.

'What if the police can't identify any witnesses? I don't imagine they'll have been collecting names and addresses last night.'

Sam glanced at the young man, mentally reminding himself that Odbayar did not know the full detail of the previous night's events. 'They'll be asking for witnesses to the bombing to come forward,' he said. 'There won't be any shortage of busybodies. And some of them will remember what they saw. Your performance was noticeable enough.' He smiled. 'But that's the icing on the cake. Worthwhile, but not essential.'

'I hope it was worthwhile,' Odbayar said. 'I was nearly gunned down. Probably would have been if I hadn't pretended that the smoke had got to me. And I've still got bruises from where those goons grabbed me.'

'They had to think it was for real, just like the police did. If they'd known it was staged, that would have been two more people we'd have had to trust.' Two more loose ends, Sam added to himself, to be dealt with. Just as he had dealt with the others.

'Even so, I'm a VIP, you know. You could have told them to go easy.'

'I did.' Sam laughed. 'Think what it would have been like if I hadn't.'

Sam seemed more relaxed, Odbayar thought, now that they had reached this point. There had been a lot resting on him, while they were setting this up. But then there was a lot resting on both of them, and it was far from over. Odbayar himself wasn't yet feeling any obvious sense of relaxation.

'So how long?' Odbayar persisted. 'When do we contact them?'

'Let's get up there first,' Sam said. 'Another couple of hours or so.'

'Will we be able to call from there? I mean, will the mobile work?'

'Mine will,' Sam said simply. 'That's all under control.'

Odbayar nodded. That was what he liked most about working with Sam; nothing was left to chance. He was a professional, and he had resources behind him, even if Odbayar had chosen not to enquire too deeply into how or where those resources had been acquired.

'Won't they be able to trace it?' Odbayar said. It was only by working with Sam that Odbayar had realised how amateurish his own approach had been.

He had been cocksure before, buoyed by his own momentum, like one of those American cartoon characters who run off the cliff, still running until they make the mistake of looking down.

Sam seemed untroubled. 'Not with my phone,' he said. 'Not until it's far too late, anyway. I've told you. Relax. That side of things is all under control.'

Odbayar settled back in the passenger seat. His mind kept running back through everything they had done, trying to spot anything they had overlooked. He had wondered whether Gundalai suspected anything. Gundalai, for all his easy-going nature, was no fool.

At one point, Odbayar had thought they would take Gundalai into their confidence. He would have preferred that. Although he would never say so explicitly, Odbayar trusted Gundalai. He trusted his judgement. He trusted his reliability. And he trusted his integrity.

That had been the problem, he supposed. He could tell himself otherwise, but he knew that Gundalai would never have accepted this. If he had known what was going on, he would have tried to stop them. At best, he would have turned around and walked away. You could call that integrity. But you could also call it naivety. It was why Gundalai would always remain just a dreamer.

And, unwittingly, Gundalai would have an important part to play in any case. His lack of involvement enabled him to be the perfect witness. He would confirm what Odbayar wanted the authorities to believe.

'You think too much,' Sam commented, glancing across at his silent passenger. 'It can be unhealthy.'

'I thought that was one of your gifts,' Odbayar said. 'Thinking things through.'

'I think when I need to. I make sure I don't miss anything. But then I stop. If you think too much, you create problems where none exist.' He paused, his hands tight on the throbbing steering wheel. In a while, he would perhaps let the young man drive again. But he was conscious that Odbayar must be tired after the rigours of the previous night. It would not help them to have an accident out here. 'And you need to be ready,' he went on. 'You cannot plan everything. Some things will happen in ways that you do not expect. If you think too much, you will deaden your reactions.'

Odbayar nodded, unsure whether Sam's words represented ineffable wisdom or empty truisms. 'You think something could go wrong?' he prompted.

'Something will go wrong,' Sam said, calmly. 'Something always goes wrong. We expect that and are ready for it.' He glanced across at Odbayar's anxious face. 'But it will be nothing important.' He smiled. 'I have made sure of that. Now get some sleep. It's been a long night. And we're only at the start.'

'I can take over the driving later if you want me to.'

'Sleep first. We need to keep our minds clear.'

Odbayar slumped back in his chair, feeling the rhythms of the road through his body. He wondered, as consciousness slipped from him, how long it had been since Sam had last slept.

'So he was framed?' Solongo said. She was facing him across the kitchen table. Her eyes were boring into his, and he seriously believed, at least for a moment, that she could read what he was thinking.

'No,' Tunjin said. 'I don't know.'

'But this was murder you're talking about? He was accused of murder?'

'Yes,' Tunjin wondered quite how he'd got into this.

'He was framed,' she said, simply. She'd missed her vocation in the legal profession, he thought. Five minutes in court with her, and he'd confess to anything. 'You said it. He was set up.'

'No,' Tunjin insisted. 'I don't know that. He was a murderer, we knew that.'

'But you had no evidence,' she said. 'Until the second murder.'

'Yes, until we found the second body.'

'And you thought that that was all just a bit too convenient. But you did nothing about it.'

'What could I have done? The evidence was there. It was what we needed.'

She watched him, unblinkingly. 'Doripalam always said you were one of the ones with integrity. Whatever other faults you might have.'

'I think he was generally more conscious of my faults.'

'But I'm right, though, aren't I?' she continued. 'You're one of the ones with some integrity?'

'There are more of us than you might think,' Tunjin said. 'But, yes, I hope so. I've done some stupid things in my time, but usually with the best of intentions.' He paused. 'Which doesn't make them any the less stupid.'

'And this was stupid, was it?' she said. 'Turning a blind eye. No – more than that. Using this supposed evidence to fit him up.'

'If you want to put it that way. Things were different in those days.'

'You don't need to tell me that,' she said. She thought back to her father, and how little attention he would have paid to these niceties. 'Okay. So I accept that, even if I don't like it. But, if you think the evidence was faked, where did this body come from? You don't just find a conveniently murdered corpse sitting on a street corner. Not even in those days.'

There was a long silence as Tunjin stirred his already cold coffee. 'No,' he said, finally. 'But you could find them. If you knew where to look.'

Solongo took even longer to reply. 'And, if you knew where to look, I don't suppose you had to look very hard.'

'Not me,' he said. 'I was just a junior officer. Did what I was told.'

'Just obeying orders.'

He shrugged. 'If you like. But we knew what Wu Sam was. We knew he'd never be prosecuted. Not here, anyway. But it would give us an excuse to have him deported. Something the Chinese couldn't create a diplomatic stink about.'

'So you couldn't just accuse him of being a spy?'

'He was a spy as well. But that would have just led to endless disputes and reprisals. And we weren't too bothered about him spying. We were bothered about him murdering young men.'

'So you had him deported so he could carry on murdering young men in China?'

'Maybe. But we didn't think it was very likely that they'd allow him to. We didn't imagine the Chinese authorities would simply turn a blind eye.'

'And did they?'

Tunjin shrugged. 'We don't know. No, that's not right. *I* don't know. I didn't want to find out. I imagine the security services would have kept tabs on him.'

'Would Nergui have known?'

Tunjin looked up, surprised by her question. 'Maybe. He was quite a bigwig even in those days. He'd been in the ministry. He'd set up the Serious Crimes Team. I imagine he could have found out if he'd wanted to.'

She nodded. 'So who was behind this? If you're right about the framing, I mean. Was that Nergui?'

He shook his head. 'I don't think so. It's not his style. Maybe he had his suspicions too, but he didn't reveal anything.'

'Which is very much his style. So who, then?'

'I don't know. The intelligence services, maybe.'

'But why? Why would they go to those lengths over some junior spy, even if he really was a murderer? I don't imagine the intelligence services shared your burning desire for justice.'

'Probably not. But they don't like things that are messy. Especially if they have international ramifications. Maybe they just wanted things tidied up, quickly and cleanly.'

She nodded, her eyes thoughtful. 'I'm missing the bit about the carpet.'

'The body – the second body – had been beaten to death. It was wrapped in an old carpet and dumped in the cellar of Wu Sam's apartment block. Along with one or two other pieces of neatly incriminating evidence.'

'But the carpet?' she persisted.

'Maybe some sort of joke.' He caught the expression on Solongo's face. 'Or a comment. Something else to point the finger in the right direction. Wu Sam was preparing a dissertation on the invasion of the Muslim empire.'

'Hulagu,' she said.

'Exactly,' he said. 'Every school child knows that story.'

'But he wasn't a Muslim? The victim, I mean.'

'I've no idea,' Tunjin said. 'I don't imagine so. He would have been a Communist, I imagine. Officially, at least.'

'So you arrested this Wu Sam and had him deported.'

'Pretty much. The evidence was there. I imagine we drew the Chinese authorities' attention to the other unproven case. I don't suppose they raised much objection. Probably just keen to—'

'Brush it under the carpet,' she said.

'Exactly.'

They sat in silence, both staring down at their half-full cups. Finally, Solongo rose and picked up the bottle of vodka from beside the kitchen sink. 'I'm going to have some of this,' she said, holding out the bottle as if proferring a refill of coffee. 'Do you want some?'

Tunjin looked at her, suspecting an undertone of irony. 'I think so,' he said.

She took two glasses from one of the kitchen cupboards and carefully poured two measures. Small measures, he noted. But there would always be the opportunity to replenish them.

She took a mouthful. 'So,' she said, 'you think what you did to this Wu Sam is somehow connected to the body at the museum?'

'I don't know. I mean—'

'Every schoolchild knows that story.'

'Yes, exactly. It might just be coincidence. Someone else trying to make some kind of point.'

'But what kind of point?' she asked. 'It occurred to me that there might be some kind of political resonance, but it doesn't really make much sense.'

'I don't know. It makes no sense to me. And then I look at what happened in the square yesterday.'

'So what did happen in the square yesterday?' she said. 'I thought you were a hero. That you'd stopped a suspected suicide bomber.'

'I don't know what I am, but I don't think I can claim to be a hero. I didn't know what I was doing even if it had all turned out for the best. As it is – well, I don't know how it's turned out.'

She took a swallow of her vodka, finishing the glass. Without a word, she poured another glass for herself and topped up Tunjin's. 'But what are you saying?' she said. 'Are you saying that – whatever it was in the square is somehow connected with the body in the museum?'

He shook his head and swallowed his own glass of vodka in a single mouthful. 'I don't know,' he said. 'And I don't know whether the supposed suicide bombing that I did or didn't prevent is connected to whatever other bombing might have happened last night. I don't know . . .' He stopped and helped himself to another glass of vodka. He waved the bottle vaguely in Solongo's direction. She shook her head, holding up her largely untouched drink.

'I don't know anything, really,' he concluded. 'I'm better at the instinctive stuff.'

'Then we'd better stick together. I lost touch with my instincts years ago. But I'm okay at logic.'

'And what does your logic tell you?'

'That there's something going on here. Something serious. And that it might well be connected to your Wu Sam.'

He gazed at her, and then finished his vodka in another mouthful. 'Funny,' he said. 'That's exactly what my instinct is telling me.'

# CHAPTER SIXTEEN

Sarangarel was trying to comfort Gundalai who, for some minutes, had seemed beyond any rational intervention. He curled in on himself, his body racked by endless rhythmic sobs. Nergui watched from his vantage point by the window, his expression suggesting he was observing some moderately interesting scientific demonstration.

It was several minutes before Gundalai became calmer. Sarangarel sat beside him, gently feeding him sips of water. Finally, he looked up. 'I'm sorry,' he said. 'It's just – well, Odbayar. We don't know where he is – what's happened to him.'

'What do you think may have happened to him?' Nergui said, softly.

Gundalai was staring at the floor. 'I don't know,' he said. 'But I've been worried.'

'Worried about what?'

'His campaigning. His anti-government campaigning. The things that were happening.'

'You think he was making enemies?' Doripalam said.

Gundalai shook his head. 'I don't think it was as simple as that. I mean, yes, he made enemies – he saw that as one of his purposes in life. But it was more that he was starting to have an impact. And people knew who he was. Who his father was, I mean.'

'What are you saying?' Nergui's tone was neutral.

'I don't know what I'm saying. I'm just saying that people were watching him.'

'You think there were people who felt threatened by him? By his actions?' Doripalam said.

Gundalai shook his head. 'No, not really. I mean, he was small-fry, really, wasn't he? There were plenty more influential figures out there.' He dropped his head into his hands, kneading his temples as though trying to stimulate his brain. 'No,' he said through his fingers, 'it was more that there were people who thought they could use him. People who thought he could give them some kind of leverage.'

'What kind of people?' Nergui's tone suggested nothing more than mild curiosity.

'I'm not sure,' Gundalai said. 'But some powerful people.' He stopped as though a thought had just occurred to him. 'I didn't believe that anyone would take *him* that seriously – not because of his political impact, at any rate. But there were people out there who thought he could help their cause.' He paused. 'Maybe even some people on his own side.'

'People opposed to the government, you mean?' Doripalam prompted.

'Who knows?' Nergui said. 'The biggest threat Odbayar poses is the risk of embarrassing his father. And there are plenty even within government who wouldn't be sorry to see that happen.'

'So what are we going to do?' Batzorig said. 'I mean, Odbayar might have been taken by persons unknown for reasons unknown. But he might not have been. And if he has, we've no clue where he might have been taken.'

'I think you've summed up the situation with characteristic succinctness,' Doripalam said. 'We can't do much more than we're doing, interviewing anyone who might have been a witness from the bombing, anyone who can corroborate or add to what Gundalai saw.'

'And that's the best you can offer?' Gundalai said. 'Endless witness interviews which just might add some tiny titbit of information to what I've already told you?' He looked around the assembled group, as though suspecting that they might themselves be impostors.

Doripalam shrugged. 'It's how it works. We don't do miracles.'

Nergui had turned and was staring out of the window. His dark-skinned face as impassive as ever, his blue eyes fixed on the distant horizon. 'And what about Wu Sam?' he said.

'Wu Sam?' Doripalam looked up. 'This supposed killer from twenty years ago? What about him? You really think there might be a connection?'

Nergui turned to face the room, silhouetted against the morning's brilliant sunshine. 'Two identical killings,' he said. 'Two bodies wrapped in carpets, replicating the story of Hulagu.'

'Not necessarily identical, from what you said,' Doripalam pointed out. 'We don't know the victim at the museum was actually killed inside the carpet. We don't know where the actual killing took place.'

Nergui gazed blankly at him. 'The scenario is exactly the same,' he said. 'The victim was killed as you describe. And then the body was wrapped in the carpet and left, partly hidden, in the basement of Wu Sam's apartment block.'

Doripalam frowned. 'But why would Wu Sam do that? Wrap the body in a carpet, I mean?'

'Who knows? Perhaps just because he was insane. He was preparing his dissertation on the Mongol's invasion of the Muslim lands. Perhaps the gesture meant something to him.'

'Did it mean anything to you?' Doripalam persisted.

Nergui looked for a moment as if he were about to respond to the question, then he shook his head. 'It was enough for us. We did not need incontrovertible evidence. We simply needed some-thing strong enough to justify our sending him back to his masters.'

He sounded almost defensive. It was a tone that Doripalam had never heard from Nergui, even when he was describing the demands and challenges of the old regime. Nergui had always traversed the minefield of moral dilemma with the most delicate of steps, and he never seemed to lack confidence in his own ethical position. There was a new uncertainty here.

'And you seriously think that the two cases might be connected?'

'We have to consider the possibility. Especially considering . . .' his voice trailed off, and he sounded uncharacteristically tentative.

'Considering what?' Doripalam said.

Nergui shook his head. 'Nothing important. It was a long time ago.'

'But something that makes you think this Wu Sam might be involved again?'

'I have reasons for thinking we should follow it up.' The words were spoken without undue emphasis, but Doripalam knew that Nergui's unspoken reasons were never wisely ignored.

'But this Wu Sam couldn't have entered the country without our knowing,' Batzorig said.

Nergui shrugged. 'It was all a long time ago. We do not know what happened after his return to China. In theory, he would be on our lists. But in practice – who knows?' As if responding to his own question, he pulled his mobile phone from his jacket pocket and thumbed in a number. 'It's Nergui,' he said. 'I need an answer to a simple question.' He laughed gently at the unheard response. 'Consider it a challenge then. We deported a suspected spy back to China about twenty years ago.' He laughed again. 'Yes, I can.' He paused, and then named a precise date. 'I could probably quote you the time and number of the flight he took, if you give me a couple of minutes. But I imagine your fancy databases can outdo that. You'll have him on record – probably just hard copy, I don't know – but there'll be a photograph and all the details. I just want to know whether the same man has re-entered the country in, say, the last month. I told you it was a simple question.' He paused, clearly listening to what was being said at the other end of the line, a faint smile playing across his face. 'Okay, I'll make it even easier for you. Forget China. Have a look at other international arrivals first.' He paused again, listening. 'I don't know. How does fifteen minutes sound?'

He thumbed off the call. 'I think some of these backroom people spend too long away from civilised company.' He moved to slip the phone back into his jacket pocket, and then stopped as it vibrated in his hand.

He held the phone to his ear, listening intently, and then looked back up at the expectant group around him. 'I suppose this is hardly a surprise,' he said, speaking to Doripalam. 'And it may mean something or nothing. But Tunjin has been true to form. He's absconded from the hospital.'

The young man was asleep now, his head lolling against the vibrating wall of the truck. Sam glanced at him, noting the trim muscular outlines of his body. Nothing like his father in that respect, though Sam could see a certain facial resemblance. In other circumstances he might have been more interested, especially given the history, but this was business. There might be time for distractions later.

He glanced at the dashboard clock. Another hour or so. Wait till they were well away from the cities, up there in the foothills. Even if they could be traced – and for all his earlier confidence, Sam knew better than to underestimate the opposition – it would take too long for anyone to reach them. If necessary, it could all be finished almost before they realised it had started, and he would be long gone.

He glanced at the satellite navigation screen. There were no real roads out here, just a tapestry of inter-crossing dirt tracks, but the equipment was pointing them in the right direction. Soon he would strike off east, heading towards the rising blue line of the mountains, driving until the grasslands grew more lush and thickets of fir trees rose around them. The land up there was less sparsely populated than these empty grasslands, but he had little concern about their being seen. Visitors, even foreign visitors, were much less uncommon here these days.

Sam had been careful to organise the hiring of a Land Cruiser similar to those used by the tourist guides. Even if someone did register their passing, there was nothing to connect this hired vehicle back to Sam. By the time the vehicle was tracked down, it would be too late.

The sun was high, and even this far north the temperature was rising rapidly. It was very different from the last time Sam had been here – the icy depths of winter, a sense of excitement, fear, auguries of impending chaos. For Sam, this society had seemed both strangely familiar and utterly alien, and he had struggled to regain a sense of control. In the end, he had been less experienced, less skilled than he had thought. They had played him, every inch of the way, while he had thought he was slipping beneath their radar.

He remembered how it had ended – the fat man he had not seen for twenty years, but whose gloating face was imprinted immovably on his mind, and the other one – the one he had seen at the end, the one with the dark wooden face. The one who could have helped and had chosen not to.

Suddenly realising that they had reached the point where they needed to strike off to the east, he peered hard at the sun-dried ground ahead of him, looking for any sign of a clear track. When he reached it, a hundred yards ahead, it was little more than a balder stretch of earth across the parched grasslands. He pulled to the right, the earth juddering beneath the truck's tyres. And then they were off again, bouncing along the endless ribbon of the dirt road, the forests and mountains growing steadily closer.

He smiled, feeling the earth's vibrations through his fingers, watching the shadows shortening as the sun rose. He knew now, finally, after all these years, how everything worked. He knew everything he needed to know.

He knew everything.

## WINTER 1988

It was worse than he could have imagined.

He had assumed that, however things turned out, it would be quick and brutal. He had imagined being bundled off at the dead of night, led anonymously on to a flight or train back home, handcuffed discreetly to some silent police officer.

Instead, the two men – police officers themselves, he assumed, though he realised later that they had shown him no identification – had walked him, back through the icy streets to an undistinguished concrete building behind the central square. They had taken him to a tiny, dingy interview room in the depths of the building. It was a bleak room: a concrete floor, grey walls scattered with disturbing stains, a single table bolted firmly into the ground.

An hour or so later the questioning began. The thin one asking him repeated insinuating questions, promising that it would all soon be over. The fat one chain-smoking cigarettes, slamming his fist on the formica table top, jabbing his finger in Wu Sam's face, blowing smoke. The threat of violence moments away.

He had no idea what they were talking about. Some body they had found. Some student. Someone he supposedly knew. Some relationship he had supposedly had.

The inquisition went on and on, variations on the same question in an endless loop – persuasive, aggressive, cajoling, threatening. Wu Sam's responses were hardly even denials, little more than blank incomprehension.

After another hour, as if at some unspoken signal, the two men suddenly rose and left the room. He sat by himself, his mind still reeling, trying to work out what was going on.

Finally, the door opened and another officer – one he had not seen before – stuck his head around the door and announced, in a grudging tone, that he was free to leave. 'For now,' the officer went on. 'But we'll be keeping tabs on you. Don't make it difficult for us.' The undertone of threat was hardly concealed.

Outside, Wu Sam stood for a moment, breathing in the icy late afternoon air.

The fat cop had emerged from the main doors of the police building, and was standing on the steps smoking. He was looking in Wu Sam's direction, but his gaze seemed unfocused, as though he was looking far beyond, at some impossible horizon.

# CHAPTER SEVENTEEN

## SUMMER

She reached for the bottle, but he shook his head, pulling it away. 'I don't think you should,' he said. 'Not this early, anyway.'

'You're ahead of me,' Solongo pointed out. 'Two glasses ahead.'

'I'm used to it,' Tunjin said. 'And nobody's ever told me it's an admirable quality. Besides, do you want to end up looking like me?'

She opened her mouth, but could clearly think of no response. 'You're right,' she said. 'Not that that helps.'

'Has this been going on long?' he said. 'The drinking, I mean.'

'Yours or mine?' she said. 'Sorry. I mean, I don't know. Not long. Not at this time of the day, anyway. I mean, in the evenings when Doripalam's delayed yet again or called back in, and I'm stuck here – a glass or two, then, I suppose. A bit more over the last few weeks – trying to cope with this bloody museum job. I don't think you can blame me.'

'I'm the last one to blame anyone,' he said. 'But I know the costs.'

She shrugged. 'I should tell you it's none of your business. But you're right. I've known for weeks.' She paused. 'Doesn't mean that I don't want another drink, though.'

'No,' he agreed. 'It never does.'

'And what about Doripalam?' she said.

He glanced sharply up at her, wondering where this was going. 'What about Doripalam?'

'His drinking,' she said. 'You must have noticed. You of all people.'

'Me of all people,' he said. 'Yes, I should have noticed. You think he's drinking too much?'

She shrugged. 'What's too much? He goes to that bar of his, most nights when he's not working. Sometimes when he says he is working.'

'You don't know that.'

'I know that. I've called the office. They've told me. Sometimes they haven't told me, but they're poor liars. And I've called his mobile. He doesn't answer. Or he calls back once he's out into the street. But I've seen him in the bar.'

'You've followed him?'

She smiled. 'Not really. I just happened to be there one evening. I went for a quick drink with some of the students from the museum. He came in, on his own. He didn't see me – we were in a dark corner. I nearly went up to him, but I got the impression he didn't really want to see anyone.'

'And did he drink a lot?'

'A few beers. But that wasn't the point.' She hesitated, as though searching for the words. 'He went there rather than coming back here. And when he did come back here, finally – I made sure I got back first – he drank some more. A few more glasses of vodka.'

This sounded pretty tame by Tunjin's standards, but perhaps not by Doripalam's. 'Just the once,' he said.

She shook her head. 'No. I went back there – the students pop in most nights. I went a couple of times. His routine was the same.'

'And what's your concern?' he said. He could feel himself slipping into the unaccustomed and unwanted role of agony aunt, but had no idea how to extract himself from the conversation. 'Is it that he's drinking too much, or that he prefers to do his drinking without you?' Spoken out loud, the question sounded too blunt.

'It's – well, it's both, I suppose,' she said. 'But mainly the second. That's what drives me to drink.'

'But you don't—' he stopped, not knowing how to finish the question. How do you ask a woman whether she suspects her husband of having an affair? A question like that, he conceded, was probably better left to someone with some tact and sensitivity. 'You don't think anything else is going on?'

She looked at him for a moment, as though mentally translating a question unexpectedly asked in a foreign language. 'You mean an affair?' Suddenly, she burst out laughing. 'Doripalam? No, I don't think so. Not unless you count his infatuation with the job.'

'I think you might reasonably count that,' he said. 'Or at least I would if I was in your position.'

She nodded, smiling now, and Tunjin began to wonder if he had a future in relationship counselling after all. But perhaps he shouldn't push his luck. 'I need to decide what I'm going to do,' he said. 'I can't stay here for ever.'

'No,' she said. 'Unless you want to wait for Doripalam. He's bound to get back eventually. I imagine.'

So much for his attempt to change the subject. 'I need to get a handle on all this. What happened in the square. What Nergui's up to. This body at the museum.' He paused. 'Wu Sam.'

'I don't understand,' she said. 'This student you deported twenty years ago. How can he be connected to any of this?'

'I don't know. But it's a hell of a coincidence, don't you think? A body in a carpet. Someone drugs me and sticks a gun in my hand. Gets me to shoot what might turn out to be an innocent man.'

'Frames you, you mean,' she said.

He nodded slowly. 'Yes, I suppose that's exactly what I mean.'

'But you weren't framed,' she pointed out. 'You did what you thought was right. You did it to save lives.'

'But I killed an innocent man.'

'Not so innocent. He was carrying a bomb.'

'A fake bomb. That doesn't make him a murderer. Or even a terrorist.'

'It gives you legitimate grounds to shoot him.'

'Maybe in legal terms. But that doesn't make it any better for me. I killed an innocent man.'

'But you were drugged. You were manoeuvred into it.'

'That doesn't make it any better,' he repeated. He picked up the vodka bottle again. Then he placed it carefully back down on the table. 'For once, I don't think that's what I need. I think I need a clear head.'

'Is it him?'

Nergui was sitting facing Doripalam's desk, looking utterly relaxed. He was in his familiar posture, leaning back in the seat, his ankles resting precisely on the desk's corner, staring hard at the photograph he was holding. He shook his head. 'I don't know. It could be, but it's difficult to be sure.'

'He's Chinese,' Doripalam pointed out.

'I'd determined that much. It was twenty years ago though. He looks about the right age. I could persuade myself it was him. But I could probably do the same with any middle-aged man of Chinese origin.'

'And it's not the best picture.'

Nergui shook his head. 'You'd have thought by now they could have got the technology right. It's hardly worth them bothering.' The photograph had been taken at the airport, part of the immigration procedure at the point of entry, each passenger's digital image captured on an automatic camera. But the image remained blurred, a scramble of pixels when blown up.

'I presumed your people were responsible for the technology. A ministry responsibility.'

'No doubt. And no doubt they purchased the technology from the Chinese or Koreans, and were royally ripped off in the process.' Nergui tossed the image on to Doripalam's desk. 'I don't know. He sounds promising, though. He flew in from the US. New York, via Chicago and Seoul. But Chinese.'

Doripalam looked again at the notes that had been sent with the photograph. 'By birth, according to his passport details. Born in Beijing, but now resident in the US. Been there since the 1990s, apparently. Has obtained his Permanent Residence card.' He paused.

'Occupation given as "professor". He's here on an exchange visit at the National University. At the faculty of Mongolian studies.'

'So far so good, then,' Nergui said, studying the back of the photograph. 'And his name is Sam Yung.'

'Supposedly.'

Nergui turned the photograph over and gazed at the glossy image. 'And that's all there is about his background?'

'So far. I think they've done well to pull this particular needle out of the haystack so quickly.'

Nergui nodded. 'They've done brilliantly,' he agreed. 'If this really is him. We don't know how much time we've got. Assuming we're not chasing shadows.'

'Assuming we're not chasing shadows, we don't know that we're not already too late,' Doripalam pointed out. 'What have you told the minister?'

'Nothing yet,' Nergui said.

Doripalam looked up at him in surprise. 'Nothing? Is that wise?'

Nergui shrugged. 'The sensible thing would have been to have told him straightaway, so that my back was covered. But it's never been my policy to be over candid with the minister.'

'Over candid? But this is his son.'

'I know. And we don't know yet that anything's happened to him.'

'We know,' Doripalam said. 'I know. You know. Something's happened to him.'

'But we don't know what. And we don't know why.'

Doripalam shook his head. 'You can be bloody gnomic, Nergui. But even by your standards—'

Nergui held up the photograph, as though to halt any further discussion. 'So this Sam Yung,' he said. 'Where is he?'

'I've got Batzorig over at the university now, trying to find out. According to the visa details, he's on a three month visit.'

'Do we know why he's here?'

'I did a bit of hunting on the internet to see if I could find anything. There were a couple of references to academic papers he'd published on the origins of the Mongol empire. I imagine he's here for the Genghis Khan anniversary.'

'Or that's his excuse for being here,' Nergui said. 'If we assume that his motives are not purely academic.'

'Quite. But, if so, why is he here? Why after all this time?'

Nergui continued to study the photograph, as though he might glean more knowledge from the blank oriental features staring back at him.

'One of your hunches? You think there's something behind all this?' Doripalam picked up the phone and pressed the speed-dial code for Batzorig's mobile.

Nergui placed the photograph carefully down on the desk. 'I'm flying blind, you know that. I'm always flying blind.'

'But usually in the right direction.' Doripalam's tone was wry.

Batzorig had just entered the vice-president's office when his mobile buzzed. The middle-aged man, rising from his desk, had opened his mouth to speak, but Batzorig held up his hand. 'I'm sorry,' he said. 'It's the chief. I need to speak to him. I do apologise, but I'm sure you understand.'

The vice-president looked as if such behaviour was far beyond his understanding but he watched unblinking as Batzorig took the call.

Normally Batzorig would have felt some discomfort at his own rudeness. But, having been kept waiting for thirty minutes after he had seen the vice-president stroll past his secretary into the office, he felt little inclination towards generosity.

'I think I did mention,' he had said to the vice-president's secretary, 'that this is a murder enquiry. And that it's potentially urgent.'

'The vice-president is a busy man. He'll see you as quickly as he can. I'm sure he appreciates how important the matter is.' Her tone implied that the vice-president's assessment of this and most other matters would differ significantly from Batzorig's own.

This was a cheap revenge, therefore, but a mildly satisfying one. Batzorig held the phone close to his ear and spoke quietly, while ensuring that the vice-president would be able to follow his words. 'Yes, sir. Well, no, not as much as I'd hoped yet. I had to wait a little while to see the relevant party, sir.' He was aware that, in similar circumstances, Doripalam would have simply walked past the secretary. Nergui would quite possibly have had both her and the vice-president placed under arrest. Batzorig still had some skills to acquire.

'No, I haven't yet, sir. No one seems to know.' Batzorig could feel the vice-president's gaze fixed on him, and wondered how long it would be before his call was interrupted. 'Yes, that's exactly what I'm doing. I would have – but, as I say, I was kept waiting for some time. Yes, I will tell him that, sir.' The final sentences hadn't been a direct response to Doripalam's actual question, but Batzorig trusted the chief would understand that he was playing to a different audience.

Doripalam caught on quickly enough. 'If you like,' he said from the other end of the line, 'you can tell the snooty old bastard that if he doesn't co-operate immediately we'll have him brought in for obstructing a murder inquiry.'

'I'll pass on your sentiments, sir,' Batzorig said. He felt able to meet the vice-president's gaze now.

He turned off the phone and smiled at the old man sitting behind the desk. The vice-president was a tall, slightly stooped individual, his swept back hair clearly dyed black. He had the air of someone who had never consciously failed to be the centre of attention, and who was on the point of reclaiming this rightful role.

'I'm terribly sorry, sir,' Batzorig said. 'It's the chief. The head of Serious Crimes. He was just emphasising the urgency of the matter, this being a murder investigation.'

The vice-president had clearly been about to express his displeasure, but now stopped and gazed at Batzorig warily. 'What does this have to do with the university?'

'Possibly nothing, sir. But you'll appreciate we have to follow up all leads.'

'I just hope that you're not wasting your time.' The words 'and mine' were as audible as if they had been spoken.

'That's the point, sir, if you'll forgive me,' Batzorig said, earnestly. He was beginning to enjoy this. 'It's never time wasted. If nothing else, it enables us to eliminate a line of inquiry. That's the nature of policework.' He had been schooled by masters in the art of patronising pompous interviewees.

'And this line of inquiry would be what, precisely?'

Batzorig paused, as though weighing up how much he should reveal. 'We're trying to track down a Mr – sorry, a Professor Sam Yung. We understand that he's a visiting scholar from the US.'

The vice-president's gaze remained constant. 'You'd better sit down, Mr . . . ?'

'Batzorig.' Batzorig lowered himself into the chair opposite, thinking that this represented a first small victory.

'I must confess that I'm a little taken aback, Mr Batzorig.'

'Sir?'

'You do realise, of course, that Professor Yung is a most distinguished academic. An honoured visitor to our country.'

'If you say so, sir. It's not really my field.'

'No, well. But you'll understand my surprise that Professor Yung—'

'I'm merely trying to contact him. That's all.'

The vice-president looked at him for another long moment, as if trying to read the thoughts of the moon-faced young man sitting opposite. 'Yes, of course,' he said, finally. 'Well, I can give you the address where he's staying. We've provided him with one of the university apartments.'

'I know that. It looks a very pleasant place.'

The vice-president allowed a momentary glimmer of surprise pass across his face. 'You have his address?'

'Yes, sir. It was given to the immigration service as part of his entry requirements.'

'Of course. And you've been over there?'

'It was the first place I tried, sir. We're just looking to talk to him informally. At this stage, I mean.' Batzorig left the final words hanging ambiguously in the air. 'There was no one at the apartment. I tried some the neighbouring apartments and eventually found someone who knew him. Another member of your faculty, I believe.' He paused, managing to imply that the presence of this second faculty member might somehow be incriminating.

'I'm afraid I don't see—'

'I was told that he hadn't been around for some time. At least a couple of weeks. And that I should visit the faculty, that you might have some idea where he was. Which is why I'm here, sir.' Batzorig was smiling now. 'I was told something about a trip?'

The vice-president looked much less self-assured. It was strange, Batzorig thought. This was a different world now, a very different society. There was no reason why foreign visitors should not travel freely wherever they wished, but the vice-president, like many of his generation, had never quite shaken off the shackles of the old regime. He was a product of the days when no foreign visitor – and certainly none of the very rare travellers from the West – would have left the city without the full knowledge of the authorities and a dutiful MIAT guide. It was clear that he felt some discomfort at being unable to account for his visitor's whereabouts. In the old days, his position would have been untenable and the tone of this meeting would have been very different. Batzorig decided to make every effort to remind the vice-president of the old days.

'I take it Professor Yung is not in the university at present?' he said, calmly. 'Do you know where he is?'

'Professor Yung is a guest of ours, and a distinguished scholar of our nation's past,' the vice-president said, in the tone that he no doubt adopted for graduation-day speeches. 'We would of course wish him to take the opportunity to explore our heritage and landscape.'

It was finely done, Batzorig was forced to acknowledge, but there was an undertone of hesitancy to the vice-president's words. 'This would be an official trip, then?' Batzorig offered. 'Hosted by the university?'

'We have organised several official trips for the professor.'

'Including this one?'

The vice-president shook his head. 'No. I understand that this excursion was organised at the professor's own request. He wished to explore some of the country for himself. The official trips can be a little formal.'

Batzorig gazed impassively at the vice-president for a moment. 'He's exploring the country on his own?'

'Not on his own.' The vice-president stopped, and then went on as if trying to extricate himself from the web of his own circumlocution. 'Look, Mr Batzorig, I've had very little direct involvement in this. We received a request from the professor to visit as part of his sabbatical. He was keen to experience the anniversary-year celebrations and exhibitions. And we were only too pleased to welcome someone of his eminence.'

'He really is a distinguished scholar, then?' Batzorig said, trying hard to keep any note of irony from his voice.

'Of course. You must understand that ours is not a field that is widely studied in the West. Genghis Khan is always of interest, but the broader study of the Mongol empire is a more specialist area of expertise. Professor Yung has written a number of well-regarded papers.'

The best we could find, then, Batzorig mentally translated. 'But his current whereabouts?' he prompted.

'I have to say that, although Professor Yung was co-operative enough in terms of our formal programme, I had a sense that his real interest lay elsewhere. That he found the structured excursions a little constraining. Perhaps understandable for one of his background.' He stopped, possibly in response to Batzorig's facial expression. 'He asked for our support in visiting one or two locations on his own. We were only too happy to assist.'

'So where is he at the moment?' Batzorig interrupted.

'Well, the last I was aware, he was travelling up to Genghis Khan's birthplace. Or supposed birthplace.'

'When was this?'

There was a moment's silence. 'It was – well, it must have been nearly two weeks ago. I'd rather assumed he'd returned, but from what you say . . .'

'I don't know, sir. I only know that none of his neighbours appears to have seen him.'

'I've certainly not seen him around the faculty. I mean, he's discharged all his formal duties – the lectures and seminars he agreed to as part of the visit – so there's no particular reason for him to be here. But I'd assumed that he would attend some lectures.'

'But you've seen no sign of him for the last two weeks?'

'He may have decided to extend his excursion.' This was said with an air of bravado, as though the vice-president were challenging Batzorig to question the validity of the statement.

'You said he wasn't travelling alone?'

'We'd organised him a guide. Someone who spoke English. Professor Yung spoke some Mongolian, as well as Chinese, but he was far from fluent.'

'He spoke Chinese?'

The vice-president nodded. 'Yes. He was born in China, in Beijing. But his family were from Inner Mongolia, apparently. Hence his interest in Mongolian history. One of those who perceive the links rather than the divisions between our two countries.'

'He had been here before?'

'Not that I'm aware. I think that was the point. He'd always been fascinated by our country; had been brought up tantalisingly close to it, but had spent most of his adult life on the far side of the world.'

'When did he move to the US?'

'I'm afraid I've no idea. I just had the impression that he'd lived most of his adult life there.'

'And the last you knew, he was intending to visit Genghis Khan's birthplace?' Batzorig paused. 'You'll forgive my ignorance, sir, but that would be where, precisely?'

'Precisely,' the vice-president said, perhaps sensing that he was moving on to more comfortable conversational terrain, 'it's very difficult to say. Imprecisely – well, it's out in the east. Up in the hills. The nearest town is Ondorkhaan.'

This meant nothing to Batzorig, who had rarely ventured beyond the city boundaries. 'How far is that?'

'Some distance. There are flights to Ondorkhaan, and it's a drive beyond that.'

'Who was the guide, sir? Who's with Professor Yung?'

'I'm afraid I can't help you there. It was organised through one of my staff, who in turn arranged it through one of his students, as I understand.'

Batzorig raised his head, thinking of Wu Sam's history, wondering if this Sam Yung might indeed be the same man. 'One of your students is accompanying him?'

'Not exactly. I mean, we often would do it that way. A lot of our graduate students speak excellent English, and are keen to earn some extra money.'

'But not this time?'

'Nobody was available. Over the summer, most of them have got jobs already.'

'So who is it?'

'I think it was an ex-student. Someone who's done this kind of thing before. I can find out.'

'I'd be grateful if you could do that, sir. As soon as possible.'

The vice-president was finally beginning to recognise the urgency in Batzorig's tone. 'Yes, of course. When do you need the information?'

'I was thinking of immediately, sir,' Batzorig said. 'Unless you can provide it quicker than that.'

# CHAPTER EIGHTEEN

The mountains were more beautiful than he had ever seen them. The sun was high in the empty blue sky, and the temperature outside was well into the thirties. He had been using the truck's air-conditioning sparingly, aiming to conserve fuel. Not that they were short. He had planned that as carefully as everything else and the rear of the Land Cruiser was lined with plastic cans of diesel. Nevertheless, his instincts, as always, were for caution.

The sparse grassland became increasingly lush as they headed east, and there were thickets of trees in the middle distance. Every mile brought them closer to what he increasingly thought of as his spiritual home. Soon the desolate steppe would give way to rich pastureland, the green shade of woodlands, the undulations of the lower hills, the silent sweep of the river.

Odbayar slept on, undisturbed by the juddering surface of the dirt road. I could kill him now, Sam thought. A single shot to the temple, a knife in the heart. He would never even know. Or I could stop here and toss him, still barely awake, out into the deserted grassland. The chances that anyone would find him were minimal.

But that was not the point. That was why he needed to apply some discipline This was about the future. Realising his dreams. Reclaiming what was rightfully his.

Odbayar stirred suddenly next to him, his body shaking as if in the middle of some vivid dream. His eyes opened wide and he stared at Sam, his expression one of terror. 'Who are you?' he said.

Sam was taken by surprise, and for a moment almost lost control of the vehicle, feeling the steering wheel slipping between his fingers as the truck bounced from boulder to boulder. He pressed his foot on the brake, knowing that the worst thing he could do was to overturn the truck on this remote track.

It seemed like an eternity before the truck came to a halt, its rear wheels twisting slightly. He looked at Odbayar, who was still staring blankly at him.

'It's me. Sam. You know me.'

'Sam?' Odbayar repeated the word as though trying out an unfamiliar sound in his mouth.

'Sam. You know where we are. You know where we're headed.' These were statements rather than questions.

'Sam.' Odbayar was speaking more quietly now, and his eyes were closing. It had simply been some dream, bubbling up towards consciousness, then vanishing back beneath the waves of sleep.

Sam restarted the engine and glanced briefly at the GPS system, reassuring himself that they were still travelling in the right direction. Then he accelerated down the dirt track, enjoying the rhythmic thud of the road, his eyes fixed on the distance, his senses already lost in the rich scent of the fir trees, the feel of the mountain breeze, the soft endless washing of the river in his ears.

'So what next?'

Tunjin gazed down into his empty glass. 'I don't think I've got the faintest idea.'

'You were looking for Doripalam,' Solongo reminded him.

'I know. I was going to throw myself on his mercy. Put myself back into the system.'

'You think your arrest was outside the system?'

'I'm not sure. Nergui usually knows what he's doing. Maybe it was for my own benefit.'

'You don't trust Nergui?'

'Do you?'

'I'm not a reliable witness. You've worked with him for years.'

'I have. And, yes, I suppose I do. That is, I trust him to do what's right. But I also think that might involve casualties.'

'And you might be one of those casualties?'

'I don't know.' He paused. 'I suppose I need to track down Doripalam.'

'I suppose you do. Though Doripalam's another one who always does what he thinks right. And who also leaves casualties.' She gestured towards the nearly empty vodka bottle. 'Take it from one who knows.'

'I should try the office again, see if Doripalam's there. Or his mobile. It's just that . . .' he rose and walked over to the window. There were a few people about out there now, a middle-aged man in a smart suit hurrying to work, an old woman in a traditional robe shuffling slowly past, not obviously heading anywhere, 'if it is Wu Sam, I want to know why he's back.'

'Doripalam will help you,' she said.

'Doripalam will hand me over to Nergui. He'll do it properly, by the book, and he'll make sure all my rights are protected. But that's what he'll do. He's got no choice.'

'If it is this Wu Sam,' she said, 'maybe Nergui's trying to protect you. Perhaps that's why he had you under guard.'

'It could well be,' he said. 'But I don't think it's that simple. If Nergui was just looking out for my well-being, there are other ways he could have handled it. This was about containment. Nergui likes to be in control.'

'You don't need to persuade me of that.'

'The question,' Tunjin said, 'is what was he trying to contain?'

'You think this Wu Sam was framed,' she said. 'There's a story there. It could embarrass Nergui.'

'I've never known Nergui troubled by embarrassment,' he said. 'Not on his own account, at least.'

There was something about the way he spoke the final words that made Solongo look up at him. 'You think he might have been concerned about someone else's embarrassment? Yours?'

Tunjin laughed. 'I think he might care marginally less about my embarrassment than his own. I don't think Nergui's mind works like that.'

'If you ever find out how Nergui's mind works,' she said, 'you must remember to let me know.'

'What drives Nergui,' Tunjin went on, 'is his sense of duty.'

'Oh, yes. Nergui the patriot. I've heard a lot about that. It seems to be the justification for everything he does.'

'It is.' Tunjin spoke simply, as though he had not registered her irony. 'It really is what he believes.' He paused, and she realised that he was pouring the last of the vodka into his empty glass. 'So,' he said, 'if Nergui is concerned about embarrassment, it's not his or my reputation that will be troubling him.' He raised the glass to eye level, as if making an elaborate toast, and then swallowed the contents in one mouthful. 'No, Nergui will be concerned about the embarrassment of the nation.'

'What about Tunjin?' Doripalam said.

Nergui was working his way painstakingly through the reports of the previous night's incidents. 'What about him?'

'I understood he was being detained.'

'He is,' Nergui said. 'Or, rather, he was. Now he's absconded. I've got people looking for him.'

'None of my people,' Doripalam said.

'I think this falls within the ministry's jurisdiction.'

Doripalam opened his mouth to respond, then shook his head. There was no point in debating any of this. Nergui would reveal his hand, if and when he chose to.

Nergui waved the wad of reports in the air. 'What do you make of this?' he said.

'Which in particular?'

'All of it,' Nergui said. 'We have a city in quiet chaos.'

It was a good phrase, Doripalam thought. There was a sense of unreality to it, as if the surface of things remained unchanged while turmoil bubbled beneath. He recalled a newspaper image he had seen a year or two before of a run-down apartment block somewhere in the city which had partially collapsed after years of structural neglect. The block had been uninhabited and there had been no casualties. But, according to the experts, the collapse could have happened at any time over a number of years, while its residents had continued their daily lives unaware of the instability of the building in which they lived.

Nergui flicked through the papers on his knee. 'How long do you think we have before this really hits the media?'

'We're doing the best we can from our side to contain it,' Doripalam said. 'Your people saw to it that nothing was reported about the incident in the square. I don't know how you managed to swing that.'

'National security,' Nergui said. 'The usual excuse. It stills works with the respectable media because they depend on us. They can't be bothered to go and hunt out any stories of their own.'

'What about the yellow press, though?' Doripalam asked, referring to the mass of cheap scandal sheets that now dominated the news stands.

'We can't do much about that. But they're generally not too interested in this sort of story unless they can find an excuse to illustrate it with a photograph of a half-naked woman.'

'But people must be talking about it.'

'Probably. There were plenty of people about. People saw the shooting. There'll be a thousand and one paranoid explanations doing the rounds. But they won't be surprised that it wasn't reported.'

Another hangover from the old regime. People didn't expect the media to report the truth. Or, at least, they expected the media to report only the most boring, uncontroversial truths. And it wouldn't matter if the story did get reported in the yellow press since no one would believe that either. The rumour-mill would churn away, but no one would take it seriously. Doripalam had once assumed that a free press would bring dramatic changes to the national culture, but it had never really happened. The media had simply polarised – on the one hand, dutiful and dull reports of proceedings in the Great Hural; on the other, wild unsubstantiated scandals about transitory celebrities. But nothing in the middle. Real, significant stories tended to emerge only when someone – usually a member of one of the opposition parties – took the trouble to leak them.

'What about the bomber?' he said. 'The supposed bomber, I mean. Have you identified him?'

There was a silence. 'It's the usual,' Nergui said, finally. 'Endless legwork. We're making some progress.'

It wasn't quite the equivalent of a formal statement to the media, but it sounded far from candid. This was Nergui going native, or perhaps reverting to type. Despite his endless capacity to surprise, Nergui remained at heart an apparatchik of the old school.

'You think he's a local, or a foreign national?' Doripalam persisted.

'We're pursuing all lines of inquiry,' Nergui said. 'As you would expect.'

'I'm sure you'll let us know if we can be of assistance.'

As always, Nergui seemed impervious to irony. 'What about your own inquiries? The two bodies.'

'The same legwork,' Doripalam said. He wondered whether, if they really had made any substantive progress, he would be prepared to share it with Nergui. In practice, the question was academic. 'But we're not getting very far. We've got the pathology reports, but they don't tell us much we didn't already know. The first was literally kicked to death. Chillingly so, in fact – I'd assumed some sort of frenzied attack, but it seems to have been more systematic.'

'The victim was dead before being wrapped in the carpet,' Nergui said. It was not a question, and Doripalam was left wondering, yet again, about Nergui's access to supposedly confidential police reports.

'It looks like it. There are lesions on his wrists and ankles. The assumption is that he was tied up in some way, and then—'

'Kicked to death.'

'Carefully placed kicks, at that. Maximising the pain. Eking out the time until the assault would prove fatal. And substantial damage to the face.'

Nergui gazed at him, unblinking. 'And what about the second body. At the hotel.'

'Stabbed. The weapon was left behind. A fairly ornate dagger – like something from the golden age of Genghis himself. We thought it might tell us something, but it's just a cheap ornament. They're selling them all over the city during the anniversary celebrations. There are hundreds out there. Made in China, ironically enough. Not much chance of finding out precisely which market stall it was purchased from. We're having it checked for prints and DNA, but I'm not optimistic.'

'He was killed in the storeroom?'

'As far as we can tell. There's no evidence that the body was moved after death.'

'Any clue as to the bodies' identities?'

'Not so far. No matches to their fingerprints. They weren't Mongolians. Not ethnically, at any rate.'

'So unlikely to be Mongolian citizens?'

'Yes.'

'Visitors?'

'Probably. Not likely to be illegals. Not from there.'

'Shouldn't be too difficult to identify, then.'

Doripalam shrugged. 'We've asked immigration to find potential fits, males who've entered the country in the last month. But it won't be easy to match the photographs.' He gestured towards the photograph of the Chinese man. 'Particularly if that's the quality of the images we have to work with. I don't know how they came up with that one so quickly,' he said. 'They've told us it's likely to be tomorrow before they have a list of possibles.'

'It's who you know,' Nergui said, smiling. 'I'll rattle the cage for you, if you think it would help.'

'Anything would help. We don't have much.'

'But it wasn't too difficult to find this one,' Nergui said. 'They were looking for males of Chinese origin who'd not entered from China.'

'Why not from China?' Doripalam said. 'You didn't know – you still don't know, if this isn't him – that Wu Sam wasn't still living in China.'

Nergui shrugged. 'One of my wild hunches. I don't think the Chinese wanted him back. I think they made arrangements for him to exit discreetly, so they could make use of him elsewhere and, if necessary, let some other government pick up the problem. Anyway, I was being pragmatic; it would take for ever to work through all the Chinese males entering from China. I thought we might as well start by looking at those who'd come in from elsewhere.'

Typical Nergui, Doripalam thought, that mix of off-the-wall intuition and common-sense practicality. 'I don't think ours are going to be so easy to pinpoint. We can't even be sure about the ethnic origin, not yet, anyway. We think Indian sub-continent, but I don't know if we can really narrow it down beyond Central Asia, or even Eastern Europe. They could have come from anywhere. We can look for suitable surnames, but their names might be totally Westernised. It's not a lot as the basis for a shortlist.'

'I see your problem.'

'And the real question,' Dorilpalam said, 'is whether any of this is connected. At a mundane level, I don't even know where to focus the resource. I mean, the urgent issue is Odbayar's disappearance, but we don't even know whether he's really disappeared.'

'Or whether it's some kind of stunt, you mean?'

Doripalam nodded.

'If so, we should know soon enough. There's not much point in publicity stunts unless you want publicity.'

'Is that why you're holding off breaking the news to his father?'

'Maybe,' Nergui said. 'Or maybe it's just another wild hunch.'

Gundalai remainded hunched in a corner of the sofa, his arms wrapped tightly around his knees, staring fixedly into space.

'Gundalai, it's going to be all right.' Sarangarel didn't really even believe this herself, so there was no reason why Gundalai should.

But there was no option other than to be positive. 'We don't even know that anything's happened to Odbayar.'

'I know what I saw.' His voice was quiet and steady.

She shook her head. 'I didn't learn much from my time in the judiciary. But I learnt one thing. You can never be sure what you saw. I lost count of the cases where witnesses gave diametrically opposed accounts of the same event. Everyone swearing blind they were telling the truth.'

'People lie in court,' Gundalai said, bluntly.

'Most people don't. They're just witnesses, with no axe to grind. They still disagree.'

'I know what I saw,' he repeated.

'Maybe,' she said, doubtfully. 'But, even if you do, you don't know what it means.'

'Odbayar was being taken away.'

'You don't know that. You don't even know for sure that it was Odbayar.' Even to herself, her words sounded unconvincing.

'So where is he?'

It was a question she couldn't answer. She turned back to the window. 'You're very close to him, aren't you?' she said, finally. 'He means a lot to you?'

She looked back and realised that Gundalai was nodding, his eyes still staring at the floor. 'More than you know,' he said.

She nodded. 'I think I know,' she said.

She was not surprised, though many of her fellow citizens would be simply baffled by the idea. Homosexuality was not illegal now, though its existence was barely acknowledged. But it was a country with a young population, and she had no doubt that many engaged in activities, legal or illegal, which would have been unknown – or at least unacknowledged – in her generation.

'Do you trust him?' she said.

He looked up at her, the question clearly taking him by surprise. 'Trust him?'

It occurred to her that, in fact, she had intended to ask whether Gundalai loved him, but she had not been able to articulate the words. But, now it had been asked, the question seemed to be the right one.

'Of course I trust him,' he went on, without waiting for her to respond. 'Why wouldn't I trust him? You don't know—'

'I don't know anything,' she said. 'I don't know you, really. My nephew. My sister's son. I haven't seen her for five, six years. I haven't seen you for even longer. I've never met Odbayar. Do you trust him?'

This time, he didn't respond immediately. 'I think so,' he said. 'He means well. He has good intentions . . .'

'But do you trust him?' she persisted.

Finally, he said: 'I don't know. That's the truth. I don't know.'

She nodded, as if this was the answer she had been expecting. 'Why don't you know?'

Gundalai was shaking his head, slowly, rocking backwards and forwards, as though trying to deny the world. 'I—' He stopped, his head still moving, the words eluding him. 'It's not the same,' he said, at last. 'He's not like he was. Nothing is like it was.' He lowered his head into his hands, running his fingers through his hair repeatedly and fiercely, as though trying to remove some foreign body.

Sarangarel had lowered herself on the sofa beside him. 'What's not the same?'

'I thought we were drifting apart. I mean, it didn't really surprise me. Odbayar was never really comfortable with . . .' He looked up at her, as if conscious for the first time of what he was saying. 'Well, you know . . .'

'With your relationship?'

'Exactly. I mean, it was different when we were students. It didn't really matter, even with Odbayar's background. It made him feel rebellious. Knowing that it was something his father would have disapproved of.'

'You don't think he took it seriously? Your relationship, I mean.'

'It's hard to tell what Odbayar really thinks about anything. And now that he's begun to take the politics more seriously, I thought

– well, I thought it was probably going to end soon, anyway.' He seemed more composed now, as if he had unloaded some burden. 'But it's more than that,' he went on. 'I think there's something else.'

'What do you mean?'

'I don't know. I thought at first that Odbayar had found someone else. But that's not the way he does things. Whatever else he might do, he'd be honest about that. If only because it wouldn't occur to him to worry about my feelings.' He laughed, mirthlessly. 'If there was someone else, he'd just have told me.'

'So what was it?' she prompted.

'He was distracted. I mean, we were going along with all the political stuff. But it was if his heart wasn't really in it.' He frowned. 'No, that's not quite right. It was still important to him. But I don't think he believed in what we were doing – the meetings, the speeches, the protests. It was as if he'd realised that he wasn't going to achieve anything that way.'

'I thought he'd made quite an impact,' she said. 'He got people out on the streets.'

'Don't get me wrong,' he said. 'He's a brilliant speaker. Even when he was going through the motions, he could get people eating out of his hand. And you're right – there was a movement starting to build. Not just through Odbayar, but he was part of it.'

There was genuine enthusiasm in Gundalai's tone. For the first time, Sarangarel realised how seriously he had taken all this. 'You really thought you could change things?' she asked, trying hard to keep any scepticism from her tone.

He looked up at her, trying to gauge whether she was mocking him. 'I still think we can,' he said. 'Things have to change.'

'Things have changed,' she pointed out. 'More than you can imagine. In my lifetime.'

'I know,' he said. 'And even in mine. But it's not enough.'

'I don't know,' she said. 'We've had two decades of change. There was a time when I really thought this country was finished. You don't remember; you were a child. There were people starving.

People out on the steppes who were killing their livestock – their livelihood – to survive. People without a roof over their heads. There was economic disaster.'

'I know,' he said. 'I've read about all that.'

'But you don't know what it was like to live through it,' she said. 'You were a child. And things weren't so bad for you. Your father had a government job. He was still being paid. There were countless people who had nothing.' She stopped, wondering why she was rehearsing all this, why it seemed to matter.

Gundalai was staring at her, surprised by the vehemence of her words.

'It was a strange time,' she said. 'We'd all had so much hope at first. We all thought that at last the country was ours again.'

'But you knew it was going to be difficult,' Gundalai pointed out. 'You must have known that once Russia withdrew its support.'

She nodded. 'We knew how dependent the country was on the USSR's money. A third of our GDP. But we had a sense of history. We had a sense of what this country had once been.'

'Then we're not so far apart,' Gundalai said. 'That's what we believe. That's what Odbayar believes. That we can make the country great again. Not like it was. But a genuine, successful independent nation, in charge of its own destiny.'

'I hope you're right,' she said. 'I'm sure, in the long run, you are right. But it's taken so long. We've had years of turmoil. We've had corrupt governments, incompetent governments. But, yes, things are improving. And, yes, things could have been much worse.' She leaned back in the sofa, feeling weary. She had been awake since the small hours dealing with Gundalai. 'But it's stability I want. Not more years of change.'

Gundalai nodded, as though reflecting on her words. 'Odbayar says it's the politics we need to change. And the politicians.'

'Including his own father?'

Gundalai smiled faintly. 'Especially his own father. I think even Odbayar would acknowledge the Freudian undertones of what he wants.'

'And what does he want?' she said. She had assumed that Odbayar's goals would be ill-defined, that he was a student activist interested in change primarily for its own sake.

'He wants politicians who are motivated by the interests of the country, not just by lining their own pockets. Who really want this country to be in control of its own destiny, not subservient to Russian, China or the West.' It sounded like a prepared speech, and Sarangeral suspected that the words were Odbayar's.

'Not all politicians are self-seeking,' she pointed out.

'Maybe not. But even if they're not, they don't have a vision. They just bumble along from day to day.'

'And Odbayar has a vision?'

'You only have to hear him speak. He could make us great again.'

'When he becomes president?'

'You're laughing at me,' Gundalai said, without bitterness. 'We're used to that. We're still young. Time's on our side.'

'I can't argue with that,' she said. 'And I hope you're right. I'm just too old and cynical now. I've seen too many young firebrands turn into everything they once despised. Perhaps that's what's happening to Odbayar,' she said. 'Perhaps that's why you thought he was just going through the motions.'

'No,' he said, firmly. 'That's not what I meant at all. I think he believed it more than ever. But he'd realised we weren't going to get there by making speeches.'

'So how was he going to get there?'

'I don't know. I just had the feeling that something was going on. Something he wasn't sharing with me.' The sense of betrayal was unmistakable. Sarangarel wondered whether Gundalai would have found the treachery less profound if the cause had been sexual or emotional, rather than political. 'Did you have some reason to think this? Something he said or did?'

'No. But I knew him. There was something he wasn't saying. And he started being secretive – taking mysterious phone calls, disappearing for the day. Not telling me what he was doing.'

'Perhaps you were right the first time. Maybe there *was* someone else.'

'Maybe. But I don't think so. There was no sense that he was – I don't know – embarrassed or feeling awkward, the way you would—'

'If you were having an affair? He might just be a better liar than you.' The words came out more bluntly than she intended, and she realised she felt protective towards the young man.

Gundalai smiled. 'Maybe. He's a politician, after all. And I know that the partners are always the last to find out. But I still don't think so.'

'He might have thought you'd cause trouble,' she persisted. 'He had his potential political career to think of. You could have embarrassed him.'

'I wouldn't have. He knew that.'

'Okay. But you think there was something going on, all the same. Something to do with his political activities?'

'I suppose so.'

'So why wouldn't he share that with you? Surely you were partners in that as much as in anything else?'

'In a way. But never equal partners.'

'He wouldn't have trusted you with whatever he was doing?'

'Maybe not. Not because I'd betray him. Just because – well, he thought I was naïve.'

'That suggests that whatever he was planning was risky or needed to be kept under wraps.'

'Anything's possible with Odbayar. I don't think he'd do anything that was illegal.' He stopped. 'No, that's not true. He'd happily do something that was illegal, if he thought it was right. But he wouldn't do anything that he thought was unethical.'

'That could still mean that he had something to hide from you. If it was something illegal, he might have wanted to protect you.'

Gundalai looked up at her, his eyes bright, as if this thought had not previously occurred to him. 'I suppose that's right. He always looked out for me.'

'So do you think,' Sarangarel said, finally, 'that any of this might be connected with what happened last night?'

It was the unspoken question that lay behind everything they had been saying, but Gundalai seemed surprised. 'His disappearance, you mean? I suppose so, but I don't know how.'

'Perhaps he was meddling in something more dangerous than he realised?'

'I can't imagine what.'

'I can imagine things,' she said. 'There are dangerous people out there.' She thought back to her own experience, a year or so previously, of coming up against one of the most dangerous. 'If Odbayar was trying to expose corruption, anything's possible.'

He stared at her, his eyes beseeching, and for a moment she thought he might burst into tears again. 'There's nothing more you can think of?' she asked. 'Nothing that might give any clues? If you can think of anything, we can pass it on to Nergui and Doripalam. It would give them somewhere to start.'

He shook his head. 'Nothing. There was nothing he said. Nothing he gave away. I don't even know if it was just my imagination.'

'You said he took phone calls? On his mobile?'

Gundalai nodded. 'I don't know who they were from. Or even if they were all that mysterious. I just had the sense that he was cutting them short if I was there. It didn't feel natural. It felt as if he had something to hide.'

'We can get the police to check his mobile account, I imagine. Check the numbers he was talking to. It might give us something.'

'It might,' he agreed. 'But if they were trying to hide something, they wouldn't make the calls easy to trace, would they?'

It was a fair point, she acknowledged. She had no idea how easy or otherwise it was to trace mobile calls, and she imagined that any professionals would know how to cover their tracks. But Odbayar wasn't a professional. 'It's worth a try, anyway,' she said. 'Doripalam's probably already got it in hand, but if not—' She stopped, realising that Gundalai was no longer listening, but staring distractedly across the room. 'What is it?'

'You've just reminded me,' he said. 'My phone. It's in my jacket pocket. There might be a message. I kept trying Odbayar last night, but his phone was turned off. If he got my messages—'

'Wouldn't we have heard it ring?'

'I don't know. The battery might be dead by now.' He shook his head, frowning as he tried to think. 'In any case, I had it set on silent so it wouldn't ring during Odbayar's speech. He might have called. There might be a message.'

She looked at him with compassion, recognising the hope that he was clinging on to. 'It's possible,' she said. 'Of course it's possible.'

His jacket, a thin cotton garment, had been thrown across a chair, forgotten since his arrival. He fumbled in the pocket and pulled out the slim mobile phone. 'The battery's not quite dead,' he said. 'But no one's called.'

He dropped the phone on to the table and slumped back down into the sofa, his face pale and blank.

'It was a good thought. I'm sure he'll get in touch as soon as he can,' she said, conscious of how unconvincing her words sounded. 'We've just got to wait.'

She was interrupted by a noise from the table. It took her a moment to recognise the source of the ugly, unexpected sound, although Gundalai was already halfway across the room.

'It's a text,' Gundalai said, as the muted mobile vibrated twice more against the wooden surface. He grabbed the phone and flipped it open. 'It's him,' he said, his voice rising an octave in his excitement. 'It's a message from Odbayar.'

It hardly felt like freedom.

Sometimes, usually around midday, he would go for a walk, tramping briskly through the frozen streets, his breath clouding the air. He had a regular circuit, down to the square, south to the park, around in a loop, and back to the apartment. The circuit felt symbolic to him – repetitive activity, going nowhere, to no purpose, but somehow unable to stop.

He returned one afternoon to find two men – the same two officers – standing outside the entrance to the apartment block.

'You've come,' he said.

The fat one pushed himself slowly away from the doorpost, grinding his cigarette out under his foot. 'You don't sound surprised.'

Wu Sam shrugged. 'You were always coming back.'

'And why would that be?'

'Because it's how you work. That's fine. I'll say anything you want me to.' He suddenly felt relaxed, as if finally it was all over.

'About what?'

'About anything. About this murder. This student. Whatever it is you want me to confess to.'

The fat one glanced over his shoulder. The entrance doors were open. Wu Sam could see other people inside – at least a couple of officers in uniforms, one with a flashlight, another by the doorway that led to the cellar steps. 'I think it's probably a little late for that, don't you?'

Wu Sam stared past him, bemused.

'I think you'd better come with us.'

# CHAPTER NINETEEN

## SUMMER

Odbayar had no idea how long he had slept. He could scarcely believe he had been able to surrender consciousness so easily. When he had envisaged this, he had seen the two of them as equal partners, sharing the burden of the driving as they made the long trek eastwards. He had imagined their easy conversation, their laughter as they talked through the plan, checking every detail, working out exactly how it would all be handled.

Instead he had slept. He had been exhausted. Not just by the events of the past twenty-four hours, but by the months of arduous toil. Maintaining the façade while developing the plans for all this.

And keeping Gundalai out of it.

That had been the right thing to do, he was sure. It didn't feel like a betrayal. Gundalai would understand when the time came.

But it hadn't been easy, practically or emotionally. He had had to drive Gundalai away from him, and he knew that Gundalai had seen that things were changing. He knew that Gundalai, without ever knowing how or why, had felt betrayed. He knew the pain he had caused Gundalai, and he knew that however much Gundalai eventually would understand and accept his motivation, that pain would never be entirely removed.

But it was nearly over. Just a few more hours.

He stretched and pulled himself up in his seat, his body aching from the hours of bumping over this harsh terrain. The truck was still thumping along at a steady rate, Sam swerving slightly from time to time as he avoided the worst of the crevices and potholes. He looked as fresh as ever, his hands light on the steering wheel, his eyes fixed firmly on the rough track ahead.

'Where are we?' Odbayar asked.

Sam glanced across. 'You're awake, then?' A smile played across his lips, as though he was recalling some private joke. 'I hope you're feeling better for the sleep.'

'I didn't mean to sleep so long. I can take over the driving now if you like.'

Even as he made the offer he realised that it was of little value. He could see through the windscreen that the landscape had changed. When he had fallen asleep, they had been driving through endless steppe, a brown sweep of barren grassland, parched by the summer sun. Now the terrain was growing hilly, the grass thicker and more lush. Ahead, he saw the beginnings of woodland and the mauve line of the northern mountains.

'We're nearly there,' Sam said, confirming Odbayar's thoughts. 'I might as well carry on.'

'How far?'

'Maybe forty minutes, maybe a bit less. It's difficult to get any speed up on this surface.'

Odbayar glanced at his watch. Nearly noon. The sun was high. It was hot, even in the truck. The air-conditioning was turned off, but Sam had opened the windows and the steady rush of air made the temperature bearable. Outside, the heat would be intense.

'When do we call?'

'We can start things moving soon,' Sam said. 'Slowly, slowly. We want to play them in, get their attention. Make sure they're taking it seriously.'

'So we start with Gundalai?'

'We start with Gundalai,' Sam agreed.

Odbayar nodded. This had all been agreed between them, weeks before. But it was no easier now that the moment had come.

He reached into his jacket and drew out his mobile. As he

switched on the phone, he saw that there were messages waiting. He carefully thumbed in the short text message that he and Sam had agreed between them. 'I'm safe but in trouble. Need help. More soon.' Nothing else. Sam had been adamant that they should keep the message short and enigmatic.

'That's it,' Odbayar said. 'It's gone.'

'That should start things moving. Get their attention.'

'They might just think it's a stunt.'

'They probably will.' Sam smiled. 'But they won't be able to take the risk that they might be wrong. Remember who you are. The police won't want to mess this up.'

The irony hadn't escaped him. He'd spent a large part of his life denying his background, pretending he was something different. It had been a burden, an embarrassment, a continual impediment to his ideals and desires. And now it had become the key to everything.

'I hope you're right.'

Sam's eyes were fixed on the track ahead of them. They were climbing uphill, a gentle but steady gradient leading them towards the edges of the forests. Odbayar began to fancy that there was a fresher taste to the air, the first scent of the mountain breezes and rolling streams.

'I'm right,' Sam said. There was a faint smile on his face, and he looked at Odbayar with a look that he clearly intended to be reassuring. But there was something in his expression that Odbayar was unable to read. 'After all these years,' Sam went on, 'I know I am.'

'I think I'm supposed to make some comment about having good news and bad news,' Batzorig said. He had been standing outside Doripalam's office for some minutes, uncertain whether to interrupt the two senior officers.

Now he was conscious that his opening line had been ill-judged, an attempt at levity which had seemed only to antagonise Doripalam.

'I'm glad you're finding something to amuse yourself with,' he said. 'Nergui and I are having some difficulty in that direction.'

'I'm sorry, sir. I didn't—'

Nergui glanced up at the young man, then looked across at Doripalam. 'Sit down, Batzorig. It's been a long night for all of us. What have you got?'

'I've made some progress, sir. But there's something else you ought to see first.'

Doripalam looked up at him wearily, with an expression that suggested that nothing would surprise him. 'Go on.'

'The newspapers.'

'What newspapers?' Doripalam had seen the early editions of the major newspapers first thing that morning. A couple had carried bland and uninformative references to the previous night's explosion, in both cases with the suggestion – which the police press office had quietly encouraged – that the likely cause was a gas explosion.

Batzorig had copies rolled up in his hand. He opened them and spread them carefully across the desk, as Doripalam moved the case files to one side. There were two newspapers, both privately owned tabloids. Not the worst excesses of the scandal sheets, but still journals more interested in sensation than the accurate reporting of news.

The two lead stories were different. One focused on the events in Sukh Bataar Square two days earlier and was headlined: 'Terrorism Arrives Here?' The other carried a large front-page picture of Odbayar and was headed: 'Minister's Son Missing?'

'At least both have the grace to stick a question mark on the end,' Nergui commented.

'But where did they get the stories?' Doripalam said. 'If it was just the one, it might simply be some enterprising hack adding two and two together and happening to come up with four, but this . . .'

'Suggests something more co-ordinated,' Nergui agreed. He looked as relaxed as ever, his chair tipped back, his eyes apparently fixed on some point near the ceiling. 'It can't be a leak. Not from here. Not from anywhere.'

He dropped his chair to the floor with a crash, his blue eyes fixed on Doripalam. 'I bow to no one in my respect for the efficiency of the media,' he said. 'But their powers stop somewhere short of telepathy, I think.' He picked up the relevant newspaper and glanced down the front page. 'It's very detailed,' he said, 'and fairly accurate. But it's not come from any of our people.'

'You can be quite sure of that, then?' Doripalam said, with a touch of scepticism in his tone. In his experience, the ministry always managed to remain beyond reproach in such matters.

'It's not come from anyone who knows anything, anyway,' he said. 'The real story is that the bomb was a fake.'

'So they've just cobbled it together from eyewitness accounts. Perhaps your appeal to national security wasn't quite convincing or threatening enough this time.' Doripalam was aware that tiredness and tension were giving his tone an unintended edge.

'Possibly, but their descriptions feel too detailed. The detail of the shooting, the number of bullets fired, an unidentified but accurate description of Tunjin. It's an eyewitness, yes, but someone who knew what they were looking at.'

'So they found a good eyewitness. What does that prove?'

'It's more than we usually manage to find,' Nergui said. 'We generally end up with twenty different versions, all mutually contradictory. But then look at their description of last night's explosion. Just as detailed. And just as accurate.'

'They have to get lucky now and again,' Doripalam said. 'Or they do have somebody on the inside here, after all. Someone who's leaking selectively – maybe holding back information to get the best price for it.'

'I think it's more likely that these stories are coming from the perpetrators.'

'The perpetrators?' Doripalam shook his head, staring past Nergui's apparently languid form to the bright blue square of sky visible through his office window. It was another scorching day. He felt as if he had been sitting in this gloomy office for days, though it was only a couple of hours since they had arrived back here. 'We don't even know that there is a perpetrator. Not one who's still alive, anyway. The supposed bomber in the square might have just been some lone lunatic. And we don't know that last night's explosion wasn't just some sort of accident.'

Nergui nodded, though it wasn't clear that he was listening. 'And then there's the minister's son,' he went on, gesturing towards the other newspaper headline. 'That's hardly a story for us, yet,' he said. 'We don't even know that Odbayar's actually missing. And yet there's the story.'

'Perhaps it's Gundalai. Maybe he's already talked to the press.'

'You know he can't have done. There was no time before he turned up at Sarangarel's door. And if he'd decided to contact the press after we went, Sarangarel would have let us know.'

'So they found another witness. After all, Gundalai saw it.'

'Which itself was a useful coincidence,' Nergui said. 'If Gundalai hadn't seen it all, we'd have no reason to be concerned about Odbayar's absence.'

'We'd have been aware of his presence at the hotel,' Batzorig interrupted. 'We've had someone working with the hotel management overnight, piecing together a list of who was in the hotel at the time of the explosion. Not easy. Their record keeping isn't the best in the world, even for the hotel residents. And there was no proper evacuation of the hotel after the blast, so there was no roll call of who emerged. We don't know about most of the attendees at the rally, for example. But Odbayar's on the list because he was the main speaker. So, even without Gundalai's account, we'd have known that he was missing.'

'Very good,' Nergui said. 'Assuming that Odbayar is indeed missing, we would eventually have known. But how long would it have taken us?'

'I don't know. We got the first list of names about an hour ago, I suppose.'

Nergui nodded. 'So we wouldn't even have known till then that Odbayar was at the hotel?'

'We've been collating names from various sources. The witnesses we've interviewed.'

'I'm not questioning the work that's being done. I'm saying only that, without Gundalai's intervention, it could have taken us a long time even to learn that Odbayar had been at the hotel. Even then, we wouldn't necessarily have assumed he was missing. We'd have had to contact his home, identify anywhere else he might have gone after the explosion—'

'Contact his father?' Doripalam said.

Nergui smiled. 'Quite possibly. But even if we couldn't track him down, our first concern would have been to confirm that he wasn't a victim of the explosion. It could have been a long time before we started to worry about him being missing in a more general sense.'

There was a moment's silence as Doripalam and Batzorig took in the implications of Nergui's words.

'You think Gundalai's made up his story?' Doripalam said finally. 'That this is something that he and Odbayar have concocted between them? Is that what you're saying?'

Nergui shook his head. 'Gundalai sounded sincere this morning. But perhaps he saw what he was meant to see. The one person who would recognise the significance of what he was seeing.' Nergui gestured towards the newspaper headline. 'In any case, it looks as if someone's keen to let us know that Odbayar really is missing.'

'Not just us,' Doripalam pointed out. 'Now that's hit the streets, everybody will know.' He paused. 'Including Odbayar's father.'

'Which might also be the intention,' Nergui agreed.

'So why haven't you received a call from on high?' Doripalam said. 'The minister must be aware of this by now.'

'No doubt,' Nergui said. 'Unfortunately, I must have forgotten to recharge my mobile phone last night. I imagine he's trying to track me down as we speak. I'll call in shortly.'

Doripalam stared at him. 'I never know what games you're playing, Nergui. But this seems riskier than most.'

'They're all risky,' Nergui said. 'The skill lies in playing the odds.'

'It's your career. What about the other story?' He picked up the second newspaper and pointed to the headline. 'You think this is a plant as well?'

'I think so. We've done a good job in keeping a lid on this story. I think someone wanted to prise the lid off.'

'It's an enormous story,' Doripalam said. 'Potentially an international story. Our first serious terrorist attack. Our first suicide bomber.'

'Except it wasn't,' Nergui pointed out. 'Well, perhaps a suicide, as it turned out. But not a bomber.'

'But will anyone believe that? Now it's out in the public domain, I mean. It's going to be difficult for us to deny the story. We might have got away with it before this appeared.' He waved the newspaper in front of him. 'Even those who saw the shooting wouldn't have known quite what they'd seen. When it failed to appear in the media, they'd just have assumed some government-led conspiracy. But now the press have got hold of this—'

'It's going to be difficult to come up with an alternative story. Quite so. And if we say the bomb was just a fake – well, it sounds too bizarre to be true.' Nergui nodded. 'So potentially we have a panic. Perhaps an international panic. Particularly if you then factor in the murders and last night's explosion. Presumably, it's only a matter of time before those stories are leaked as well.'

'Assuming that all this is linked.'

'Assuming that all this is linked,' Nergui agreed. 'If not, it's a hell of a coincidence. But I don't know how it's linked. And I don't know how it's linked to Wu Sam, that's if our visitor really is him.'

Batzorig coughed quietly. 'Sir.'

Nergui looked up, his expression suggesting that he had momentarily forgotten the young man's presence. 'Batzorig,' he said, 'you had some good news, too, as I recall. I hope it compensates for all this.' He pushed the newspapers away across the desk.

'I'm not even sure it is good news, but—'

'It must be better than this. Go on.'

'Well, sir, it's about Wu Sam. Or at least about Professor Sam Yung, if he turns out to be the same person. It seems that Professor

Yung is something of an expert on Mongolian history. He's here on sabbatical – timed to coincide with the Genghis Khan anniversary.'

'And where is he now?' Doripalam asked.

'He's away. They'd organised the usual round of official sightseeing for him. But he was keen to do more than that, apparently. Wanted to go off on his own.'

'On his own?' Nergui's tone suggested that this was a highly unorthodox proposal.

'Well, with a guide. A former student who spoke decent English, I understand.'

Nergui nodded. 'A young man, then?' he said, his toneless voice betraying no hint of his thoughts. 'And where did they go?'

'North,' Batzorig said. 'To Genghis Khan's birthplace.'

# CHAPTER TWENTY

The vodka bottle was empty, but Tunjin showed no obvious ill-effects. If anything, his mind felt clearer than earlier in the day when he had still been recovering from the after-effects of whatever narcotics had been used on him. He felt calm, as if the drink had taken the edge off his anxiety. That was why alcohol was such a pernicious drug. Half a bottle of vodka, and you could actually persuade yourself that the stuff was good for you.

Not good for Solongo, though. He wasn't sure how much she'd drunk before his arrival, but it was more than anyone, or rather anyone who wasn't like Tunjin himself, should have been drinking at this time of the day. And she looked tired. Not just physically tired, but worn down, as though some long-standing struggle was finally becoming too much for her.

'What about the exhibition?' he said, finally. His mind was still wrestling with his own predicament, trying to work out what he should do next, but the possibilities eluded him. It was easier to focus on someone else's troubles. 'Shouldn't you be at the museum?'

Solongo had retreated from the kitchen back into the larger living room. Through the open doorway, Tunjin could see her sitting in a corner of a large sofa, her legs neatly tucked under her. She had a box file open on her knees and was carefully sorting through a pile of crumpled papers. She looked up.

'Of course I should,' she said. 'I decided they could probably manage without me for an hour or two.'

'Very wise,' Tunjin said. 'You had a shock yesterday. Maybe more than you realised.' Perhaps that's why she'd been drinking this morning, he thought. But somehow he doubted that it had been solely attributable to the previous day's experience. Either way, Doripalam really ought to have been here. Ought to *be* here, looking after her.

'But I need to go back,' she said. 'We've only got three days till the opening.'

'But everything must be ready,' Tunjin pointed out. 'More or less, I mean.'

'You mean if we're not ready now, we never will be,' she said. 'Well, that's true enough. And we're at the stage where we could open without causing too much embarrassment to anyone,' she shook her head. 'Embarrassment, again. Do you ever think we place too much emphasis on all that? Our good name, our national pride. All that stuff?'

Tunjin sat himself on the opposite end of the sofa. 'I don't think I'm the one to ask,' he said. 'It's never been that important to me, all that national identify stuff. I've never done too much to enhance the Mongolian image.' He stretched out his large limbs, feeling the frame of the sofa creaking under his weight. 'But it's hardly surprising, is it? We have to cling to something.'

'But all this birth of the Mongol empire stuff, what does it mean now?'

'You're supposed to be the expert. I think it's just something we have to – I don't know – to reclaim before we can move forward.' He stopped, conscious that his words sounded uncharacteristically earnest.

Her expression suggested that she was taking his sentiments seriously. 'I suppose it could be something like that. I hope it is, and we're not just getting mired in the past, pretending we can somehow recapture ancient glories.'

'It depends who you are,' Tunjin said. 'There are plenty who'd like to think that way. Looking for a new Genghis Khan ready to take control.'

'If he's out there, he's keeping very quiet,' Solongo commented.

'Probably just biding his time,' Tunjin said. 'Waiting for his moment.' He stopped suddenly, his fogged mind trying to reach for some thought. 'And perhaps this is it,' he went on, not sure what he was saying. 'Perhaps this is the moment.'

'What do you mean?'

'I don't know,' he said. 'But I was thinking if some modern-day Genghis Khan was out there – or someone who thought they were – well, now would be their moment, wouldn't it?'

'The anniversary, you mean?'

'The anniversary and everything that goes with it. Your exhibition. The new statues. The Genghis Khan memorial. All the pageantry. Everything that's been lined up for this summer. If that wasn't their moment, when would be?' He paused, rubbing his hands through his sparse hair. 'Perhaps that's what this is all about. The anniversary.'

'I don't understand,' she said. 'This is what what's all about?'

'What's happened,' he said. 'The supposed bombing in the square. The body in the museum.' He paused. 'Me being framed. Wu Sam.'

'You think Wu Sam sees himself as the new Genghis Khan? How does that work? He's not even Mongolian.'

'He is,' Tunjin said, frowning. 'I remember that. Ethnically, he was Mongolian. He was from Inner Mongolia. He'd moved to Beijing as a child – his father was some kind of Party apparatchik. But they were Mongolian. That was why he developed his interest in Mongolian history.'

'Wouldn't that have been rather suspect? In Communist China, I mean?'

'Who knows? The ways of the Party have always been a mystery to me. But that kind of thing can cut either way. It depends on your motivation. It depends on how you're perceived.'

'That's true enough,' she said, thinking back to her own father's time as a senior Party official. As a teenager, observing his activities with the cynical detachment of youth, she could never comprehend the subtle shifts in official mood that led to individuals being in or out of favour. Her father had been as deft as anyone at riding the waves of change. But that was probably how everyone felt until the unexpected undercurrents finally dragged them under. Her father's reputation had definitely been on the wane near the end. Even she, as a teenager, had been able to sense his declining confidence, his increasing paranoia. Ironically enough, it was the sudden arrival of democracy that had given him the opportunity to reinvent himself one more time.

'But I still don't understand,' she said. 'Where does Wu Sam fit into this anyway?'

'I'm not sure,' Tunjin admitted. 'Maybe he doesn't at all. Maybe I'm chasing ghosts.'

'But you think there's something?' She had put aside the box file and was watching him intently, as though she could read something in his expression.

He looked back up at her, surprised by her seriousness. 'Yes,' he said, finally. 'I think I do. I don't know whether it's Genghis Khan or—' He stopped, wondering what he was saying. There was silence in the room, a sudden intensity, as though a storm was brewing. But the sky through the broad windows was as blue as ever, and the dust motes drifted slowly in the unwavering beams of sunlight.

Tunjin opened his mouth to say something more. And then, almost as unexpected as if there had been a clap of thunder outside, the room was filled with a sudden piercing noise.

For a second Solongo looked almost as startled, as if she had forgotten where they were. Then she shook her head and pulled herself slowly to her feet. 'There's someone at the door downstairs.'

Another mile or two brought them into the first real shade. Sam steered the truck carefully into a cluster of fir trees and drew slowly to a halt. 'We can stop here for a few minutes,' he said. 'I need a comfort break. There are some bottles of water in the back if you want one.'

Odbayar pushed open the passenger door. Outside, the heat was as intense as he'd expected, despite the shadow of the trees. For a moment, it left him breathless, as though the oxygen had been sucked from the air.

The day was as still as he'd ever known, with no breath of breeze to alleviate the temperature. Other than the sound of Sam's footsteps as he walked slowly away, the silence was almost complete. Somewhere in the trees ahead, Odbayar could faintly detect the sound of birdsong. And somewhere beyond that, there was the sound of water on rocks, the far-off murmuring of a stream.

The thought of water made Odbayar conscious of his thirst, and he made his way round to the back of the truck. The body of the vehicle was almost too hot to touch and a shimmering heat haze rose from its roof. Odbayar pulled open the rear doors and stared gratefully at the rows of bottled water that Sam had stacked down one side of the available space. There were cans of fuel, too, and some cool-boxes which Odbayar presumed contained food. It had all been carefully planned.

He pulled out one of the bottles and, unscrewing the lid, took a deep swallow of the liquid inside. It was luke-warm from the sun, but after the hours of driving tasted better than anything he had ever drunk. He swallowed some more, and then straightened up.

'Don't drink it too quickly.'

Odbayar turned, taken off-guard by the proximity of the voice. He had not heard Sam approaching. 'We seem to have plenty,' he said. 'You've planned it well.'

Sam nodded. 'But we do not know how long this may take. We need to be cautious.'

As so often in Sam's company, Odbayar felt mildly chastised for his naivety. 'I suppose so,' he said.

Sam removed the bottle from Odbayar's hands and took a swallow himself, then pointedly screwed the top back on. 'We need to ensure that we're the ones in control. If this drags on, we must be prepared for that. The longer it takes, the more they'll feel the pressure.' He replaced the bottle in the rear of the truck, then leaned further in and eased up the lid on one of the boxes. 'You must be hungry,' he said. 'I brought some food. Nothing fancy – just enough to sustain us. Bread, biscuits, some dried fruit. Stuff that will keep.'

'Some bread would be good,' Odbayar said. He was less hungry than he would have expected, but that was probably just the effect of the adrenaline.

Sam reached into the box and pulled out a loaf of bread. He tore off a piece and handed it to Odbayar. The bread was already dry, but tasted fine. 'There's some dried meat, if you'd like it,' Sam offered.

Odbayar shook his head. 'This is enough.' He pointed towards the rear of the truck. 'What's in all the boxes? More food?'

Sam looked at him, his gaze unwavering for several seconds. Then he said: 'There's plenty of food. Enough to keep us going, so long as we're careful.'

Odbayar noticed that his question had not been answered. 'How much further now?'

'Not far,' Sam said. He turned and pointed ahead. In the distance, the trees thickened across the landscape, dark knots of fir trees, as the land rose towards the hills. 'Maybe half an hour. Maybe a little more.'

Odbayar nodded, wondering again why all this was necessary. Why did they have to come here? He understood the symbolism, and understood the practical reasons for needing to be away from the city, but did they really have to come all the way up here?

He knew that Sam had secrets and they were here because of them and because of Sam's background. That was why they would be able to do this. Odbayar had no idea how Sam had co-ordinated all the required activities, and he had no wish to find out. That was why you worked with professionals, because they knew the things you didn't.

But there was more. He was no fool, and he was much less naïve than Sam might think. Sam was an agent. He was doing a job, not just for Odbayar but for the distant masters who had always run his life. Odbayar had had no direct contact with them, had no definite knowledge of what they might be looking to gain from all this. One of the challenges he was going to face, if this all worked out, was ensuring that they were happy but that the price wasn't too high. He had assumed there would be scope for some deal that would keep all parties happy.

Was he being too complacent? Perhaps he really was getting involved with something he couldn't handle. Was Sam working towards a different end-game? He didn't think he was, but he'd always known that he was running that risk. However, Odbayar could not shake the feeling of unease; there was something about the way Sam looked at him that had haunted his dreams even during their endless drive up here.

Something personal.

For the first time, standing in the baking heat of the sun, under the inadequate shade of the shabby firs, Odbayar felt a chill of fear. It was an unfamiliar sensation. It had never occurred to him that he had any real reason to be afraid. Sure, he was taking risks. But they were professional risks – to his reputation and livelihood, risks to his future. Not risks to his own life.

Suddenly, looking across at Sam, he realised that he had been naïve; he had no idea who this man was, what his real motives were for getting involved in this escapade, what he might be expecting to get out of it.

What he would do if anything should go wrong.

Sam would have thought everything through. He would have identified any potential problems, anything that might throw them off track and he would have a plan to deal with every contingency. Which meant that, even at the worst, Sam would get out of this safe and sound. He would walk away. No loose ends.

Odbayar shook his head and pulled open the truck door. He was being ridiculous. He had worked closely with Sam for weeks. Sam had been recommended by people who knew what they were talking about. He had planned this to the last detail. Nothing would go wrong.

Sam had already climbed into the driver's seat and was watching Odbayar curiously. 'Everything all right?'

Odbayar looked back at the older man, as calm and punctilious as ever in his white shirt and neat college tie. 'Just hot.'

'Not far now. It'll be cooler once we get properly into the trees. And when we get some altitude.' Sam smiled, though his eyes gave nothing away.

'Do you want me to drive? You've done it all so far.'

Sam shook his head, still smiling. 'No. Just relax. Enjoy the scenery. Enjoy the peace.' His smile broadened, as though some pleasant thought had just struck him. 'After all, everything's just about to start.'

'Eight missed calls in the last hour,' Nergui said, holding out his mobile phone. 'And that's not counting the ringbacks from the voicemail service.'

'The minister?' Doripalam asked. He was staring intently at a detailed map of the north of the country.

'All "number withheld",' Nergui said. 'So I imagine so.'

'You'd better call him back. He's clearly keen to speak to you.'

'Clearly,' Nergui agreed. He was in his characteristic posture, stretched back in his chair, his ankles resting delicately on the corner of Doripalam's desk. 'I suppose I had, actually,' he said. 'This is his son we're talking about after all.'

Doripalam shook his head, trying to read the older man's typically blank expression. 'There are depths to your compassion I've never recognised,' he said.

'A son is a son, I imagine. Even for the minister.' He pulled himself slowly to his feet. 'I'll find somewhere quiet to call him.'

Meaning, Doripalam thought, that you don't want the likes of me listening into the conversation. 'You can stay in here. I've things I need to sort out with Batzorig.'

'Thank you,' Nergui said, with apparent sincerity. 'It won't take long.' He paused. 'How much do we want to tell the minister? It's your call. Your case.'

'About Wu Sam, you mean? Or Professor Sam Yung, assuming they're really one and the same. It's hardly my call, even if it is my case. It's your career on the line. But my inclination is to say nothing, unless you really think you should. We don't even know for sure that Odbayar really is missing, let alone that this guy's got anything to do with it. As for the rest of it, who knows?'

Nergui nodded. 'I'm very good at playing dumb in such matters,' he said. 'You'd be surprised.'

'I'd be astonished.' Doripalam rose and crossed to the door. As he closed it behind him, he saw Nergui resuming his familiar posture, his legs stretched out again, the phone clamped to his ear, looking completely relaxed.

Batzorig was in his own office, also engaged in what looked to be an intense telephone conversation. Doripalam watched through the open door, conscious of how the younger man's confidence had grown since his promotion earlier in the year. He had always been bright and capable, but he had previously been too easily intimidated by authority, real or assumed. As had been demonstrated by his handling of the university vice-president, he was overcoming that particular shortcoming.

'I don't care,' he was saying calmly. 'We need it now. No, that's not good enough. Yes, you've explained the situation very clearly. But we need it now.' He paused, listening to another blast of self-justification from his interlocutor. 'Yes, from the chief.' He looked up at Doripalam. 'Well, if you'd like him to repeat his request in person, I can. Of course. No problem. When will you be ready? Okay, that's fine. No, really, thanks for your co-operation.' He was smiling broadly as he replaced the receiver.

'That was good,' Doripalam said. 'So what have I requested?'

Batzorig had the grace to look mildly embarrassed. 'I'm sorry, sir. I knew he wouldn't really want to talk to you.'

'Well, who would?' Doripalam agreed. 'But I trust that whatever I've requested was worth all your efforts.'

'I hope so, sir,' Batzorig said, with some eagerness in his voice. 'It's a helicopter.'

'A helicopter?'

'Yes, sir. The city unit has use of one. It's the military's, strictly speaking, and that's where they borrow the pilots from. But they've been experimenting with it for handling stuff out on the steppes or the desert. Much quicker than taking a truck.'

'I'm sure,' Doripalam said. 'How do you know all this stuff?'

'I just read the circulars, that's all, sir.'

'I always knew there was something different about you, Batzorig.' Doripalam stopped, his tired mind only now absorbing what Batzorig had said. 'Now just remind me precisely why it is that we need a helicopter.'

'Genghis Khan's birthplace, sir. It's up in the north, near Ondorkhaan. A long way. I assumed we'd want to go there.'

Doripalam nodded. He still couldn't understand how Batzorig managed to remain so enthusiastic after what was rapidly heading towards a forty-eight-hour turn of duty. 'I suppose we do,' he said. 'Or somebody does. If that's where Sam Yung, or Wu Sam, or whoever the hell else he's supposed to be, was last sighted.'

'That's what I thought, sir. The only other option was to wait for the next scheduled flight, but that wouldn't be till tomorrow. I'd assumed it was more urgent than that.'

'So you commandeered a helicopter for us?'

'Well, borrowed, I think. It's theoretically available to all parts of the police service if you go through the appropriate channels.'

Doripalam gestured towards the phone. 'And that was you going through the appropriate channels?'

Batzorig blushed faintly. 'I short-circuited them slightly, I suppose.' Then he smiled. 'But only at your request, sir. As you'll recall.'

Solongo stepped out into the hallway. Tunjin followed her, wondering how to handle this.

'Who do you think it is?'

She shook her head. 'Haven't a clue. I'm not expecting anyone.'

'Perhaps it's someone for me,' he said. 'Maybe they've tracked me down.'

'How could they have? No one saw you come here, did they?'

'I don't think so. I mean, nobody followed me from the hospital.'

'Nobody knows you're here. It's probably just a delivery or something.' Between them, the buzzer sounded insistently.

'Are you expecting a delivery?' He'd developed a finely honed sense of paranoia during all the events of the previous year, when that gangster Muunokhoi and his cronies really had been out to get him. Paranoia had saved his life then, and he'd seen no good reason to underestimate its value ever since.

'I don't know. It could be something from the museum or—'

Tunjin watched her closely as she moved to the door. If he was honest – and this was definitely the paranoia talking – he had no particular reason to trust Solongo. He'd turned up here on one of his usual badly conceived whims. He hardly knew her and she was not, to put it at its mildest, exactly his type. And he'd found her knocking back the vodka first thing in the morning. He couldn't blame her if her priority had been to get him out of her apartment. Perhaps she'd found some opportunity to contact Doripalam.

The buzzer sounded a third time, a rapid staccato succession of buzzes, as though the caller was becoming impatient. 'You'd better answer,' Tunjin said. If it really was Doripalam's men out there, they'd batter the door down if they thought Solongo was in danger.

She nodded and pressed the intercom. 'Yes?'

The answering voice was metallic, devoid of character. 'Police. We need to speak to you.'

Solongo glanced at Tunjin. She seemed genuinely surprised. If she had called Doripalam, she was clearly a skilled actor. She put her finger to her lips, indicating that Tunjin should be silent. 'I don't understand,' she said into the intercom. 'What police? Why do you want to talk to me?'

There was a moment's pause. 'It would be helpful if we could come up,' the voice said, finally.

'I'm sure it would,' she said, calmly. 'But I'm not in the habit of allowing uninvited callers into my apartment without identification.'

There was another pause, a brief crackle of static on the line. 'We can show you ID when we come up,' the voice said.

Solongo took her finger off the intercom button. 'I don't like the sound of this,' she said. 'I don't know what they want, but it seems official.'

'Maybe it's the murder,' Tunjin said. 'Maybe they're just after another witness statement.'

'But those would be your people, wouldn't they? I mean, Doripalam's people. Surely they'd have said so.'

'I'd have thought so. They must be here for me. Maybe they're Nergui's people. I don't know how they found me here, but . . .' He shrugged. His experience with Muunokhoi had taught him never to underestimate what people might know, or how they might have come to know it.

'What do you want me to do?'

Tunjin looked at her gratefully, feeling guilty for his earlier suspicions. 'Buy me some time, if you can. I don't want to end up in Nergui's hands just yet. Not till I've got some idea what's going on here. Go down and keep them talking for a bit. Challenge their ID or something. Ask for a phone number so you can check up or them. That kind of thing.'

'You'd be surprised how resourceful I can be,' she said.

'I don't think I would. Is there another way out of the building?'

'There's a rear staircase. It brings you out into an alleyway at the back. Follow it round and you'll get to the main road.' She stopped and reached into her pocket. 'Tunjin.' She stopped, as if weighing up an idea. 'Look, I'm going to regret this. But my car's out there. One of those little Daewoo things, parked at the side of the building.' She told him the registration. 'You should be able to get to it without them spotting you.' She looked at him closely. 'Are you in a state to drive?' she asked. 'I don't think I would be.'

'I'm ashamed to say I've driven in much worse states than this,' he said. He felt scarcely affected by the vodka he had drunk earlier, though he knew that that was little more than a delusion. On the other hand, the prospect of being picked up by Nergui's men was a great aid to sobriety.

The buzzer sounded again, held down for a long moment.

Solongo pressed the intercom again. 'I'm sorry,' she said, brusquely. 'What is it you want?'

'We need to speak to you, madam.' The last word was added apparently as an afterthought. 'If we could just come up.'

'I'll come down,' she said. 'Then I can check your ID before we do anything else. I'm sure you'd want me to be prudent.'

The voice said, 'Madam—' But Solongo had already released the button and was opening the door. Tunjin followed her on to the landing. 'The back stairs are there,' she said, pointing down the corridor. 'It's a fire exit, so once you're through you won't be able to get back. I'll go down and keep them talking as long as I can.'

Tunjin smiled. 'Thanks. I owe you one.'

'You also owe me for the vodka,' she said. 'Good luck. I'm hoping I'll be able to have another drink with you one day.'

Tunjin opened his mouth, as though he was about to say something about that. Then he shook his head. 'I hope so, too. Like I say, I owe you one.'

## WINTER 1988

It was simpler this time. There was no hesitation, no game-playing. Just question after question after question. A relentless barrage from the fat cop and his thin colleague. The first time, they had seemed tentative. Now, they were confident. Sure of their ground.

But to Wu Sam it made no more sense.

There was another body, he gathered. Another student. There had been a tip-off, and the body had been found in the cellar of his own apartment block. And they had incontrovertible evidence that Wu Sam was the murderer.

Except that he wasn't. He still had no idea what they were talking about. He had no idea what kind of proof they could have.

But why go to these lengths? They could plant whatever evidence they needed. They could take any steps they liked to render his confession unnecessary.

And then, as the two men endlessly circled his chair, barking out their questions he realised that this was just another case to them. If he was being framed it was being done elsewhere, by someone else. By the contact.

These men were, like himself, just pawns in the game, playing their part. Working to break him, to get him to confess. To make it all official.

'So take us through it one more time,' the fat one said. He was sitting down now, rocking the metal chair back on its legs, blowing casual smoke rings around his cigarette. 'How did this body come to be in your cellar?' His tone was calmer now. Earlier, he'd been aggressive.

'I don't know,' Wu Sam said, trying to keep his voice calm. 'I know nothing about it. It's not my cellar. It's just part of the block.'

'The block where you live,' the fat one pointed out. 'You're doing research into – what was it again?' He spoke as if making conversation at a party.

'You know what I'm researching,' Wu Sam said. 'I've told you everything I can.' His mind was beginning to work again, after the initial shock of being dragged back in here. He had some leverage, after all. He knew who the contact was, he knew what the contact had been doing. The challenge was to find someone who might believe him.

The fat one was regarding him thoughtfully, as though he had some inkling of what was passing through Wu Sam's mind. 'Okay,' he said, wearily, 'let's try this again, shall we?'

'I'm being set up,' Wu Sam said, suddenly. The words had slipped out of his mouth before he had thought through what he was going to say. 'Can't you see that? I'm being framed.'

The fat one stared at him, and for a moment it looked as if he might start laughing. 'You're being framed, are you?' He glanced up at his colleague. 'Well, that's original. Don't think we've heard that one before, have we?'

'Not today,' the thin one said.

'A set up,' the fat one said. 'Well, we'll bear that in mind. But let's come back to the body, shall we? Just tell us—'

He stopped suddenly as the door of the interview room swung open. Wu Sam looked over the fat one's shoulder, expecting some underling bearing a message for his interrogators, but whoever the new arrival might be, he was no underling. He stood silently in the doorway, gazing fixedly at Wu Sam. His face was dark, his skin shining in the dim light like polished wood, an unyielding mask. But his eyes were a piercing blue, and Wu Sam felt as if they could see into his soul.

The fat one twisted in his chair, clearly surprised by their visitor. 'Sir, we were just—'

The man nodded. 'That's fine, Tunjin. You two go and get a break. I'll look after this for a while.'

# CHAPTER TWENTY-ONE

## SUMMER

He was still at the window, staring out at the empty street, the silent grasslands, the low line of the far mountains.

'I've been trying to track down Nergui,' she said from behind him. 'He's not answering his mobile, but I've left messages. And I've phoned Doripalam's office. They'll get in touch and then we can get this moving.'

Gundalai remained motionless. 'They won't do anything,' he said, quietly.

'They will,' Sarangarel said. 'It's their job.'

'But that's all it is,' Gundalai said. 'It's just a job. They won't take it seriously. They'll think this is some kind of stunt.'

'They might be right, you know. Have you considered that?'

His eyes looked dead, unfocused. 'You think so as well?'

'I don't think anything. We have to take that text message seriously but it doesn't really say anything, does it? Just claims that he's in trouble and tells you to call the police. If he really is in trouble, how come he's in a position to send you a message? And if he can send you a message, why can't he give you more information? I don't know. Odbayar's an activist. This wouldn't be the first time he's tried to grab the headlines.'

He turned away and walked across the room, throwing himself down on to the sofa. Suddenly, he looked much younger than his years. 'But he'd have told me. He wouldn't have done this without me.'

'I'm sure you're right,' she said, without much conviction. 'Anyway, it doesn't really matter, does it? We have to treat that message seriously. I'm sure that's how Nergui and Doripalam will see it.' She paused. 'In any case, you know Nergui can't afford to take any chances with this.'

'Odbayar being who he is, you mean? Well, no, I wouldn't expect Nergui to take any risks with his career.'

'I can't think of many people less concerned about their career than Nergui,' she said. 'But it's because of who Odbayar is that we – and they – have to take this seriously. If he has been kidnapped, it's most likely because of his father. Why else?'

Gundalai stared at her, as though about to argue. 'I just know that I'm worried about him. I think something's happened to him. I don't know why or how. But I'm worried.'

'You might not think it,' she said, 'but if anyone can find him, Nergui can.'

He nodded, but looked unconvinced. 'If you can manage to get hold of Nergui, that is,' he said. 'We need to be doing something. It must be possible to track where that text was sent from. They must be able to pinpoint where his phone is.'

'I've no idea. I don't imagine it's easy. It probably takes time.'

'Especially when nobody's even trying to do it,' he said, bitterly. 'I just wish I had some idea of where to go, what to do. I thought he might send something else. But there's just silence.'

'I know it's difficult,' she said. 'But we have to wait.'

Gundalai jumped up and strode over to the window. 'I can't just wait—' he stopped suddenly, as though frozen. 'That's my phone.'

Sarangarel had heard nothing, but Gundalai was already fumbling in his pocket. He pulled out the mobile and stared at the screen. 'It's him,' he said. He looked up and his face seemed to have come to life again. 'It's another message. He's telling us where he is.'

★

'This was your idea, right?' Nergui said.

'Batzorig's,' Doripalam said, jerking his thumb towards the young man engaged in discussion with the official in the small wooden cabin. 'That's why I insisted he come with us.'

'Very wise.' Nergui nodded. 'There's no reason why he shouldn't suffer as well.'

'It's the vertigo I'm worried about,' Doripalam said. 'I've never been up in one of those things.'

'It's a new experience for all of us. That's the great thing about working with the younger generation.'

They were standing in a small military airfield at the northern edge of the city. There was a line of small hangars along one side, a pre-fabricated hut that provided office accommodation, and the small cabin containing the uniformed young man in charge of tracking the aircraft movements. Somewhere off to the right, there was one of the innumerable *ger* camps that ringed the urban centre like a besieging army, line on line of the distinctive round tents.

Batzorig was repeating his earlier telephone conversation, although now his hand was strengthened by the presence of Nergui and Doripalam. Finally, he straightened and turned back towards the two older men.

'All sorted,' he said. 'Ours for twenty-four hours. Fully fuelled and with pilot.'

'That's good to know,' Doripalam said. 'I'd hate to have to take it up on my own. Who's paying for all this?'

'There's some sort of inter-agency recharge arrangement,' Batzorig said.

'You don't know, then?' Doripalam said. 'I don't know that I've got a budget to cover it.'

'The ministry will no doubt pick up the tab if necessary,' Nergui said. 'Assuming that I'm still in a position of any influence by the time we get back. And if I'm not – well, the cost of this probably won't matter too much.'

Doripalam had not asked how Nergui's conversation with the minister had gone. When he'd returned to his office, Nergui had still been sitting at the desk, flicking aimlessly through the various case files. He had looked untroubled, and had dismissed Doripalam's initial polite enquiry with a smile. There was no obvious way for Doripalam to return to the subject after that.

'Do you think this is really necessary?' Doripalam said, gesturing towards the helicopter.

'I think Batzorig's right. If our suspicions are correct – or even if they're not – we need to track down Professor Sam Yung as soon as possible. We could waste a lot of time trying to do that.'

'Even with this, we may waste a lot of time,' Doripalam pointed out. 'I've already got the local force up in Ondorkhaan trying to find him. I don't know that we'll be able to do much they can't.'

'How many men do they have up there?' Nergui asked. 'A handful? And no doubt the usual local incompetents. I can't imagine they'll be putting a lot of effort into it.'

'Maybe,' Doripalam said. 'But maybe we're better off here than going off on some wild goose chase.'

'Why? You've got all the bases covered as far as you can. You've got a team tracking down all Odbayar's friends and contacts, another team investigating the hotel explosion. You've got the forensics reports due on the murders, but we haven't even identified the victims yet. I don't see what else you can do for the moment. And if anything breaks in the meantime, this thing will get us back quickly enough.'

There was no arguing with Nergui's logic. But, as always, Doripalam had a suspicion that it was the operational thrill that motivated Nergui, another chance to escape the routine of his desk job and get his hands dirty.

'What about Tunjin?' Doripalam asked. 'Have you tracked him down yet?'

'No, but I've got people looking. There aren't many places he can go.'

'I still don't know what you're up to, Nergui, though there's nothing new in that. But you know Tunjin well enough not to underestimate his resourcefulness.'

Nergui made no response, but gestured out towards the helicopter. 'I think it's time for us to be boarding.'

'You sure we're both allowed to ride together?' Doripalam said. 'Doesn't the ministry have rules about that kind of thing?'

'No doubt,' Nergui said. 'The ministry has rules about most kinds of thing.'

Batzorig, proprietorial about the whole adventure, confidently led the way across the scrubby grass of the airfield. The pilot looked up and signalled to acknowledge their approach, and then indicated where they should sit, helping them with seatbelts, handing out the headsets that would enable them to converse above the noise of the rotors.

'If this is as uncomfortable an experience as I'm fearing,' Doripalam said, 'you may be saying goodbye to a promising career, Batzorig.'

There was a moment's silence, while the pilot fiddled with the controls. Somewhere, over among the scattering of *gers*, Doripalam could hear a goat bleating, an incongruously bucolic and comforting noise. A second later, the pilot started the engine, and all other sounds were lost beneath the scream and roar of the engine, the deafening clatter of the blades.

The ascent was smoother and less terrifying than Doripalam had feared. He watched the ground fall away, suddenly seeing the *ger* camp spread out like a map. The helicopter banked, and then the whole city was below them. Rows of grey concrete tenements, open squares and parks, the newer and more striking buildings of the city centre and the business areas, the ornate gold temples. As they rose, he could see the central square, the statue of Sukh Bataar, the squat new likeness of Genghis Khan. The edges of the square were draped in canopies and awnings, in preparation for the impending anniversary celebrations and the annual Naadam Feastival. And there was the new memorial, finally almost complete after frantic last-minute construction work.

It was a small city and it still seemed unsure of its own permanence, as if settled living might be only a temporary aberration in their long national history. As the helicopter rose still higher, he could make out, on all sides of the city, the spreading rash of *gers*, the dotting of white resembling some kind of organic growth, an uncontrollable mould spreading around the ordered ranks and squares of the city centre.

In those tall office blocks, there was all the paraphernalia of the twenty-first century – computers, mobile phones, wireless networks. And living alongside them there were people with no running water, no permanent sanitation, huddled round wood stoves even in the depths of the Mongolian winter. It was a growing problem, and the nature of the problem changed with the seasons. In the winter, the challenge was the bitter cold – deaths through starvation and hypothermia. Now, in this brief baking summer, the stench of poor sanitation indicated a different threat.

'You look as if you're about to be sick,' Nergui said, his voice metallic in Doripalam's earphones.

Doripalam looked up, startled out of his reverie. 'Speak for yourself,' he said. 'I'm actually rather enjoying this.' He leaned forward towards Batzorig, who was sitting next to the pilot. 'Your career's safe for another day, then.' Batzorig looked back over his shoulder and gave an enthusiastic thumbs-up.

'It gives you a whole new perspective,' Nergui said. 'Different from being in a plane, even.'

Doripalam nodded. They were rising higher now, banking away from the city to begin their journey, heading east. The endless grassland lay beneath, browner than usual after the extended hot weather. Paler lines stretched across the empty landscape, indicating crude dirt roads apparently leading nowhere. In the distance, the land darkened towards the edges of the forests and mountains. Doripalam could see the shadow of the helicopter, the shape distorted by the angle of the afternoon sun, scurrying across the steppe, chasing after them like an eager dog.

'How long will it take us?' Nergui asked.

'Best part of a couple of hours, apparently. We should sit back and enjoy the view.'

Nergui twisted his head and took in the vast empty vista spread out before them. 'One hell of a view.'

Tunjin heard the fire door click softly shut behind him. No way back.

The rear stairway was functional rather than decorative, not intended for public use. The stairs were bare concrete with a plain iron railing, the walls a dull beige. There were no windows, and the only illumination was the dim glow of emergency lights to provide direction in the event of a fire.

Tunjin made his way down the stairs, taking two at a time but trying to make his movements as silent as possible.

It took him only a few minutes to reach the bottom. The rear lobby was as unprepossessing as the rest of the stairway – an empty hallway with a tiled floor, one grimy window, and, opposite the bottom of the stairs, a double fire door. Tunjin lifted himself to peer out of the window.

There was nothing much to see. The fire doors opened on to a small courtyard, with a narrow alleyway beyond. As far as Tunjin could tell, the courtyard was deserted. He pushed open the door and stepped out. Even in this shady spot, after the relative cool of the building the heat of the day struck him immediately. The fire door shut firmly behind him. Definitely no way back now.

He stepped forward and peered into the alleyway. It was narrow and dark, running between two adjoining apartment blocks, with a glare of sunlight at the far end. He scurried quickly down the alley, then stopped and peered around the corner. From there, he could see the main entrance. Two men, dressed in dark grey suits, were standing next to a black, official-looking car, engaged in discussion with Solongo.

Tunjin had already spotted Solongo's Daewoo, parked a few hundred yards from the entrance. With any luck, he should be able to reach it without being seen. They'd hear the engine starting – and there were still few enough cars passing here for that to be conspicuous – but he'd buy himself a few minutes.

He turned back towards Solongo and the men, trying to judge when the moment might be right to make his move. Although he was too far away to make out the words, the conversation seemed to be becoming heated. Tunjin assumed that Solongo was doing her utmost to be difficult.

Thanking her silently, Tunjin began to jog towards the car, the keys clutched firmly in his hand. Further up the street, Solongo shouted something, and for the first time he caught a snatch of her voice.

He reached the car and stopped, his hand on the hot metal of the door handle. Keeping his head low, he looked back. She had sounded genuinely distressed. Distressed and angry. Something more than even the most skilful of acts.

Moving slowly around the car, keeping his large body hidden, Tunjin peered cautiously over the top. Solongo was definitely shouting now, waving her arms as if trying to attract attention. Other than himself, there was no one to respond.

Suddenly, one of the two men grabbed her arm and pulled her forcibly towards their car. She struggled for a moment and then stopped. For a second, Tunjin thought she'd been struck. Then he realised why she had stopped moving. The second man had come forward, his arm extended, something in his hand.

Tunjin stood for a moment, feeling as if the breath had been knocked from his body, wondering what to do. I owe you one, he thought. He hadn't expected that he'd need to pay it back quite so quickly.

He stood frozen, working out the possible options. He could try to intervene, hoping that his presence would be enough to scare them off. But if these men were prepared to snatch the wife of the head of the Serious Crimes Team in broad daylight, they were unlikely to be disturbed by an overweight superannuated policeman.

He was still hesitating when the man with the pistol pulled open the rear door of the car. The other thrust Solongo inside. She fought back briefly, her heel grinding brutally against the man's shin. And then the man with the pistol thrust it hard against her head and drove her back into the car, forcing himself in beside her. The other man pulled open the driver's door, threw himself in and started the engine.

Tunjin fumbled with the keys to Solongo's car and finally succeeded in opening the door. Behind him, he could hear the other car executing a clumsy U-turn, its front wing scraping noisily against a street sign. Perhaps Solongo was still causing them trouble. In any case, the minor accident – and the need to reverse and extricate the car – gained Tunjin a precious few seconds. He found the ignition, started the engine and, keeping his eyes on the black car, prepared to pull into the road.

He waited a moment, hoping that, even in these quiet back streets, he would be able to avoid drawing attention to his presence. Ahead of him, the black car straightened and then, as the driver floored the accelerator, disappeared up the street.

Immediately, Tunjin pulled out, in time to see the rear end of the black car disappear round the next corner. Perfect, he thought. Close but not too close.

In his better days, Tunjin had trained as a high-speed driver. The booze had put paid to all that, just as it had to his career as a marksman. His own choice, in both cases. Nobody else seemed to have noticed that his reactions were shot, or that his aim wasn't as precise as it had been. But Tunjin had been aware that it was only a matter of time before he killed somebody. Before he killed the wrong somebody.

The somebody in the square, perhaps.

He put the thought from his mind and pressed the accelerator. He reached the corner just in time to see the black car turning right at the next junction. They were heading out of the residential district towards the centre of town. Once out of these quiet back streets, it would be easier for Tunjin to remain unnoticed, but harder to keep behind them.

There was nothing else he could do. He had to keep close. There was no time to stop and call for assistance. No time for anything.

Not for the first time that day, Tunjin wished he'd thought a little harder before deciding to leave the hospital.

At least, then, he might have remembered to bring his phone.

# CHAPTER TWENTY-TWO

Everything was silent, except for the steady hum of the engine and the constant rattle of their wheels across the harsh terrain.

Sam smiled softly at the figure in the passenger seat. Asleep again. Though hardly surprising this time, given the sedative that had been added to the bread he'd eaten.

The timing was just right. Not too large a dose, nothing too risky. But enough to keep Odbayar asleep till they reached their destination. And beyond. It was important to keep Sam's options open.

He was relieved not to have to endure any more of Odbayar's fatuous conversation. Still, at least Odbayar understood where things had to go, even if he was supremely deluded about his own potential role in taking them there.

The sun was high, but they were entering the edges of the forests and the air felt cooler. As soon as he was sure that Odbayar was unconscious, Sam had stopped the truck and dug out the mobile phone from Odbayar's jacket. He had flicked through the list of numbers until he had found Gundalai's and then carefully composed a second text message.

The message sent, he had slipped the phone carefully back into Odbayar's jacket, watching the young man sleeping, his head slumped against the side window. Everything was slowly moving into place. He had checked his own phone, and there was a series of text message, sent over the previous hour or so, confirming that everything was running to plan.

He started the engine again, driving forward into the emerald gloom of the forest, his eyes fixed on the rough road ahead, the rising terrain, the looming trees. The endless empty landscape.

'We can use my car,' Sarangarel said. 'We can be there in fifteen minutes.' She reached out and held Gundalai's shoulder. 'Don't worry. He must be all right.' She wished that she felt as confident as she sounded. 'We need to find out what's happening. But we need to tell the police. I mean, if he really is in some kind of trouble—'

'But he said not to. He said we shouldn't tell anyone yet.'

'It doesn't make any sense,' she pointed out. 'He says he's in trouble, but doesn't say what kind of trouble. He says he needs help, but doesn't say what kind of help he needs. He asks you to meet him, but doesn't want you to tell anyone else. What's it all about?'

'I don't know,' he admitted. 'It must be something only I can help him with. Or something that he can't let anyone else find out about.'

'And what sort of thing would that be, do you think?' She knew she was being harsh, that this kind of logic had no currency in the young man's heart. But she felt they were being manipulated, increasingly sure that this was just some stunt that Odbayar had cooked up. And she was angry that Gundalai – trusting, honest, helpless – was being suckered into it.

Gundalai was already on his feet, grabbing his jacket, his phone clutched in his hand. 'I don't know,' he said. 'I don't know what any of this is about. But if Odbayar really is in trouble, we can't just leave him.'

'If he really is in trouble, we need the police,' she said. 'If he isn't – I mean, if this is just some kind of—'

'You don't believe him either,' he said. 'Just like Doripalam, just like Nergui. You all think he's just playing games.'

She grasped his shoulders and swung him round to face her. 'But that's just it,' she said. 'He plays games. He's a politician; that's what they do.'

He shook his head fiercely, looking on the verge of tears. 'Not with me,' he said. 'He doesn't play games with me. If he says he's in trouble, then he is. He needs me to help him. He needs to know he can trust me, that I won't betray him. That I won't go rushing to the police.'

She loosened her grip, knowing that there was no point in arguing further. 'Okay,' she said. 'Let's go.'

'What do you think?' Doripalam said. 'Another hour?'

Nergui nodded. 'Something like that. Surprising how quickly you can get bored with the view, isn't it?'

They had travelled some distance already, but the landscape remained unchanging. The journey had brought home to him, as if for the first time, quite how vast this country was, with its mile upon mile of uninhabited plains.

The steppe was spread out before them, folds and billows of green, with only the occasional white scattering of a *ger* camp or brown line of a road to mar its emptiness.

This country telescopes distance, Doripalam thought. The sheer absence of landmarks draws the horizon to you. He was familiar with this phenomenon in the Gobi, and knew how deadly it could prove for those lost to the elements. You see sanctuary in the distance – a camp, a scattering of trees indicative of clean water, livestock – and you start to walk, assuming you can reach it in safety. But the miles stretch on, and your target grows no nearer. And eventually the sun, the heat, the dehydration catch up with you. A metaphor for life.

Nergui was watching him, his expression quizzical. As so often, it was as if he had some conduit to Doripalam's thoughts. 'You think we're wasting our time?'

Doripalam shook his head. 'I don't know. It's all so tenuous. We don't really even know that there's any cause for concern.'

'I think we do know that,' Nergui said. He leaned back in his chair, and peered out of the helicopter towards the ground, far below. 'I have not been entirely frank with you.'

Doripalam shuffled round in his seat, trying to take in what Nergui was saying. It was as if he wants to wrong-foot you, he thought. He picks his moments. Way up in blue heaven, the air throbbing with noise, your senses dulled by the miles of nothingness, your mind drifting to blankness. 'What are you talking about?'

'I have told you the truth,' Nergui said. 'But not the whole truth.'

Doripalam couched forward in his seat, pressing his hands to his forehead, wanting to lose himself in the endless rhythmic drone of the rotors. 'You know,' he said at last, 'I don't find that too surprising. I wonder if you've ever told anyone the whole truth.' There was an edge of bitterness to his last words that he did nothing to conceal.

'Probably a justified comment,' Nergui said, his voice toneless through the earphones. 'But you know I have my reasons.'

Doripalam saw no reason to bite back his anger. 'You always have your reasons, Nergui. But you need to recognise that now and again you have to deal with us mortals. Maybe you should cut us a little slack.'

Nergui was staring out at the landscape, watching the skittering of the helicopter's shadow over the plain. His deep brown face was as expressionless as ever, his blue eyes unblinking. 'Old habits die hard,' he said, finally. 'Self-protection, I suppose. And the protection of others.'

'Okay, so tell me what this is all about.'

'It's the story of Wu Sam,' Nergui said. 'The whole story.'

Doripalam watched the older man, realising that for once Nergui was lost for words; his eyes, fixed on the far horizon, looked haunted. For a moment, he wondered whether to intervene, offer some anodyne words, but all his police training suggested otherwise. Hold the silence. Let the other person break it. It's easier to tell the truth than to say nothing.

'We arrested him,' Nergui said, finally. 'We knew his background, why he'd come here. We thought we knew what he'd done. We had enough evidence.'

'And what did you have?'

'We had a set up,' Nergui said. 'We didn't realise it at first. We were seeing what we wanted to see. A low-grade informer – not even a proper spy. Someone paid peanuts to relay back whatever scraps he might stumble across.'

For a moment, Doripalam thought that Nergui really had lost the thread, his mind distracted by the incessant booming of the rotors, the ancient tangles of his own story.

'We assumed we had a psychopath on our hands, and we wanted him dealt with as quickly as possible.' For the first time, he looked directly at Doripalam. 'We wanted a result. We believed what we wanted to believe,' he paused, half a beat, 'what we were encouraged to believe.'

'I don't understand,' Doripalam said. His patience was wearing thin. Here he was, once again, chasing some half-explained intuition of Nergui's. Some phantom who might turn out to have nothing to do with all this in the first place.

'I lost focus,' Nergui said. 'I didn't pay attention.' A smile played across his face, flickering like the shadow tossed by the helicopter across the steppe. 'My political sense failed me. I've been more careful since.' He stopped. 'I'm sorry. I think this has haunted me more than I realised. What I knew. What I should do about it.' He took a deep breath. 'It began when we interviewed Wu Sam. We interviewed him as we would any suspect. He wasn't a diplomat, so he had no formal immunities. We treated him like any foreign national suspected of a serious crime, so the Chinese couldn't accuse us of political machinations.'

Doripalam resisted the urge to comment. 'And the interview?'

'The second murder,' Nergui said. 'The evidence was unequivocal, but he seemed genuinely baffled by it.'

'He wouldn't be the first suspect to deny the obvious,' Doripalam pointed out.

'Of course not. What I mean is, I found myself believing him. Tunjin and another officer were conducting the interview. I was watching from the observation room. And, after a while, I began to believe what he was saying. That he was innocent. That he hadn't committed the murders.'

'If you were right about what he'd done, he was a psychopath. A born manipulator'

'Perhaps. But I'm no fool. All my instincts told me that he hadn't committed the murders. But that he was implicated in some more complex game.'

Nergui paused, apparently gathering his thoughts. 'They interviewed him for that first day. Then at the end I went in on my own. They were getting nowhere, and my unease was growing all the time. I felt we were further away from the truth, rather than closer. He'd started to talk about being set up. So I went in, and he spoke to me.'

There was a sudden shout from the front seat of the helicopter. Batzorig was twisting his head back over the seat, gesturing ahead of them. 'This is it,' he called back. 'Pilot reckons we're just about there.' He pointed off to their left. There was a moderate-sized cluster of wooden buildings, the odd pale dots of *gers*, two larger buildings apparently fabricated from corrugated iron, faint trails of smoke rising into the clear sky. 'That's Ondorkhaan. The airfield's just beyond the town, but I'm assuming we don't need to go there. The pilot's asking where we should put down.' He pointed off to the right, where the land rose towards the forests. The terrain was rich and verdant, the afternoon sun glinting on the sinuous line of a river. 'That's the birthplace, supposedly. Do we want to head up there?'

Nergui nodded. 'Get as close as we can. It doesn't look like the easiest place to land.'

Batzorig spoke briefly to the pilot. The helicopter banked in the air, the green earth sweeping away beneath them.

Nergui looked back at Doripalam, who was watching him quizzically. 'Wu Sam told me a story.' He gestured towards the landscape below them. 'That's why we're here. I still don't know for sure if the story was true. But if it was, I want to know how it ends.'

PART 3

# CHAPTER TWENTY-THREE

For a moment, as they entered the wider central thoroughfares, Tunjin almost lost them. The black car turned a sharp left into Peace Avenue, not slowing, its speed perfectly judged to merge seamlessly with the line of oncoming vehicles.

Pretty impressive driving, Tunjin thought. The black car was already disappearing into the commuter traffic circling the centre of the city.

He crunched the gears of Solongo's car, cursing its lack of acceleration, as he reached the corner with Peace Avenue. The traffic had thickened, and he was forced to slow. Losing patience, he slammed down the accelerator. With a barrage of horns behind him, he pulled sharply across into the outer lane. They were in the commercial district, the avenue lined with newly erected office buildings, studded with the increasingly familiar Western logos.

Tunjin hovered between lanes, incurring the wrath of the surrounding motorists, searching for the black car ahead. At last he spotted it, in the outer lane, eight or nine cars ahead. For once, Tunjin felt grateful for the sedate pace of Mongolian driving.

The black car was moving left, preparing to leave the avenue towards the city centre. Tunjin put his foot down, keeping it in sight as they emerged briefly into the road alongside Sukh Bataar Square. The far side of the square, where the new Genghis Khan memorial was being completed, was closed to traffic. For a moment, Tunjin wondered where the car was heading, then it turned to the right, behind the state museum.

Tunjin was still only a car behind, and had no difficulty in following. But the car had already moved to the left, preparing to turn into the rear of the museum. Behind him, a horn blared as Tunjin hit his brakes. He twisted the wheel to the right and, ignoring a further succession of horn blasts, he pulled into the kerb and stopped, his wheels at an angle across the pavement. A car passed, the driver shouting obscenities from his open window.

Tunjin climbed awkwardly out of the car and peered at the imposing museum building. Its carved stone frontage looked out over Khuldadaany Gudamj, one of the avenues that criss-crossed the city centre, the broad central square off to the left. The rear of the museum was gloomy and utilitarian, with a functional courtyard for delivery vehicles.

He crossed the street and peered through the museum gateway. The black car was parked in front of the rear entrance, and there was no sign either of Solongo or the others. The wide loading bay was closed, its heavy metal shutter firmly locked, but a smaller door beside it was wedged ajar.

The museum would be open, as far as he knew, though the public areas would probably be quiet on a weekday. In any case, a large section of the building was currently closed off, as Solongo and her team completed the preparations for the anniversary exhibition.

The open door led into the loading area, which was in darkness and apparently deserted. To the left, a gloomy corridor stretched into the interior of the building with more doors, mostly closed. Tunjin moved cautiously down the corridor until he reached a dimly lit stairwell, with concrete steps leading up to the rest of the building. He peered up the stairway and began slowly to climb.

At the top of the stairs, a further corridor stretched out, again with an array of doors, some open, some closed. The first open door he passed led into an office, with two desks set against the opposing walls. Both were clearly in use, but there was no sign of any occupant. The walls were lined with the familiar likeness of Genghis Khan, pictures of Karakorum and numerous other images relating to the Mongol empire. At the far end of the room, a book-shelf was crammed with academic-looking volumes.

He continued his slow progress along the corridor, stopping at each closed door to listen for any sound. The silence seemed unnatural, as if the museum's inhabitants had been mysteriously removed.

Finally, at the far end of the corridor, he heard something. He stopped, straining his ears. The sound of a voice, a male voice. Perhaps more than one.

Ahead, the corridor widened into a lobby, more brightly lit and salubriously decorated. Beyond the lobby, there was an antiquated-looking elevator and a set of marble-faced stairs – the entrance from the administrative area into the public sections of the museum.

To one side, there was a new-looking leather couch, with a polished wooden coffee table set in front of it, and two further doors, both half-open. Their brass fittings suggested that they led to more impressive offices than those Tunjin had already seen.

The voices were clearer now – two of them, both male. Tunjin could make out no words, but the speakers were engaged in some kind of dialogue, their respective tones clearly distinguishable. One was low and murmuring, calm and deliberate. The other was higher pitched, emotional, though it was hard to pinpoint what emotion was being expressed. Perhaps anger. Perhaps anxiety.

Tunjin stopped opposite the first open door, positioning himself to peer inside without betraying his presence. As far as he could judge, the office was deserted. Two desks were visible, both topped with slightly out-moded computer monitors.

He moved towards the second door. The door was ajar, but he could not see what lay behind it. He stepped forward again until he was parallel with the doorway.

The voices were increasing in volume, the contrast between the two speakers becoming more pronounced. Tunjin listened harder, trying to discern any words. Finally, inches from the door, he could make out some of what the first speaker was saying. 'Ridiculous . . . outrage . . . half-baked . . .' All hissed in the same intense half-suppressed whisper.

There was a small gap between the door and the frame, allowing Tunjin just enough space to peer between the hinges. Trying hard not to move the door itself, he peered through the tiny aperture.

It was a plushly appointed office, presumably that of the absent museum director. At the far side, below a large window, there was an expansive dark-wood desk, with a brass lamp, a telephone and little sign of any working clutter. Closer to hand, there were two black leather sofas, set facing one another across a glass-topped coffee table. There were people sitting on both sofas, as well as a figure propped on a high-backed chair.

Tunjin moved slightly, trying to make out more detail. Both sofas were set at right angles to him, and he could see some of the faces ranged opposite each other. All but one was male. The woman was sitting at the far end of one of the sofas, only her shoulder and the side of her head visible. Solongo.

There were four others, apparently of varying ages. The man on the high-backed chair was relatively young – probably late-twenties – and dressed in the dark suit and dark glasses that, in Tunjin's experience, was the standard uniform for a certain type of higher-class thug. The other men on the sofas were older, dressed in similar dark suits but looking more comfortable in the formal attire than their younger colleague.

The voices belonged to two men facing one another across the low table. Tunjin could see the face of the more relaxed speaker. His expression was at one with the tone of his voice – faintly smiling, his eyes unblinking, occasionally shaking his head gently as though in polite acknowledgment and dismissal of what he was hearing.

Tunjin could see less of the other speaker. His head was turned slightly away from the door, and only a small part of his face and the back of his head were visible. His hair was dark and sleek – dyed, Tunjin guessed – and his movements matched the intense tone of his voice, his head jerking backwards and forward, his forefinger stabbing the air.

There was something familiar about him. This was a man he had seen before, quite recently.

It took him a moment to realise where and, when the answer came, it explained nothing. Because the man in the room was, indirectly but ultimately, his own boss. The man who, in his official role, was responsible for the safety and well-being of the entire nation. None other than the minister of security.

# CHAPTER TWENTY-FOUR

The singing was both familiar and yet unearthly, echoing amongst the empty stands and out into the wide parkland and the steppe beyond.

The afternoon heat hit Sarangeral after the cool of the car's air-conditioning. She stood for a moment, her hands on the hot metal of the car roof, captivated by the extraordinary resonances of the music. Beside her, Gundalai's face was blank, as if he had no more idea of why they were here than she did.

She turned towards the large expanse of the Naadam Stadium. It was still a few days before the start of this year's Naadam Festival, and preparations and rehearsals were underway. The remarkable undulating singing that had greeted their arrival had, for the moment, died away, replaced by a more familiar aural tapestry of banging and shouting – the usual noises associated with the logistics of a major public event.

As she locked the car, the singing rose again, momentarily dominating even the vast spaces surrounding the stadium. This was *khoomii*, throat singing, the remarkable vocalising that produces notes of different pitch simultaneously. The low notes resonated around the stadium, echoing and re-echoing, mingled with the higher pitched counterpoints to create an all-embracing sound.

For a second, Sarangarel felt lost, suspended in this sonic landscape. Like all Mongolians, she had grown up with the sound, but it still struck her as something ancient and alien. It was as if the music pierced all this country's pretensions to modernity, laying bare something much older and far more strange.

She turned and looked at Gundalai. 'This is where he said?' she asked, gesturing towards the stadium building.

It took him a moment to process her question, and then he nodded. 'That's what he said.'

'There was nothing else?' she said. 'Nothing that might tell us where to look?'

Gundalai shrugged. 'He'll be here somewhere.'

She nodded, unbelieving, and turned to look back at the stadium. It was an impressive edifice, set against the backdrop of the city and the surrounding hills. Days from now, it would be hosting the annual festival, the major celebration of the three 'manly sports' of archery, horse riding and wrestling. It was always a major event, a modern-day version of the traditional nomadic assemblies, gathering crowds from the surrounding regions. Other towns would be celebrating their own festivals over the same period, but this was the big one.

And this year's would be the largest of all, with additional celebrations for the anniversary of the Mongol empire. The coming days would see an unprecedented gathering of crowds, military displays, music, artistic performances and sporting contests. There would be an opening ceremony in Sukhbaatar Square, the symbolic transportation of the nine yaks' tails – representing the nine tribes of the Mongols – to the stadium, and then two extended days of sports and celebrations.

It was a celebration which Sarangarel had dutifully attended on numerous occasions, although neither the ceremonials nor the sports were particularly to her taste. The contemporary event was a mix of the traditional and the contrived, some of it no doubt designed more to appeal to modern tourists than to reflect historical precedent.

The current dates of the festival had been fixed under the old regime to commemorate the communist revolution, and the celebrations had been transformed into People's Revolution Day. There was an ironic symbolism about the way in which the celebration had, over the years, been appropriated by both sides of the political divide. The politicians were only too keen to link their causes to what, in every other respect, was simply a celebration of life and physical pleasure. By the end of the second day, when the taking of alcohol was the primary interest, physical pleasure would be the exclusive objective of many participants.

Various trucks and vans were lined up alongside the stadium walls, and groups of hefty-looking men in shorts were unloading equipment. She could hear more music now, too – not *khoomii* this time, but a traditional instrumental with the horse-headed *morin khur* fiddle to the fore. The sound was less other-worldly than the throat singing, but the melodies rippled ethereally through the sunlit air.

Sarangarel turned back to Gundalai. 'Why would he be here, though?' she said. 'What's this all about?'

Gundalai shrugged again, in the manner that, for all her sympathies, she was beginning to find infuriating. 'He'll have some plan.'

'I don't doubt it,' she said. 'But what part are we expected to play?'

They walked through the entrance into the arena and looked around. The arena trapped the afternoon heat, and the interior was baking hot. She wondered what this place was going to be like in a few days' time, thronged with people. For the athletes, the horsemen and the wrestlers especially, it would be even worse.

She had no idea where to go or what to do next. There was an administrative area – cabins and two *ger* tents – at the far end, but both looked deserted. Various individuals were striding around the arena with an official-looking air, carrying files or talking earnestly into mobile phones, but it was impossible to judge their respective status or to know whether any of them would be worth approaching. In any case, what would she say?

She walked slowly into the centre of the arena, trying to get the most complete view of the surrounding stands. She wanted Gundalai to know that she was at least taking his predicament seriously.

Off to her left, targets were being erected for the archery competitions. Beyond those, there were the tracks for the horse racing. On the opposite side of the arena, a stage was being constructed for musical or dramatic performances. Behind the stage, two large screens had been erected to enable the festival's events to be magnified for the whole arena. This was technology she had not seen here previously, but the anniversary celebrations were taking everything up to a higher level. She scrutinised each area in turn, searching for any sign of Odbayar.

But of course there was nothing. She turned back towards Gundalai, preparing to tell him that this was a waste of their time. But Gundalai was not looking at her. His head was down, and he was staring at the screen of his mobile phone.

'What is it?'

He held out the phone. 'It's him.'

'Another message?' she said, drily. 'Perfectly timed.'

'He knows we're here. He must be around here somewhere.' Gundalai gazed eagerly around the stadium, as though expecting to see his friend waving back at him.

'What do you mean?' she said, her patience wearing thin now. 'How does he know we're here? What does he say?'

Gundalai again waved the phone in her direction. 'Not much. The text just says, "You're here. Now we can begin."'

Behind them, someone had switched on the recorded music again, and the unearthly sounds of the *khoomii* began to echo through the stands, the sound eerily distorted by the emptiness of the building.

'Now we can begin what?'

It was a beautiful place. The forests thickened ahead, rising up towards the mountain peaks. Behind, the land fell away, dappled shadow and sunlight down to the vast steppe below. Far to the left, disappearing into the afternoon haze, he could see the distant scattering of buildings that made up the town of Ondorkhaan, the dots of *gers* in the surrounding grassland. To the right, there was the curve of the river, the pale strip of water broadening out into the expanse of the plain.

The cradle of the empire, he thought.

He looked down towards the river. Fifty metres or so from where he stood, there was a shallow point, where the edge of the water was lined with flat rocks.

He could not have found a better spot. Not immediately visible, and partly concealed even from the air by the overhang of the bank. But once you reached this point, as any visitor up here eventually would, everything was exposed.

He had parked the truck up in the forest, its dull green paintwork invisible in the deep gloom. Odbayar was still in there. It was unlikely that he would wake from the sedative just yet.

Quite soon, he would need to fetch Odbayar and set things in motion. He had received the texted signals from the city. Everything was in place. Things could start to move.

He looked up again at the empty sky. He could hear nothing yet, despite the silence of the windless day. But he fancied that he could see it now, far off in the pale distance.

They had proved slightly more resourceful than he had imagined. But, if you were a professional, you made your own luck. Everything played into your hands. Because here they were, on their way to join his party. To be the participants he needed.

Even better than he had planned, this would not all be filtered through the constraining lens of technology.

It would be witnessed. Live.

As they banked, the land dropped away, green and gold in the afternoon sunshine. The buildings and tents of the town disappeared behind them as they headed up towards the forests and mountains. Doripalam could make out the line of a river, twisting down from the hills to the undulating plain.

Batzorig twisted in his seat and called back to Doripalam and Nergui, 'That's where we're heading. That curve of the river. He'll get us as close as he can.'

Doripalam looked at Nergui, wondering whether he would take the opportunity to complete his story. But Nergui was staring out of the window, his eyes on the empty landscape.

The pilot leaned over from his seat and gestured forwards. Batzorig nodded. 'He's planning to touch down over there,' he said. 'By that upper bend in the river. Does that look okay to you?'

Nergui nodded to Batzorig. 'That's fine,' he called. 'That's the supposed birthplace. Get as close as you can, we can walk the rest.'

The helicopter began to descend rapidly, the grassland gathering detail as they dropped towards it – a rough tapestry of peaks and troughs, scattered with rocks and hollows. It was easier now to see why the pilot was selecting his landing place with caution.

They landed more smoothly than Doripalam had expected, settling gently on to the firm grassland. The pilot turned off the engine and they sat as the rotors slowed.

Outside, in the baking afternoon, the silence was stunning after the incessant noise of the helicopter. As they disembarked, Doripalam stretched his arms, his body stiff from the cramped cockpit. The land rose above them for perhaps fifty metres, before dropping again into the broad river valley. The ground was thick with verdant grass, dotted with a tapestry of wild flowers. Perfect grazing land, Doripalam thought. No doubt, somewhere out in that landscape would be nomads, drawn up here for the quality of the pastures.

Nergui had already begun to stride up the hillside, his characteristic energy undaunted by the steep gradient. Batzorig glanced at Doripalam, then shrugged and began to follow. Doripalam turned to the pilot. 'I don't know how long we'll be.'

The pilot shook his head. 'No concern of mine.' He gestured towards the helicopter. 'I'd like to get this back by the end of the day, though. It's needed again tomorrow.'

Doripalam looked up at the hillside, the tall figure of Nergui striding away from them. 'I don't think we'll want to be here all night.'

He turned and began to follow his colleagues. Nergui was already nearing the edge of the valley, Batzorig trotting willingly behind him. Nergui had the air of knowing where he was going. As he took the first steps down the far side into the river valley, Doripalam saw his impenetrable face silhouetted for a moment against the deep blue of the sky.

Doripalam hurried up the last few metres to the summit, conscious of the sweat dripping inside his shirt. Nergui and Batzorig were already some way below. The surface of the river glittered brilliantly in the sunshine. Doripalam scrambled down the incline, stumbling as stones tumbled beneath his feet. A moment later, he reached Nergui and Batzorig, and his eyes followed Nergui's pointing finger towards the dazzling water.

Squinting against the reflected glare, it took Doripalam a few moments to identify the object of their gaze. There was a cluster of rocks, dotted with reeds and other vegetation, at the point where the river curved closest to them. On the furthest rock, positioned to be clearly visible from the surrounding hillside, there was a body.

# CHAPTER TWENTY-FIVE

Tunjin peered through the narrow gap between the door and the frame, transfixed by what he was seeing.

Even from this limited vantage point, he had no doubt that this was the minister. He had seen that misleadingly benign face often enough; the minister was not shy of publicity.

'Satisfied your curiosity now?' a voice said from behind him.

He started to turn, but felt something hard pressed against the small of his back.

'I think you'd better get a proper look, don't you?' the voice said. Tunjin felt himself pushed forward into the office.

'We have a visitor. He was lurking at the door.' Tunjin looked back. Another identikit thug in the standard dark grey suit.

The other men in the room were watching Tunjin with curiosity, but no obvious anxiety. Whatever they were up to, they looked entirely in control. The young man on the high-backed chair had a pistol hanging loosely between his fingers. Solongo was on the sofa, her face expressionless. She had not looked up at Tunjin's entry.

The minister was staring at Tunjin. 'What the hell is this?' he snapped at the man opposite. His voice had risen from the whisper that Tunjin had heard outside. 'I mean, are you clowns capable of organising nothing? Who the hell is this?'

There was a protracted silence. Clearly, nobody had an immediate answer to these questions. Tunjin felt the prod of the gun in his back again. 'Go on. Tell the gentleman who you are.'

'I'm a police officer. A member of the Serious Crimes Team,' Tunjin paused. 'And if it wasn't for the fact that you've got a gun stuck in my back, I'd be telling you that you're under arrest.'

The man behind him laughed. 'Lucky for me, then. Though I think your boss over there might have something to say about it as well.'

The minister looked unamused. 'I'm glad you're amused. This whole bloody thing's spiralling out of control. We've got the whole works – up to and including a fucking policeman with a gun in his back. This isn't quite how I'd envisaged it.' His voice was quieter now, but sounded all the more threatening as a result.

None of this made much sense to Tunjin but, seeing no other options available, he decided to stir things up a little more. 'I don't understand this,' he said, gently. 'I don't know why you're here. And I don't know why you've brought this lady here. Of all people.'

He had the minister's attention now. For all the old man's bluster, Tunjin had begun to sense that the minister was out of his depth. 'What are you talking about?'

'Let me introduce Solongo,' he said. 'Wife of Doripalam, the head of the Serious Crimes Team. An interesting choice of kidnap victim.'

Tunjin looked at Solongo, whose expression had, for the first time, begun to reveal some emotion. He wondered whether her earlier consumption of vodka had helped her to retain her calm. But she appeared sober enough now, and he could see she was calculating how best to play the situation. Finally, she succeeded in raising a smile and turned on the sofa to face the minister. 'Pleased to meet you at last,' she said. 'My husband's said so much about you.'

The calm irony proved too much for the minister, who pulled himself to his feet and crouched over the man opposite. 'What the *fuck* do you think you're playing at? You told me you had all this under control. You've told me a crock of shit since this all started, and I was stupid enough to believe you.'

He stopped and jerked his head back, almost as if the man had struck him. It took Tunjin a moment to realise that the metaphorical blow had been nothing more than the other man's untroubled smile. Whatever the minister might say, this man simply didn't care.

The man's smile broadened. 'Sit down, old man. Relax. We're here to help you. Everything is under control.'

The minister straightened slowly with the cautious stiffness of one accustomed to maintaining his dignity even in the most challenging of circumstances. 'You're full of shit,' he said, softly. 'You and your boss. I don't think you have a clue what you're doing.'

The other man was watching him, still smiling, his eyes unblinking. 'Sit down, old man,' he said again. This time, there was an undertone of menace to his words. 'We know much more than you imagine.'

Her first reaction was to storm out. Just walk out of here, get back into her car, and leave all this nonsense behind.

It was only the expression on Gundalai's face that stopped her. No matter what happened, he continued to believe. He really thought something important was going to happen. Not just some idiot stunt pulled by an overgrown student politician.

'So what are we waiting for?' she said.

He looked wildly around the stadium. The bustle of preparation continued as before. 'I don't know. Something—'

Suddenly the rhythmic modulation of the *khoomii* cut off. There was a loud sharp crackling across the PA system, as if it had been affected by an electrical storm.

At first, there was no discernible effect on the individuals scattered about the stadium, most continued with their activities, assuming that the sound had been affected by some technical glitch.

A moment later, there was another loud electrical crackle and the two large screens burst into life. There was a brilliant dazzle of light from each, a blurred scattering of brightly coloured diamonds, and the two screens displayed an identical image.

With a comical synchronisation everyone in the arena looked up simultaneously. Silence spread slowly as the spectators ceased whatever activity they had been engaged in and watched the screen.

It took a while for them to understand what they were seeing. It appeared to be a live broadcast. But it was clearly not a film of the stadium or any of the surrounding area.

For a moment, a jumble of pale blue and turquoise lozenges danced diagonally across the shot. Then slowly the camera panned round and came into focus, as though an amateur cameraman was slowly gaining control of the instrument.

The fractured white and blue was revealed as sunlight and sky reflected on a rippling body of water. The curve of a broad river.

The camera pulled back further and the screen was filled with rich blue and green. The vast empty bowl of the Mongolian sky, the green of the plush northern grasslands.

The onlookers began to lose interest, assuming that this was some travelogue for tourists. Some had already turned back to their former activities.

Then there was an audible intake of breath from the remaining observers, as they realised what the screen was showing. A murmur of puzzlement spread slowly across the arena.

The camera had zoomed slowly in towards the river. There was an expanse of grass, a cluster of rocks stretching out into the middle of the current. The camera zoomed further and it was possible to discern an object spread out on the flat stone.

Sarangarel leaned forward, trying to work out what was being shown. Was this Odbayar's stunt? She braced herself for something unexpected. Some satirical joke.

But it was no joke.

The camera jerkily moved forward again, and the nature of the object on the rock became clear. Gundalai cried out something behind her. Though Sarangarel could not make out what he had said, his startled tone was echoed around the stadium.

The object was a human body, its limbs spread out as if it were a sacrificial victim, its head twisted at a grotesque angle. The camera moved forward and, in close-up, the state of the body became clearer. The face was dark and bruised, already affected by decay.

The voices of the onlookers around the stadium were becoming more strident. Whatever this might be, it was clearly no test transmission. Sarangeral turned to say something to Gundalai, but the young man was no longer behind her. She looked around the arena, but could not see him. She glanced back up at the screen, waiting for some denouement to the scene. But the camera simply held for long seconds on the damaged face. A young man, she thought, once good looking.

Then the camera tipped back, focused now beyond the rock and the body, towards the far bank of the river and the grassland above it.

And the three figures making their way towards the water's edge.

# CHAPTER TWENTY-SIX

An offering, Nergui thought. A sacrifice to some unimaginable deity.

He had paused, trying to make sense of the scene spread out below. Doripalam and Batzorig had stopped too, transfixed by the grotesque tableau.

'You were right, as ever,' Doripalam said. 'Though I didn't expect you'd prove it quite so easily.'

Nergui's attention had already moved from the supine body, and his eyes were scanning the far bank. 'Nor did I,' he said. 'I wonder why we're being offered this.' He gestured down towards the river. 'I feel uncomfortable when our work becomes too simple.'

Doripalam nodded. He and Nergui shared the same uneasy memories of the last time this kind of display had been prepared for them, two years before in a deserted warehouse in the back-streets of the capital. 'What do you think?'

Nergui was still gazing intently at the far bank. 'If this has been prepared as a welcome,' he said, 'someone is waiting.'

Doripalam followed the direction of Nergui's gaze. 'Maybe we should get some shelter,' he said. 'We're pretty exposed here.'

'If he wanted to shoot at us, he could have done so by now. I don't think that's it.'

'Over there, sir,' Batzorig said, suddenly. He had taken Nergui's cue and had been carefully scanning the landscape.

The other two men looked where he was pointing. There was

something up there, just inside the shade of the thickening tree-line, almost invisible against the afternoon sun.

Batzorig squinted. 'It's metallic. I can see the sun shining on it through the trees.'

'Metal or glass. And something moving in the trees,' Nergui said.

'It could be a gunsight,' Doripalam pointed out.

'Or binoculars. Or a camera,' Nergui said. 'Let's not panic until we've good cause.'

Doripalam shook his head, recognising that this was not the moment to respond to Nergui's provocations. 'So what do you suggest we do?' he asked. 'Instead of panicking.'

'We could have a look at the body.' Nergui began to stride down the bank, passing Doripalam and Batzorig. 'See if it's who we're assuming it is.'

'Which may be exactly what's expected. Maybe he wants us in range.'

There was no arguing with Nergui. One day he would finally be proved wrong. Doripalam wasn't sure whether or not he wanted to be present when that happened. Reluctantly, he followed Nergui down towards the water, Batzorig trailing a few steps behind.

The body was decayed but not in a bad state. It didn't look like a body that had been sitting out in the summer heat for a week or more. The white face was discoloured with bruising, the neck twisted, but there was no major decomposition. Out here, too, the body would surely have been attacked by animals or birds.

It was casually dressed, Western-style – blue jeans and some sort of sweat-shirt, trainers on the feet. There were brown spots of blood scattered across the pale cotton of the sweatshirt. A young man, Mongolian, probably in his early twenties, thick dark hair swept back from his forehead.

Nergui glanced back over his shoulder. 'Do you think it's him?'

Batzorig had managed to track down a photograph of the missing graduate student, Sunduin, among the university records. It was an unhelpful photograph – several years old and cropped from some larger picture.

'He's the right age, certainly. And has the right kind of looks. But then so do lots of young men.'

Nergui was at the edge of the water, peering more closely at the body. He turned to Batzorig. 'Can you call the local police? We need someone out here to deal with this.' He glanced up at the sun. 'Soon, I think. And make sure they have someone who can deal with the evidence properly.'

'For what it's worth,' Doripalam said. 'Do you think it's likely to tell us much? This hasn't been left here by accident.'

'Who knows?'

The sudden explosion was shattering in the silence. Doripalam threw himself to the ground, closely followed by Batzorig, both assuming that this was gunfire they had been half-expecting.

Only Nergui seemed unmoved. He had turned back towards the river and, Doripalam realised, was calmly watching the opposite bank.

There was a man standing, twenty metres or so up the far slope, as calm and motionless as Nergui. He was slightly built, a hunched figure dressed in a black tee-shirt and black trousers, Chinese in appearance. He was holding a smoking pistol in his left hand.

'Wu Sam,' Nergui said.

The man bowed slightly. 'Professor Sam Yung,' he called back, 'from the University of Syracuse in New York.'

'So I understand,' Nergui said. 'It is always pleasing to meet a true authority.' He gestured towards the supine corpse. 'This is your work, I take it.'

Sam bowed his head again. 'Symbolic, really. Though he will not be missed.'

Nergui turned to look at the body, the bruised figure of the young man, as though preparing to challenge this assertion. 'It captured our attention, certainly,' he said, finally.

Sam nodded. 'I had not expected you to come here. Not so soon. But it's good that you have come.'

'I am sure we are pleased to be of assistance.'

Sam stepped slowly down the bank, the pistol hanging loosely in his hand. 'You are here as witnesses.'

Nergui glanced up at the shadow of the trees behind Sam. Following his gaze, Doripalam noticed for the first time a video camera standing on a tripod a little way up the slope. It was trained on the rock where the body lay, taking in their own figures as well as the rear of Sam's body.

'You already have a witness,' Nergui said, nodding towards the camera.

'Many witnesses,' Sam agreed. 'It is a clever piece of kit. It is amazing what my countrymen are capable of producing these days.'

'Your countrymen?' Nergui said. 'In the United States?'

Sam laughed. 'Some of the technology is no doubt American. But the Chinese duplicate it more cheaply.'

'So I understand. Not always legally.'

'My countrymen are rewriting the rules in many areas. That is why we are so successful.'

'No doubt. So you have a camera. You have a transmitter?'

Sam nodded, a touch of eagerness in his manner, as though he was pleased to be demonstrating his ingenuity. 'A satellite transmitter. Very neat. But the clever part is elsewhere. I can claim only a little credit for that.'

'Elsewhere?' Nergui had moved to the river's edge. He casually dipped the toe of his shoe into the clear swirling water. The river was relatively deep here – perhaps a couple of metres or more. It would be difficult to cross without moving substantially further downstream.

'I don't wish you to feel self-conscious, Nergui. But you are being watched. Initially by – I don't know, a few dozen people. But shortly by thousands.'

Nergui looked up at the camera as if with mild curiosity. 'I think it would take more than that to make me self-conscious,' he said. 'Who are these thousands?'

Sam gestured behind him. 'It's very simple,' he said. 'I've had our transmission from here patched into the closed-circuit broadcasts at the Naadam Stadium. Our conversation is being televised on the large display screen in the stadium.'

'I'm honoured,' Nergui said, bowing faintly towards the camera. 'Even though I don't really understand.'

'They – and you – are my witnesses,' Sam said, smiling now. 'It is important that everything is out in the open, that everyone sees what happens. This time.'

There was a moment's silence. As the sun beat down from the empty sky, it struck Doripalam that some understanding had passed between Sam and Nergui. Something was working itself out here. Something more complex and personal than Doripalam had imagined.

'Witnesses to what?' Nergui said, quietly.

'I've spent a long time preparing,' Sam said. 'All my time in the US. Not wasted.'

'Not wasted,' Nergui echoed. 'You're a respected academic, a journalist. An authority on our country and your own.' It was as if he was trying to remind Sam of another life. Something that Sam might have forgotten.

Sam nodded. 'As you say. It was a useful position to occupy. In all kinds of ways. A sleeper.'

Nergui gazed at Sam across the shimmering water, as though trying to read his thoughts. 'So what have you prepared?'

'I've thought this through very carefully. I had assistance. Some of it willing. Some of it – well, still willing, but perhaps misguided.'

'Odbayar,' Nergui said.

Sam looked at him, his face for the first time betraying some emotion. It was the surprised recognition – familiar enough to Doripalam – that Nergui was, if not yet a step ahead, perhaps fewer steps behind than Sam might have imagined. 'Odbayar. He has been of great assistance to me. He isn't to be blamed; he has done what he thought best for his country.'

'I'm sure he has,' Nergui said. 'Where is he?'

Sam gestured behind him. 'Up there,' he said. 'There is a truck parked just above the tree-line, in the shade. I thought it would be inhumane to leave him out in the heat.'

Doripalam recognised the significance of Sam's words and had no doubt that Nergui had done the same, though there was no change in the older man's expression. Odbayar was here and, for the moment at least, was alive.

'We can see him?'

Sam smiled. 'Very shortly. You will need to see him. To be witnesses.' He gestured to the camera. 'You and everyone out there.'

'There won't be many people in the stadium,' Nergui pointed out. 'The festival hasn't started yet.'

'I considered delaying this until the festival, that would have had more impact.' He shrugged. 'But the time did not allow. And I think the security would have been more problematic once the festival had begun.'

'But you need your witnesses?' Nergui said. There was method in the way he was talking, Doripalam thought. This notion of witness somehow lay at the heart of whatever Sam was up to.

'I have witnesses,' Sam said. 'There are people in the stadium. Some are there by accident – those preparing the stadium for the festival. Some are there at my beckoning. The young man's friend, for example.'

'Gundalai,' Nergui said. Gundalai had been with Sarangarel. She would not have left him alone. If Gundalai had somehow been summoned to the Naadam Stadium, Sarangarel would be there as well. Another witness.

Sam nodded. 'Gundalai. And I have arranged for the media to be there. A camera crew, to film this.'

'I hope your faith in our media is not misplaced. I do not think they would attend such an event without good reason.'

'I have given them a good reason,' Sam said. 'Despite the best efforts of yourself and your colleagues. They are aware now of the shooting in Sukh Baatar Square, the hotel bombing, even of the two bodies. I have given them some potentially lurid explanations.'

'Terrorism?' Nergui said, calmly. 'I don't know if that kind of explanation is likely to be very credible.'

'Who knows? You're a nation of storytellers,' he said. 'It's what you do. Your mythic past and your make-believe future.' He stopped and glanced at the camera. 'But I think there's enough to guarantee that the media will be here. Now it's my turn to tell the story.'

The minister was slumped back on the sofa, looking as if the mental fight had been knocked out of him. Tunjin was still standing, acutely conscious of the weapon inches from his back. Solongo was as stone-faced as ever, but Tunjin knew that, below the surface, she was terrified.

He recognised the type of man who was sitting opposite the minister. A well-heeled thug. A hanger-on to the new elite in energy or minerals or international trade. Not making serious money himself, but squeezing a good living from those who were. Someone who got things done. The things his betters wouldn't soil their hands with.

Which raised the question of what kinds of services the minister had been expecting from these people. Whatever the answer, it was clear that he was no longer in control.

'You've finished, old man?' the man said brutally, staring at the crumpled figure opposite.

The minister glared back at him. 'Are you going to tell me what's happening?'

The man smiled and stretched out his legs. 'You thought you were using us, didn't you? Must be a shock to find you're the one being used.'

The minister glanced up at Tunjin and then across at Solongo. 'I've no idea what you're talking about.'

'It's all very simple, really. Nothing flash. Just plain old-fashioned extortion.'

'If you're thinking of trying to blackmail—'

The man laughed, harshly and unexpectedly. 'I don't think so, old man. You don't have much of a reputation left to lose. Not if you hang around with people like us.'

'You—'

The man held his finger to his lip, gesturing for the minister to be silent. 'Enough. It is nearly time, anyway.' He twisted in his seat and glared at Tunjin. 'You,' he said. 'The fat one. Sit down over there.' He waved his hand towards a hard-backed chair by the large desk. 'Keep an eye on him,' he said to the man with the gun. 'Though I don't imagine he'll move too quickly even for you.'

Tunjin sat down heavily on the chair. The man with the gun pulled across another chair and straddled it, keeping the pistol pointed towards him.

'Good,' the man on the sofa said. 'So we're all settled.' He pulled a mobile phone from his jacket pocket and thumbed one of the keys, glancing at the screen. 'The message has arrived,' he announced, speaking as if everyone else in the room would understand.

He rose and made his way to the corner of the office, where there was a large, flat-screen television. He glanced at Solongo. 'Your former director looked after himself very well. I'm sure you appreciated it.'

The man turned and beamed, with the air of a master of ceremonies introducing the top of the bill. 'I'm reliably assured that the moment has arrived.' He pointed the remote control at the television, which burst into life with a gentle click. 'Let the show begin.'

# CHAPTER TWENTY-SEVEN

Nergui.

Even given the poor quality of the image, there was no mistaking that dark chiselled visage. He was facing the sun, the intense light catching in his dark hair, his glinting eyes.

The camera steadied and the scene on the large screens became clearer. Nergui was standing at the river's edge, looking at the man whose head was silhouetted in the foreground. A few feet behind stood Doripalam. Off to the right, there was a third figure – the young officer, Batzorig.

Like the rest of the small crowd, Sarangeral was trying to make sense of what was being shown. For several minutes, there was no sound, so the scene resembled a surreal silent movie. Perhaps a Western, Sarangeral thought, Nergui looked the part, standing dark-suited and motionless in the hot afternoon sun.

Keeping one eye on the screen, Sarangarel anxiously tried to spot Gundalai in the crowd. He was an adult and ought to be capable of looking after himself, but something about his unexpected disappearance, combined with the eerie sight of Nergui's silent figure on the screen, left her profoundly uneasy.

A loud crackle brought her full attention back to the screen. The noise lessened and resolved itself into a babble of speech, at first indecipherable but slowly coalescing into meaning.

'. . . a nation of storytellers,' the voice said, booming around the nearly-empty stadium. 'It's what you do. Your mythic past and your make-believe—' The sound cut out again for a second, replaced by a burst of static.

There was a sudden commotion at the far end of the stadium. A truck had driven through the large open gates, and two eager-looking young men were unloading a television camera and other pieces of equipment. There was an argument going on with another camera crew who were already in place with a camera pointing up at the screen. A poised young woman – presumably a television reporter – was watching the exchange with some amusement.

It appeared that the media had been alerted. Had she been right all along, then? Was this some stunt by Odbayar?

There was another crackle from the loudspeaker system, and the voice from the screen resumed '. . . It's my turn to tell the story.'

Finally, the man on the screen turned to face the camera. It wasn't Odbayar, as she had half-expected. In fact, it was no one she recognised. A small, slight man, Chinese in appearance, though with a shape to his face that suggested some Mongolian blood. He had moved to the side of the shot, so that it was possible now to see the glittering river, the rock with the spreadeagled body, and the far bank with the motionless figures of Nergui and his colleagues. For a moment, the shot appeared staged, as if the participants were posing for a bizarre portrait.

The man, staring straight into the camera, looking not unlike a news reporter himself, gestured behind him. 'I owe an apology to this young man. He was not responsible for his actions or for his own death. He is a victim of your country. A victim of its deca-dence, its descent into corruption and decay.'

It sounded like a prepared speech, something he had rehearsed and repeated to himself, waiting for the day when he would finally get the chance to deliver it. She assumed that this was some convo-luted political allegory that Odbayar had cooked up, some metaphor that would reveal its meaning before much longer. But she couldn't begin to imagine how Nergui had ended up participating.

It was obvious from a rising murmur of chattering that some in the stadium were already losing interest. The two television crews were now talking more amicably to one another. Perhaps they had begun to suspect that they were not after all in competition to secure some major scoop.

'But this,' the man on the screen went on, 'is merely a symbol. You can think of it as the end of an old order, a discredited world. My purpose today is to look forward into a brighter future.'

He sounds like an evangelist, Sarangeral thought. Another of the born-again Christians from the United States or Europe. This man had the same unyielding certainty about his own role and purpose in the world.

The man walked up towards the static camera, leaving behind the golden strand of the river and the matchstick silhouettes of Nergui and his colleagues. He was still talking as he trudged up the steep slope, his voice short of breath. 'I am not here simply to tell you stories – though I have many stories that will surprise you. I am here to take action. In a moment, you will see the power I have at my disposal.'

The man was close to the camera, his eyes staring fixedly at the lens. For the first time, Sarangarel felt a tremor of fear. This no longer felt like a stunt. This felt like madness. There was a look in his eyes that she could not read, an emptiness unmistakable even through the blurred transmission. The man's expression had transfixed those around her as well. The growing murmuring died away; and faces turned back to the screen.

The man reached forward and the image juddered wildly on the screen. It took Sarangeral a second to realise that he had picked up the camera and was striding up the hillside, pointing the lens towards the trees in front of him. The soundtrack was a muffled thumping – the sound of the man's footsteps as he headed up the slope.

Then his voice re-emerged. 'I need to show you,' he said, sounding breathless, though it was unclear whether this was the result of physical exertion or a growing excitement. The confusion on the screen resolved itself into a shot of rising grassland, dark fir trees, a boundary of bright light and deep shadow. In the middle, almost obscured by the shade, was a black Land Cruiser.

The shot was held for a second, and then the image bounced again as the man walked forward to open the rear door of the vehicle. 'The first item I have to show you.'

At first, the rear of the truck appeared empty. Then the camera zoomed in towards the area behind the front passenger seats. A box, with wires. Sarangarel was no expert. But it was clear to her that they were looking at an explosive device – or something mocked up to resemble such a device.

Around her, all eyes were fixed on the screen. At the front of the arena, Sarangarel could see that the attitude of the television crews had changed yet again.

The man's voice boomed around the stands. 'A bomb. Quite a sophisticated bomb. And capable of doing considerable damage.'

The camera panned back from the device, then moved out of the truck's interior and along the side of the vehicle. 'But you may wonder,' the voice continued, 'what could be damaged out here. Some trees, the truck itself.' There was a pause. 'Myself. And my associate.'

The front of the truck came into shot. The camera focused on the side window, moving closer until it was possible to discern, through the glass, the figure of a young man in the passenger seat.

At the same moment, there was an anguished shout from somewhere at the front of the stadium. Saranageral looked around frantically, trying to spot Gundalai. There was another, louder shout, a disturbance breaking out at the rear of the giant screens. And then both screens went blank.

'What does the pilot think?' Nergui was staring out across the river. Sam was up there somewhere in the trees, but it was impossible to see what he was doing.

Batzorig caught his breath. Even for one of his youth, it was a hot day to be running uphill. 'There's nowhere immediately on that side of the river, and further up you get into the forest. It would have to be down towards the plain. Probably half a mile or so down there.' He pointed to the flatter land where the river widened and curved towards the steppe.

Nergui looked down towards the spot indicated. 'It's going to lose us time.'

'There's no alternative. The river's pretty deep until you get down to the plain.'

'Okay.' He glanced up towards Doripalam, who was already making his way back up the slope. 'Let's go.'

Minutes later, the helicopter was ferrying them over the river. The pilot shouted back to Nergui and Doripalam. 'He's picked his spot pretty smartly. Not even sure how he got the truck up there. But there's no way I can land within a half mile or so.'

'Get as close as you can,' Nergui said.

Eventually, the pilot pointed towards a flatter area some distance below the edge of the trees. 'That's as close as I can get,' he said.

The landing was perfect, positioned directly in the centre of the selected area. Almost before the engine had stopped, Nergui jumped out and scuttled up the hillside, keeping his head down below the slowing rotors. Doripalam and Batzorig glanced at one another, and then followed.

They caught up with Nergui some distance short of the trees. 'Can you see him?' Doripalam said.

Nergui shook his head. The full width of the valley had opened up to their left and the rocks and the splayed body were below them. 'But we must be close.'

They proceeded cautiously, listening intently for any sound, until they finally heard Sam's voice, declaiming into the microphone. A moment later, they spotted him. He was standing by the front of the vehicle, pointing the camera towards the front window.

'Do we rush him?' Doripalam whispered.

'Too dangerous,' Nergui said. 'We don't know what he's up to. We can't risk running into something we don't understand.'

Doripalam stopped. 'You seem to understand all this better than the rest of us,' he said. 'I want to know what I'm getting into.'

Nergui turned away. At first, Doripalam thought that he was

not going to respond. 'In the helicopter,' he prompted, 'you said it was a fit-up. What did you mean?'

'Wu Sam was a spy,' Nergui said. 'But not quite in the way we'd imagined. He was working for us.'

'For us? What do you mean?'

'A double agent. Supplying information on the Chinese.'

'I don't understand.'

Nergui took a step or two further up the slope, he craned his head as his eyes scanned the trees ahead of them. 'It was the usual hall of mirrors. Wu Sam was a lot more influential than we – than I, that is – had given him credit for. He was a young man, but he had the right Party connections. A rising star in the Chinese intelligence service.'

'And he was working for us?' Doripalam repeated.

'In part. Sam's loyalties were more complex than his masters had realised. His father was a Party official in the capital, but his family on his mother's side were ethnic Mongolians. From occupied territory, as he saw it.'

'He was a traitor,' Doripalam said.

'Nothing so simple. His grandfather had filled him with stories about the great Mongolian empire. About how Genghis Khan was the father, not just of our nation, but also of modern China.' It was a familiar paradox – that China had seen the Mongol empire as its great enemy, but had also appropriated Genghis Khan as one of its founding fathers.

'So who was he working for?'

'Himself, mainly. Or his supposed ideals. He wanted our two nations to become one. To merge Mongolia and China.'

Doripalam was struggling to make sense of this. 'But he regarded Inner Mongolia as occupied territory.'

'And he regarded our territories as occupied too, by the Russians. An occupation of finance and resources, rather than force of arms. But an occupation nonetheless. Given the choice of two evils, he felt that China was the lesser. He wanted a new Mongol empire but knew that, realistically, such an empire would be ruled from Beijing not from Ulaan Bataar.'

'It's insane,' Doripalam said.

'Probably. But they were insane times. No one expected the USSR to collapse like a house of cards, but everyone felt that change was possible. And there were the first democratic protests in China—'

'Quickly crushed,' Doripalam pointed out.

'But these were all straws in the wind. Plenty of people – in the USSR, in China and in our own government – were considering their positions. Working out how to play this to their advantage. Forging alliances that they might call on if the need arose.'

'And Wu Sam?'

'He was a young man with ideals, but also a young man on the make. He knew that if the Soviets pulled out our economy would collapse. And he thought that was his best chance to realise his vision of unification.' Nergui had started to walk slowly up the hill, dropping his voice almost to a whisper. 'He had trained as an academic, specialising in Mongolian history, but he worked as a senior analyst on the Mongolia desk in Beijing. He'd been security cleared, so they saw his expertise as a positive. They encouraged him to build relationships with contacts on our side of the border.'

'He had our agents working for him?'

'Who was working for whom? I'm not sure even those involved really knew. Each side thought they were using the other, with Russia as the common enemy.'

'So who were his contacts?' They were close to the edge of the forest, the westerly sun throwing the shadows of the trees into the interior.

'I don't know the full story,' Nergui said. 'But Wu Sam was a trusted agent. He'd been pushing his masters at home to send him out into the field. He wanted to make contact, to build up his personal allegiances. To start to realise his vision.'

'With official backing?'

'That's not how these things work. Everything is deniable. But they wouldn't have discouraged him if it might bring dividends for them. So he came and made contact. And it didn't go as he'd expected. Perhaps a clash of visions.'

'What happened?'

'He made contact with his most influential source. Each of them trying to use the other. Wu Sam to progress his own ambitions, and his contact – well, he had a different agenda. At best, he was building alliances for the future. At worst – if Russia remained dominant – he might gather some information that would give him some bargaining chips.'

'So potentially a triple agent?'

'A realist. A survivor.' There was something in Nergui's tone that rang alarm bells in Doripalam's mind. 'But Wu Sam didn't like being used. He was a young man, still. Impetuous. And I suspect there were other, more personal factors involved.'

'And you're saying that that was why he was framed? How can you *know* all this, Nergui?'

They stood motionless, whispering in the lowest of voices, their ears straining for any clue to Sam's position.

'I don't know it,' Nergui said. 'Not for sure. I'd begun to get suspicious when we arrested Wu Sam. His response wasn't right. And when I looked at the evidence, it was all just too convenient. There were witnesses in all the right places. So I challenged him.'

'But if he'd been framed, surely he'd be shouting it from the rooftops?'

'We never gave him a chance. And he knew that both countries would want to bury the problem. The best thing he could do was keep his head down and wait to get shipped back home. But his career was over. Even if his masters accepted that the charges were nonsense, they'd see him as a failure, as a security risk. Someone who'd compromised their position.'

'So what did he say when you challenged him?'

'He told me he'd been framed. He wanted me to help him.'

'Help him how?'

'Let him stay. Allow him to rebuild his life and career this side of the border. And in return he'd give me evidence on his contacts – those who'd betrayed our country.'

'Why you?'

'Because he knew that I'd been set up as well. He was no fool. He recognised that I wasn't part of the game. That I didn't know who his contact was.'

'And did you help him?'

Nergui looked back and gazed at the younger man for a moment. 'No,' he said, finally. 'There was nothing I could do.'

'Even though his contact was a traitor?'

'I don't believe the contact gave away anything of real value. He was just wheeling and dealing. That wasn't the issue.'

'So what was?'

There was a look on Nergui's face that Doripalam had never seen before, as if he had unburdened himself of some baggage. He looked more human than Doripalam had ever seen him.

'The issue,' Nergui went on, 'was that, if Wu Sam had been framed for the murders, then he wasn't a killer. And that meant that someone else had murdered those students.'

'The contact?'

'Yes, the contact. Not personally. This was someone with resources to call on. Not a killer.'

'But a realist and survivor.'

'Exactly.'

'So why didn't you do something?'

'Because I'm a realist too. There was nothing I could do, nothing I could prove. I knew better than to try.'

Nergui looked up, his expression suddenly changing, as if he had sensed or heard something. His body tensed, his eyes fixed on the thick woodland ahead of them. But then he said: 'The contact. He was as senior as they come. The chief of the security services. Now your boss and mine. Bakei. The minister.'

He strode forward into the green shade, apparently unmindful of any noise he might be making. And, at that moment, the crack of a gunshot reverberated around the valley slopes.

# CHAPTER TWENTY-EIGHT

She felt suddenly that there was something terribly wrong. There was a disturbance under the large screen, but she could not see what was happening. There were more shouts, and the television crews had shifted their attention away from the screen towards some occurrence at ground level.

Sarangeral grabbed the shoulder of a young man in grey over-alls. 'What's happening?'

'No idea. Some drunk, probably. Don't they realise that some of us have got work to do?'

She pushed past him into the milling crowd, forcing her way forward until the crowd thinned around her, and she found herself in an open space, a few yards from the base of the screens.

The screens flanked a wooden stage which would be used for performances during the festival. Behind the stage, a portable office unit provided a home for the administrative and technical support staff. Its twin wooden doors were closed, and there was no indication that the unit was occupied.

She was reaching forward to see whether the doors were locked when she felt a movement behind her, warm breath on the back of her neck, and a hand clasped firmly around her mouth.

'I think you'd better come inside,' a voice said.

'Shit.' The man was stabbing the remote control with his fore-finger, repeatedly changing channels as if he might make something different appear on screen. He switched back to the state television channel. 'He told me he had all this under control. Where the fuck is it?'

He glared at the other dark-suited men sitting around the room. Suddenly, Tunjin thought, he looked much less in control. The cool arrogance seemed to have evaporated.

'Maybe it's coming,' one of the other men said, with a vague shrug.

The first man stared at him. 'Coming?' he said. 'We are supposed to *be* the news, not second fiddle to some presidential visit to a hole in the ground.' He gestured towards the screen, which was showing images of the president visiting a new mining complex in the south.

Tunjin could only guess at what might be happening. It seemed that their hosts had been expecting some significant coverage on the state television news. Whatever they had been expecting, it was clear that they were disappointed. The state television news was doing what the state television news generally did – giving respectful and unremittingly dull coverage of state affairs.

The museum system provided access to cable television, as well as the limited range of local terrestrial channels, and the man had rapidly flicked through the available selection. But all he had found was the usual mix of imports, Western and Eastern – dramas, soap operas, pop videos, garish talk shows.

The man kicked one of the hard-backed chairs across the room. It bounced off the coffee table, narrowly missing the legs of one of his colleagues, who looked up at his apparent leader. 'So what are you suggesting we do?' he asked.

'I don't know. We're fucked. We need to get a message to him. Find out what's going on. Check that he really has got it under control.' There was an undertone of deep scepticism in his voice. 'You got the number?'

'He said not to contact him. The number wouldn't be operational. He's been swapping SIM cards so no one can track him . . .'

The man walked forward slowly and stood over his colleague. 'You know,' he said, quietly, 'I'm not an idiot. What made you think I might be?'

'I'm only saying.'

'Just give it a try.'

The second man pulled out his mobile phone and keyed in a number. 'Nothing. It's dead.'

The first man was still gazing at the television, which was playing silently on the far side of the room. A female reporter was standing in the Namdaal Stadium, rows of empty seats stretching behind her. The man turned on the volume, and the reporter's voice crashed, initially too loudly, into the room '. . . no cause for concern. But, following the recent spate of so far unresolved incidents in the city, the authorities will be looking to tighten security at this year's festival. Back to you.'

'That was it?' the man said. 'They were there, but – nothing.' He looked back at his colleagues. 'What the fuck is he playing at?'

'I think we cut out losses,' the man on the hard-backed chair said. 'What do we really know about this guy?'

'We know what kind of backing he's got.'

'*Says* he's got.'

The man shook his head. 'No, I saw it.' He glanced at his watch. 'But we're in the shit if it goes wrong, whatever.' He waved his hand towards the minister. 'We have the small matter of our friend here. If we pull out, we need to decide what to do with him and his friends. We give it thirty minutes. If things are still on track, he'll be in touch. Maybe he's playing it some different way.'

'And after thirty minutes?' the other man said.

The man looked round again at the minister, then at Solongo, and finally at Tunjin, his eyes resting on each for several seconds. 'Then you're right,' he said. 'We cut our losses.'

## CHAPTER TWENTY-NINE

For a moment, they could see nothing but the solid hulk of the Land Cruiser. Beyond the trees, the afternoon sun was as dazzling as ever. Here, the thick foliage created an undersea world, textures of green scattered with golden pinpricks of light.

The echoes of the gunshot had died away, and the silence had returned. Nergui peered into the gloom, poised to react at any sign of movement. Doripalam moved silently up behind him. Somewhere behind him, Batzorig was standing, tensely watching.

Nergui moved forward slowly, his feet silent in the bushy grass. It was a little cooler here in the forest shade, but the air was dank and humid.

They were a few yards from the truck when they heard a groan from the other side of the vehicle. Nergui pulled out his handgun and slid cautiously around, feeling the bodywork warm against his hand.

Sam was crouched on the ground, his ungainly stance looking almost comical. His stomach was stained red with blood, an uneven patch spreading down the sleeve of his pale shirt. He held a pistol loosely in his right hand. There was another object – a slim box – grasped firmly in his left.

'Stupid, stupid of me,' Sam said. He smiled up at Nergui, clearly struggling to sustain the expression. 'After all this time.'

For a moment Nergui assumed that Sam had somehow managed to shoot himself. Then he realised that the passenger door of the truck was partially open, a head lolling against the window.

'Put the gun down,' Nergui said. 'You need help.'

'I don't think so, Nergui. Not now I've come this far.'

'What are you going to do?' Nergui said, calmly. 'You can't even drive in that state.'

Sam tried to shrug, though the movement was impeded by his injury. 'We'll see. Maybe you can give me a lift.'

'Maybe we'll have to. Who's in the truck? Odbayar?'

Sam glanced up at the figure half drooping out of the passenger seat. 'Stupid,' he said again. 'I thought I'd left the gun in the back, out of his reach. I should have kept more of an eye on him.'

'He's dead?' Nergui asked.

Sam looked surprised by the question. 'I was trying to get the gun off him. That's when he shot me. I beat him round the head with it.' He raised his left hand, still holding the small box. 'This hand's strong enough. Didn't realise he'd shot me at first. Then it suddenly hit me.'

'You need help,' Nergui said, again.

Sam shook his head. 'Not me,' he said.

'What's this all about?' Nergui asked.

Sam lowered himself back on to the ground, sitting awkwardly. The bloodstain was expanding across his chest. 'You know what it's about, Nergui. You know what happened to me.'

'I know what you told me.'

'But you believed me,' Sam said. 'And you've lived with it ever since.'

Nergui stood motionless, staring at Sam. 'And so have you, no doubt.'

'Every minute of every day. He destroyed me. He destroyed my career. My life'

'You have a career,' Nergui pointed out. 'A very respectable one.'

Sam nodded. 'Back home, they wanted me out of their hair. Not because they thought I was a killer. Nobody believed that. But because I'd compromised their contact. And because I knew too much.' Sam, paused. 'They used me. I was a young man. They took advantage of me. I was supposed to play the game. Just one in a long line.'

Nergui laughed, unexpectedly. 'I don't doubt it,' he said. 'He has a nose for weakness, and he would have exploited yours. But you weren't so innocent. It was a game and you lost.'

Sam nodded. 'I lost. I was shipped home in disgrace. And they shipped me out again. Cultural exchange with the US.' He laughed, mirthlessly.

'Not such a bad outcome.'

'You think that? Removed from my home, my heritage. Shipped off to some liberal New York institution prepared to indulge my worst weaknesses.'

'You're ashamed of yourself,' Nergui said. 'Of your own inclinations.'

'It's rotting society from within,' Sam said. 'Even here.' He gestured up towards Odbayar in the car. 'Look at this one and his – friend. Look at that one down by the river.'

'You killed him,' Nergui said. 'Why? Because he succumbed to your advances, or because he didn't?'

Sam shook his head. 'You don't understand, do you, Nergui? Yes, I have my own weaknesses. I'm only human. But that's a tiny part of all this. I've been working on this for years. Realising the vision that was snatched away from me.'

'Bringing us back into the Chinese fold? But you don't work for the Chinese any more, Sam.'

'You know better than anyone, Nergui. You never leave this game. I've always been on the payroll. Biding my time. Building up my contacts.'

'A sleeper,' Nergui said, his voice sounding dismissive.

'They never told me what to do. But they let me know what they expect of me. I've been watching your country change. Watching the Russians lose their grip. Watching the forces of change come seeping in. Watching the frustration of your people grow because they realise that their government is betraying them, selling them down the river.'

'Waiting for your opportunity?'

'I've been closer than you could imagine, Nergui. I've had people working for me, watching you. I've even watched the fat one. But you're all small beer. Most of all, I've watched him – the one behind all this. I've watched his corrupt power grow. I've seen the people he uses to achieve his ends. I knew that if I offered them the right price they'd betray him just as he betrayed me. Yours is a society on the edge of breakdown. It needs just a tiny spark to light the fuse.'

'So you've been trying to light the fuse?' Nergui said. 'That supposed suicide bomber in the square, that was you? So why have Tunjin shoot him?'

Sam tried to smile again. 'Partly just my ironic joke. Framing your fat friend, just like he would have framed me. But really just stirring up confusion, tension, paranoia. I didn't want to cause mass deaths – my quarrel isn't with your people – but I wanted people to feel they were under siege. It seemed an elegant solution.'

'And the body in the museum?'

'I had three students that I'd encouraged to come over on exchange visits. Young Muslims on the edge of fundamentalism; young men looking for a cause. I wanted to draw attention to them, suggest that they were behind all this, that there was some clandestine battle going on between the forces of Islam and the right-wing nationalists here. I thought the Hulagu story was a neat reference.'

'Perhaps just a little too clever for us,' Nergui said. 'And you killed them like you killed the young man by the river.' He paused. 'And perhaps for similar reasons. One was the supposed suicide bomber. One was the young man in the carpet. The third, I presume, was the young man found in the hotel. He planted the bomb there.'

'He helped me, yes. His body was supposed to be found next to the incendiary device. But the explosion happened before I could organise things properly.'

'You've not been lucky in this, Sam,' Nergui said. 'Or perhaps just not quite as well prepared as you thought.'

'Those were just the preliminaries,' Sam said. 'This is the main act.'

'Kidnapping Odbayar?' Nergui said. 'You selected that hotel because you knew that Odbayar was speaking there. You grabbed him in the confusion.'

'He came willingly,' Sam said. 'We've worked together on this. He thought he was part of the plan. Undermining his father's government to give his type their opportunity.'

'He's a young man,' Nergui said, echoing Sam's earlier words. 'You took advantage of him—'

'Like his father tried to take advantage of me. But this time I've won the game.'

Somewhere behind him Nergui could hear the faint movement of Doripalam's footsteps in the grass as he stepped closer. Otherwise, the silence was almost complete. There was no breath of wind, no sound of birdsong.

Sam rolled backwards, trying to ease his body. It wasn't clear whether or not his chest was still bleeding. The bloodstain covered half his torso, but seemed to have grown no worse.

'So what are you planning to do, Sam?' Nergui asked quietly.

'Revenge,' Sam said, simply. 'And a step towards realising my vision.' He shrugged and gestured off to his right. For the first time, Nergui noticed that the hand-held video camera was lying on the ground, apparently broken. 'Though perhaps not quite as fully as I'd envisaged. The bullet caught the camera. I don't know how much they saw.'

'Saw of what?' Doripalam said. He had been standing just behind Nergui, peering passed him into the interior of the truck. He was pointing towards the explosive device tucked behind the front seats. 'You showed the people in the stadium that?'

'I hope so,' Sam said. 'I wanted them to realise what was at stake. I wanted them to see that I was prepared to blow it all up. Genghis Khan's supposed birthplace – only of symbolic value, I suppose, but then, in this environment, what else matters? And of course the son of their security minister. Even if they don't know the full reason why he has to die.'

'You said all that to the camera?' Doripalam asked, thinking about the potential effect of all this on the crowd, on the wider television audience. On a volatile population.

'I don't know how much they heard. It doesn't matter. They'll see the chaos soon enough.'

'The chaos?' Doripalam felt a chill run down his back.

Sam leaned back, and for a second it genuinely looked as if his injury was no longer troubling him. 'The chaos,' he agreed. 'We have a bomb here, which will kill Odbayar and destroy the surrounding area. And I have a bomb placed in the Naadam Stadium. It will detonate before the festival – as I say, my quarrel is not with the ordinary people, so I wanted as few casualties as possible – but I think the symbolism will be clear. Oh, and I have placed another bomb in the national museum, in the new exhibition. More symbolism, you see.'

He paused, and a smile played across his face. 'But more than symbolism. You see, I've made two other small arrangements. First, with a little help from his supposed friends, I ensured that the minister would be there. And second,' he turned and nodded his head towards Doripalam. 'I arranged for your wife to be there. It seemed appropriate, and not only for her role in turning the mighty Mongol empire into a tawdry commercial sideshow.' His smile was full now. 'You see,' he said. 'I really have been keeping tabs on you.'

Doripalam's head was reeling with the horrifying absurdity of all this, and he was hardly able to comprehend the notion that Solongo might somehow be caught up in it. 'But why?' he said. 'Why do this?'

'Destroying so we can rebuild.' He paused, grimacing, the wound now beginning to trouble him. 'People will believe your country is under siege. Nothing is safe. Not your security minister. Not your most precious historical artefacts. Not your festivals. And no one will believe the government. You shot down a suicide bomber and suppressed it. Muslim fundamentalists are killed, but this does not reach your media.' He gasped again, clearly in pain now. 'You have tried to suppress the chaos but you have only made it worse.'

Nergui smiled faintly. 'And you will destroy to rebuild.'

'Your government is corrupt. You have betrayed your history. People will see that. We will be celebrating this anniversary, this great anniversary, by bringing down this crumbling edifice. Then we can restore the Mongol empire, the legacy of the great Genghis Khan.' He fell back slightly.

'And who will do this restoration?' Nergui asked. 'You?'

Sam's face was pale. He appeared scarcely capable even of speaking more. 'I don't matter,' he said. 'I am just setting the scene for others.'

'Your masters at home?' Nergui said. 'You think they will rebuild the empire here?'

For a second, Sam seemed unable to respond. 'They are building their own empire. The future lies with them. I am just doing what I can to hasten the day.'

He was virtually horizontal now, his body splayed back on the grass. The blood covered half of his chest, his shirt stained crimson. The pistol was held loosely in his hand, no longer a threat.

Nergui started to move forward. But Sam held up his right hand, which still clutched the thin black box. 'Stay there,' he said. 'This is a remote control device. I've primed it already. As long as I stay holding it, nothing happens. If I let go or loosen my grip . . .' he looked up at the car. 'So if you shoot me or try to stop me, well, you know what will happen.'

Nergui took another half step forward, his eyes fixed on the other man's face. 'Give me the device. We can get Odbayar out of the car. We can stop all this.'

'And what?' Sam said. 'This is what I've lived for. To be a catalyst.'

'A catalyst for what?' Nergui said. 'You said it yourself. For chaos.'

Sam shook his head. 'No. For change. To bring back what we once had. To start all over again.'

Nergui moved forward another step. But again Sam held up his hand, pointing the remote control device towards the car. 'It's up to you, Nergui. It's all over now. For me. For Odbayar. Probably for you and your colleagues, if you come any closer. But I want you to live with your failure. With what will come after all this.'

For the first time, Nergui took his eyes off Sam's crumpled body and glanced behind him at Doripalam and Batzorig. 'Get back, you two. Get back and get down. Now.'

Doripalam hesitated momentarily. 'You too, Nergui. There's nothing to be gained.'

Nergui shook his head and remained motionless, as Doripalam and Batzorig began to back away down the slope. There was a low hillock twenty or so yards down the hillside, a row of trees. The only place where they might have a chance, Doripalam thought. He was moving more quickly now, Batzorig just ahead of him.

Behind them, Nergui turned back to face Sam. He was slumped back, his eyes tightly closed, his mouth half open as though he was about to scream in pain. Even as Nergui focused again on the supine body, Sam's right hand opened and the remote control slipped softly from his fingers.

The man looked at his watch for perhaps the fourth time in as many minutes. 'This is no good,' he said. 'He made us promises. We're holding the fucking minister of security against his will. This was supposed to make us all rich. I say we cut our losses now.' He pulled a handgun from his pocket. 'No one knows we're here. We can just get rid of the evidence and leave.'

'Get rid of the evidence?'

The man walked forward slowly and placed the gun against the minister's neck. 'The evidence,' he repeated, calmly.

The minister looked up at him. He was, Tunjin thought, remarkably calm. If they were prepared to shoot the minister, they were unlikely to have any qualms about doing the same to himself or Solongo. Tunjin looked across at her. Her face carried the same frozen, glassy-eyed expression that he had noted when he had first entered the room.

Was there anything he could do? At most, he could cause some sort of distraction, maybe create an opportunity for Solongo to escape. There was little chance of saving himself or the minister. But there might be an outside chance of getting Solongo out of this mess. The main question, looking at her blank expression, was whether she had any inclination to help herself.

The man was pressing the barrel of the gun harder against the minister's neck. Finally, the minister looked up. 'You haven't got the nerve,' he said. 'You're a small-time thug. All you're good for is doing my dirty work. You're out of your depth. Miles out of your depth.'

'Shut up, old man. You're finished, don't you realise that?'

Despite the pressure of the gun barrel, the minister managed to twist his head, regarding the man with an expression of contempt. 'Maybe. But you've never even got started. You're just a loser. And it looks to me as if you've just lost again.'

If Tunjin was going to try something, he had to do it now. Inches from where he was sitting, there was a small stone statuette, which had been adapted as a pen-holder. With a speed and dexterity that belied his massive frame, Tunjin suddenly moved, sweeping up the statuette into his hand and throwing himself forward. The statuette made contact with the gunman's head, the stone striking his skull with a dull thump.

The man fell forward instantly, stumbling against the coffee-table. He tried to regain his balance, before toppling sideways, landing awkwardly between the table and one of the sofas. The gun flew out of his hand and, with a perfectly timed movement, Tunjin caught it. Before anyone else could react, he grabbed the man's collar and pulled him back, slamming the barrel of the gun hard against his temple. Then he looked up.

One of the dark-suited men on the sofa reached into his jacket, but Tunjin pressed the gun harder against the head of the man in front of him. 'You know,' he said, 'it's less than two days since I shot a man down in the middle of Sukh Bataar Square. Just over a year ago, I shot and killed the most powerful man in Mongolia. Do you want me to make it three in a row?'

The man on the sofa slowly withdrew his hand from his pocket.

But then he smiled at Tunjin. 'That was very impressive,' he said. 'But if you think we give a fuck about what happens to him, you're wrong. Shoot him in the head for all we care.'

Tunjin had been watching the hand that had been reaching into the jacket. But the man raised his other hand, and there was already a handgun in it. Still smiling, the man placed the gun barrel, very gently, against Solongo's neck. 'On the other hand,' he said, 'I'm willing to bet that you might give a fuck about what I do to this fine lady here. So put that gun down, you fat bastard, and we can start this all over again.'

At first, Sarangarel tried to resist, but her captor was too strong. If she were able to scream, someone in the arena might hear her, but a hand was clasped firmly across her mouth. She was dragged backwards, her feet stumbling on the sandy ground.

A moment later, the figure behind her pulled open one of the doors of the office unit and thrust her inside. She staggered, only just retaining her balance, and fell against one of the desks.

Gundalai was sitting on the floor in front of her. His face was bruised and there was blood dripping from an ugly-looking graze across his cheek. To his left, there was a man, dressed in Western-style jeans and white tee-shirt, holding a pistol.

She turned and regarded her own assailant. He was similarly dressed; anonymous gear for anonymous-looking men. Probably late twenties or early thirties, clean-shaven, neat hair. Nothing memorable about them at all.

'Found her outside,' the man behind her said. 'Being nosy.'

'This is getting too deep,' the other man said. 'I didn't expect this. Just a technical job. Get in, get it running, get out. There wasn't supposed to be anyone in here.'

'There wasn't,' the other man said. 'Till this guy turned up.'

Gundalai sat sullenly at the man's feet. 'Where is he?' he said.

The man stared at him for a moment. 'You don't give up, do you?' he said. 'I thought I'd beaten some sense into you.'

'The man on the screen. I need to find him. I need to find the man in the car.' His voice rose, a note of panic crackling just under the surface.

'We're just here to do a job,' the man said. 'Get the satellite link working, and get it up on to those screens. Technicians, that's all.'

'Pretty violent technicians,' Sarangeral pointed out.

The man shrugged. 'I didn't start it. He attacked me. We were expecting this to be a little more low-key.'

Sarangeral gestured towards Gundalai. 'It was his friend, in the car.'

'In the film, you mean?'

She suddenly realised how little these men knew about what they were involved in. 'It wasn't a film,' she said. 'Do you know what it is?'

'A protest. Against the government selling off the mineral rights. That's what we were told.' He frowned, sensing her disbelief. 'Some sort of propaganda. We were going to do it at the festival itself, but then it got brought forward, thank God. It would have been a nightmare to get in here while the festival was on.' He paused, as though trying to take in what was going on. 'But that's all we were supposed to do. We had a portable satellite receiver, a designated channel we were supposed to use, and then we were supposed to show – well, whatever it was. I thought it would be a link to a live protest somewhere. I didn't understand what was being shown, some sort of mock-up perhaps.'

She shook her head. 'No. It was live. And real.'

'Real?' She could see that he was only just taking in the significance of what she was saying. 'You mean the body . . . ?'

'The body,' she said, 'and the bomb.'

The man looked across at his colleague, who was pacing up and down behind Sarangeral. 'We've been set up,' he said. 'Well and truly fucking set up.'

'Who asked you to do this?'

'We don't know. Friends of friends of friends. We went on a few anti-government protests. Someone heard we had the technical skills. You know how it is.'

'Someone must have told you what was required.'

'A middle man,' he said. 'No one we knew. Gave us instructions, provided the equipment. Promised us everything would be ready. Gave us a down-payment. More money when it was done.'

She had no idea whether to believe him, but the story made sense. 'So you don't know where all that was taking place? You don't know where the man in the car is?'

The man looked between her and Gundalai. 'I'm sorry,' he said. 'I don't know anything except what we were told.' Sarangarel could see that there was something else in his mind.

'What else?'

'I don't know. The guy who paid us. He said we should do our job here and then get out. That there'd be something even more spectacular to follow.'

She stared at him, thinking about the man who had appeared on the screens. About Odbayar in the car, and the device strapped to the seats behind him. About the stadium and the impending festival.

'Oh, my sweet heaven,' she said.

# CHAPTER THIRTY

Doripalam held his breath, waiting for the force of the explosion to hit them. His body was flat to the ground, but he had little confidence that the gentle gradient would offer any real protection. He breathed in the sweet scent of the grass, his ears straining for any clue as to what was happening. He moved his head slightly, squinting to his right. Batzorig was in a similar posture, his body spreadeagled further along the same hollow.

Doripalam had no idea how much time had elapsed. Batzorig had raised his head and was looking back at him quizzically. At last Doripalam risked peering out.

Nothing had changed. The Land Cruiser was in the same position. There was no sign of Nergui or Wu Sam. Other than the occasional ripple of birdsong, the silence remained complete.

'Anything?' Batzorig whispered.

Doripalam shook his head. He was beginning to feel embarrassed at their hurried retreat down the slope. But who knew what was happening up there?

The question was answered almost immediately. There was a bang from somewhere on the other side of the Land Cruiser. Doripalam started and got his head down, but realised almost immediately that the sound was simply that of a car door being slammed.

He peered over the edge of the bank. Nergui emerged from behind the vehicle, his face set in a grimace of exertion. It took

Doripalam a moment to realise that he was dragging something –
a body, Nergui's arms wrapped under its armpits, its feet scraping
along the ground.

'Come and give me a hand,' Nergui said. 'It's safe for the moment.
At least, I think it is.'

Doripalam had assumed that the body was Sam's, but as he
drew closer he realised that it was the young man. Odbayar. He
grabbed the dragging feet, helping Nergui move the body further
down the slope. Batzorig arrived a second later and began to help
with Odbayar's upper body.

'We need to get as far down the slope as we can,' Nergui gasped,
the exertion making him breathless. 'I don't know how much time
we've got.'

Nergui was still stumbling down backwards, the young man's
torso clutched in his linked arms. For the first time, Doripalam
noticed that between Nergui's clasped palms there was a slim black
box. The remote control.

Nergui looked back over his shoulder. 'If we can get to those
rocks, that should be okay.'

Some fifty metres away there was a small cluster of trees
surrounding three large rocks, dumped at the riverside by some
prehistoric glacier.

They zigzagged awkwardly down the uneven slope. Finally, they
reached the shelter of the rocks and placed the limp body safely
on the ground, the three men slumping down beside it.

Nergui held up the remote control. 'Keep your heads down,' he
said. 'I'm holding this down so it shouldn't detonate the device,
but I don't know what—'

As if on cue, his words were cut short by a sudden roar from
above. For a second, Doripalam was surprised by the sound –
more gentle than he might have expected. But then the force of
the blast struck them, a physical wind that buffeted them heavily
even in the lee of the rocks, a shattering noise too loud to describe.
Some large object – presumably part of the truck – flew over their
heads and landed with a crash beyond them. Doripalam kept his

head down, his face buried in his arms, feeling something scattering against his hair and back.

The noise of the explosion terminated as abruptly as it had begun, its echoes lost in the open terrain. Doripalam's ears were still ringing, and he looked around confusedly. Nergui was crouched over Odbayar's body, protecting the young man from the falling debris. Batzorig was staring at a line of blood welling up on the back of his hand.

'Are you okay?' Doripalam asked.

Batzorig looked up, then back down at his hand. 'I think so,' he said, finally. 'It's just a scratch. A piece of glass.' His expression suggested that the minor injury had brought home how lucky they had been.

Doripalam looked across at Nergui. 'How's Odbayar?' He presumed that they would not have risked their lives if the young man was already dead.

'I think he's okay. He's been sedated, but he seems to be breathing all right.'

'What happened up there?' Doripalam gestured up towards where the Land Cruiser had been. Above them, under the canopy of the trees, a cloud of smoke had gathered, dimming further the thin sunlight that filtered through the leaves.

'Sam was haemorrhaging blood pretty fast from that wound. Assuming that he was telling the truth about this,' Nergui held the remote control device loosely between his fingers, 'I was concerned about what might happen if he lost consciousness.'

'And did he?'

'I got as close as I could. He was in no state to shoot me. When I saw his eyes starting to close I threw myself forward and hoped that I'd be in time to grab this before he lost his grip on it.'

'Which you did.'

Nergui looked down at the slim device. 'There was a moment when I thought I'd lost it. Or there was some delay on the device detonating. I don't know.'

'But you had time to get Odbayar out?'

'Only just.' Nergui shuddered, as if the shock was only just hitting him. He peered over the top of the rocks. 'I think we can assume that, one way or another, we don't need to worry about Sam any more.'

There was little left of the Land Cruiser. Part of the chassis, with an axle and one of the wheels visible, was standing in the clearing, and there were twists of jagged metal scattered around it, thick smoke guttering into the air. It was impossible to see what remained of Sam's supine body.

'We should go and see,' Doripalam said. 'He might still be alive.'

Nergui shook his head. 'I don't know how much fuel was on board, but we might have another explosion on our hands. There's nothing we can do for Sam. He was beyond help a long time ago.'

'This is madness,' Doripalam said. 'What was he trying to achieve?'

'What he said,' Nergui said. 'To be a catalyst. And he may still succeed.'

Doripalam stared at him. His relief at their escape had been so overwhelming that he had forgotten what Sam had been saying. 'You really think he's planted other bombs?'

'He's done enough already to suggest that we shouldn't underestimate him.' Nergui glanced back up the hill, his eyes following the rising plumes of smoke. 'The worst of it is that he wasn't even the professional he thought he was. He was a bungling, incompetent madman. He was probably promoted above his level of ability even when he first came here. But that made him even more dangerous.'

'Because you don't know what he was capable of?'

'With professionals, you know there'll be some limits. With Sam – well, who knows?' He reached into his pocket and pulled out his mobile. 'We need to get the stadium and the museum cleared and searched.'

Doripalam's mind was racing back over what Sam had said. 'He said that Solongo was there,' he said. 'Why would he want to involve Solongo in this? To get revenge over me? He doesn't even know who I am.'

'No,' Nergui said. His head was down, as he thumbed through the call on his mobile phone. 'But he does know who Solongo is.'

Tunjin was still standing over the unconscious man, the gun held to his head, trying to work out some further option, anything he might be able to do to retrieve the situation. The man on the sofa had the barrel of his own pistol pressed firmly against Solongo's neck. As though by instinct, the minister had edged further away from both of them.

'Okay,' Tunjin said, finally. He carefully placed the gun on the desk, away from the reach of any of the dark-suited men. He wasn't going to make it too easy for them.

'Very smart,' the man on the sofa nodded. 'Okay, now get back from my friend there. Go back to your seat. And we'll have a think about what we do next.' He smiled. 'Or what some of us do next. I think we can probably forget about him.' He gestured towards the man still slumped on the polished wooden floor. 'I think the best thing we can do is cut our losses and go.' He paused. 'Taking this lady with us for insurance purposes.'

'I don't think so,' the minister said, unexpectedly. 'Not just yet, anyway.'

The man twisted, still holding the gun against Solongo's skin. 'You're going to stop us?'

'Possibly with a little help from my associate over there.' He looked across at Tunjin. 'Pick up that gun again, will you?'

Tunjin looked bewilderedly from the minister back to the man with the gun. 'I'm not sure that's a good idea.'

'I think it's an excellent idea,' the minister said.

The man on the sofa shook his head. 'It's quite simple. If he picks up that gun, I shoot her.'

The minister shrugged. 'So shoot her.'

Tunjin stared, horrified, at the grey-haired old man. Was this just more posturing? Calling the gunman's bluff on the assumption he wouldn't have the nerve to go through with it?

'If you shoot her,' the minister went on, 'then you've shot your bargaining counter. You can only shoot her once.'

Tunijn didn't know whether Solongo was really taking all this in. She still seemed to be in a daze, her eyes fixed on some point in the middle-distance. There was no sign that she realised that her life was being debated.

The gunman himself looked baffled. He clearly hadn't expected events to move in this direction. He shook his head. 'So then you become my hostage,' he said.

The minister nodded. 'And you think I care whether you shoot me or not? And I'm sure he doesn't.' He gestured towards Tunjin. 'Pick up the gun,' he said again to Tunjin.

There was a faint look of panic now in the gunman's eyes. Somehow his authority was slipping away. He looked across at Tunjin and pressed the gun hard into Solongo's neck. For the first time, she showed some reaction, grimacing slightly and trying to pull away. 'If you pick it up, she dies.'

Tunjin made no move. Perhaps the minister's judgement was sound, but Tunjin didn't feel inclined to take the risk. Not on Solongo's behalf, at least.

'If he doesn't pick it up, I will,' the minister said, making a motion to rise from the sofa.

'I'm telling you—'

The minister turned, his eyes unblinking. 'And I've told you. Go ahead and shoot, if you must.' He climbed slowly to his feet.

By now, there was no doubt about the gunman's panic. He looked wildly from the minister to Solongo, uncertain what to do next. At last, he jumped to his feet, pulling Solongo along with him, the gun now pressed to her temple. 'I'm telling you,' he said, 'if you make one more move, I'm pulling the trigger.'

'So do it,' the minister said, moving calmly across to the table.

The gunman stared at him, beads of sweat trickling down his forehead. He looked down once at Solongo, hesitated for a second, and then finally, frantically, he squeezed his forefinger around the trigger and pulled.

'What are you talking about?'

Sarangeral pushed past the two men. 'You saw what was on screen,' she said. 'He was talking about some kind of explosive device.'

'But that was – well, wherever that was being transmitted from. And we don't know if any of that was real.'

She shook her head. 'That was for real. Whether the bomb itself was real – well, who knows? But I wouldn't want to take the risk, would you?'

'So what are you saying?' the man said. 'That he's planted a bomb here as well?'

'Well, if he told you that there was going to be something else here . . .'

'This whole thing is crazy. I just want out of it.'

'Then go,' Sarangeral said, dismissively. It was clear that she was going to get no support from them. It was equally clear, as she gazed down at Gundalai's battered, forlorn body, that help wouldn't be forthcoming from that direction either. The two men stood awkwardly for a moment, uncertain what to do. Finally, they looked at each other, and one of them stepped forward to pick up a tool-box from the desk. 'Look,' he said, 'if there was anything we could do—'

'Just go,' she said. The man shrugged and pushed open the office door, his colleague following closely behind. In the doorway, the second man stopped, looking back. 'Good luck,' he said. Then the door swung closed and they were gone.

She stood silently, despair sweeping over her. If there really was some kind of explosive device in the stadium, how long did she have? It might be that any bomb would be timed to detonate at the height of the festival, when the stands would be thronged with spectators.

But the two men had been told to make themselves scarce. If anything was going to happen, it would happen soon.

She pulled out her mobile. Nergui, she thought. Everything had been happening too quickly, and, since she'd left the messages earlier, it hadn't occurred to her to try to contact him again. She had no idea why he'd been present on the large screen, but it might mean that he'd discovered something.

She keyed in his number and waited anxiously, but the call cut straight to his voicemail. 'Nergui,' she said. 'It's Sarangeral. I'm at the Naadam Stadium and I need to talk urgently. Call me back as soon as you can.'

She thumbed off the phone and looked down at Gundalai. 'How are you feeling?'

'Battered,' he said. 'But okay.'

'Good. We've got to get this place evacuated. We need to find out who's in charge.'

She was turning towards the door as the blast struck. The sound was extraordinary, a roar louder than any thunderclap, ripping through her body. The frail unit shook around them, and Sarangeral flung herself to the ground, rolling under one of the desks, wrapping her arms around her knees as she tried to compress her body into the smallest possible space. Across the room, she could see Gundalai scrambling into a corner, his face ashen with fear.

The unit's windows crashed inwards, and something unseen hit the floor behind her. She could hear shouting and screaming, a shrill repeated cry of panic. And then everything stopped and, in the aftermath of the explosion, there was a sudden, unnerving silence.

# CHAPTER THIRTY-ONE

'What's going on here, Nergui?' Doripalam said. 'How could Solongo be involved in something like this?'

They were airborne again, heading back towards the capital. The sun was low, the hills and mountains throwing elongated shadows across the steppe. Batzorig had been left behind, co-ordinating the arrival of the local force who would be dealing with the two bodies and the aftermath of the explosion. Doripalam had asked for the whole area to be cordoned off and treated as a crime scene and had ordered post-mortem examinations of the bodies, but with no real expectation that this would reveal anything worth knowing.

His mind was in turmoil with thoughts of Solongo at the museum. Nergui had already asked Doripalam to send a team there, and had arranged for two of his own men, including Lambaa, to join them. 'We need to be careful,' he said. 'We don't know what might be happening.' The comment was scarcely comforting.

A further team had been deployed to the Naadam Stadium, with arrangements for the arena to be evacuated as discreetly as possible. Bomb disposal expertise was being sought from the military to attend at both locations.

It was all they could do, but the lengthy journey back to the capital remained a deep frustration. For all Sam's incompetence, his plan had been cleverly orchestrated. Whatever they had done, they would have been in the wrong place.

'Tell me, Nergui,' he said again. 'Where does Solongo fit into this?'

Nergui turned from the window. 'When we were talking before, about Wu Sam, I said that his contact here was the head of the security services.'

'Our friend Bakei. The minister.'

'Exactly. But that wasn't the whole truth. He was only an agent.'

'An agent for whom?'

Far below, Doripalam could make out the white scattered dots of a nomadic camp, the shifting patterns of their livestock. 'For a senior Party member,' Nergui said. 'Someone in a position of great influence and authority. Someone who was more powerful than the government he supposedly served.'

It took Doripalam a moment to comprehend what Nergui was saying. 'Solongo's father,' he said. 'Battulga.'

'I fear so.'

Doripalam shook his head, struggling to take this in. 'You're saying he was a traitor?'

'That's a strong word,' Nergui said. 'He was like Bakei. A survivor. Ready to bend with the wind, whichever way it might choose to blow.'

'But he was selling secrets to the Chinese?'

'Nothing so crude. I think he was in negotiation with them. He had found in Bakei a kindred spirit, but someone who had a more active vision of what he wanted to achieve. I don't think Battulga wanted to initiate anything. He just wanted to ensure he wasn't caught out by whatever future might emerge. He pulled the strings and provided the resources from above, but was quite happy to let someone else make the running. Bakei was a lot more self-interested.'

'I'm not sure I understand,' Doripalam said. Sometimes he suspected that, faced with the world that Nergui seemed to inhabit, he would never understand.

'Battulga was quite happy for someone to do his dirty work for him. He was even happier to find someone with the will and energy to initiate that dirty work for themselves. He didn't need to tell Bakei what to do. Bakei was already out there, working towards his own warped vision of Mongolian–Chinese – well, what shall we call it? Co-operation? Co-existence? All Battulga had to do was watch from on high, give the strings a small tweak where necessary, provide some resources from time to time. But always staying detached, making sure that, if the wind blew in a different direction, it was Bakei who would be left exposed.'

'But Bakei's a smart operator. He wouldn't have allowed that to happen.'

'They're all smart operators. They're all busy playing games.'

'So what do you think happened?'

'What I said before – there was some falling out between Wu Sam and Bakei. I think Bakei was accustomed to making use of the young men who were sent here over the border. One of the perks of the job, you might say, supplied by his paymasters over the border.'

'The minister? That great advocate of family values?'

'He's a politician,' Nergui said, as if that fact would explain any shortcoming. There are things that he has to – if you'll pardon the pun – espouse. But I think that Wu Sam was not the first young man he propositioned. And perhaps not the first to refuse him.'

'You think that's what this was all about?'

'Bruised pride? No, more than that. Once Wu Sam rejected Bakei's advances, he was a loose cannon. He knew too much. Bakei was smart enough to know that the Chinese were happy to feed this appetite of his because it made him more controllable. His behaviour was still illegal in those days. It was another lever they could pull if they needed to. But I don't think Bakei was too worried, so long as the arrangement was mutual – he no doubt had plenty of levers of his own. But Wu Sam wasn't part of that game. There was a real risk that he might take some unilateral action to expose Bakei.'

'So he planted a dead body? It sounds an extreme way of dealing with it. Wouldn't it have been quicker and cleaner just to have arranged for Wu Sam to be deported?'

'That's what I thought,' Nergui said. 'It was what made me

dismiss Wu Sam's story. I thought it was a last ditch attempt to save his own skin.' He looked directly at Doripalam. 'But it depends, doesn't it? If Wu Sam wasn't responsible for the murder of those two students, then someone else was. As I say, Wu Sam may not have been the first to reject Bakei's advances.'

'You think that Bakei . . . ?'

'I've no evidence,' Nergui said. 'Nothing that would stand up in a court of law, anyway. I don't think Bakei killed them himself. But he was – he is – a powerful and ruthless man. I don't know whether the other two students were also Chinese operatives, or just local victims of Bakei's tastes. But I suspect that he was already being blackmailed. He saw this as an opportunity to clear up a mess on his own doorstep, and destroy Wu Sam at the same time. Perhaps it was also a warning to the Chinese that he wasn't someone they should mess with. And I think there was something more. I think that Wu Sam had discovered that Battulga was involved.'

'You said that Battulga was careful to keep his distance.'

'He tried to. But that's the story through all this. Clever people playing games. Thinking they're the ones pulling the strings. And the strings get tangled.'

'And if Wu Sam had threatened to expose Battulga?'

'That would have been disastrous. Battulga was a powerful man. More powerful than many people realised. He was never a public figure – never president or even a minister but the most powerful people never were. He was a key fixer for a generation or more. He kept things on the road, did the deals. The people who stood up in the Great Hural or on the podiums were just figureheads – people who could make the speeches, look good. But it was Battulga, and the apparatchiks behind him, who did the real work. He kept the balance, made sure that no faction became too powerful. And he didn't seek the limelight himself. Qualities that made him immensely influential.'

Doripalam had met Battulga only a few times, in his early days of courting Solongo. The old man had been impressive, even though Doripalam hadn't much liked him and had assumed that this sentiment was largely reciprocated. Battulga's behaviour towards Doripalam had barely even risen to disdain. He seemed hardly to have noticed his daughter's young suitor. Doripalam had occasionally wondered about how Battulga would have reacted to a request for his permission to marry Solongo. The question had never arisen because the old man had died before Doripalam had proposed, but Doripalam found it hard to imagine that an impoverished young policeman would have been welcomed with open arms.

'Bakei was a protégé to him,' Nergui went on. 'Battulga saw Bakei becoming an equally safe pair of hands, someone who could do his dirty work for him and, I think, towards the end, Battulga was losing his touch a little.'

'You mean the drinking?' Doripalam said.

'There were rumours,' Nergui said. 'Perhaps more than rumours within the family?'

Doripalam shook his head. 'I never saw anything. But, well, I put two and two together.'

'I think Bakei was protecting him more and more towards the end,' Nergui said. 'Wu Sam would have been the final straw. If it had emerged that Battulga was trying to do some deal with China, however good his intentions, that would have been all the ammunition his enemies needed. And, in those uncertain times, if Battulga had fallen the result would have been chaos. The turmoil came soon enough, in any case, once the Russians pulled out.'

'So Bakei framed Wu Sam to protect Battulga?'

'And himself. He was in a position to do it, as head of the security services. I don't know about the murders, but it wouldn't have been difficult for him to find someone to take the necessary steps.'

'But it would have left Battulga in his debt?'

'Again, nothing would have been explicit. But Battulga would have pulled some appropriate strings. The minister is very able. He would have risen to his current eminence in any case. But it does no harm to have a helping hand.'

'But where does all this fit in?' Doripalam said. 'Wu Sam's return? Whatever it is that's been going on?' He paused. 'Solongo?'

'I've been trying to put it all together,' Nergui said. 'We heard what Wu Sam said. We have a confluence of interests here, everyone playing their own little game and hoping to come out on top. Sam wanting his own revenge. His masters at home hoping to destabilise our government.'

'You really think the Chinese would do that?'

'There are some who, quite publicly, speak of our country becoming part of the greater Chinese People's Republic. They would not show their hand openly – not unless things changed significantly between our counties – but they would not discourage actions which might move things in their desired direction. I've no doubt that they funded Wu Sam's escapade, however indirectly. But we will never be able to prove it.'

'And the minister?'

'I think the minister was very neatly set up,' Nergui said. 'He has been building bridges with the Chinese – just as, in fairness, he has with the Koreans and the Russians and the Americans and any other nation that might consider investing. But there've been rumours about his links with China for some time. His involvement in the free-trade zone in the south, for example, supposedly building economic links with the Chinese. There were those – and, ironically, his son was one who articulated this very publicly – who thought that all this was a betrayal. I suspect that the betrayal might have been more than merely economic. I think he might have been happy to go along with a plot to destabilise our society, to cause panic and confusion, to suggest some sort of terrorist threat.'

'To allow the Chinese to invade?' It sounded like madness to Doripalam.

'Not quite,' Nergui said. 'But if there was a perceived threat to us – the increasing possibility of terrorism, some kind of historically justified jihad, increasing civil unrest among our own people – it would give the Chinese an excuse to strengthen the military on our borders. It would give them the excuse to take over the jointly administered free-trade areas. Over time, it might give them the excuse to extend their influence to some of the mineral-rich areas over the border. And – well, you know how it goes.'

'But why would the minister have become involved with Wu Sam, after all their history?'

'Because he didn't know it was Wu Sam. He thought he was playing his own games. Wu Sam thought he was pulling the strings. And the truth probably was that both were being manipulated.'

'So what happens now?'

'That's what worries me. Wu Sam told us about a bomb in the Naadam Stadium, a bomb in the museum. I don't think he was bluffing. By now, the minister must know that he's been set up, but he won't know how much this has exposed.'

'And Solongo?' Doripalam said.

'I think initially just Wu Sam's black sense of humour,' Nergui said. 'As he said, he kept close tabs on things while he was in exile. He followed the remainder of Battulga's career, and kept an eye on his family. He probably saw the opportunity for some potential mischief when Solongo married you and you took up your current role, particularly as I'm sure he was keeping tabs on me too. And I imagine that when Solongo took on the job at the museum that was too perfect an opportunity to miss.'

'Opportunity?'

'He'd have got the minister there on some ruse or other – Bakei is used to dealing with dubious characters, so I don't imagine it was too difficult. And then I think that, at some point in his broadcast, Wu Sam would have confronted him with the daughter of his old associate and then revealed that his own son was a potential victim. If Wu Sam had succeeded in broadcasting all that stuff to the stadium, with a television crew present, he'd have got immediate nationwide coverage.'

Doripalam let out a low whistle. 'But what about Odbayar?'

'Bakei and Odbayar were effectively lured into the same trap. For Odbayar, the whole thing was a glorified stunt. Like his father, he thought he was playing the part of an unwilling victim, supposedly kidnapped because he was Bakei's son. He thought that this, combined with a small campaign of non-lethal smoke bombs – which he understood had been planted at his own rally – would be enough to raise questions about national security and put the nationalist cause back on the agenda.'

'Sounds pretty naïve,' Doripalam said. 'Though I suppose it would have severely embarrassed his father, if nothing else.'

'Make of that what you will,' Nergui said. 'Sam's objective wasn't that different. Just a lot more deadly and a lot more cynical. He was always planning to kill Odbayar – that was his real revenge on Bakei.'

'But how did Sam think he'd escape? Even if he'd been able to keep himself and the truck undamaged, if Odbayar's death had been witnessed on TV, we'd surely have been able to apprehend Sam before he could leave the country.'

'Who knows?' Nergui said. 'It's a big empty country. Perhaps he originally intended to take the bomb and Odbayar away from the truck, so he'd be in a position to drive off afterwards. Perhaps he'd arranged to be picked up by air from somewhere in our borders – he could probably have managed it before we'd got our act together. Maybe he changed all his plans once he discovered we were on our way up here.' Nergui paused. 'But I think actually he never meant to leave. I think he always intended to die up here. I think this was always his grand finale – leaving his chaotic legacy behind him.'

Doripalam stared out at the passing landscape. Far off in the distance, ahead of them, he could make out the dark hazy smudge of the capital. The elongated shadow of the aircraft ran far ahead of them, as if as eager as Doripalam to be reaching their destination. 'So what will the minister do now?'

'He must know that it's all over, that he can't cover it up or bluff his way out of it. He's a smart man, and he's not prone to panic. But he doesn't have many options. I imagine that his strategy will be to try to negotiate his way out, and call in some favours from the Chinese. I don't see any alternative now for him but a one-way trip to Beijing.'

'But what has he got to negotiate with?'

Nergui looked at him, his face blank. 'He doesn't have much,' he said, finally. 'But he has Solongo.'

Tunjin closed his eyes, his body braced for the inevitable explosion.

But instead there was a gentle click and then silence. Tunjin opened his eyes. Nothing had changed. The man on the sofa was still holding the gun to Solongo's head. Her eyes were closed too, her face scrunched in terrified anticipation. Finally, after what felt to Tunjin like minutes, she opened her eyes and peered round at the gunman. He pulled the gun back and moved to take another shot.

'Don't bother,' the minister said. 'It's not loaded.'

The man stared at the gun, then up at the minister. 'What do you mean?'

The minister gestured to Tunjin. 'Pick up that gun,' he barked. 'Quickly, before any of these fools makes a move.'

Tunjin grasped the pistol from the desk, pointing it towards the man on the sofa. The third man started to make a move, but Tunjin waved the gun towards him. The man's hand paused, halfway to his jacket.

The minister shook his head. 'Don't worry,' he said. 'Yours isn't loaded either. Just that one.' He waved his hand towards Tunjin, and then reached into his own pocket. 'I'm not an idiot,' he said, pulling out a handgun of his own. 'I thought I'd set this up with your friend over there.' He pointed to the unconscious man still lying stretched out on the carpet. 'Though it looks as if I was the one being set up.' A look of vague regret passed across his face. 'It's always the way. You can't do everything yourself, but you can't trust anyone else to do it.' He appeared to be in a momentary reverie, but his arm jerked sharply towards the man on the sofa who was reaching into his own jacket pocket. 'If you have some other weapon in there, I'd advise you not to go for it. Bring it out slowly and throw it on the table.'

The man scowled and did as instructed. The minister leaned forward, took the second gun and climbed to his feet. 'You see, it was all play-acting. I was supposed to have been taken hostage while chaos exploded on the streets. I would be battered and maltreated, but would ultimately emerge the hero. Ready to take control of a confused and besieged nation. All set up nicely. But my own condition was that, other than your friend over there, I didn't want any of you really to be armed. He couldn't tell you what was going on if you were to play your parts realistically. But I've seen too many operations go wrong because some idiot panics and starts shooting.' He moved out from between the sofas, and bowed gently towards Solongo. 'I'm very sorry, my dear, that we had to go through that little charade. It must have been very distressing for you.'

'Bastard,' she murmured softly. It was not clear whether the word was addressed to the man sitting next to her or to the minister.

'Now,' the minister said, 'the fact that nothing appeared on the television news suggests that these carefully laid plans have gone astray. And it's difficult to see how that might have happened without leaving my own position exposed.' He paused. 'I might be able to bluff my way out of things. It wouldn't be the first time. But I think I'd be better just making my exit.'

Tunjin was still standing, his gun pointing towards the man on the high-backed chair, wondering what to do. Everything he'd understood had been turned on its head. He could try to stop the minister, but that would just put them back at the mercy of this bunch of thugs. But if he allowed the minister to go – well, he didn't know what the implications might be.

The minister was now standing behind Solongo. 'You really don't need to worry,' he said to the dark-suited men. 'I really have no interest in you. I'm very happy for you to just slink back into whatever dark alleys you emerged from. I need a few minutes to get out of here, and then you can just quietly slip away and put this down to experience.' There was a smile playing across his face now, as if he had been mentally working through the options and had settled on his next step. 'As for you . . .' He turned and gestured with the gun towards Tunjin. 'Thank you for your assistance. I'd advise you not to try anything, unless you feel like trying to bring these gentlemen to justice single-handedly. You would be wise not to try to stop me, but just in case you should decide to be foolish . . .'

He leaned forward, grabbed Solongo's wrist and pulled her up in front of him, his gun now pressed to the side of her head. 'I really am sorry,' he said, apparently speaking now to Solongo. 'I really shouldn't be treating you like this, knowing who you are.' Her eyes flickered sideways as she tried to look at him, her fear giving way to bafflement. 'But I suppose that just makes it fitting. Perhaps it's finally a way for your father to pay me back, after all these years. I'm sure he'd enjoy the irony.'

He backed towards the door, still holding Solongo. 'Let's say fifteen minutes,' he said. 'I want none of you to move for fifteen minutes. That's all the time I'll need. If any of you emerges before then, I'll have no hesitation in shooting this young lady.'

It was some minutes before Sarangeral realised that the silence was far from complete. Slowly, she was able to pick out sounds. In the distance, someone screaming. Another person barking instructions. Behind all that, the sound of a siren.

She raised her head. Gundalai was lying motionless, his body curled into a foetal position. For a moment, she thought he was injured. But then he raised his head and stared at her, his eyes wide.

'Are you okay?' For some reason, she found herself talking in a whisper.

'I think so. Some of the glass caught me, but I don't think I was cut.'

She dragged herself to a sitting position, and for the first time it occurred to her to worry about her own well-being. Her light-coloured suit was filthy, covered with dust from the explosion and the office unit floor. But otherwise she seemed to have suffered no adverse effects. She pulled herself to her feet and moved cautiously to the window. There was no telling whether the initial explosion would be the precursor to further blasts.

The stage obscured the stadium, so she could not see what kind of state the arena might be in. Through the shattered glass, she could hear the external noises more clearly – shouting, some panicked, some more authoritative. The sound of sirens was growing louder, but still some distance away.

'What shall we do?' Gundalai said from behind her. 'Stay here or try to get out?'

'My instinct's to get out, but that might not be the smartest move if there are other bombs.'

Gundalai was brushing the broken glass from his clothes. 'On the other hand, if there are other bombs, staying here might not be the smartest move either.'

'Shall we risk it, then?'

She opened the door of the unit, peering into the sunlight. With Gundalai close behind her, she stepped cautiously out. Overall, the impact of the explosion had been much less severe than she had envisaged. A small part of one of the nearby stands had been damaged, leaving a gaping black hole and a scattering of broken wood. In the midst of the festival, the blast would have killed or injured numerous spectators. Today Sarangeral could see no sign of any serious casualties.

There were few people left in the arena, other than one or two onlookers by the main entrance. Even as she watched, a uniformed official began to move them further back.

'Come on,' she said to Gundalai. 'Let's get over there.'

They jogged briskly across to the wide main entrance. The man in uniform looked at them quizzically and seemed about to speak, but they moved quickly past him into the stadium car park. There were clusters of people standing at the far end of the concreted area. The sound of sirens was loud in the air, and she assumed that police and ambulances would be arriving shortly.

The atmosphere was strangely calm, very different from the panic she had feared. As they crossed the car park, she saw some casualties being dealt with by the arena's own medical staff. One young man was sitting on the ground, ashen-faced, a nurse applying a dressing to his cheek. Another was lying, conscious but motionless, on a hastily-strewn blanket, his leg being bandaged by another medic. Both looked shocked, but not seriously injured.

Beyond these individuals, a thicker crowd had gathered. This was largely comprised of those who had been evacuated from the stadium, although they were being joined by a growing number of curious passers-by. The atmosphere seemed one of enthusiastic interest, rather than fear or panic. Most seemed to have assumed that the worst risks had passed, or at least that they were now at a safe distance. It was an assumption that caused Sarangerel some unease. If there were more bombs, why should they have been planted in the stadium itself? Wasn't it possible that a device could have been hidden out here, perhaps in one of the cars or trucks?

She looked around, in the hope of spying someone in authority. Finally, she pulled out her mobile and keyed in Nergui's number again. As before, she was transferred immediately to his voicemail. She quickly left a message, succinctly informing Nergui about the explosion, reassuring him, if he should be concerned, that both she and Gundalai were unharmed.

The sirens were loud now, just a street or two away.

It suddenly occurred to her to think about the approaching emergency crews. She had heard the first siren only seconds after the explosion had died away. How could the emergency services have been summoned so promptly?

The question was answered almost immediately. A line of marked police cars, sirens wailing, appeared in convoy on the main road that ran along the north side of the stadium grounds. Two screamed to a halt, scattering dust, and parked nose to tail, blocking the two lanes of the road. A third pulled up beside them, covering, though not yet blocking, the entrance to the stadium itself. Whatever their purpose might be, the drivers were not primarily interested in the bombing.

It was a few minutes before an ambulance arrived, pulling up beside the small group of casualties. The two ambulance men helped the injured into the back of the vehicle, then the ambulance turned and sped back along the concrete track towards the main road, the siren recommencing its distinctive whoop.

As it disappeared, the third police car moved into position, fully blocking the entrance to the stadium, preventing any other vehicle from entering or leaving. The main road – the key route from the city centre to the south-west and the international airport – was completely closed.

A battered truck approached the roadblock from outside the city. A uniformed policeman climbed languidly from one of the cars and leaned down to speak to the driver. A moment later, the truck did a rapid U-turn and sped back down the road, as the driver either abandoned his planned trip or sought some alternative route.

It was clear that no traffic would be coming past this point in the immediate future. Something was happening, Sarangeral thought, and its focus was not the explosion. The explosion had been a symptom, and these people were waiting for the cause.

'Move!'

Solongo stumbled slightly as he drove her down the wide marble steps in the museum's main hall. She thought she was going to fall, but she regained her balance and continued down the remaining stairs, aware of the steely grip of his hand on her wrist, the gun barrel inches from her head.

She had been in a daze since she had been bundled into the back of the car. Perhaps partly the merciful effects of the morning's alcohol, deadening her sensitivities. But more likely it was shock. She had always been aware of the risks that Doripalam faced, but she had never seriously believed that those risks might extend to herself.

And now she found herself stumbling through a deserted museum, a gun at her head, dragged by an apparent madman. A madman all the more terrifying because his demeanour seemed utterly calm and in control. She had recognised the elderly man as soon as they thrust her into the room at the museum, not only from the television but she had seen him, from time to time, at functions that Doripalam had attended in his official capacity. But she could make no sense of this terrifying turn of events.

The clattering sound of their footsteps echoed around the empty halls of the galleries, deserted now in the late afternoon. The minister was moving faster, his eyes fixed determinedly on the side exit ahead of them. Sunlight from the high windows barely illuminated the gloomy interior. They passed silent eyeless statues, cluttered displays, the inevitable image of Genghis Khan staring disapprovingly down from a giant poster.

Finally, they reached the exit. The door was wedged open, and the minister pulled it back and thrust her out into the dazzling daylight.

She wondered then if there might be a momentary opportunity to escape, to pull away and seek help in the main thoroughfares, but the door opened on to a narrow side street, and an official-looking car was waiting a few metres away. As the minister emerged into the daylight, she heard the engine start.

The minister grasped her wrist more tightly and whispered harshly in her ears. 'Act normally. I'm going to put the gun in my pocket, but it'll still be aimed at you and I won't hesitate to use it. On you and on the driver, if necessary.'

She stared at him for a moment, wondering what normal might mean in these circumstances. Then she turned and made her way, a few steps in front of him, to the car.

The uniformed driver was presumably one of the official ministerial pool, who had brought the minister down here and had been waiting to take him on to his next assignment. It was difficult not to be impressed by Bakei's confidence, she thought. He had come to the museum on this clandestine errand, and yet had no hesitation in using ministerial facilities. And why not? He would have aroused much less suspicion by making full use of the trappings of his office than if he had tried to skulk around on his own.

Her only immediate hope was that the driver would respond to her presence in some way that might provide her with an opportunity for escape. But no doubt official drivers were encouraged to turn a blind eye to anything they didn't understand, particularly if their boss turned up unexpectedly accompanied by a member of the opposite sex.

Sure enough, the driver offered no reaction, but simply climbed out to open the rear doors. Solongo looked at his face for a moment, hoping that a silent spark of telepathy might somehow jump between them. But he simply gazed blankly back at her, his eyes shaded by his peaked cap.

'The airport, next,' the minister said. 'As quickly as you can.'

Solongo climbed reluctantly into the rear seat. Bakei followed her, allowing her to glimpse the hard round barrel of the gun jutting against the material of his jacket.

Moments later, they were back in the main streets, maintaining a steady but rapid pace through the late-afternoon traffic around the central square. The driver knew what he was doing, timing perfectly the changes from lane to lane. They were unlikely to encounter any significant delays.

She had no idea what the minister's plan might be. His behaviour suggested desperation, a last throw of the dice. Perhaps a long-planned exit. It was clear that something had gone badly wrong. The minister looked like the kind of man who would have prepared, very carefully, for just such a contingency.

They sped down the western side of Sukh Bataar Square, heading south on to Chingisin Orgön Chölöö, the main avenue that swept south and then west past Nairamdal Park, then the Naadam Stadium and out towards the international airport. Already the city centre was behind them, the faded greenery of the park stretching off to their left, the squat tower of the Bayangol Hotel to their right. She could see couples walking in the warm weekend sunshine, clusters of old men draped in the familiar heavy *dels* despite the summer heat, children running across to the play area or down to the lake. She felt as if she could just wind down the car windows and call out to them, telling them what was happening. But the car sped by, and crossed the junction with Teeverchidin Gudamj, the road along the southern edge of the park.

As they passed, something caught her eye, and she looked at the minister to see if he had spotted it. He was staring straight ahead, his eyes fixed on the hazy surface of the road, as if he was already envisaging his own escape.

She risked a glance over her shoulder. She had been correct, even though she had only glimpsed the movement in the periphery of her vision. There were two parked police cars, one on each side of the junction. As she watched, the cars pulled foward, now blocking the two carriageways of the road behind them.

At the same instant, the minister let out a sudden grunt of anger. She followed his gaze and looked through the windscreen. The road stretched out ahead, converging lines disappearing into the haze of the summer sunshine. The dark shape of the Naadam Stadium rose to their left.

At first, everything was lost in the shimmering heat. Then she saw what the minister had already seen. A flickering line of blue lights across the road. A roadblock.

The minister leaned forward and tapped the driver on the shoulder. 'Looks as if the road's closed for some reason. Something to do with the festival, maybe. Turn round and we'll find another way through.' His voice sounded remarkably calm, as if this was just another minor irritation in his busy day.

The driver shook his head. 'I don't think so, sir. I think we'll just carry on, if it's all the same to you.'

The minister's mouth opened but, for a second, no sound emerged. 'What the hell do you think . . . ?' But then something about the driver's tone struck him. 'You're not one of the usual drivers, are you?' he said.

'Not really, sir. But don't worry, I'm fully trained.' The driver placed his foot more heavily on the accelerator and the car picked up speed towards the roadblock. 'I'd advise you to throw the gun into the front of the car, sir. Gently, if you please. We don't want it going off accidently.'

The minister was staring at him, his face white. 'Who the hell are you to—'

'I can understand your irritation, sir,' the driver went on. 'I'd appreciate it if you don't make it any more difficult than it needs to be.'

The minister was twisting his head, trying to spot another escape route. They were now only a few hundred metres from the line of police cars. There was a cluster of officers, some armed, crouched behind their vehicles.

'I'll be damned if I'll let you tell me what to do,' Bakei said. He had pulled the pistol free of his jacket pocket. For a moment, he waved it in the air, as if unsure how to deploy it. Then he thrust it firmly into the driver's neck. 'Turn back,' he said, calmly.

'No point,' the driver said, his voice equally steady. He had slowed slightly, but there had been no other obvious effect on his driving. 'Look back. There's another block already in place.' He paused and added, sadly: 'I really hoped that you'd respond more sensibly, sir.'

'Okay, pull off here. Towards the stadium.' Although the main roads into the stadium area had already been blocked by police cars ahead of them, there were a couple of dirt tracks leading into the open ground alongside the arena. It was difficult to see where they might lead, other than towards the car park and the arena itself. But it was clear that there were no other options.

'If you insist, sir,' the driver said. Solongo was becoming absurdly irritated by his insistent use of the word 'sir'. She couldn't work out if it was ironic or simply habit, but it seemed inappropriate in the circumstances.

The driver twisted the wheel hard to the left, and they pulled off the main road, bumped uncomfortably across the broad gully, and then hit the dirt track towards the stadium. The car bounced in the air, throwing the minister and Solongo back into their seats. Ahead of them, she could see that the men around the police cars had noted the change of direction. The car that had been covering the main entrance to the stadium turned and began to head along the entry road, clearly intending to intercept them.

The driver glanced back over his shoulder, smiling broadly. 'Where now, sir?' he said.

Nergui's body was twisted so that he could peer out at the cityscape spread out before them. From here, the capital looked small, its scattering of old and new buildings dwarfed by the sheer scale of the surrounding steppe. The sun was low behind them, and the taller buildings threw the heart of the city into rich shadow. Ahead of them, he could make out the green expanse of Nairamdal Park, the dull vermillion of the lake, the land stretching out to the Naadam Stadium.

Doripalam was listening to a radio message that the pilot had relayed through the headphones. 'They think they've spotted him. The roadblock's in place. And they've confirmed the message you picked up from Sarangarel. There was an explosion in the stadium, but there don't seem to be any serious casualties.'

'We can be thankful for small mercies, then. I just hope there are no more devices in there. As for the minister, well, I don't know how he'll react,' Nergui said. 'He's not one of life's losers. He won't come quietly as long as he thinks there's some chance of getting out of this.'

'Don't you think he'll try to bluff his way out?'

'He knows it's too late for that. I imagine he's had an exit route planned for a long time.' Nergui paused. 'There's a private jet based at the airport. Belongs to one of the entrepreneurs for whom the minister's done a few favours over the years. I've had a man out there keeping an eye on it. The pilot took a call about thirty minutes ago and has been organising permission to take off. Destination Beijing. All the formalities cleared.'

'By the minister?'

'By the minister. I can't even block it. No one can, unless we escalate it up to the prime minister or president. But I don't think that will be necessary.'

'What about your man in the car?' Doripalam said. 'Does he know what he's doing?'

'Lambaa?' Nergui shrugged. 'There's no one better. Present company possibly excepted.' He looked across at Doripalam. 'You know how it is,' he said. 'You more than anyone. There are no guarantees. But Lambaa will do what he can. And he can do more than most.'

'And this is assuming Solongo is still with him.'

'I think we can reasonably assume that, from what Tunjin told us. She's the only bargaining chip he's got.'

'That's very reassuring, Nergui.'

'Not my strong point, reassurance, as you know. But it does mean that there's every reason for Bakei to keep her alive for as long as possible.'

'You're right about reassurance not being your strong point,' Doripalam said. 'But I see what you mean.' He hoped that he sounded calmer than he was feeling. He had always admired Nergui's professional detachment, but now he began to suspect that the older man's lack of emotion verged on the inhuman. Doripalam could feel panic welling up inside him, as he struggled to maintain the composure that he knew his job demanded.

The call from Tunjin had reached them just a few minutes earlier, confirming all they had feared and more. Tunjin himself was safe. He had half-expected some trouble with the dark-suited men, but the two who were still standing were interested only in saving their own skins. The man on the floor had been left behind, still semi-conscious. He needed medical help, and they seemed quite happy to leave that to Tunjin. Tunjin had called police HQ, discovered that Doripalam was in transit with Nergui, and then called Nergui's mobile with the news about the minister and Solongo. In the end, he didn't know whether he had helped protect Solongo or had simply driven her into deeper trouble. But now he had to depend on Doripalam and Nergui to get her out of it.

A similar thought was running through Doripalam's mind as the helicopter hovered high above the Naadam Stadium. He could see the line of police cars far below, the flickering of blue lights along the roadblock. A scattering of trucks and cars in the stadium car park. And then, to the north of the stadium, a single car heading at speed over the rough terrain, trailing clouds of dust. Another car was speeding from the main road to intercept it.

Doripalam felt an icy clutch of fear in his stomach. 'I hope your man Lambaa knows what he's doing.' Doripalam said. 'We need to be down there.'

'On the other side of the stadium, I think. We don't want to spook the minister into doing something stupid.'

Doripalam's own instinct was to get close to the speeding car, but he recognised that Nergui was right. 'Or something even more stupid.'

There was a movement from the front seat. Odbayar had been slumped against the side of the cockpit, still sleeping, for the whole journey. Now, finally, he was stirring. His eyes opened and he stared around, frantically, trying to work out where he was. 'What's happening?' he said. 'Sam?' Then he paused, and a look of bafflement ran across his face. 'He must have drugged me – I don't know . . .' The puzzled expression was replaced by one of panic.

Nergui leaned forward and rested a hand on him. 'Don't worry. You're safe. We're police officers. We're bringing you back to the city, that's all.' He glanced across at Doripalam, clearly wondering how much more to say.

Odbayar seemed to be at least momentarily calmed by Nergui's words. He leaned forward and peered out of the window. 'That's the Naadam Stadium,' he said. 'What's going on down there?'

Nergui looked across at Doripalam, perhaps in the hope that the younger man would take up the story. But Doripalam's gaze was fixed on the ground below, his mind wrestling with how they could intercept Bakei.

Nergui leaned forward again, speaking softly into his headset. 'It's a long story,' he said. 'But I think I should tell you it before we touch down. You need to know.'

Sarangeral had been watching the roadblock, wondering what was happening. Clearly something serious, she thought, looking at the lines of armed police crouched behind the cars, until finally the gathering crowd was moved back behind some hurriedly erected barriers.

It was then that she had received the return call from Nergui. He explained briefly his and Doripalam's position, his voice metallic through the helicopter's radio.

'You're coming here?' she said.

'You can probably see us by now,' Nergui had pointed out. She could hear the throbbing of the engine down the line but could not, as yet, discern its real-life counterpart. But then she saw a small black dot appear in the northern sky, a sudden glitter as the rotors caught the rays of the lowering sun.

'But keep well back,' Nergui had said. 'If the minister's heading in that direction, he'll be pretty desperate.'

It sounded absurd, she thought. The avuncular elderly man she had seen so often on the television screen, now fleeing with Solongo as a hostage.

'What about Odbayar?' she had asked, glancing across at Gundalai who was gazing at her anxiously.

'He's fine,' Nergui said.

She nodded to Gundalai, smiling, and watched an answering joyous smile spread across his face.

'Try and keep him that way, won't you?' she said, as Nergui cut the connection.

★

'So where do you suggest we go?' Lambaa said, struggling with the steering wheel as the car bounced on the uneven ground. Solongo noticed that he had finally given up on the 'sir'.

The minister peered out of the rear window, then turned back to look at Lambaa. 'Just keep going,' he said. 'Get to the stadium, and we'll take it from there.'

'With respect,' Lambaa said, 'there must be an easier solution. With someone of your status, it must be possible to concoct some sort of deal. Nobody's going to want this to come out.'

'That's what you think, is it?' the minister said. 'It might have been true once but not today. There are too many people who want to destroy me.' It was amazing, Solongo thought, that even in these circumstances, the politician's rhetoric and self-regard still came to the fore. 'They don't want a quiet deal, knifing me in the back and shipping me silently into exile. They'll want to bring me down with as much noise as possible. They don't just want to destroy me. They want to destroy the government. Our democracy.'

Solongo struggled to reconcile the minister's impassioned espousal of democracy with the gun that was pressed firmly into Lambaa's neck.

They were close to the stadium now. The police car that had been moving to intercept them had paused, fifty yards ahead, the driver waiting to see what would happen next.

'So what are we proposing to do?' Lambaa asked calmly.

'Get close to the stadium. Over there. Then stop.'

'If you say so.' He pulled the wheel to the left, slowing as they reached the shadow of the arena. 'This do?'

'Perfect,' Bakei said. He leaned back in the rear seat, the gun still inches away from Lambaa's neck.

Lambaa turned off the engine, and glanced back over his shoulder. 'So what now?'

'Now we stay here,' the minister said. He laughed, unexpectedly. 'It's only just occurred to me that it's the safest place. I know these cars. Bullet-proof. Blast-proof. Pretty much impenetrable from the outside so long as you keep it locked. Designed to protect the likes of me. Ironic, isn't it?' He smiled. 'So I can just sit here and negotiate with those people out there until they let me through. This is going to be easier than I thought.' He pressed the gun harder into Lambaa's neck. 'You'd better give your colleagues a call to break the good news.'

The helicopter hovered briefly over the stadium, and then began to descend, aiming for a clear space in the car park on the opposite side from where the minister's car had come to a halt.

Nergui had completed his summary of the events that had brought them all to this point. Odbayar was blank-faced, looking like an overwhelmed teenager rather than the demagogue who had paced the stage at the previous night's rally. It was difficult to tell what affected him more – his betrayal by his supposed political ally, Sam Yung, or the revelations of his own father's more substantial treachery. He had the air of a young man who had had all his illusions stripped away at once.

'So what's going to happen?' he said, finally. 'To my father, I mean.'

'I think that depends on him,' Nergui said. 'There would have been a time when someone like him would have been allowed a quiet exit.'

'Handed a revolver, you mean?' Odbayar said, bitterly.

'Maybe. Or, more likely, a one-way ticket to Beijing or Washington, whichever was appropriate. But I fear those days are gone. One of the disadvantages of democracy; we're held to account.'

Odbayar gazed back at him with an air of deep cynicism. 'When it suits, yes. Democracy always seems to be a convenient excuse.'

'Not to me,' Nergui said. 'I tend to find it deeply inconvenient. But necessary. As to what will happen to your father – well, if he's arrested, he'll no doubt be tried.'

'But you don't think he'll be arrested.'

'It's not his style. He wants to be the one in control.' He paused. 'Whatever the cost.'

'It sounds like a variant on the loaded revolver,' Odbayar observed.

'Maybe. He'll do his best to find a way out of this, but if that fails – well, as I say, he'll try to keep control.' Odbayar opened his mouth to speak, but Nergui interrupted. 'And you should know, before you say anything else, that he may have a strong hand.' He gestured towards Doripalam. 'We understand he has a hostage. My colleague's wife.'

Odbayar turned and stared at Doripalam. 'Your wife? I didn't realise . . .' He stopped. 'I'm really sorry,' he said, as though the fault was his own. Then he added, with sudden vehemence: 'The stupid *fucking* idiot.'

'What do you want me to say?' Lambaa asked. His voice carried the unhurried nonchalance of someone seeking directions.

The minister pressed the gun barrel into the back of Lambaa's neck. Solongo watched the whitening of the skin around the grey metal. 'Just tell them what's happening. And what I want.'

'And what do you want?'

The minister glared at him for a second, rattled by Lambaa's calmness, unsure whether Lambaa knew something he didn't. 'A safe passage through the roadblock to the airport. And then to be allowed to leave the country unhindered. That's all.'

'It doesn't sound a lot,' Lambaa said, 'but they might object anyway.'

'Just tell them.'

Lambaa shrugged, as if absolving himself of any responsibility for the minister's actions, and then reached forward to pick up his mobile from the passenger seat.

The movement was so quick that Solongo hardly saw it. In one elegant turn, Lambaa spun in his seat, pulled his head away from the gun barrel, grabbed Bakei's wrist in both his hands, and twisted it hard. The minister let out a high-pitched scream of agony and dropped the pistol. It fell neatly into Lambaa's waiting hand, and Lambaa jammed the gun into the side of the minister's startled face.

Lambaa was still holding the old man's wrist with his right hand. He twisted the wrist again, watching the minister writhe in pain.

'Now this time I really do suggest you sit still,' Lambaa said. 'Because if you don't I'll blow your fucking head off.' He reached round with his free hand and pressed a button on the dash. 'That's it, Solongo. Get out of the car. Go across to the police, as quickly as you can.'

For a second, he thought she was too bewildered to follow his instruction. Then she shook her head, still staring at the minister. Finally, as if suddenly released from shackles, she drew back her hand and struck him in the face with her closed fist. The minister emitted another shrill shriek and collapsed forward, clutching a bleeding nose.

Lambaa smiled gently at Solongo. 'Very good. But I think you'd really better get out now. I don't want to have to arrest you as well.'

She smiled back at him, suddenly looking relaxed, as though the punch had been cathartic, then opened the door and stepped out into the warm late-afternoon sunshine.

Lambaa watched as she made her way, with increasing speed, across towards the police. 'Now,' he said to Bakei, 'we need to get you out of here.' He pushed open his own door and climbed out, keeping the pistol trained through the doorway.

Holding the gun steady, he began to open the rear door. But this time the minister was too quick. He rolled backwards and frantically pushed at the door on the far side of the vehicle. Forcing it open, he staggered out and ran, weaving, towards the stadium.

Lambaa cursed his own complacency, and then aimed the gun across the roof of the car. He could have brought him down easily enough, but he hesitated. He was unsure of the protocol of gunning down a government minister, particularly one who had not yet even been arrested, much less brought to trial or convicted. He certainly knew that it was unlikely to play well in the private media.

On the other hand, he suspected that there were few who would share his reticence in circumstances like these.

'He's all right, though?' Gundalai said. 'He's really all right?'

'He's on the helicopter. Nergui didn't say very much, but, yes, he's fine.'

'I want to see him, then,' Gundalai said. 'I *need* to see him.' He sounded like a small child demanding some treat from a reluctant parent.

'It won't be long,' she said, aware that she was already allowing herself to slip into that parental role.

'I know,' he said, 'it's just that I want to be sure.'

'It won't be long,' she repeated. 'Nergui said we should stay well back. It could be dangerous out there.' Even as she said the words, she realised that she had made a mistake.

'That's what I mean,' Gundalai said. 'Odbayar's safe for the moment, but anything could happen.'

'Nergui's there,' Sarangarel pointed out. The words sounded reassuring to her, but she was conscious that they would carry little weight with Gundalai. 'He'll make sure that Odbayar's safe. There's nothing more we can do.'

'That's your generation's mantra, isn't it?' Gundalai said. 'There's nothing more we can do. That's why people like Odbayar do what they do. Because they believe there is something we can do. Instead of just wringing our hands.'

She realised there was little point in arguing. In a way, he was right; her generation was complacent. Unlike some, they hadn't had to fight for their freedom. It had just been thrust upon them. And now, perhaps, they were allowing the potential to slip away. Standing by, while politicians did deals, selling off the past, mortgaging the future. Odbayar's idealism, however misguided, was perhaps something to be cherished.

She turned, preparing to offer some conciliatory word to Gundalai. But he was already gone. He was twenty or thirty yards away, running furiously across the concrete, his scrawny limbs jerking awkwardly.

She opened her mouth to call him back, but it was too late. And perhaps he could do something. Or, at least, perhaps he should be allowed to try.

Lambaa's hesitation was enough to allow the minister time to reach the corner of the stadium. He flung himself round the building, aware that at any moment he might be struck by a bullet.

Beyond the stadium, there was an open field. A helicopter, which he had watched descending as they had sped across the open land, was standing two hundred metres away. There was a single police car parked near the main entrance to the arena, but no other sign of life.

It was all over, he thought. It really was all over. While he had still been in the car, he could delude himself that he might somehow manoeuvre his way out of this. But now there was no chance. Now, there was likely to be only one way out.

He fumbled in his jacket pocket, checking to see whether the key to that particular exit was still there. His fingers touched the cold metal of the second gun, the one he had taken to the museum with him. Then it had been his insurance polcy. Now, it was his last resort.

He was almost at the main entrance to the stadium when something caught his eye, a flicker of movement in his peripheral vision. He slowed his run slightly and turned to look. A young man had been running from the far side of the car park, initially heading for the helicopter. His progress had been hindered by the still-spinning rotors, and he had hesitated momentarily, then continued running to his left, avoiding the blades but trying to attract the attention of whoever was in the aircraft.

The minister watched the young man, now only a short distance away. He looked familiar. They had met somewhere, sometime. Maybe a friend of Odbayar's.

The thought of his son stopped the minister in his tracks. He had long ago ceased to think of himself as a family man – his wife long dead, his son a grown-up political embarrassment, both in any case little more than public-relations appendages. The neat nuclear family that had been expected of the senior Party official, and that had been expected no less of the elected politician he had subsequently become.

But his son was a real person. A good person, probably, if the minister had had any idea of what that might really mean. An idealist. Someone far removed from his own opportunistic pragmatism.

It was as if the young man had been sent to him – another innocent who might provide his passage home.

The minister paused by the stadium entrance, and then called and waved. The young man turned, clearly baffled as to who was calling him. He saw Bakei standing, still breathless, in the shadow of the arena.

It was clear that the young man had recognised him, and for a second Bakei thought he might have misjudged the situation. Perhaps this was just another plain-clothes police officer. Perhaps he had inadvertently handed himself in.

But the young man's expression was not that of someone about to effect an arrest. He looked angry, anxious.

'Where is he?' he shouted, across the expanse of concrete.

The minister had no idea what the young man was talking about, but he could already see distant movement across the car park. Police cars moving into position. The helicopter's blades had slowed now, too, and at any moment the young man's attention might revert to his original objective.

'Come here,' the minister called, 'and I'll show you.'

Odbayar, staring blankly from the window of the helicopter, spotted him first.

'There,' he said. 'That's Gundalai.'

Nergui stared past him, out across the sunlit concrete, towards the shade of the stadium. 'Your friend?' he asked.

Odbayar looked back, momentarily baffled as to how Nergui should have known Gundalai.

'We met him,' Nergui explained. 'He was very concerned about your whereabouts.'

'I—' Odbayar stopped, clearly at a loss for words. 'But what's he doing here?'

'He's here looking for you,' Nergui said. 'The more immediate question is what he's doing over there?' He glanced back at Doripalam. 'I told Sarangeral to keep well back.'

'Let's hope she has,' Doripalam said, his own thoughts still fixed on his wife, anxiety grawing at him.

'In any case,' Nergui said, 'I think we have a situation here. Look.'

There had been some kind of scuffle outside, Doripalam could see now. The young man – presumably Gundalai, though it was impossible to see – had moved towards the stadium, and had been grabbed by another figure. It took Doripalam a moment or two to adjust his eyes to the relative gloom of the stadium precincts. Then, his throat suddenly dry, he muttered 'Bakei?' His mind was reeling, wondering what had happened to Solongo.

Nergui nodded. 'I fear so. I think duty calls.' He gestured to the pilot, who opened the side doors. In a moment, Nergui was out on the concrete, Doripalam behind him.

'You should stay here,' Nergui said to Odbayar, who was also climbing out.

Odbayar shook his head, firmly. 'Not if it really is Gundalai. I've let him down too often.'

Nergui gazed at him for a moment, then nodded. 'Okay.' He glanced at Doripalam. 'Let's go.'

He looked familiar, Gundalai thought. He had definitely seen the elderly man before somewhere. He associated him with something important – some sort of celebrity, someone on television.

It was only as he drew close that Gundalai suddenly knew the answer, and by then it was too late. The elderly man was pointing a pistol steadily towards him. 'I think you had better stop there,' the man said calmly.

Gundalai stopped, his heart pounding both from the exertion and his growing fear. The minister of security. Odbayar's father. They had met face to face only once, at some semi-official party. Odbayar had introduced them, with an unprecedented expression of embarrassment. The minister had shaken his hand – the contact could scarcely have been briefer – and then turned away. The look on his face had not even been disdain, just uninterest.

He seemed more interested now, though, and there was a suggestion in his eyes that he recalled Gundalai after all. That would be a politician's gift. Perfect recall of anyone who might vote for him.

Gundalai glanced over his shoulder towards the helicopter. The rotors had stopped, but there was no sign of anyone emerging.

'That way,' Bakei said, gesturing towards the main entrance to the stadium. 'We'll see if we can buy a little time. You might be my ticket out of here after all.' He was smiling now, but the smile was anything but reassuring.

Gundalai began to walk forward, wondering whether he should make a move against the minister. After all, he must have forty years on the old man. But he didn't have the gun. Youth and fitness were unlikely to count for much compared with one squeeze of that trigger.

The arena was deserted following the earlier evacuation. Gundalai could feel the presence of the minister behind him, the gun barrel inches from his back.

He risked one more glance over his shoulder. There was activity around the helicopter, the doors opening, though Gundalai could not see who was emerging.

'Keep going,' Bakei said quietly from behind. 'Over there by the stage.'

Gundalai shuffled forward into the sunlit arena, waves of heat rising from the sand. Suddenly, absurdly, he felt like a performer, the focus of attention for a non-existent crowd. About to put on the show of his life.

'What's he up to in there?' Odbayar said from behind them, a faint note of hysteria in his voice.

'I don't think he wants to discuss politics,' Doripalam said grimly. He looked back at the young man. 'Look, I know how you're feeling.' He paused, feeling suddenly breathless. They had so far received no news of Solongo, though the unexpected appearance of the minister was a sign that there had been some development. Some development, he thought. The usual neutral police language. 'But please keep back. It won't help anyone if we don't approach this calmly.' His words sounded hollow even to himself.

At the entrance to the stadium, Nergui and Doripalam paused, peering into the vast empty space. The minister and Gundalai were some twenty yards away, close to the raised wooden stage. The minister was standing close behind the young man, holding the gun barrel to his head.

'Minister,' Nergui called, his voice echoing round the empty stands. Then, in a different tone, 'Bakei.'

The minister looked up and a momentary look of surprise crossed his face. 'Nergui,' he called back. 'It would be you. You've known all along.'

Nergui walked forward into the brilliant sunlight. 'I suspected,' he said. Then he seemed to think for a moment. 'No, you're right. I suppose I knew.'

'Then you're as guilty as I am, Nergui. You're a traitor, too. You've done my dirty work for years.'

Nergui's face was blank as ever. 'I've done many people's dirty work. It's my job. And it's my job to prevent it becoming too dirty.' He paused, as though a thought had struck him. 'I respected your good intentions,' he said. 'At the time.'

The minister laughed. 'We all had good intentions,' he said. 'At the time.'

'It doesn't need to be like this, Bakei.'

'You're not a fool, Nergui, and neither am I. Don't treat me like one. It's too late. My only option is to persuade you to let me make a discreet exit as I'd planned.'

'And you think your friends in Beijing will welcome you with open arms?' Nergui said. 'It's one thing to slip away unnoticed but you're an embarrassment now. They'll already be making new friends here.'

'Friends like you, perhaps, Nergui?' Bakei said, a touch of bitterness in his voice.

'I hardly think so.' Nergui smiled. 'I'm far too insignificant for their purposes.'

'I've no illusions,' the minister said. 'There might have been a time when I could have expected to be treated with some honour down there. That won't happen now. They'll just want to shuffle me silently into the wings.'

'There is more than one way of doing that,' Nergui pointed out. 'At least here your treatment will be open and honest.'

'An open and honest public humiliation? I think I'd rather take my chances with the clandestine.' He pressed the gun harder against Gundalai's neck. 'I'd appeal to your better nature, Nergui, but I'm not sure you have one in matters like this. Just your warped sense of duty. I can't complain. It's served me well. If you can't get me out of here, no one can.'

'One last professional duty?' Nergui said. 'And if I don't?'

'I shoot this boy. And then I shoot myself.'

There was a noise from behind Nergui as Odbayar tried to push himself forward. Doripalam had been holding him back, but it was too late. He elbowed Nergui aside and threw himself into his father's line of sight.

'You can't do this,' he said. 'It's insane. You're insane.' His voice was thin and high pitched, but it carried across the empty arena with authority. Nergui watched him calmly, making no move to stop him.

The minister stared, startled, his gun wavering momentarily in his hand. 'Odbayar?' he said. He peered, squinting, as though unsure of his son's identity.

'That's . . .' Odbayar struggled for the right words. 'That's my friend.' The noun sounded less like a euphemism, Doripalam thought, than a word chosen with careful precision. It was the only possible word. 'Let him go.'

'You don't—'

'No, you're right,' Obayar walked further forward. 'I don't understand any of this. I've respected you. Not agreed with you, most of the time. But respected your abilities. What I took to be your intergrity. Acting for the right reason, even when you were doing the wrong thing.' He showed no trace of anxiety now. 'That's why I don't understand this.'

His father opened his mouth, but for a moment no words emerged. Then he said, 'It's not what you think.' The tone was that of an errant husband caught *in flagrante*.

'I don't know what I think any more,' Odbayar said. 'Except that the future of this country is too important to be left in the hands of those who were responsible for its past.' He was now only yards from his father. 'Hand over the gun. Let him go.'

Bakei gazed back, shaking his head. 'No,' he said. 'I can't. Not like this.'

He lowered the gun and held it in front of him, staring down at its dull metal shape. Then he slowly raised it, clutched firmly in his hand.

It was impossible to tell what he intended to do, and there was no time to find out. Some instinct or intuition gripped Nergui and he grabbed Doripalam firmly by the shoulder. 'Get down!' he hissed, pulling the younger man alongside his own body, as his chest and stomach struck the hard sandy ground.

A moment later, the explosion ripped the wooden stage apart.

# CHAPTER THIRTY-TWO

'How much longer?' Doripalam said.

'Hours, I think,' Nergui said. 'Why? Do you mind?'

'Not really. It's pretty relaxing, after everything.'

'If you say so.' Nergui leaned back on the wooden bench and gazed impassively at the makeshift wooden stage. 'Yes, I suppose I see what you mean.'

'Continuity,' Doripalam pronounced. 'Everything as it's always been.'

'Hardly,' Nergui said. 'It's all a confection, filtered through every different regime we've had over the last century.'

'Like everything else, then. But relaxing, all the same.'

They were both on duty. At least, Doripalam was on duty. He supposed the same must be true of Nergui, but it was difficult to be sure. With Nergui, it was always difficult to be sure. But, to judge from the scowl on Nergui's face, it was safe to assume that his presence here was not entirely voluntary.

It had been a long morning already, Doripalam acknowledged. The transfer of the banners from Sukh Bataar Square, the endless processions, acres of people in traditional robes carrying their own ornate flags and decorations. A glittering ocean of reds and greens and golds, shining in the noonday sun. And the endless speeches – the president, the prime minister, invited guests from Russia, from Korea, from Europe and from the US. And, of course, from China.

The stadium was thronged with policemen, uniformed and plain-clothed. Soldiers lined the roads, their rifles prominent.

There was no reason to expect any more incidents, but that was hardly the point. The point was a visible show of security. Reassurance for a crowd united only in its cynicism at any attempt to reassure them.

That was why Doripalam was on duty. It was why, presumably, Nergui was here in some official capacity.

Nergui's career seemed to have survived so far. But that was hardly surprising. Politicians came and went, just as Bakei and Battulga had done. It was people like Nergui who held things together.

The thought made Doripalam shudder inwardly. 'How do you think Odbayar is?'

Nergui turned to look at him. 'Physically? As well as can be expected, I think. They think he's likely to walk again, eventually. But they're not prepared to commit themselves as to when that might be.'

'That's good, I suppose,' Doripalam said. 'But I wasn't really thinking of physically.'

'I didn't really imagine you were. Mentally, psychologically, who knows? It's difficult to get close enough to him to find out. Difficult for me, anyway.' He paused, as though disentangling his own thoughts. 'He seems to be coping, but it's early days.'

Doripalam gazed impassively at the stage. More music now, throat-singing, the eerie vibrato hanging in the sun-drenched air. 'How's Sarangarel taking it?'

'Gundalai? It's hard. I mean, at one level she barely knew him – she'd only met him a few times. But she'd grown fond of him in that short time after he turned up at her apartment. And she blames herself.'

'It wasn't her fault,' Doripalam said.

'Of course not. There was nothing she could have done. But she thinks she should have stopped him chasing after Odbayar.'

'He was an adult. He was in the wrong place at the wrong time. That's all.'

'That's not how she sees it. Not at the moment.' Nergui stared out at the arena. Not for the first time, Doripalam wondered about Nergui's feelings for Sarangarel, whether – for all its tragedy – this incident might bring them together again. But, as ever, Nergui's blank dark-skinned face gave nothing away.

'It's awful, though,' Doripalam went on, aware that his words were vacuous even as he struggled to move the conversation on. 'So young.'

'Perhaps he died content, seeing Odbayar try to save him.'

'And maybe I've misjudged your cynicism all these years.'

'I always tell you – I'm a realist. There aren't many pleasures or consolations we can look forward to. Perhaps that was one of them. And perhaps a better option than Odbayar faces, living on alone, unsure whether he'll walk again. Knowing that, except for the explosion, his respected father would have been exposed as a crook and a traitor.'

'Okay, I concede,' Doripalam said. 'Your cynicism is undiminished. The explosion, though? Wu Sam's last joke?'

'Perhaps. He'd concealed the device well. We might not have found it down there in the earth under the stage. The other explosions had all been relatively small, and we'd written off Sam as a half-crazed incompetent. He claimed that he wanted to avoid civilian casualties. But if that device had gone off in the middle of this . . .' He gestured around at the heaving festival crowd. The festival itself had, unprecendentedly, been postponed for several days to allow the stadium to be repaired, as well as to ensure a further thorough checking for other devices. 'But if it was his last joke, the joke was still on him.'

'How do you mean?' Doripalam had one eye on the crowd, watching for any sign of trouble, any indication of problems. The music had ended and been replaced by an individual in a heavy-looking golden *del* reading an apparently interminable poem about Genghis Khan. The familiar, oddly benevolent-looking image was projected on to the large screens behind the stage.

'The spirit of the nation,' read the poet, 'the one thread that binds us together through history, the one touchstone for our identity and our future.'

'Without the explosion, the minister would have shot Gundalai or Odbayar or himself, and quite possibly all three. It would have been difficult for us to keep that quiet. And perhaps Sam was right. In many ways, this society is a powder keg. Maybe that spark – Bakei's betrayal of his country and his own son – would have been enough to set it alight. As it was, Bakei apparently died as the tragic victim of an explosion caused by a poorly maintained gas pipe.'

'You think anyone believes that?'

'I doubt it,' Nergui said. 'Not the gas-pipe part, anyway. Two gas-related explosions in the stadium in the space of an hour is stretching credibility a little, even given the standards of maintenance in this city.'

'Not to mention the other explosions.'

Nergui shrugged. 'Nobody would have known about the one we witnessed. As for the hotel – well, they might have bought the gas explanation for that one. But it doesn't really matter.'

'Doesn't it?'

'Who believes the authorities anyway? Everybody assumes they're being lied to, and often they are. And most of these people' – he gestured vaguely at the crowd around them – 'most of these people will already have come up with a story that's more interesting even than the truth. Sam was right about that, at least. We're a nation of storytellers.'

'And that's okay, is it? You're happy that we live in a state of permanent fiction and mutual suspicion?'

'My happiness doesn't come into it,' Nergui said. 'It's the way things are. We've a long way to go before they change.'

Nergui, for his part, looked as relaxed as ever, dressed in his usual dark suit, his feet stretched out on the bench in front of them. Pale lemon socks today, Doripalam noticed. 'And what about the past, Nergui? Was Bakei right? About you doing his dirty work? You knew – or you suspected – about his relationships with Sam, about Battulga. Even about how Sam was framed. But you did nothing.'

'What could I do?' Nergui said. 'I had no proof. There was no point in trying to obtain any. These things don't work like that. All I could do was limit the damage, try to keep a lid on things.'

'While they were allowed to get away with murder? What about the killings that were used to frame Sam?'

'Bakei was the head of the security services. They were not nice people in those days.'

'Not nice people!' Doripalam could feel his sense of outrage mounting. It was impossible to know how seriously to take Nergui's words, impossible to know how his undoubted sense of morality equated with his pragmatism.

Nergui smiled. 'Not like today, I mean. They were different times. Things were done which would not be done now. Bakei was a product of his times. But he had his own sense of ethics.'

Doripalam opened his mouth and then closed it again, unable to think of any coherent response.

'Because I don't believe he was self-interested. Or at least not only self-interested. I think, in part, he was genuinely trying to do what was right for the country, however misguidedly. He knew the old order was collapsing, and he was making plans for the future. Keeping the show on the road.'

'You really believe that?'

'Maybe. He was betrayed in the end by a half-baked lunatic, but he couldn't have foreseen that.'

'A lunatic who was working for his friends over the border.'

'So we surmise. But we'll never prove it. We think he had too many friends and resources to have been acting alone, but who knows? We'll never know for sure.'

'It's worrying, though, if they really were behind it.'

'It's the way it is. The price of our autonomy and potential.'

'And you think we'll retain our independence?'

'It depends what you mean by independence. When I look at some of the deals we're doing, I wonder whether commerce is just subjugation by other means.'

'You sound like Odbayar.'

Nergui laughed. 'Odbayar's is one vision of the future.'

'His vision?' Doripalam gestured towards the massive image of Genghis Khan. The poet was still chanting somewhere below.

'He's just a symbol now. He means whatever we want him to mean. For this poet, he's a romantic ideal who inspires some dull verse. For Sam, he was a romantic ideal who justified the over-throw of our government. For most of us, he's something we cling on to. He gives us a sense of identity in a world that seems to have few ideals left.'

'That doesn't sound like you.'

'I look back at Battulga and Bakei, and I don't know what to think.' He was quiet for a moment. 'I'm sorry. I'm not thinking. Speaking of Battulga, how is Solongo? How is she taking every-thing?'

There was a long pause. Doripalam had been waiting for and dreading this question. The truth was that he did not know the answer. He shook his head. 'Badly, I think. It was all a shock: the kidnapping, finding out about her father. She's thrown herself back into her work at the museum over the last couple of days, getting all the final stuff ready for the launch. She's exhausted. She was already feeling the strain. We both were. Now – well, I don't know.'

Nergui looked hard at him. The expression on his immobile face was as close to sympathy as Doripalam had ever seen it. 'It's hard,' he said. 'It will be, I know. If there's anything I can do?'

'I'll let you know,' Doripalam said, more brusquely than he had intended.

'Do that,' Nergui said, his voice unexpectedly gentle. 'Make sure you let me know. Before it's too late.'

Doripalam turned to him, suddenly lost for words, unable to equate this man with the imperious figure who had burst into Tunjin's hospital ward, days before.

The poet had been replaced now by the keening sound of the *Morin Khuur*, the horse-head fiddle, being played expertly below. The stern image of Genghis Khan was still on the screen. Just a symbol, then, with countless different meanings, conflicting visions of the state and its future.

And behind all that, people like Nergui and himself. Bringing those visions to life, doing the dirty work needed to keep things clean. Keeping the show on the road.